SASSAFRAS

SASSAFRAS

A NOVEL

TRISH HEALD

GLASSWING
—MEDIA—

 GLASSWING
M E D I A ——————

304 S. Jones Boulevard, #1218
Las Vegas, NV 89107

This is a work of fiction. Names, characters, businesses, places, events and incidents are either the products of the author's imagination or used in a fictitious manner. Any resemblance to actual persons, living or dead, or actual events is purely coincidental.

Printed in the United States of America

First Printing, 2019

ISBN-13: 978-1-7332268-0-6

Library of Congress Control Number:2019910025

For Paul

No man ever steps in the same river twice, for it's not the same river and he is not the same man.

— HERACLITUS

SASSAFRAS

Freestyle Lifestyle

Champs cracked open a lukewarm can of beer and stared at the golden scattering urn that contained his dead wife. It was his first urn—the other dead people he knew had been buried —and he didn't have the foggiest idea of what to do with it. With her. With Pat. When he'd brought the urn back from the mortuary a month ago, he'd placed it in the center of their laminate dining table like a vase of flowers.

It was the only focal point in the assisted-living cottage he'd shared with Pat for the last two years. Of her life. She hadn't had time to make her decorative mark in their new home. That was fine with Champs. As far as he was concerned, this was no home. It was a final resting place, where an urn was the perfect ornament.

"Things sure didn't work out like we'd planned. Did they, Pat?" Champs asked the urn.

It was an understatement. He wished they'd never laid eyes on

Egret's Pond. He'd decided moving there was the instigating factor in Pat's death. Egret's Pond should have come with a warning label: *Enter at Your Own Risk* or *Dangerous Curve Ahead*. Even without the signs, he'd known right away that something didn't smell right about the place. If only he'd obeyed his instincts from the start.

Champs remembered the brochure he'd picked up when he and Pat had arrived for a tour. He could still feel its glossy pages in his hands. Egret's Pond claimed to be the retirement community with a "freestyle lifestyle." The slogan was written in swirly red letters next to a photo of horny-looking fortysomethings playing strip poker at a fancy card table. At least that was what Champs had seen. He'd turned the page for more.

Page two extolled the benefits of the SPARK program next to a snapshot of a hot nurse bending over a silver-haired man in tight swim trunks. That man had a smile on his face like the cat who'd got the cream and then some. Champs had allowed himself to fantasize about medical advances in erectile stimulation for the over-sixty-fives. He was ready to sign on the dotted line. But his excitement had been short-lived. The SPARK program comprised three "freestyle" activities: yoga, a weekly alcohol-free cards night, and a recycling club. He hadn't been able to think of a worse combination. Unless they'd included golf. Champs hated golf.

But before he could sneak out of the lobby, the facilities director had approached them. Dressed in a white pantsuit, carrying a clip-board, her brown hair pinned back from her face in swoops, she'd resembled Nurse Ratched.

"Hello, Mr. and Mrs. Noland," she'd said in an overly cheerful voice like a kindergarten teacher on the first day of school. "Welcome to Egret's Pond! We hope today will turn out to be the first day of the rest of your life!"

"Jesus Christ, Pat. Why didn't we run for the hills?" Champs asked the urn.

He took off his bifocals and rubbed his sunken blue eyes. In the mirror across the room, he examined his reflection: a slightly hunched-over, balding man with wispy strands of gray-blond hair and patchy stubble. He used to be a handsome man—if he did say so himself—with a bronzed, weathered look and taut muscles from days of year-round fishing exposed to the elements. Today, he saw a withered man with pale skin and flaccid forearms. The last two years had taken their toll.

"Say cheese," he said to the man in the mirror. But the corners of his mouth refused to budge.

When he'd gone to collect the urn, they'd given him a booklet, "What to Expect When You're Grieving." Earlier in the week, exhausted but unable to sleep, Champs had opened the booklet to the section called "Are You Depressed?" He liked quizzes, so he'd completed the diagnostic questionnaire. His final score landed him in the "moderately depressed" category. There were only three categories: depressed, moderately depressed, and clinically depressed. The treatment for all three was a combination of counseling services, support groups, and a pick-and-mix list of prescription meds. Suspicious, Champs had examined the fine print on the back cover and discovered the booklet was produced by a major pharmaceuticals company. "Depression, my ass," he'd mumbled before grinding the whole booklet down the garbage disposal.

He had his own methods of coping: drinking cheap beer, talking out loud to his dead wife, and drifting in and out of memories. As much as possible, he kept his eyes trained on the golden urn. Any moment now, he expected, Pat would pop up like a jack-in-the-box or a genie in a bottle and tell him what the hell he was supposed to do with her. What the hell he was supposed to do with the coagulated feeling in his chest, as if his organs were packed tight in aspic. Any moment now.

"Tell me what to do, Pat. I sit here day after day and you say nothing. I've got a life sentence on death row in front of me. I need some answers," he demanded, and downed the rest of his beer.

Champs was fed up with the urn's stubborn silence and angry with his wife for conning him into moving to deadly Egret's Pond in the first place. Though, generally speaking, she'd never been much of a con artist, he had to admit. As they'd approached the ripe old age of seventy, Pat had convinced him to put their family home on the market and find a suitable retirement facility. She'd called it "downsizing" and said they'd have more freedom to explore new interests, meet exciting people, and enjoy their final act together.

"There's no sense us rattling around in this big house now," Pat had said. "It's more than we need and too much work for you. Besides, it will be fun to reinvent ourselves."

The expressions "downsizing," "final act," and "reinvent ourselves" had alarmed Champs. But at the time, he couldn't think of any reasonable objections. He was used to doing whatever Pat said was best. She always knew how to take care of things. Take care of him. To make the idea palatable, he'd decided what Pat really meant was he'd have more time for fishing and crabbing on the Sassafras River.

The Sassafras River, a tidal tributary of the Chesapeake Bay, stretched twenty-two miles long on the Eastern Shore of Maryland. Champs owned a seasonal cabin there. It wasn't much more than a shack, but it had been in the family for four generations. He was devoted to it. Champs was a fisherman before all else—a Sassafras fisherman. He'd looked forward to spending as much time as possible on the water, where he belonged.

Satisfied he wouldn't need to reinvent himself or meet exciting people, Champs had whittled down fifty years of family belongings, consolidated finances, updated wills, and sold their three-thousand-square-foot house in Downingtown, Pennsylvania. He and Pat had moved into a small independent-living cottage at Egret's Pond. "Here we are," he'd said. "The first day of the rest of our lives."

Champs had soon realized that when you stripped away the glossy brochures, clever euphemisms, and overly cheerful voices, an adult living facility boiled down to two words: "game over." You wouldn't be passing "Go" anymore once you landed here, no matter how many doubles you rolled in the Monopoly club. In fact, you wouldn't be doing much of anything anymore. Anything useful, that is. Champs remembered his third day at Egret's Pond, when he'd pulled out his lawn mower to mow the grass around their cottage.

"Stop! Stop!" their new neighbor had shouted, running across the lawn dressed in a pompous golf outfit and waving a nine-iron. "You're not allowed to do that here. It's all done for you. The landscaping team will be here tomorrow at ten a.m. for that. Leaves us more time for golfing, eh?" He'd given Champs a friendly wink and a nudge to the shoulder.

Champs hated golfers even more than he hated golf. Golfers who wore plaid knickers with a matching beret and bow tie were the worst. Idiots, all of them.

"If I were in charge, Pat, I'd make them call it what it is: a goddamn assisted-dying facility. Makes no sense pussyfootin' around the matter," Champs told his dead wife, cracking open another beer and clunking it on the urn in a macabre "cheers" gesture.

No matter where you lived at Egret's Pond, your home was called your "unit." There was a full spectrum of units available on "the compound." That's what Champs had nicknamed it when Pat wouldn't let him call it a prison. She wouldn't let him call their unit a "cell" either, but that's what it felt like to Champs. A cage. A trap.

It was all part of the "continuing care" services they advertised. Independent-living cottages like theirs were units at the top of the food chain. As you shriveled and shrank, you slid to the assisted-living apartments in Ruston Hall. Champs had nicknamed it "Rust in Hell." Some fought their change in status, but very few escaped the tyranny of continuing care. From Ruston, you might go in for a cozy little number in the memory-support units on Rosemary Lane. Rosemary for remembrance, he'd guessed. As if. Or you might get a stay of execution in the rehab units after a close but not fatal encounter with the grim reaper. And eventually, if you didn't draw a get-out-of-jail-free card, you spent the rest of your life in a hospital bed at Heron's Nest. "The Nest" came with twenty-four/seven nursing care and a free ticket to hospice, the bottom of the food chain. That was where Pat had died. Four weeks and two days ago.

Champs remembered sinking into a lumpy corduroy recliner in the living room area of Heron's Nest the night she'd died. The curtains had been left open, and the windows stared back at him—black, cold, and barren. A muted TV hung on the wall over a mock fireplace, the

Weather Channel breaking the news of a blizzard somewhere. He'd thought it ironic that if you weren't in the living room at the Nest, you were in one of the dying rooms. Those were the only units available there.

He'd been told by the nurse to take a break from his wife's bedside, where she was rotting away with cancer. Pat had been officially diagnosed a mere three months after they'd arrived at the compound. "Treatment," the doctor had said at first. "Hospice," he'd said after a while. "Not long now," he'd said earlier that day. Pat had taken her last breath while Champs dozed in the living room chair. He could still feel the nurse's touch on his shoulder. Her gentle shake as he'd opened his eyes.

"Mr. Noland? Mr. Noland. She's passed now."

He'd walked numbly into Pat's dying unit and placed his hand over hers. He couldn't recall now how long he'd sat next to her, staring at a butterfly-shaped stain on her hospital blanket, unable to feel anything at all. He did remember the nurse moving his hand away before rigor mortis set in. It was daylight by then.

"And here we are," Champs announced to the metallic jar. "Ashes to ashes, dust to dust."

His beer can was empty but he didn't have the energy or desire to get up for one more. Instead he drifted into another memory. This time a happier one—when he and Pat had first met.

Nineteen years old and home from college for winter break, Champs had gone skating on Blue Marsh Lake one full-moon night with a group of his buddies and plenty of cheap beer. He'd never been a good skater and alcohol did nothing to improve his skills. After three minutes on the ice, he'd stumbled and landed hard. White skates and a sparkling spray of little stars cut to a stop in front of him. A pair of yellow mittens reached down to pull him up. At the end of the mittens was a smiling, golden-haired farmer's daughter called Pat. He'd almost slipped again, but she'd held him upright with strong arms and warm-hearted confidence. Deaf to the wolf-whistling of his drunken friends and the giggles of Pat's girlfriends, Champs didn't let go of her until midnight. By then, she'd taught him to skate, and he'd fallen in love.

The house phone rang, interrupting his reverie.

"Should I answer that?" he asked Pat, picturing her under the full moon in her white skates, short pleated skirt, and banana-yellow mittens.

She said nothing.

Champs didn't want to answer the phone. But he didn't want someone to show up at his door because they couldn't reach him over the wires. It was compound policy to place a weekly check-in call on single-occupied units. If Champs didn't answer or return the call within twenty-four hours, Egret's Pond dispatched a special SWAT team to the cottage.

He'd already been through that twice.

They'd arrived in golf carts with fake sirens on top. Their mission, as far as Champs could tell, was to pound on his front door and barge inside like hooligans just in case he'd fallen and couldn't get up. He didn't have Life Alert. Or in case he was dead. When, on both occasions, the uniformed special forces had found him alive—if inebriated —at the kitchen table, they'd looked disappointed. Champs had offered them a beer as a consolation prize, but apparently, that was against the rules.

"Hello?" Champs yelled into the phone. He wasn't deaf or taken to shouting, but it pleased him to act his age if there was any chance it might annoy the caller. He had to get his kicks somehow.

"Champs, it's Laura. You're not annoying me," said Champs's daughter, who was all too familiar with the ploy.

His children never called him Dad or Daddy or Papa; it was a family tradition. And he was the fifth Champs in the Noland line. Or the sixth. Nobody was sure. Champs had been reluctant to rock the boat with his elders. So Pat had gone along with their children's calling him Champs but she'd insisted on giving their firstborn son his own name, thereby ending the legacy. Pat had always known how to strike a good bargain.

"Oh. Laura. What do you want?"

"I'm fine, Champs. Thanks for asking. How are you?"

"Fine." It was his standard answer to prevent further questions about his well-being.

"Why didn't you answer your cell phone?"

"Huh? Cell phone? What cell phone?" Champs hated cell phones and had switched his off weeks ago. He didn't even know where it was.

"Whatever," said Laura. "I'm calling to remind you I'll pick you up outside reception at eleven o'clock today."

"Huh? What for?"

"I really don't have time for this today. Please just shave and put on some clean clothes. I'll pick you up outside the main building at eleven. Don't be late." She ended the call.

"How about you come with me, Pat?" Champs asked the urn. "You like Blue Claw, and I know you want to see the kids. There's no reason why you shouldn't be there today. Even if you didn't get a formal invitation."

Laura had set the outing up two weeks ago. "It's something for you to look forward to," she'd told Champs as she marked it in red pen on the wall calendar.

Egret's Pond provided every unit with a wall calendar. Each month had an inspirational quote under a photo of a sunset. The quote for March was "It's not about the destination, it's about the journey." Champs had scoffed when he'd seen that. He didn't think it was either that mattered when you lived in an "expirement home," in "Regret's Pond." After all, the destination was death and the journey was a long, slow slide into death. At least for him.

The lunch date at Blue Claw, his favorite restaurant, was the only thing written down in March; you really couldn't miss it. But Champs was suspicious of calendars and refused to consult them. He could perfectly remember where to be and when, unless he didn't want to be there. Plus, he hated the concept of marking time at this stage of his life. Especially in alarming red ink.

"I forgot it on purpose," he admitted to Pat with a shrug.

Champs loved his adult children and he loved the biscuits at Blue Claw possibly even more. What he didn't love was the real agenda of the luncheon. He knew Laura, along with his son Jeffrey, would push him into staying at the compound for the rest of his life. A grim prospect. At least it wasn't three-on-one today, Champs thought. His oldest son, David, lived in California and wouldn't be there.

"Let's get this over with," he said to the golden urn, and headed for the shower.

2

Blue Claw

A t eleven a.m. sharp, Laura pulled up in a brand-new, shiny
silver Lexus RX, courtesy of her lease agreement. Champs
didn't believe in leasing. In his view, if it ain't broke, why
get a new one? It baffled him how the younger generations seemed to
act as if shininess were one of the cardinal virtues and newness were
the equivalent of the Holy Grail.

"Leasing, my ass," he mumbled to Pat before climbing into the car.

He'd tucked the urn inside his bulky winter coat right next to his
heart before leaving his unit. Worried that she might pop up suddenly
at lunch—or spill out—he'd taken care to secure the lid with masking
tape.

Laura had a new haircut, Champs observed. The severity of the
chin-length style made him imagine her hacking off her long, blond
hair with the hedge shears in a fit of rage. Laura had seemed angry for
some time now—angry with him, in particular.

"Nice haircut," he offered. Pat had taught him to notice things like new haircuts or new shoes and give a small compliment. He usually stuck to "nice" to keep things simple.

"Thanks," Laura said with a weak smile.

He noticed she'd lost weight, too. Always slim, Laura was now so thin that her collarbones stuck out like a chin-up bar. Champs knew better than to comment on her weight. Pat had taught him that, too.

"You can relax, Champs. This car has antilock brakes and I'm not even going that fast."

She was referring to the way he braced himself on the armrests as if expecting a collision at any moment. But it wasn't fear of an accident that kept him tensed in an upright position. The new leather seats in Laura's car were so slippery he had to hold himself in place to keep from sliding out from under his seat belt. Next time, he thought, he'd bring double-sided duct tape so he could affix himself to the seat.

At Blue Claw, the hostess offered to take his coat, but Champs acted like he hadn't heard her and barged through the restaurant. He'd spotted Jeffrey already seated and staring into a laptop screen.

"Hi, Champs," Jeffrey said, and rose to greet him with that hand-shake and clap-on-the-shoulder thing men did. Champs hated it and stepped back to protect the urn.

Jeffrey shrugged and reached down to angle the computer screen so that it faced Champs.

"Hi, Champs," said David's head, appearing on the screen courtesy of video-chat software.

So David would join them after all, thought Champs before step-ping out of view of the camera. He couldn't stand being filmed. He feared that the replay could show up anytime, anywhere, making a fool or a liar out of him.

"I know you're there, Champs," said the voice from the computer.

Champs turned the laptop around to face the door to the men's room. He then took a seat at the far end of the table.

"Hilarious," said David's voice. "Turn me around, Laura."

She moved the laptop onto the plate opposite Champs. The phrase "bring me his head on a platter" came to his mind.

David was forty-five this year. His blue eyes were hooded and bloodshot, and he hadn't shaved in weeks. Champs thought David resembled a hungover insurance man about to face the gallows. He noticed the wrinkled suit and tie and calculated the time in California. David must have just arrived at his San Francisco office.

A waiter appeared, and Champs gestured to the screen as if inviting him to take David's order first.

The waiter looked confused.

Laura looked annoyed.

"I'll start," she said, and asked for a glass of chardonnay and a garden side salad with everything on the side.

Champs wondered what was left in the salad bowl of a garden side salad if everything was served on the side. Before he could ask, it was his turn to order.

He squinted and craned his neck forward to read the waiter's name tag. He knew they hated it when some geezer insisted on using their name over and over. It was one of his favorite "act like an old man to annoy people" moves.

"Well, Jesus," said Champs. "I'll have a pint of Dogfish Head 60 Minute IPA. Thank you, Jesus."

"Champs, it's 'hay-seuss,' not 'jee-zus,'" Laura hissed.

"Hey what?" said Champs.

"'Hay-*seuss*.'"

"Bless you." Champs offered Laura his napkin and received a fiery glare in return. He thought he saw Jeffrey and David snicker but he wouldn't have sworn to it.

"It's okay," said Jesus with a shrug. "It happens all the time. What else can I get you, sir?"

"I'll have the Blue Claw sandwich special with a side order of cheesy biscuits. On the side," said Champs, mimicking Laura. Last time, they'd brought him fries instead of biscuits. He'd had to drag the manager out of the break room to clarify things.

"Did you want fries or a garden side salad with that?"

"He'll have the fries," said Laura.

Champs scowled. He didn't need Laura to speak for him, and she might have confused the whole order. He'd once again get fries and not cheesy biscuits. On the plus side, maybe he'd get both; that would be a bonus.

The waiter turned to Jeffrey, who ordered a steak-and-ribs platter.

Jeffrey was the Noland "oops" child, born almost ten years after his sister. An easygoing man, he had the ruddy good looks and height of a Hollywood Paul Bunyan. Today, though, Champs thought he looked more like Bigfoot, with his glowering eyes, greasy hair, and straggly beard. When was the last time he'd seen Jeffrey smile? Not that he was smiling much either these days, come to think of it. None of them were.

While they waited for the food, Champs's children chatted about the weather and current events. He hadn't turned on the news or picked up a paper since Pat's diagnosis two years ago. Tuning out their conversation, he tried to lip-read the jacked-up sportscasters on the bar TV yapping about the March Madness tournament. College basketball didn't interest him, but neither did small talk. That had always been Pat's department. His department was drinking beer. He risked a peek inside his coat to see if she had anything to say about that. Nope.

The food arrived. His children let him get halfway through his IPA and onto his third cheese biscuit before they pounced. Champs thought they'd done well to hold back that long. He also thought his children sounded well-rehearsed, as if they'd written their speech out in advance and practiced. There didn't seem to be any lines for him in this play, and that was just fine. He had nothing to say. He mounted his defense by folding his arms across his chest and peering over the top of his glasses.

"We think it would be best for you to stay at Egret's Pond. It's your home now," Laura said. She spoke with her serious lawyer voice, honed in her family law practice, where she'd specialized in wills and estates. She'd quit several years ago to be a stay-at-home mom to her two young daughters. Champs missed his granddaughters and wondered when he'd see them again. Laura's husband, Brian, was a hotshot lawyer in his father's environmental law firm, which specialized in defending Big Ag bad guys. Champs liked Brian well enough even though he was more of a preppy sailing type than a fisherman.

"Yes, and clearly the cottage is too big for you now," David's head said. "When you downsize to an assisted-living unit in Ruston Hall, you'll save, let me see here . . . yes, that's correct . . . two hundred thirty-one dollars and fifteen cents a month, according to my spreadsheet."

Spurious accuracy, thought Champs. He wasn't a fan of decimal places. He could never figure out why David was paid so much to calculate them all day for a company known only by its initials: KPMG. Champs found that very suspicious. In fact, all initials and acronyms raised his suspicions. Except for "IPA" and "POW." He had once asked Laura what the "RX" stood for on her car. "Radiant cross-over," she'd told him. Radiant bullshit, more like, he'd thought. KPMG sounded like a Russian spy outfit if you asked him. Maybe David had just returned from a dangerous Siberian mission and that was why he looked like crap.

"But it's not all about saving money, Champs," Jeffrey chimed in.

Unlike his other kids, Jeffrey had never taken to college or a career. He'd dropped out of Penn State and gone into construction for a while. Then he'd worked in a boatyard on the Chester River, where he'd learned the craft of wooden-boat building until the business went bust. Now he lived at a lakeside resort in the Poconos, where he built and maintained a fleet of wooden canoes, his passion. The only thing Jeffrey loved more than boatbuilding was the Sassafras. He was teth-ered to it, Champs had observed. Unlike the women he dated. Jeffrey preferred a "catch and release" scheme concerning girlfriends—so far there hadn't been any keepers.

Jeffrey continued, off script now. "It's more about you being where you're comfortable. Where you can rest in peace."

"Do I look dead to you?" Champs barked, and then broke wind.

"Of course not," Laura responded, unable to keep her face from twisting in disgust. She waved her hand in front of her nose, giving Champs the distinct feeling she was trying to wave away more than just a bad smell.

He felt sorry for her but didn't know what to say. She'd always gone to Pat with her problems. Champs had an urge to give her the urn, as if he were holding back the one thing she needed most: her mother. He reached for the zipper on his coat but Laura continued talking and the moment passed.

"What Jeffrey meant to say is that you won't have to worry about anything or go through the hassle of getting used to a new community. It's all done for you at Egret's Pond. You're already settled and in a good routine."

Champs caught the waiter's attention and signaled for another beer and more cheesy biscuits. If he had to listen to this crap, he reasoned, he sure as hell needed more carbs.

"Well," David's head said, "what do you think, Champs?"

"I think I need the men's room," Champs replied.

He stood up, supporting Pat with a bent arm tucked up against his body under the urn. In the bathroom, he took an empty stall and sat down. Peering inside his coat, Champs spoke to his dead wife.

"I'm not staying at the compound, Pat," he said. "I thought you should be the first to know. So I'm telling you now. I won't stay. Whole place smells like piss. No offense."

"You all right in there, Champs?" called Jeffrey. "Who are you talking to?"

"For chrissakes, Jeffrey—can't a man have privacy in the goddamn head?"

"Sorry. I was just wondering if you needed any help, that's all."

"No, I don't need any help. For your information, I'm still perfectly capable of wiping my own ass!"

"Right. Got it," Jeffrey said, and left the restroom.

Champs shook his head and sighed at the urn. "Guess you have nothing to say, Pat. So there it is. We leave tonight," he said.

"Did you wash your hands?" asked Laura when Champs got back to the table.

"Really, Laura?" said Jeffrey.

Champs was fed up with the patronizing. He remained standing and downed his fresh beer in a messy series of gulps like a frat boy at a keg party.

"I'm not staying at Egret's Pond!" he thundered, and slammed the empty pint glass down on the table.

Dead silence in the restaurant. Everyone stared at Champs as if he'd shot a gun. He felt like the mighty Thor, brandishing Mjölnir on top of a rock in Asgard. Thor was his favorite Avenger.

3

The Goldfinch Plan

T he feeling didn't last. A balding old man losing his temper in Blue Claw couldn't keep the attention of anyone raised on *Terminator* movies, especially if an AK-47 wasn't involved.

"But where else is there, Champs?" Laura whined. She'd lost the attorney act and now sounded like her ten-year-old self, complaining that things weren't fair. Nothing ever seemed fair by Laura's standards. "I mean, I'd love to have you," she said, "but our house isn't set up for an extra person, and the girls are—"

"And I know you don't want to live in California," interrupted David. "That leaves Jeffrey, and since he's practically homeless, it makes sense if you stay at Egret's Pond. It's a reasonable thing to do. You probably have friends there now anyway, right?"

Champs shook his head and stared at Jeffrey's battered hiking boots. The friends—more acquaintances, really—that they'd made in their short time at Egret's Pond were because of Pat's interests and willingness to be social. Champs realized now that she had been in a rush to create pals for him so he'd have people to lean on after her death. The thought made him wince. He remembered how Pat had filled their schedule before she got too sick. She'd made him get out of their unit every day for at least one group activity. He'd made it as hard as possible, like a petulant child who dragged his feet when it was time to go to school.

"You're such a delay fish," Pat would say. She was a huge fan of *Finding Nemo*.

Then she'd drag him along to a slide show on Greek islands or a tiresome walk around the man-made pond with the on-site naturalist. It hadn't gone well. Champs thought slide shows were excellent opportunities for a good snooze and he'd doze off as soon as the lights dimmed. As far as the pond was concerned, an unfishable body of water was just a puddle on an ego trip, according to Champs. He'd informed the walking group that there were no egrets at Egret's Pond except for those "suspicious fakes"—here, he had gestured to the painted wooden birds placed on the banks of the pond. He'd elaborated that there were no waterfowl at all because there were no fish in the damn puddle to attract them. The naturalist hadn't appreciated Champs's observations, and Pat had stopped taking him on the nature walks.

He chuckled now at the memory of the Sierra Club man's face and glanced inside his coat to see if Pat was laughing, too.

"This isn't funny, Champs," Laura said. "And what are you trying to hide from us in your coat? Do you think we haven't noticed how you keep looking in there? You're sweating like crazy, take it off!"

"Leave him alone," said Jeffrey. "Stop ordering him around like he's your child."

"Shut up, Jeffrey," Laura shot back. "You're supposed to be on my side. I'm the one making decisions here."

"Here we go again," said David's head. "You're always in charge, Laura. It's like you think you have a monopoly on what's best for everyone—especially since Mom died. Here's what I think—"

"I don't care anymore what you think, David," Laura interrupted.

"After the decisions you've made in the last several months, I can't even trust you to tie a shoelace, let alone—"

"Whoa, Laura. Stop right there." It was Jeffrey's turn to interrupt. "We don't need to bring David's personal life into . . ."

Champs let them carry on while he ordered and drank another IPA. It had always been Pat who'd wrangled their children's arguments into compromises and apologies. He didn't have the energy to attempt it today and was afraid to peek into his coat to see if Pat-in-the-urn had any advice to offer in case Laura noticed her. He gave the urn a comforting squeeze instead. The line between his wife and her ashes was increasingly blurry.

"Look, Champs," said David's head after the manager came by to ask them to quiet down. "This is hard for all of us. But it's what Mom wanted. It's what's in the plan."

The plan. Champs had been wondering when they'd bring that up. Pat had prepared everything for her death and written it down in a small notebook with a goldfinch sticker on the front cover. She'd talked them through it when the family had gathered at her bedside last summer, six months before she'd passed away.

The death plan was comprehensive; there had been hardly a paper to sign before he was handed Pat's ashes in the golden scattering urn, and all the financial and legal requirements had been completed. She'd specified no funeral or ceremony, telling them it would be too much to take care of and too upsetting for everyone. And as for Champs, Pat had assumed he'd want to remain at Egret's Pond, where they could look after him for the rest of his life. She'd assumed wrong, thought Champs.

He had tried to comply with her wishes. He really had. But being a widower on the compound meant a new set of social obligations that left him weary and reluctant to leave his unit. As soon as a man lost his wife at Regret's Pond, he became fresh meat for all the widows. They wheeled, hobbled, or rattled toward him whenever he entered the main facility to run an errand or visit the coffee shop. They batted their eyelashes over milky eyeballs and petted him like he was a lost lamb, hoping to win his affections. Some men rose to the occasion, so to speak, but Champs couldn't think of anything worse. As far as he was concerned, he was a crab who'd lost a claw. He wasn't interested in a prosthetic. He would make do. Like he always did. Like Pat always did.

Worse for Champs had been the steady intrusion of the more independent widows, who rang his doorbell at all hours bearing foil-wrapped baked goods or casseroles. At first, he'd gone to the door to accept the food and grumble his thanks. But he'd soon realized this allowed the do-gooder to get her foot in the door, pummel him with nosy questions, and insist he try "just a little taste" of the homemade food she'd brought.

One woman, whom Champs had never seen before, had brought her famous Meatless Meat Mystery Stew and introduced herself as "Harvey's widow. You remember Harvey, don't you?" He didn't. Harvey's widow had bulbous earlobes punctured with pearl earrings the same tea-stained-enamel color as her dentures. He'd been wondering if they'd come as a matching set, a special deal maybe, a "twofer," when the woman had asked after his BMs.

"My what?" he'd said.

"Your bowel movements, dear. I know I took a while to get regular after Harvey died, until I found this great little remedy," she'd replied with a dancing pinkie finger. Champs had insisted his BMs were just fine, thank you very much, and shown her to the door.

Then there'd been portly Mrs. Williams's famous Gluten-Free Macaroni and Three-Cheese Balls. She'd heated one up in the microwave for him and served it in one of Pat's teacups, swimming in grease, like an orange turd in an oil slick. "We knock 'em back one at a time," Mrs. Williams said. Champs closed his eyes and let the slimy thing tumble down his throat. When he dry-heaved, Mrs. Williams took the rest of her cheeseballs and stormed out of the unit. Champs spent that night on the toilet with decidedly runny BMs, shouting obscenities at his dead wife for putting him through the whole ordeal.

Widow Candice, who resembled a spider, was so curious about the cremation process she'd asked Champs if she could lift the lid of the urn and "see how big the pieces are." He'd been holding one of her famous Sugar-Free Vegan Chocolate Chippers at that moment. His fist closed on the cookie. As the dusty crumbs landed on the table, he'd remarked, "About that big." Nonplussed, Candice had replied, "Well, I guess that's just the way the old cookie crumbles!" Funny damn spider, Champs thought before showing her to the door.

Champs had finally stopped answering the doorbell. At night he'd sneak out to collect his foil package *du jour*. He'd had great fun flushing the congealed (or crumbling) unsweetened foodstuffs down the toilet. Until it backed up. After that, he'd crammed the food into the freezer and refrigerator. It was why he drank warm beer now— there was no space for his brew in the fridge.

"I'd rather drink skunked beer all day long than deal with those crazies and their famous food. More like infamous, I'd say," he'd told the urn.

Last week, Champs had left Mrs. Wick's Famous Strawberry Lentil Shortcake untouched on the porch. Nobody had made any further offerings. He'd forbidden the weekly cleaners from removing the cake but now wondered what the Regret's Pond warden would think about that come spring and warmer temperatures.

"Well, that won't be our problem, will it, Pat? We'll be gone by then," Champs muttered into his coat collar.

"Okay, he's mumbling and incoherent," declared Laura. "It's raining now, and I have to get home and pick up the girls from school, so this meeting is over. The plan is the plan, and that's that." She slammed down the laptop like a gavel on a striking block, and David disappeared.

Champs agreed to pay the bill if Laura left the tip. He had no idea what waiters expected for tips these days and didn't want to undertip or, worse, overtip. She dug around in her cowhide shoulder bag and retrieved a purple lizard-skin wallet. What was it about people who hated hunting but couldn't wait to buy animal skins to tote around all their crap? He wondered if lizard hunters got paid by the hour.

Laura extracted a fifty-dollar bill and placed it under her untouched glass of chardonnay. Champs was about to make a comment but Laura stomped ahead of him out of hearing range. He turned around in time to see Jeffrey knock back the wine and exchange the fifty-dollar bill for a twenty. Champs raised his eyebrows, but Jeffrey only shrugged and walked past him with his head down.

Back at Egret's Pond, Champs slid himself out of Laura's car.

"So, it's settled, then," Laura said. "I'll get the paperwork started so you can move into an apartment in Ruston Hall as soon as possible. I'll let you know when it's time to pack, okay?"

She wasn't expecting a response, Champs gathered as she reached across the car, pulled the passenger door shut, and zoomed away. He stood there in the pelting rain like a left-behind child, hugging his urn, watching Laura disappear down the highway.

In his mind, the only thing settled was that he wouldn't spend another goddamn day at Regret's Pond, no matter what the plan said and no matter how convenient it was for his children. Champs had another idea. One he hadn't mentioned at lunch.

He'd decided to live year-round in his summer fishing cabin on the Sassafras. On his own. With no continuous care. What could Laura do, after all? Physically remove him from his property? She'd get used to the idea—they all would—and besides, she was only an hour away should anything happen to him. Which it wouldn't.

In fact, he relished the opportunity to get back to his familiar comforts, where nothing ever happened, nothing ever changed, and no social interactions were necessary. He'd spend the rest of his life on the river—fishing, crabbing, and drinking beer. Paradise.

Champs walked back to his unit and crashed on the couch, still clutching his dead wife. He didn't wake until three a.m. Unhindered by the time or his snarling stomach, he threw some clothes and the urn into a battered Samsonite suitcase.

As he left the unit, he stomped on the strawberry lentil shortcake. Inside his rusted, first-generation Ford Windstar, Champs put on a baseball cap that read "Fish Slayer," revved the engine a few times for effect, and made his great escape. Apart from the stinky ooze on the bottom of his shoe, he felt better than ever.

4

#2 Mepps Spinner

As the Windstar rumbled down the dark, empty interstate, Champs let his mind wander back to his early memories of the Sassafras.

It had all started with Ol' Champs, Champs's grandpa, who brought his family down to camp at Queens Point for summer weekends and vacations on the river. They joined several other camping families, all with ties to the Sun Oil refinery, where Ol' Champs and then Champs Senior, Champs's father, had worked as operators. The men and older boys on the campground would rise at dawn, back their boats into the river, and put out for the daily catch. They landed plenty back then: stripers, largemouth bass, white and yellow perch, shad, channel catfish, and American eels. The eels were chopped up and stored in paint buckets packed with rock salt for use as crab bait. Whatever their haul, the men had a preternatural sense of smell that drew them back to camp at ten a.m. for hot coffee, bacon, and blueberry pancakes cooked up by the wives on rudimentary propane camp burners.

Unless it was a crabbing day, afternoons were spent at leisure in the sweltering sun and humidity or torrential downpours of a passing thunder-and-lightning storm. Just like their father, Champs and his brother, Peety, had grown up paddling canoes, cannonballing off rickety docks, working the minnow nets, shooting ducks and squirrels with BB guns, waterskiing, and building forts. The Noland boys and their friends had left not one inch of the Sassafras or its local creeks, marinas, forests, and farmlands unexplored.

In those days, children returned to camp hungry for dinner, looking like swamp creatures—moldy and damp, splintered, scraped, and sunburned, pockets full of crushed blackberries or muddy clams they'd dredged from the riverbed. As teens, they came back to camp with hickeys on their necks and moonshine on their breath. Everyone ate the fish caught that morning along with juicy red tomatoes still warm from the field and tender, sweet, just-picked corn from the local farm stand. Tall tales were rampant, and so was the beer that kept the men lit like fireflies late into the night. Those were the good ol' days, the provenance of nostalgia, the embodiment of the "gone fishin'" spirit of the American dream. At least on the surface of things.

Champs was eleven when he first joined the other men in the boat at dawn. It was his initiation day as a Noland fisherman. For many boys from other families, this event was cause for celebration. But Champs remembered walking down the dock as a doomed man might walk the plank. It wasn't his fishing skills he doubted. He'd practiced thousands of times from his deck at home, casting his lure out to a warped paddling pool he used as a target. And he'd been fishing every summer on the Sassafras from the docks, shorelines, and rowboats, diapers and all, as soon as he could stand. He lived for fishing like most of his peers lived for baseball.

But there had been way more at stake than his angling prowess that morning. This first trip would test his manliness, his worthiness to be on the boat with a fraternity of tried-and-true, hard-ass fishermen. Champs had felt the pressure to live up to his father's expectations on other occasions and had failed. Still, he dreamed of proving himself more than worthy this time on account of his instinct for fish and his ability to take up very little space. He stepped off the time-worn dock onto the family fishing boat with a belly full of bile and a heart full of hope.

He kept his mouth shut, rigged his own line, and caught three catfish, which he removed from his hook without fuss or injury using a pair of needle-nose pliers he pulled from a pocket of his fishing vest. When he switched to a #2 Mepps spinner and realized he was reeling in a monster of a rockfish, he'd let the line go slack so it could slip away. He knew better than to outdo his father, who'd already been bragging he'd caught the biggest fish of the day. Champs didn't lose a lure, snag his line on shore, or cross another man's line. He fished where he was told, despite knowing they gave him the worst positions and had him casting into spots where he was unlikely to get any bites. No one spoke to him except to ask him to pass the donuts or beer or to hold a rod so they could take a leak off the other side of the boat.

Champs recalled the sequence of nods and winks among the men in the boat as they'd returned to the dock that morning. Ol' Champs lowered the throttle through the no-wake zone approaching the Sassafras River drawbridge. Champs Senior reached into the cooler and cracked open the last hissing can of beer. He handed it to Champs and said, "Congratulations, son. You passed." Champs took a tentative sip of beer while his father beamed at him. Golden, heady, and metallic with a hint of sweetness, it was the best thing he'd ever had—not the beer, but the first, last, and only taste of his father's approval.

He snapped out of his memories as he drove up too fast on a night-time construction project blocking traffic on I-95. Slamming on the brakes, Champs reflexively reached out with his right arm to shield Pat from the impact. The Windstar came to a severe stop just in time to avoid crushing a red Mini.

With a sigh of relief, Champs looked over to make sure Pat was okay. Real Pat, not the one in the jar. But she wasn't there. Pat was gone. Not for the afternoon, or dinner, or the weekend. She was gone forever. She was dead. Real dead.

With the urn and his imagination, he'd kept her alive, albeit in a somewhat diminished form. Until now. Champs felt someone stab him in the chest with an ice pick. He slumped over the steering wheel trying to breathe while static filled his head. He would have blacked out save for the blaring horn of the truck behind him—traffic was moving again. Champs forced the truth about Pat back into a mental tackle box and tied it shut tight with a double fisherman's knot. It was the hardest knot in the world to untie. In his experience, the truth didn't always set you free. His chest pain subsided and he was soon breathing normally again.

5

We're Not in Kansas Anymore

Champs drove in the daze that follows a nasty shock the rest of the way to his cabin at Deadrise Cove, a small community of a few dozen homes, a private dock and launch ramp, and a sliver of beach. Deadrise Cove had nothing to do with pirates even though some folks still showed up with oyster rakes hoping to dredge sunken treasure from the mucky silt at the bottom of the river. The cove was actually named in honor of the Chesapeake deadrise, a traditional waterman's workboat. Champs preferred the illusion of pirates. Watching the idiot treasure hunters dig up clam after clam was a hoot.

In 1953, Ol' Champs had purchased a double lot with one cabin in Deadrise Cove. Much later, a second cabin had been built on the property deep in the woods, lower down on the hill that led to Hill Beach. Ol' Champs had passed ownership to Champs Senior, and Champs had inherited it when his father died. He would pass it on one day to David or Jeffrey. Proud of this legacy, he took great care to ensure that everything stayed, as much as possible, original to the way it was in his grandpa's day. Pat had called it his labor of love.

Champs turned the Windstar into the overgrown, rough cement tracks of the cabin's driveway. He had to slam on the brakes again as a gleaming silver travel trailer appeared in his headlights, blocking the way.

"What the hell is this?" he muttered.

Squatters in Deadrise Cove were common as many of the residents left their cabins after the summer season. But this moron had crossed a line by parking in Champs's driveway. This was outrageous behavior! Goddamn freeloaders! Why hadn't Larry, his neighbor and the president of the residents' association, called him about this? Larry and his wife, Josanne, were year-round residents and it would be hard for them to miss a twenty-foot-long, ten-foot-high block of humming aluminum just outside their front door.

"Son of a bitch!"

Champs turned off his headlights and backed the Windstar out of the driveway and onto the front lawn, avoiding the large crepe myrtle tree. He cut the engine, retrieved a long flashlight from under the passenger seat, and climbed down from the van, leaving his key in the ignition in case he had to make a hasty retreat.

With his weapon in hand, Champs approached the trailer. He intended to scare the bejesus out of its occupants and make them get the hell out of his driveway. This was a private residence. He paid the taxes here, and he expected to park next to his own damn house. He smacked the heavy flashlight against his palm like a night cop with a billy club. Now, this was the "freestyle lifestyle" he was looking for— defending his property from intruders, taking the law into his own hands. To hell with bridge club and golf carts!

He banged on the back of the camper with the end of his flashlight, startling an owl from its perch in a leggy dogwood tree. Otherwise, silence. Champs crept around to the side of what he now realized was one of those fancy Airstreams. He whacked at the window on the entry door until a network of cracks formed inside the shatterproof glass. No answer. Champs was disappointed the squatters weren't there. Although given the condition of the camper, it dawned on him that perhaps these weren't squatters. Maybe it was Larry who'd parked his Airstream in Champs's driveway, not expecting him to arrive just before dawn on April 1, a mere month after his wife had died.

Champs sighed and let the flashlight fall in the dewy grass. What the hell was he doing here? Suddenly, it didn't feel like such a good idea. He was exhausted to the bone and needed a beer, so he walked to the screened porch at the back of the house. There was sure to be a beer or two left over from last summer. It was dark, but he knew the layout—it never changed.

When Champs stepped onto the porch, he veered to his right to avoid the picnic table and bench pushed up against the back of his house. His toe caught on the edge of an unknown rug. He stumbled into something bulky, then fell forward, smacking his shin on a hard surface before tumbling sideways into a cushioned couch.

"Damn it!"

Dizzy and disoriented, he pushed himself up to a seated position. Everything felt wrong, as if he'd driven up to someone else's cabin by mistake. Was he right now trespassing on someone else's three-season porch? Perhaps Laura was right and he was better off in continuing care at Egret's Pond. He had lost his way and maybe even his marbles! What the hell had he been thinking? Where was Pat?

Desperate for a drink, Champs made one more attempt to reach the hallowed ground of the beer fridge. Just in case. He'd come this far. You never knew. He felt his way around the unfamiliar furniture and shuffled across the porch with his arms outstretched like a zombie. When his hands contacted the surface of a refrigerator, he was almost moved to prayer. The handle, like everything else, seemed odd. Maybe he'd just forgotten the feel of things in the two years he'd stayed at Regret's Pond right by Pat's side.

Champs opened the fridge. Inside, he could just make out the shape of a few glass bottles. He disapproved of bottled beer. It was quick to skunk, and broken glass was a menace on the boat deck and in the river. As far as he was concerned, it was on tap or in the can only.

Bottled beer was for idiots. Except for growlers—sixty-four ounces of take-out craft beer in a glass jug was fine by him.

Desperate times called for desperate measures, so he grabbed a bottle, twisted off the top—grateful he didn't need to find a bottle opener—and chugged. Several swallows in, he noticed a suspicious taste. Like . . . watermelon? He spat out the last mouthful and ran his fingertips over the glass like a blind man reading braille. He felt the ridges of a familiar logo. This was no goddamn beer. This was Laura's Perrier! Flavored Perrier!

Champs spewed a string of curse words across the stillness of almost dawn. He threw the offending bottle across the porch, where it shattered into pieces on the old concrete floor.

He wasn't usually a thrower, but the adrenaline coursing through his veins felt great.

He chucked another Perrier grenade into the blackness, where it smashed on his gas grill in the corner. He was reaching for another when he noticed the glare of his neighbor's porch light behind the Airstream. Then he saw Larry, backlit on the other side of the screen door, aiming a twelve-gauge Remington shotgun right at him.

"Don't move or I'll shoot," Larry said.

"Don't shoot me, you son of a bitch," said Champs.

Larry lowered his gun barrel to the ground and shone a flashlight onto the porch. "Champs? Is that you?"

"Of course it's me."

"What are you doing here?"

"It's my goddamned house. I don't have to explain why I'm here. And stop blinding me with that flashlight."

Larry turned it off and pulled open the screen door. "No need to get hot under the collar there, Champs. We heard a lot of banging and yelling and glass breaking, so I came over here to check it out."

Champs felt around for the small stool at the end of the picnic table, hoping it was still there. It was.

"Why didn't you cut the lights on, darlin'?" said Larry's wife, Josanne, who came in behind him and flipped a switch.

Bright light flooded the porch. Champs put a hand over his glasses to shield himself from the onslaught. Ceiling fans whirred overhead, and he thought he heard water trickling out in the dark yard. He peeked through his fingers and saw Josanne in a white flannel nightgown and army-green rubber rain boots. Her platinum-blond hair was wrapped around dozens of spongy rollers tight up against her head. To Champs, it looked like her scalp was being eaten alive by fat caterpillars.

"If I'd known there was a light, I would have," he snapped, dropping his hand shield. He tried hard not to stare at the hairy larvae making a meal of Josanne's head.

"Well there's no need to pitch a hissy fit, Champs," Josanne scolded. She'd grown up the daughter of a Methodist pastor in South Carolina. Although she hadn't been back there in forty years, she'd kept the accent and sayings of her childhood. It annoyed the hell out of Champs.

With the porch illuminated, Champs took a good look around. He was flabbergasted. He sat on an entirely different porch than the one he'd known like the back of his hand. The picnic table and benches were in the right place, but someone had had a field day with a can of whitewash. Who the hell would paint solid wood furniture in the exact same color as the bird shit that decorated the tops of pilings and marina docks up and down the river? On the Sassafras, seagulls were known as "government painters" for the shit job they did decorating the woodwork. What kind of idiot would do a government paint job on their indoor porch?

The mismatched collection of webbed lawn chairs, collapsible camping chairs, and plastic Adirondack chairs was gone. The overturned paint buckets and crates that functioned as side tables had vanished. In their place was the furniture Champs had stumbled over minutes before. He couldn't believe his eyes: a matching set of tan wicker club chairs and sofa upholstered in pale blue fabric, throw pillows in sickly pastel colors, and an impractical glass coffee table he'd already met.

The rug he'd tripped over resembled a macramé of old mooring ropes as far as he could tell. There was another one further down on the porch where the red vinyl card table and folding chairs used to overflow with soda, beer, life jackets, forgotten tackle, and back issues of *National Geographic* magazine. A jigsaw puzzle, Scrabble game, and deck of cards were neatly stacked on a wooden table with four chairs around it, all painted in the same slovenly manner as the picnic table. New bamboo shelves stocked with expensive beach towels and life vests lined the cabin side of the screened porch. His old beer fridge had been replaced with a spotless aqua-colored one with the suspicious initials SMEG on the door. It had been built to look like it came straight out of the 1950s. Who the hell replaces a working old beer refrigerator with a brand-new one designed to look old?

Last but not least, in the far corner where his gas grill, meat table, extra propane bottles, and barbecue supplies had once been stood a marble fountain, the source of the trickling water sound. Champs could not fathom the point of an indoor water feature on an outdoor porch next to a goddamn river. The whole place looked staged. If he were a girl with braids in a checked dress carrying a cairn terrier, he might have said something about not being in Kansas anymore. But he wasn't.

"What a hellhole," Champs said in response to his redecorated porch.

"Lord have mercy," Josanne said, indicating Champs's bleeding leg and the broken glass everywhere. She lifted a too-well-plucked eyebrow at Champs.

Champs gave Larry a pointed look, hoping to signal him to get Josanne back to her own house. He had little patience for her at the best of times. And now was not the best of times. No, now could not possibly get any worse, Champs was thinking, when it got remarkably worse.

Larry's terry-cloth robe fell loose, exposing his privates to the glaring overhead lights. He was a tall man, but that wasn't how he'd earned his nickname, "Larry the Long," at community college.

"Larry, goddamn it. Put it away!" Champs said.

"My gun?" Larry asked, looking down the barrel.

"No, not your gun. Your . . . your johnson!" Champs hissed.

"Oh, right," Larry said. He leaned his Remington against the porch door and chuckled while he wrapped the robe around his body. Champs didn't find it remotely funny.

Josanne straightened the furniture and picked up the larger shards of glass. "Well now, Laura didn't tell us you'd be coming down for a visit. If I'd known I would have had coffee ready and a batch of my old-fashioned honey muffins warm from the oven. I've got some in the freezer, though. You want me to put one or two in the microwave for you?"

Then she gasped and turned an Ivory-soap shade of white. "Sweetheart, I'm so sorry! I nearly forgot. Champs! Champs, darlin', I'm so sorry for your loss. Poor Pat. We all prayed for her, you know—at church, in sewing group, at association meetings. It was all so terribly sad. How are you feeling, honey?"

"There'll be plenty more time for that, Josie-Ann," interjected Larry before Champs had to respond. "Now, you go on back to bed, and I'll finish cleaning up this mess and make sure Champs gets settled in real good."

"Do you have a key, Champs? Laura put in locks at the end of last summer. There were break-ins over there in the Skipjack development. And, well, the police couldn't find anyone. But Sue? Y'all remember Sue? From Otwell's, down yonder? Course they don't call it that anymore. Well, bless her heart, she told me that—"

"My love, why don't you go on now and get the key," Larry said. He opened the screen door and herded her out.

Larry offered to get Champs's bags from the Windstar, but Champs waved him off. He accepted the key from Josanne when she returned and stepped into his cabin. Exhausted, he crashed on the narrow sofa just inside the door.

6

Naked Newts

Three hours later, Champs woke to the smell of hot coffee and fresh bacon. His empty stomach responded. He fumbled around for his glasses and "Fish Slayer" cap as unknown voices and laughter drifted in from the porch. Champs tried to remember why he'd slept on the sofa in his clothes but drew a blank.

"Pat?" he called out.

He stood up and stumbled to the door that led onto the screened porch. Poking his head out, he shouted, "Pat?"

Two strangers looked up from the picnic table laden with home-made coffee cake, thick slices of back bacon, and a steaming pot of coffee.

"Where's Pat?" he demanded.

They looked alarmed, as if they'd seen a ghost.

"Here you go, darlin'. Come on out and have a cup of coffee. It'll do you a world of good," said the curly-haired blond woman wearing a peach-colored, silky blouse cut just low enough to reveal the creamy beginnings of an ample bosom. Champs pulled his eyes away with some effort.

"I don't want a damn cup of coffee! What's going on? Where's Pat?"

The lady chuckled. "Good one, Champs. April Fool's! You sure got us going there."

Champs glared at her.

The lanky man with a green "Duckaholic: Quack Addict" cap stood up and took a deep breath. "Champs? Pat is gone. She passed away about a month ago. You drove here last night by yourself, remember? From Egret's Pond?"

Champs's eyes darted around the porch as he tried to get his bearings. Nothing looked familiar. A shard of green glass reflecting the morning sun caught his attention. It reminded him of the smooth surface of the Sassafras, the week after Labor Day, heading downriver past the marinas with not a breath of wind or another boat in sight. At those times, every eagle, every osprey that crossed his bow, was two: the real bird and its reflection in the emerald mirror of the river. Champs squeezed his eyes shut as time warped and the ground beneath him pitched. His head filled with static. Was he real? Or just a ghostly reflection of his former self?

Larry reached him as he buckled over, saving him from a painful landing on the concrete. When Champs came back to life, he was laid out on the porch sofa he remembered falling into earlier that morning. The events of the last twenty-four hours rushed back. Josanne and Larry regarded him with some concern.

"What happened?" Champs barked.

"You blacked out," Larry answered.

"It's perfectly normal," said Josanne. "After what you've been through, hon, plus driving all the way out here in the middle of the night. It's only natural you'd be a little outta kilter."

Champs heaved himself to his feet, refusing Larry's help, and sat down at the picnic table. Josanne held out a steaming mug of coffee.

"Humph," he muttered, accepting the coffee.

He felt embarrassed by his weakness in front of his neighbors.

They weren't laughing at him, but he flushed, ashamed to be an object of pity. What the hell were they doing eating breakfast on his porch, anyway? It was an invasion of privacy, and Champs considered ordering them to leave. But he was hungry and his mouth watered. He loaded a plate with bacon and Josanne's famous coffee cake, smearing it with slabs of cold butter. It was the best thing he'd eaten in two years.

"Have you blacked out before, Champs?" asked Larry.

Champs shrugged off the question. Couldn't they leave well enough alone? He wasn't about to tell them about his blackouts. Especially the first one.

He had been about eight or nine. It was a stinking hot morning with a sun that would "sear the skin off a newt in three seconds flat," as his grandpa Ol' Champs used to say. Champs had imagined dozens of pitiful naked newts, blind and pink like baby mice, racing around the sand trying to find shade, their skins abandoned on the beach like little black raincoats. He feared something was wrong with him; a normal boy wouldn't have those kinds of thoughts. Who cared about newts anyway?

That morning, the Noland family went crabbing at Eastern Neck in the Chesapeake Bay. The water there was salty, clear, and shallow with patches of undulating eelgrass. It was the perfect environment for big Maryland blue crabs looking to mate. Which also made it a favorite destination of cownose rays looking to hunt. Their triangular fins broke through the surface of the water as they approached the shore. Champs didn't know about the rays and screamed, "Shark! Shark!" his pulse racing, one of his worst Sassafras nightmares come true. They laughed at him then—Champs Senior and Ol' Champs—called him a "Sally" and a "landlubber." The insults stung Champs like the barb on a skate's tail, pointing to his lack of experience and weakness in and out of the river. He felt his face burn with shame.

He stood on the shore with the blazing sun bearing down on his head like a bully. A massive oak tree offered shade, but young Champs heard the threatening buzz of hornets and spotted their monstrous, egg-shaped, papery nest dangling from a branch. He felt dizzy and feverish.

Champs watched his grandpa standing ankle-deep in the Chesapeake untangling a trotline. Ol' Champs's gnarled brown toenails were magnified in the water. He seemed impervious to the biting blackflies. Rivulets of blood trickled down his hairless, translucent calves like tributaries racing to the bay.

All of a sudden, the cancerous sun, stench of rotting chicken, and anxiety brought on by the rays caught up with Champs. Sweat poured down his face as the droning of the hornets got louder and louder. He felt the beach heel beneath him, and then everything went black.

Young Champs woke up drenched. Six-year-old Peety stood over him, delighted by the opportunity to dump a whole pail of water on his older brother. Champs's father laughed his ass off and told Champs he looked like a washed-up perch gulping for air.

Josanne fussed around the picnic table, gathering the remains of breakfast. Despite relishing her food and coffee, Champs considered her an irritant. He scowled and hoped she'd get the message. Instead of leaving, Josanne sat back down with a look of pity on her face. Champs flinched—pity was an attack on his composure.

"Honey," she began in a soft voice, reaching out to place her hand on top of his. He yanked his away at the last minute and crossed his arms on his chest.

"I know this is a delicate subject," she continued, leaving her hand on the table in front of him. "And you're still in mourning. Course you are. But I'd simply love to make you a cross-stitch sampler to honor Pat's life. It's the least I can do. We'll sit down and have a good long chat. Talking about a lost loved one is a healing experience. And also, well, not to toot my own horn, but my samplers are considered treasured family heirlooms by most of my clients."

Champs put his fist to his mouth and belched under his breath.

He recalled that Josanne was renowned for turning her three passions—the Lord, cross-stitching, and minding other people's business—into what she called "an honest living." Popular in Methodist congregations in three counties thanks to her baking skills and willingness to write church newsletters, Josanne never had a problem finding her beloveds. That was what she called folks who paid up to $1,000 for a framed, hand-stitched sampler honoring the life of a loved one, person, or pet. She'd pour tall glasses of her sweet tea and have "good long chats" with her beloveds. Josanne had memorized a series of questions about the deceased's hobbies, favorite colors, and significant life events. This was how she customized her premade layouts. Champs had seen Josanne at work on her veranda, as she liked to call it, many times over the years.

"This is the Lord's work," Josanne would explain to anyone gathered. "It's my special calling."

Champs remembered one particular time when she'd explained her unique gift. Larry had had a few too many beers and grinned. "The way I see it," he'd said, "Josanne here, what she does, well it's all about making a killing on the memorial market." Champs had choked on his beer. Good thing Larry wasn't a stand-up comic, he'd thought, taking in the stern faces of Josanne's new church friends around the table that night.

Yawning, Champs stretched his arms in the air, but Josanne didn't get the hint. She seemed content to carry on all morning about Pat and how much good it would do Champs to talk about her. When she'd exhausted that subject, she moved right on to sewing babble, asking him what colors of floss he'd like in the sampler. Champs didn't know dental floss came in so many different colors. On and on she went.

He had no desire to sit with his neighbor, no matter how appealing her breasts, and "chat" about his dead wife. That was Pat's department —doing the talking and arranging of things during whatever crisis was at hand. Come to think of it, he felt put out that his wife presumed he could take care of her memorial sampler, for chrissakes. If she'd wanted one, if it had mattered to her at all, she should have written it down in her goddamn death notebook.

"I think she liked goldfinches," Champs said, and left the porch in search of his boat.

7

The Crappie

H ead down, Champs hustled across the backyard to the pull-through, double-story boathouse. They called it a boathouse, but it was really only a shed stretched out like a shoebox with a pitched roof that allowed for a half-finished loft space. Jeffrey had been home for the summer during his sophomore year in college when the builders, two local guys, had put him to work. They called Jeffrey the "wood whisperer" because right away his carpentry skills verged on craftsmanship, despite the shoddy materials Champs had rounded up.

"Just like Peety," Champs had said to Pat, recalling his brother's way with wood. "Shame they'll never meet."

"It doesn't have to be that way," Pat had replied.

Champs bent down to lift the garage door at one end of the boathouse. He was excited to reunite with *his* beloved—a 1992 Sea Nymph fishing boat. Rusted and pockmarked with mold, Laura had nicknamed it *Tetanus*. Champs didn't care. His boat was his mistress, and he felt confident that once he was on the river with her, everything would be right again, everything would make sense again. He pictured himself cutting through the green-brown chop, wind racing at his face, raising a can of beer in a toast to the Sassafras. Now, that was a "freestyle lifestyle," all right.

He tugged at the garage door handle, but the rolling aluminum panel didn't budge.

"It's dead-bolted on the inside," yelled Larry. He was loading his shotguns and target stands into an ancient GMC Jimmy. "The house key opens that old door on the side there. All part of Laura's security plan after the break-ins last summer."

"Figures," muttered Champs.

He watched Larry pull out, headed for the shooting range at Elk Neck State Forest. Champs lifted his cap, scratched behind his ear like a dog with a flea, put the hat back on his head, and adjusted it. Three years ago he'd been king of this castle. Things had worked the way he wanted them to work, the way they'd always worked, the way they were meant to work. And now? How locked out of his own life could a man get?

Scanning the backyard, Champs was struck by what was missing. Like the daffodils in Pat's flower garden that used to give way to a profusion of black-eyed Susans, white butterfly bushes, and daylilies later in the season. He noticed the missing pile of timeworn crab traps and the butcher-block fish-cleaning table that used to occupy the corner of the yard under the shade of a beech tree. The old rotary clothesline was gone. That would've taken some doing given it had been anchored in cement. The raised vegetable beds built by Ol' Champs back in the day had been removed. Two rectangles of dead grass marked the spot where Champs should have been leaf-mulching three feet of soil to plant seeds this time of year.

He headed back across the lawn to retrieve the boathouse key. He'd forgotten to ask Larry about the Airstream in the driveway and hoped he hadn't noticed the cracked window. That was another thing he had to add to his mounting list of things to do. He also needed to get to Otwell's in town for beer and groceries. Plus get Pat and his suitcase out of the Windstar and settle into the cabin. And, he supposed, he ought to turn his cell phone on and let Laura know he'd escaped. But first things first: he needed a whiz.

Champs stopped at the cabin door. He hadn't been in it yet except to sleep, wake in a daze, and rush onto the porch in search of Pat. Given the hideous transformation outside the cabin, he feared what might be waiting for him on the inside. But it had to be done. He pushed through the door.

"Well, son of a bitch!"

In front of him was the same narrow sofa that had been there forever. Except it had been re-covered in light blue fabric with a seashell print. A sand-colored faux-leather recliner stood in place of his grandma's rocker. Matching suede, turquoise club chairs had replaced the 1970s peeling brown chrome ones. The shipping trunk that used to hold their TV set was gone, and a freestanding flat-screen took up one whole corner of the living room. Two useless side tables fashioned out of bent bamboo stalks made poor substitutes for the stacked cinder blocks that had always done the job. Seagrass shades had been installed on the windows, replacing the olive-green valances that his grandmother had sewn. The orange shag carpet had been ripped out, replaced with whitewashed, wood-effect laminate. Worst of all, Champs's collection of framed fish prints—including the crappie that had hung on the outside of the bathroom door—was gone. The walls had been painted light green and featured a trio of watercolor seascapes. An overpowering scent of coconut potpourri engulfed him like diesel fuel exhaust. Champs felt sick.

He ran for the bathroom and vomited into the sink. In the mirror over the basin, he noticed a new rail with an ocean-themed shower curtain in place of the clothesline and tarpaulin screen they'd rigged up years ago. After relieving himself, Champs sat down on the fancy new toilet lid to fume in silence. This was Laura's doing, he knew. Here was a woman who believed in the expression "Revenge is a dish best served cold." Three years cold, Champs thought with a bitter taste still in his mouth.

That was how long it had been since the big blowup. Champs still didn't understand it. Out of the blue, Laura had arrived at the cabin that summer with a bee in her bonnet about hygiene standards and her nose in the air about the trailer-trash look of her vacation home. Nothing was good enough for her anymore and she'd kept on carping about it. She'd reminded Champs of the barking sea lions he'd seen at Fisherman's Wharf in San Francisco when he and Pat had visited David and his family one year.

Laura had refused to go out on the Sea Nymph—in fact, that was the year she'd named it *Tetanus*. She wouldn't put so much as a toe into the river. Laura had spent half a day in rubber gloves scouring the cabin with paper towels and a bottle of Mr. Clean. She'd worn the rubber gloves whenever she was on the porch or in the cabin. Laura had followed her girls around slathering their hands with an antibacterial solution. She'd forbidden them from sitting on the rug in the cabin or the concrete floor of the porch. She'd banned lunchmeat, lettuce, crabs, and barbecue from the menu because they were too likely to expose the family to E. coli. When Laura returned from Save-Cave one day with plastic tarps to cover the furniture, Champs had had enough. He'd told her to stop acting like a hothouse flower or not to bother coming back next summer.

"Hothouse flower?" she'd screamed at him, indignant. "You have no idea, Champs! I can't stand this. I can't stand you! You have no right! If it weren't for this germ-infested cabin, I'd never . . . he never would've . . . ." She'd burst into tears and locked herself in the safe confines of her brand-new Lexus.

Stunned by the outburst, Champs had yelled for Pat, who sat in the car with Laura while she sobbed, shouted, and pointed a finger like a hot poker in his direction. When Pat got out of the car, she gathered the girls, buckled them in their car seats, and loaded the trunk with two packed duffel bags. Champs stood there helpless. He felt wrongly accused as Laura backed out of the driveway, her face haggard, still wearing the rubber gloves.

"What the hell just happened?" Champs asked when the car disappeared.

"It's nothing," Pat said. "She's just having woman's problems.

Don't worry—she'll be back."

"I hope with an apology." Champs had cracked open a fresh can of beer.

But she hadn't come back that summer, although they saw her, their grandkids, and Brian at Laura's home as usual on Thanksgiving, Christmas, and Easter. The next summer, Champs and Pat had been too busy selling the house and moving into Egret's Pond to get down to the cabin. And the summer after that, Champs had stayed at Egret's Pond with Pat while she battled cancer. He wouldn't leave her side, and she'd never regained enough strength to weather the Sassafras again.

Champs's anger mounted. He wondered what his next move should be. How dare Laura change everything he cherished, everything he relied on? For the sake of what? Decorative finishes? Who was she trying to fool? She ought to have known you can't make a silk purse from a sow's ear. This was his fishing cabin, goddamn it, not her private vacation resort she could do whatever the hell she liked with. Was she that ashamed of the place? Of how she'd grown up? Of him? After everything he'd provided?

His temples pounded. The edges of his vision blurred. Head spinning, he got off the toilet, removed his clothes, and stepped behind the glossy beach curtain. Champs stood under a cold shower until he felt in no danger of blacking out. He dried off and dressed with a new sense of resolve. It was his responsibility to make the cabin right again. He would do it all on his own. It would take a while, maybe the rest of his life, but he would put back everything the way it had been, the way it was supposed to be.

Champs left the bathroom in search of his car key. He noticed that the kitchen area, with its orange Formica countertops and pine cabinets, remained intact, although he could still smell the bleach Laura had obviously used to clean it. It sparkled like a showroom kitchen. Champs opened the refrigerator, hoping beyond hope to find a forgotten beer. The fridge was empty apart from a jar of Miracle Whip and one lone can of Guinness. He sent a silent thank-you to his son-in-law, Brian, who had a passion for stout, corned beef, and cabbage. Brian was part Irish and had the red hair to prove it.

The Guinness spurted open, and the creamy head overflowed onto his hand. Champs was glad no one was around to witness the way he licked, sucked, and gulped the second-most exceptional beer of his life. With renewed vigor, he swaggered to the screen porch to make a start on transforming his cabin back to its original state. He grabbed an index card and pencil to start a to-do list. To hell with Laura.

But the weather had changed. Champs frowned at the darkening sky and fat raindrops. The smell of the gathering storm triggered a memory of Pat's rushing out to pull the beach towels off the clothesline. He heard the kettle whistling on the stove. He smelled the spicy orange tang of her Constant Comment tea and her cedar-scented wool sweater as she sat down at the picnic table with a crossword puzzle. He heard himself complain to her about the damn weather. And he felt himself smiling as she replied that it was good for the garden and nodded toward his newly planted seeds: kale, red-leaf lettuce, scallions, peas, and radishes.

A crack of thunder knocked Champs back into real time, where there was no clothesline, no teakettle, no garden, and no Pat. His heart constricted and he wondered if he'd been hit by lightning, so searing and electrifying was the jolt of pain. He collapsed in one of the cushioned wicker chairs, wrapped his arms around a pillow, and rocked himself back and forth.

Champs realized he could gut the whole place, find his old furniture in a junkyard somewhere, rehang his fish prints, rebuild the vegetable beds, and plant new seeds. He could make everything authentic again, the way he liked it. Yes, he could do that. But it didn't matter how hard he worked, how many ocean shower curtains he tore down; he'd never be able to bring back Pat. And there was no damn point in restoring the past when the person who'd made it all worthwhile couldn't be there. Couldn't be put back in place like a cinderblock side table. Plus, he hated to admit it, but the new porch furniture was very comfortable.

He pushed Pat out of his mind, moved to the sofa, and dozed off to the sound of rain.

8

Survival Blanket

By the time Champs woke, the storm had passed, and the sun neared the horizon, leaving behind a blushing rose and lavender sky. Pat used to call it the pinking hour. It was the time of day when she mixed herself a gin and tonic and sat on the porch to husk corn or top-and-tail green beans for dinner. Champs's stomach grumbled. He would need to make a trip into town if he wanted to eat.

Fortunately, Larry appeared at the screen door holding a Galena Pizzeria box and a six-pack of light beer. Champs waved him in.

"Josanne's worried about you and sent me over here with provisions. Mind if I join you?" asked Larry.

"Suit yourself," Champs replied, wishing Larry would drop the goodies and leave him alone.

Larry set the pizza down on the glass coffee table. He sat in a wicker chair, cracked open a beer, and passed it to Champs.

"Thanks," said Champs.

Larry opened one for himself. "Sorry about Pat."

Champs nodded once in acknowledgment.

They drank in silence for several minutes while crickets chirped and frogs croaked. Larry opened the pizza box and lifted up a slice of pepperoni with jalapeño peppers, Champs's favorite. Josanne sure knew a thing or two about food, he thought.

"Been meaning to ask you about that Airstream," Champs ventured. "Is it yours?"

"That thing?" Larry looked over his shoulder. "Not mine. No. Laura and Brian parked it there the summer you and Pat moved to Egret's Pond. They use it like another cabin when they come down here with the girls. Assumed you knew about it."

"Nope," said Champs, biting into a slice of pizza.

"That mean you didn't know about all the other changes she's made to the place?" Larry popped open another round of beer.

"Not till today."

Larry exhaled with a whistle and shook his head in commiseration.

They finished the pizza and leaned back into their seats with the last of the beer. Night fell. Lightning bugs came and went. After a while, Larry spoke again.

"Been out to see the new boat?"

"What new boat?"

"For chrissakes, Champs. You mean to tell me they dumped your Sea Nymph at Swansong Marina and bought a brand-new deck boat without even consulting you?"

Champs choked on his beer. His face mottled with anger. He stood up like a ramrod, knocking the pizza box onto the coir mat underfoot.

"I think you better leave now, Larry," he said, trying hard not to explode.

"Hey, look here, Champs. I shouldn't have said anything. Just let's calm down a minute before we jump—"

"Get out *now*!"

Larry backed away with his arms outstretched as if facing a panicked wild animal, then disappeared into the night.

Champs paced back and forth across the porch, clenching and

unclenching his fists. Redecorating his cabin was one thing, but condemning his fishing boat to the marina where all good intentions went to die? Unforgivable. He felt attacked by his daughter and betrayed by his other children and Larry, too. Pat must have known about this all along, and it pained him even more that she'd allowed this to happen behind his back, no matter how sick she'd been. He didn't deserve this. Did they think he wouldn't find out about this? How dare they keep secrets from him. What was a fisherman without his goddamn fishing boat? Laura might as well have chopped off his balls or drained the river while she was at it.

His legs tired of pacing, though his mind still spun like a tumble dryer. Champs couldn't face entering the airy, pastel nightmare that had once been his musty, practical fishing cabin. He couldn't face the bedrooms, where he imagined his life with Pat was bleached out as if they'd never lived there at all. Never lived at all. So many rugs had been pulled out from under him in such a short space of time. The only touchstone he had left, it seemed, was his ramshackle Ford Windstar. He fled to it, hoping to calm himself down by driving around in the dark.

He drove to Middletown on autopilot, a solid twenty-minute drive to come up with a new plan. By the time he pulled into the discount Save-Cave parking lot, he knew precisely what the situation called for. Pushing a cart with a cranky wheel, Champs entered the floodlit cement church of the cheap and nasty. Up and down every aisle, he filled the cart with the necessities for his new life.

Two hours later he approached a checkout lane with a sack of potatoes, a large bag of powdered eggs, two tubs of pretzels, a variety four-can pack of cheese spray, a dozen cans of chili with beans, ten tins of sardines, an eighteen-can pack of Vienna sausages, two boxes of saltine crackers, a twelve-pack of canned peaches, another of green beans, a forty-eight-count variety box of instant oatmeal, two twelve-ounce cans of jalapeño-flavored SPAM, a propane tank, an extra-large squirt bottle of mustard, two canisters of Chock Full o'Nuts coffee, a king-sized foil survival blanket, four cases of store-brand beer, a bar of soap, several packs of different-sized batteries, a gallon of kosher dills, and a twelve-ounce bottle of Blue Bonnet squeeze butter—because everything tastes better with Blue Bonnet on it.

"You stockin' a bunker? Preparing for a siege?" asked the cashier, a pimply guy with long hair, man boobs, and fingernails bitten down to the quick.

"Something like that," said Champs, grabbing a fistful of Peperami packages from the display at the checkout line. "You want one, uh"—Champs squinted at the man's name tag—"*Danielle?*"

"Danielle, that's right. I'm in transition," Danielle explained with a shrug, and accepted the stick of pork meat from Champs. "Thanks."

"Oh, sure," said Champs. "Good luck with your move."

He thought he'd best get out of there. Peperami was one thing, but he'd almost sprung for a deck of cards at the last minute, too. Damn those impulse displays! And who the hell did he have to play cards with, anyway?

On the way back to Deadrise Cove, Champs explained his plan to Pat, still in her yellowish metal urn in the Samsonite suitcase.

"We'll sleep in the Windstar tonight. Tomorrow, I'll raid the boathouse and get the family tent and camping supplies out of storage. If my gas grill isn't there, I'll come back here and buy a new one. I'll hitch that new boat trailer to the Windstar and rescue the Sea Nymph from the Swansong Marina dumping grounds. We can just go back to living like we used to at Queens Point before the cabin. Guess you weren't with me then, but you'll get used to it. We'll make do until things get back to normal."

Champs parked in the backyard between the upper and lower cabins. After a late-night snack of Vienna sausages and warm beer, he relieved himself in a tangle of tree roots, rotten logs, and poison ivy. Back in the van, he wrapped himself in the survival blanket and reclined the seat as far as it would go.

"Night, Pat."

Fruit of the Looms

After a restless night, Champs rose with the sun and slurped his way through a can of peaches for breakfast. He was itching to fish, but it was too early to save the Sea Nymph from her premature grave. Instead, he decided to set up his living accommodations.

The key slid into the lock on the side door of the boathouse. Champs flipped on the lights to reveal a twenty-one-foot, royal-blue Yamaha speedboat. It looked like it had never seen the water. He observed the features and trim and came up with a rough estimate: sixty grand. The boat was a beauty, there was no denying it. Super fast, too. But Champs found it difficult to celebrate a vessel perfect for every water activity—skiing, tubing, swimming, tanning, diving, racing (there was even a goddamn barbecue)—except the one that mattered most to him: fishing.

"Humph," he muttered, and opened both ends of the shed.

Josanne rushed over with a hot cup of coffee and a blueberry muffin wrapped up in a paper towel. "Well, there you are, darlin'. You didn't come home last night. We worried about you. You fixin' to take the new boat out this morning?"

"That thing?" Champs pointed to the Yammy with his muffin hand, then took a gratifying gulp of coffee. He felt the hot caffeine rush through his veins like a mild current stimulating his nerve endings to attention.

"You sure you're all right there, Champs?"

"Good as gold, Josanne. Got a lot of work to do, so I'd better get moving along."

Champs retreated into the boathouse and set his breakfast on a workbench before pulling down the stairway to the loft.

"Toodle-oo," Josanne called out.

Champs heard her front door close and breathed a sigh of relief. The whole idea of coming back here had been to live his life free from the intrusions of well-meaning but irritating people. Why couldn't they mind their own damn business and leave him alone?

At the top of the ladder, he scanned the loft space, where nothing had changed. Camping cots, each with a pillow and sleeping bag, lined up like railcars across the far wall. A TV, an Atari gaming unit, and beanbags were coated in dust at one end. Next to the TV stood an unplugged minifridge and microwave. The rest of the space contained storage cabinets, shelves, and labeled boxes full of the flotsam and jetsam of four generations. Champs noticed his framed fish prints in a cardboard box. He spotted his grandma's rocking chair in the corner and dusted off the boxes containing their old camping supplies.

As he clambered down the ladder to finish his coffee and muffin, it occurred to him he could move into the loft instead of setting up camp. But he didn't want the inconvenience of climbing up and down the ladder multiple times a day. Not to mention walking around that ridiculous excuse for a boat to get up there.

His fishing caps were lined up in a neat row on the top shelf of his tool bench. He chose a red "Kiss My Bass" one and settled it on his head. Now he felt ready for business.

It was one o'clock by the time Champs had moved the speedboat out, brought down all the supplies from the loft, set up camp, and rescued the *Tetanus* from the marina morgue. The owner had waived the storage and removal fees because he knew Pat had died and he couldn't take money from a man in the throes of grief. Champs would have preferred to pay any amount of cash to avoid the pitying look and the arm thrown around his shoulders. What was it about death that compelled grown men to put their hands on him? He considered getting a T-shirt made that said, "Touch me, and I'll kick you in the nuts."

Champs staked out the old, square green tent against the hedge of invasive English ivy and honeysuckle that ran along the side of the yard. The tent had patches of mold here and there but was otherwise in good enough shape. He rigged his crappie fish print to hang inside. Next, Champs repurposed a large tarp, spare guylines, and tent poles to create a covered kitchen area furnished with the red card table he'd found in the loft and a Coleman stove. He stacked his canned goods underneath the table. A plastic storage box held all the pots, pans, cutlery, kitchen utensils, and enameled dishes—white with red trim— they'd used decades ago at Queens Point camp.

At some point, Laura had bought a pop-up screen tent meant to keep her and the girls free of sun, sand, and flies on long afternoons at the beach. As with most things Laura bought, it was a deluxe model. Champs had plenty of room for his grandma's rocking chair, two card-table chairs, and a tree stump he rolled up from the lower cabin lot for a side table. He brought his trusty flyswatter inside and felt right at home.

Two power cords poked through a hole in the screening on the real porch. One fed into the tent to charge his phone and various batteries. The other connected to a tangled cord of Christmas tree lights that Champs had clipped onto his tarp kitchen awning with wooden clothespins. He couldn't wait to see the effect once it got dark.

After a lunch of tinned sardines, squeeze cheese on saltine crack- ers, and a couple of beers, Champs got the suitcase out of the Windstar and unpacked in his tent. He didn't know where to put the urn, so he leaned it into a corner near his cot. The clothes he'd thrown into the suitcase included a towel, four pairs of dirty underwear, two T-shirts, and an extra pair of cargo shorts. Perfect. Champs took the towel, the laundry, and a bar of soap down to the outdoor shower that was still operational on the uncollapsed side of the lower cabin.

He was hanging his wet Fruit of the Looms on a clothesline between the cabin and a cedar tree, buck naked apart from the towel wrapped around his waist, when he heard a car pull up in the driveway behind the Airstream.

"Hello? Laura? Hello?" called out a young woman dressed in a short black skirt and high heels. She hobbled her way to the backyard and caught sight of Champs and his dripping underwear. She halted in her tracks and stared at him. Champs stared back.

"Oh, I'm sorry. I must . . . I must be at the wrong house? I'm looking for Laura?" said the woman.

"She's not here," replied Champs.

Just then, Champs heard another car engine, a slammed door, and the annoying "beep-beep" of an alarm being set. As if you needed a car alarm in Deadrise Cove.

"Hello? Amanda? Are you back here?" called Laura as she rounded the corner. There was a moment of stunned silence broken by Laura's two-ton slaughtered-cow handbag sliding off her shoulder onto the ground.

"*Champs?*" she said as if he were an alien version of himself who had just walked out of a UFO.

"Hi, Laura," said Champs. "This lady here . . . Amanda, I'm guessing? She's looking for you." He returned to his task, whistling "Heigh-Ho" from *Snow White and the Seven Dwarfs*.

"What in the hell is going on here?" yelled Laura. "You're supposed to be at Egret's Pond. What have you done to the backyard?"

"What have you done to my cabin?" he retorted.

Amanda stood on the lawn, staked in by her high heels, and swiveled her head back and forth between Laura and Champs like a spectator at a tennis match.

"Your cabin? What are you even doing here? Why aren't you dressed? Are those *Christmas* tree lights?" Laura exclaimed. "Oh my

God, this isn't happening. This can't be happening. Have you gone insane?"

"Um, Laura?" said Amanda. "This seems like a bad time? I'll head back to the office and call you tomorrow, maybe? Okay?" She stepped out of her shoes, yanked them from the ground, and scampered on tiptoe back to her car.

"Great," said Laura. "You've ruined it, Champs. Once again, you've ruined it. That woman was meeting me here to inspect the beach cottage I've spent an inordinate amount of time and money fixing up for you!"

"Beach cottage now, is it? Inspect it for what?"

His first thought was termites, but Amanda hadn't looked like a typical pest control type. She hadn't worn coveralls with her name sewn on the front, not to mention an Orkin hard hat.

"Inspect it for renting, Champs. For income. But who the hell will rent a vacation beach cottage with a homeless encampment attached?" Laura demanded.

"Renting? What are you talking about? You can't rent out the cabin without my permission. I live here! I own this cabin! Did you think I wouldn't notice? Do you think I'm a goddamn moron?"

"No. We thought you'd be pleased. We thought we had time to get the whole thing operational while you transitioned into the apartment at Egret's Pond. We didn't want to stress you out any more than you already are."

"'We'? Who's 'we'?"

"Me, Jeffrey, and David. Who else would it be? We agreed before Mom died that since you wouldn't be spending much time down here anymore, if any, it was a good idea to set it up as an Airbnb. That way, you'd have a small income stream to pay for any extra care you may need," explained Laura.

Champs was speechless. What the hell was a "hair-being-bee"? There were so many things wrong with what Laura had just stated, he couldn't breathe, let alone think or respond.

"Like I said before," she continued. "We thought you'd be pleased. It was supposed to be a nice surprise, but now you've ruined it.

Honestly, Champs—I don't get you. You seem determined to make everything difficult for us. As if it isn't difficult enough with Mom gone, and . . ." Laura trailed off then, kneading her forehead with clenched fingertips like talons. Champs could tell she was trying hard to hold back tears, or something worse.

It didn't work.

"Go to hell!" she cried, her face a twisted mess of anger and pain. She broke out in sobs and ran to her car. Champs heard the tires spitting gravel as she sped out of Deadrise Cove.

Head pounding, he brought a six-pack of beer onto his fake porch and guzzled one down. He was dumbstruck and hurt by her outburst. The way he saw it, Laura was the one determined to make everything difficult for *him*, not the other way around. He was adjusting to his new circumstances—transitioning—without bothering any of his children. So what the hell was Laura so upset about? And why lash out at him?

If only Pat were around to help him. To help Laura. Champs didn't know what he was supposed to do. He felt defeated at every turn.

Several crushed cans later, he passed out in the rocking chair, chin to chest. A thin line of drool pooled on his faded T-shirt.

10

Peregrin Wethered

Champs woke to a low rumbling sound. It took him a minute to realize where he was. He sat up straight in the pedestal fishing chair mounted on the stern of the Sea Nymph and finished the can of beer still gripped by his hand. He'd gone catfishing at Lloyd Creek early in the morning. Apparently, he'd dozed off waiting for a bite.

It had been nearly two months since Laura's hissy-fit visit. Almost June now, and Champs still hadn't caught a single thing. Had she cursed his fishing because he hadn't reached out to apologize? Her words still stung, and although he'd picked up his phone more than once to check on her, he'd lost his nerve each time and had never made the call.

Champs sighed and reeled in his line to find the bloodworm long gone.

The next drumroll barreled upriver. He assessed the clouds and sniffed the air like a hound dog. It was a thunderstorm, not test bombs from the Aberdeen Proving Ground, a US Army facility on the other side of the bay. Grunting, he stood up and leaned over the boat to pull up anchor. The Sea Nymph rocked from the wake of a twenty-five-foot aluminum crab hauler, *Emi-Lee*, returning from the Chesapeake with its daily catch.

Back in the day, Champs had known the owner, Frank Pruitt, and his then-wife, Beverly. Frank had christened the hauler in her name —*Bever-Lee*—hoping to win her over to the crabbing life. She wasn't impressed. Especially when the locals called her "the beaver" and made rapid sucking sounds with their front teeth stuck out whenever they saw her. Beverly wasn't known for her sense of humor.

One night, Frank came home late from his poker game to find a bushel of jumbo Jimmies scuttling around on his side of the bed, claws extended, pinching at the air. He never saw Beverly again. But the next day, Frank seasoned the crabs with Old Bay, steamed them up real good, and invited friends and neighbors over for a feast. Among them was Emily, and he'd married her soon after. Frank painted "Emi" over the "Bever" part of the crab boat, and that was the end of that. Champs wondered who was operating the *Emi-Lee* now. Not Frank, who would be in his late eighties, if he was still alive at all.

The anchor came up, Sassafras muck clinging to the rode, as the first raindrops landed on Champs's Dogfish Head Brewery cap. The river turned steel gray and choppy in the rising wind. *Tetanus* sputtered loud and rough, then settled into a rumble. Champs followed the *Emi-Lee* toward Turner's Creek to take temporary shelter. It was too late to make the five-mile trip home now.

He moored his boat at the rotting public wharf that supported an old wooden granary with a corrugated steel roof dating back to the late 1800s. The storehouse had been built to hold tobacco, then later, corn or wheat until the steamboats arrived to take it to market.

Champs had an affinity for historic structures that once served a vital purpose and now sat dormant across the watershed areas of the Chesapeake Bay. This particular granary had stayed in the family of its original owner, Peregrin Wethered, until 1974, when his descendants sold it to the commissioners of Kent County. Except for minor repairs, it had been left alone to the ravages of time. The structure had what Champs considered a beautiful patina, a soft, weathered grace that it took time to create and was hard to find anymore in this day of shiny surfaces. Most folks saw it as an eyesore or safety hazard. Champs knew it wasn't long for this world. But neither was he.

It was raining hard as he hoisted himself out of the boat and jogged for cover under the park pavilion on a small bluff above the public landing. How many times had Pat distracted the cold, wet, and hungry kids here when a nasty weather front caught them out on the river? How many times had he stood here as a child throwing oyster shells at his brother, Peety, while his mother and Champs Senior, or Granny and Ol' Champs, counted the seconds between lightning and thunder to figure out how close the storm was?

A stark white bolt zigzagged against the gunmetal sky. Champs counted, "One one thousand, two one thousand, three one—"

The bone-shattering smack of electricity and hot air startled him, even though he knew it was coming. Champs longed for the companionship of his pipe, which Pat had insisted he give up for health reasons decades ago. Instead, he dug out a bag of peanuts from the pocket of his drab cargo shorts and munched through them until he was thirsty for another beer. He figured it was around noon. For lack of anything else to do, Champs opened his clamshell phone to check the time. Eleven fifty-one. He stared at the fluorescent numbers until the display showed 11:52. Irritated, he snapped the lid of the phone back into place. In his opinion, digital clocks were always trying to get one over on a person. He treated them like spies, suspicious of their spurious accuracy. Who the hell needed to know more than that it was around noon anyway?

The Sassafras had been empty of activity even before the storm gathered. It was a Thursday morning, and although the summer season had officially opened, most of the pleasure boats, recreational crabbers, and fishermen wouldn't appear on weekdays until the schools let out. Champs's mind wandered back over the last two months of forging his "freestyle lifestyle" outside the confines of Regret's Pond.

He'd enjoyed the first week of camping life, reuniting with his boat and the river. The Christmas-light awning had proven to be very snazzy at night, carnival-like. But in the weeks that had followed, Champs had been plagued by moments of confusion, dizzy spells, stabbing pains in his chest, and lung-crushing inertia he couldn't escape. The days and nights had run together in an endless cycle of drinking, fishing, and passing out with little to revive his dampened spirit. Others had reached out, but with few exceptions, Champs had insisted that he was A-okay and didn't need company or help. "I'm fine on my own," he'd told anyone who'd bothered to ask.

David had left three or four voice messages on the clamshell that Champs hadn't bothered to play. One child telling him to go to hell was enough. He didn't want to risk a confrontation with David that could end on the same note.

Jeffrey had driven down every week from the Poconos on Sunday evening, bringing hot meatball sandwiches from Galena Pizzeria. He stayed overnight and went fishing with Champs the next morning, then left after lunch, when Champs retreated to his tented porch to sleep off the morning's beer. The first time Jeffrey showed up, he'd made no comment about Champs's escape from Egret's Pond or the homeless encampment he now inhabited. That had been fine by Champs. But recently, Jeffrey had asked some uncomfortable questions.

"How is this any better than Egret's Pond?" he'd inquired a couple weeks ago.

"The fishing," Champs had replied. "No fish in that damn puddle they call a pond."

"You don't catch any fish here, either."

Champs had considered telling him to get lost, but there were the meatball sandwiches to consider. Instead, he'd shrugged and opened another beer.

Larry had offered more than once to help Champs trade in the Windstar for a great deal on a preowned car at the used-car dealership he'd once owned. But Champs waved him away. He had no interest in getting rid of the Windstar; it may have been old, but it worked fine. Champs had informed Larry there was no point in trading a used car for another used car with payments tacked on. Did Larry think he was some kinda sucker just because he lived in a tent? Undeterred, Larry had switched to guns and offered to teach Champs how to shoot game birds. Despite the promise of a pint of IPA in the bar afterward, Champs told Larry he was no more a gunman than a golfer, and besides, he didn't look good in camouflage. Larry had left Champs alone after that.

Josanne hadn't given up on her plan to make a memorial sampler. Champs had tried to be blunt with her. He'd told her he didn't need a sampler because he didn't need reminding his wife was dead—he still had her ashes in an urn right inside his tent. Maybe she'd like to see them? At the time, Josanne had been holding a decadent slice of real strawberry shortcake. He'd reached out to take it and she'd pulled it back.

"Well, bless your heart, Champs. Tell you what. You come on over to my veranda, and I'll give you this cake and a glass of my famous sweet tea. All you have to do is keep me company while I work on my samplers. Deal?"

"Deal." Champs was already salivating. Whether because of the cake or her cleavage, he would have been hard-pressed to say.

After that, Josanne had baked for him every Wednesday afternoon. She only allowed Champs to partake if he'd sit with her while she worked on her samplers and shared the stories of her beloved customers. He'd refused to discuss Pat, but his knowledge of embroidery floss and the sorrows of the local Methodist community had grown considerably. As had his waistline. He now looked about nine months pregnant.

Champs rubbed his protruding belly in memory of the excellent sour cream coconut cake he'd enjoyed yesterday. The rain sputtered out, and the grim clouds yielded to a penetrating sun and a pure blue sky. Within minutes, sweat trickled down his forehead. He huffed it back to the wharf.

It was like that on the Sassafras. After a few days, rain, sweat, river, and tears mingled on a person's skin with sun cream, mosquito repellent, and spilled beer. Champs referred to it as the Sassafras sheen, a human patina of sorts. Even after showering, something dank and elemental escaped from your pores when next exposed to the heat and humidity. There wasn't a deodorant in the world that stopped the stink wafting from the pits of men and women alike after a day on the river. He'd gotten used to it years ago.

Champs eased himself into the soaked Sea Nymph and cast off from the wharf. With the motor coughing, he took off his cap and mopped his head before setting it down tight for the ride back. He hammered the throttle and sped for home, anticipating a cold beer and a nap in his screened tent.

Twenty minutes later, Champs idled into Deadrise Cove. Someone stood on the shoreline, tossing sticks into the river. For a moment, Champs thought it was his brother, Peety, whom he hadn't seen since that terrible stormy night back in '75. He squinted for a closer inspection, then frowned when he realized it was Jeffrey.

Why was Jeffrey here unannounced on a Thursday?

Champs hated surprise visits. In his experience, unplanned visitors arrived bearing bad news. He avoided the temptation to turn the *Tetanus* around and hightail it out of there. Why couldn't people just leave him the hell alone?

Millie Moves In

C hamps cut the motor and tied off the Sea Nymph while Jeffrey walked down the dock and onto the splintered floating finger on the port side of the boat. A six-pack of light beer was tucked under one arm, and a bedraggled dog was draped over the other.

"Hey," he said.

Champs nodded once and reached over to yank a beer can out of its plastic ring. His movement tipped the dock finger and the boat, but he and Jeffrey remained balanced. As lifelong watermen, they were comfortable with the pitch and yaw of life on the river, if not so much on land. Champs popped the tab, enjoyed the brief fizzing sound, and gulped half of it down. His stomach rumbled.

"Did you bring the meatballs?" he asked, making eye contact with Jeffrey.

Champs had first laid eyes on his son after rushing over to Brandy-wine Hospital during his lunch break the morning Jeffrey was born. At the far end of the maternity ward, Pat held what appeared to be a four-month-old baby. She'd swaddled him in the fluffy receiving blanket that his other children had kicked off in a squalling fit when they'd been born. He remembered being annoyed about that: he'd practiced for hours swaddling a chipped Betsy Wetsy doll when Pat was pregnant with David. What a waste that had been. But this new baby wrapped up in Pat's arms looked content. He had soft wisps of black hair and a healthy complexion.

Champs hesitated before running over to them, unsure of himself. To be fair, it had been nine years since Laura, and he was out of practice. But there was more to it than that. He'd expected a tiny infant, jaundiced, wailing and bald, punching and kicking at the world from the get-go. Like David. Like Laura. This one seemed, well, wrong somehow. Champs couldn't put his finger on it and felt an uneasy sense of doubt rise like a red flag in the back of his mind. Had they given Pat the wrong baby by mistake? Waved over by his beaming wife, he crossed the worn and well-bleached floor. She lifted the bundle to him. He took it as if receiving an unwanted gift.

"His name is Jeffrey," Pat announced.

On cue, baby Jeffrey opened his eyes and looked straight through to Champs's soul. Jeffrey's eyes were the exact color of the Sassafras: a murky yet reflective green-brown. Champs felt pulled into his son's gaze, under the river's surface and through the swaying pondweed, down to the sucking, silky muck below. Abruptly, he handed the baby back to Pat, hoping she hadn't noticed his odd behavior. He kissed her on the forehead, made his excuses, and went back to work.

"No meatballs today," Jeffrey said.

He wore a faded black *Queen* T-shirt familiar to Champs because his brother, Peety, used to wear it. Why was Jeffrey wearing Peety's shirt?

"I got kicked out of the resort this morning and moved into the lower cabin," Jeffrey announced.

"That explains the T-shirt," said Champs. Peety used to live in the lower cabin and must have left some clothes behind.

The dog, a brown and white spaniel, whined.

"And the dog?" Champs asked, gesturing to the mess that hung like a wet fur coat in the crook of Jeffrey's arm.

"I guess she lives here now, too," Jeffrey replied.

"Humph." Champs scowled at the animal, who maintained a drippy, woeful expression.

He grabbed his cooler, stepped onto the main dock, and plodded back to the Windstar on shore. Jeffrey followed. A great blue heron glided to the shaded bank of the river and perched on the branches of a felled tree. Champs glowered at it.

"Goddamn pterodactyl! Get outta here!" He swung the cooler as if to swat the intruder away.

The bird didn't move.

Most folks couldn't get enough of the beauty and nobility of the great blue heron. It was the signature bird for every Eastern Shore tourist brochure, guesthouse, and "Save the Bay" campaign. But the heron's greedy appetite for fish had made it the bane of every recreational fisherman's existence—and the greatest culprit ever for having a bad day on the river. Champs turned to address the spaniel still hanging from Jeffrey's arm.

"See that there? That stupid excuse for a waterfowl? That's the reason we don't eat fish tonight! Got it? He ate 'em all. Him and all his goddamn buddies over there on Hen Island!" Champs paused to draw breath. "If you're gonna stick around here, Millie, you better—"

"Millie?" Jeffrey interrupted.

Champs shrugged.

"Millie?" Jeffrey repeated. "You just called the dog Millie."

"So what?"

The spaniel wiggled free of Jeffrey's arm and belly-flopped into the river with a giant splash that sent the heron flying away.

"Good dog," said Champs as Millie surfaced.

She doggie-paddled to shore, keeping pace with Champs as he continued to stomp down the dock.

"Well, for a start, that's not her name, Champs," Jeffrey called out to him.

Without breaking stride, Champs swiveled his head around. "It is now."

His next step forward brought him smack into the down-filled vest of a tall, ropey-looking man who'd appeared out of thin air at the end of the dock.

"Whoa there, Champs. Nearly ran me over," said the feather-breasted man as he stepped back. He tried to steady Champs, who reeled from the collision.

"Jesus Christ!" said Champs, and swung his cooler again as if to ward off the latest irritant.

He scanned the man in front of him. A ruddy, stubbled face. Greasy salt-and-pepper hair pulled back into a ponytail under a stained cap that read "Cluckin' Good Poultry Grit." Flannel shirt. Worn-out jeans. Farm boots. He looked familiar, but Champs couldn't place him.

"It's me. Ray?" said the man. "Chicken Ray? Your fisherman friend who happens to raise the best-tasting birds on the Eastern Shore? We're all organic now."

Champs made no move to acknowledge Chicken Ray. Weariness seeped into his bones. He didn't want to deal with any other surprises today. It was too much. Everyone seemed determined to block his way to an afternoon of serious beer drinking in his favorite rocking chair on the tent porch. The sun reflected off the water into his eyes with the precision of laser shafts. His head filled with a buzz-saw sound.

He was about to black out when Millie reached his side and shook herself, splattering him awake with muddy river water and strands of bright green algae scum. Jeffrey stepped off the dock and placed a steady hand on Champs's back. The dog skulked over to the Windstar, ears down and tail between her legs. She avoided the shade and flopped against a steamy black tire, draping a paw over her muzzle.

"Weird dog," said Chicken Ray.

"Hi, I'm Jeffrey, Champs's youngest," Jeffrey said, and extended his hand out to Chicken Ray. "I'm pretty sure we've met before."

"Of course," said Chicken Ray, accepting the handshake. "Jeffrey. Been a while. Good to see you. I was just about to put the ol' lady in the drink and baptize this coffin-billed crankbait. There's a striper out there with my name on it."

He dangled the lure at the end of his rod for emphasis.

"Champs here will tell you it's too late in the day to catch anything, but sometimes I get lucky after a summer squall. You two wanna join me? I got plenty of beer."

Champs had no intention of joining Chicken Ray, the most notorious arsonist on the Eastern Shore.

The Ballad of Chicken Ray

He'd first met Chicken Ray when he was twelve.

"He's about your age, I reckon," Champs Senior had said one day. "He and his twin brothers are living with Hessie over there at the wooden-boat repair yard. Turns out they're Hessie's nephews. He took 'em in after their trailer burned down, killing their ma and pa. His name's Ray. I told Hessie you'd get him situated with the other kids."

Champs Senior knew Hessie from the River Rats poker club, where they both gambled and got shit-faced on Friday nights along with several other locals. Hessie was only twenty-two years old when he took in his orphaned nephews. He'd done what he could to raise them. But his passion for cards and Harley-Davidsons meant his parenting skills left a lot to be desired. Although the community pitched in and did what they could, Ray and his younger brothers had, for the most part, been left to their own devices. You could say they'd been raised by the river.

As instructed by his father, young Champs had pulled Ray and his twin brothers into the group of year-round and summer-season kids and teens on the river. They reunited each year for three sweltering months to wreak havoc on each other and the Sassafras. As time wore on, some bonded as fishermen and members of the River Rats poker club. Ray joined at sixteen, but Champs's mother put her foot down—she had enough to worry about with one confirmed alcoholic gambler in the house.

Hessie's boat repair yard went out of business around the same time Ray's brothers came home from Vietnam in twin coffins. In order to make ends meet, Hessie and Ray opened a bait shop out of Hessie's garage, a short walk up from the boat-launch ramp in Fredericktown. Ray stopped making a living selling clam snouts and got into the poultry business after winning a burned-down chicken farm from its meth-addicted owner in an illegal game of Texas Hold'em out in Cecilton. The main shed had exploded in flames the week before, prompting the local paper to declare, "BBQ'd Chicken (and Farm) for Sale." Rumors flew that Ray had set the chicken farm alight, knowing he could beat the owner at cards and win the property.

Ray knew nothing about chickens, but he knew a lot of guys in construction who owed him favors of one kind or another. The chicken sheds and other farm equipment went up in a matter of weeks. Pat offered to help him with the chickens and share her "free range" farming expertise. At the end of the summer, Ray's first flock of broilers sold out to local stores and restaurants. He landed on the front page of the *Kent County Crier*, with the headline "No Fowl Play: Chicken Ray's Cluckin' Good Luck." The nickname stuck.

Shortly after, Uncle Hessie died in a suspicious hotel fire in Ocean City, Maryland. He'd racked up substantial debt in a casino operated by a violent motorcycle gang—so the story went. According to the police report, the surviving desk clerk had sworn on the Bible he'd checked Hessie into his room that night and hadn't seen him leave. There were no traces of Hessie's body. And no evidence of *Nadine*, Hessie's meticulously polished Harley.

Local folks started telling tales of a phantom Hessie haunting the abandoned boatyard, which rotted plank by plank into the Sassafras silt. Another rumor spread that Hessie, with the help of Chicken Ray's arson expertise, had staged the whole thing and was living down in the Florida Keys smoking gator meat for a living.

Chicken Ray inherited the riverfront boatyard and Uncle Hessie's old Victorian house, along with six boxes of live bloodworms, two poly barrels of pickled eel, and a twenty-gallon bag of bull lips—all that remained of the fish-and-bait business. The *Kent County Crier* featured him again with the headline "Going Cheap, Cheap, Cheap: Chicken Ray's Haunted Wharf." Speculation about who would buy the old warehouse with its decrepit docks and cormorant-topped pilings was the talk of the town. But Chicken Ray held on to it.

Champs and Chicken Ray had gradually drifted apart. Occasionally, Champs saw Ray on the river and got updates from Larry, who'd joined the River Rats and saw Chicken Ray most weeks. According to Larry, Chicken Ray had continued to moor Hessie's Chesapeake Bay deadrise, the *Duchess,* at the old boatyard until someone set her ablaze several years later. Ray was away at a poultry industry conference at the time, but that didn't stop locals from speculating. His notoriety grew.

Chicken Ray cashed in his insurance policy and bought a used fishing boat and a preowned Dodge pickup with a reliable hitch and boat trailer. The second *Duchess* was a Tidewater center-console boat with a canvas bimini over the cockpit. About two years ago, Larry had mentioned to Champs that Chicken Ray was regularly launching his boat from Deadrise Cove. He wasn't a resident and didn't pay dues, but no one seemed to care. He was Chicken Ray after all. His status as a celebrity arsonist had earned him all kinds of privileges and connections up and down the Sassafras. If you needed something done fast, cheap, and off the record, Chicken Ray knew a guy who'd get the job done.

Champs rolled his eyes as Jeffrey accepted Chicken Ray's offer of an afternoon of fishing and beer with the enthusiasm of a kid invited to Disneyland. What was so goddamn special about a fire-starting poultry clown?

"Champs, did you get that?" Jeffrey asked. "Chicken Ray here's gonna take me out on the *Duchess* for a little fishing. Can you do me a favor and take Sal—I mean Millie—home with you?"

Champs refused to commit.

"Tell you what, I'll pick up those meatball sandwiches when we're done fishing. What d'ya say?" Jeffrey pleaded.

Champs didn't respond.

Chicken Ray cleared his throat. "Good to see you, Champs. I heard you were back in town. Glad to run into you, so to speak." He attempted a chuckle, but the joke fell flat and so did his face as it morphed into what Champs perceived as pity.

Nothing could be worse.

"I'm sorry about Pat," Chicken Ray said. He clasped Champs's shoulder, anchoring him to the ground. "I don't . . . I don't know what to say."

An awkward silence intensified the afternoon heat. Champs predicted a long, hot, and humid summer. A yellow perch jumped out of the water and plopped back under the surface. The heron flew back to its tree branch.

"How are you holding up?" Chicken Ray finally asked.

"Fine," replied Champs with gritted teeth as he wrested himself out of Chicken Ray's grip.

He turned away and stomped across the stony parking lot toward Millie. He had nothing to say to Chicken Ray and hated the pretense that they had been good buddies once. They had only ever been acquaintances, men who loved to fish and shared a river and occasionally a beer. And that was way back. So what if Pat had helped him with his goddamn chickens? That meant nothing anymore. Champs didn't see the point of making nice with the locals—particularly the kind who put a hand on his shoulder and asked how he was holding up with his dead wife. How do you think, asshole?

13

DEFCON 1

Millie couldn't jump into the Windstar, so Champs opened the passenger-side door and lifted her onto the front seat. He roared up the hill, eager for a much-needed afternoon of solitude and suds. As he approached the cabin, he slammed on the brakes. His arm flew out in a protective gesture and stopped Millie from catapulting into the dashboard. Laura's silver Lexus was parked behind the Airstream.

"For chrissakes, what now?"

Millie whined.

Champs gripped the steering wheel and set his jaw to DEFCON 1 before parking at the back of the lot between the upper and lower cabins. He was reluctant to get out of the van. Hadn't he been through enough today already?

"Millie," Champs said. The filthy mop dog in the passenger seat waited for Champs to continue. Flies buzzed around her muzzle and he spotted a bulging tick burrowed in her neck. "You have my full permis-

sion to bare your teeth if Laura approaches either of us with a disinfec-
tant or weapon of any kind. You understand?"

Millie growled.

"Good dog."

Champs breathed a sigh of relief when he found his campsite
empty. He took a few beers from the cooler he'd set up when the
weather had turned warm. Just as he zipped himself inside the tent
porch, Laura and the girls emerged from the Airstream and crossed the
yard to greet him. Champs sat down in his rocking chair. Millie barked
through the screen.

"A dog!" screamed six-year-old Zoe. She broke free from her
mother and appeared to mount an imaginary horse, which she galloped
straight up to the tent, her red hair coming loose from its pigtails.

Millie stopped barking and wagged her tail.

"Awww," Zoe said. She dismounted her horse and bent down,
smooshing her hand against the screening, where Millie covered it with
dog kisses.

"Zo-Zo!" Laura reprimanded her as she caught up with her daughter. "Stop that! You don't know if that dog is friendly or not. We talked
about this." Laura whipped out an antibacterial wipe and bent down to
pry Zoe's wet hand away from the screen and give it a good scrubbing.

Zo-Zo fought and refused to give up her hand.

Millie bared her teeth.

Champs looked up from the scuffle to meet the gaze of nine-year-
old Hannah. She crossed her arms and rolled her eyes as if fed up with
the antics of her mother and sister. Champs motioned for her to walk
around to the back door of the tent porch, unzipped it, and let her in.
He handed her a beer and offered up a chair. They cracked open their
cans in unison. Hannah studied Champs as he sucked up the thin foam
on the top of the can. She did the same, but not without a grimace.

"All right. Fine, then. You win," Laura said, and let go of
squirming Zo-Zo, who ran to the evaporating rain puddles where the
raised garden beds used to be.

Laura stood and wiped her own hands before unzipping the tent-
porch door and stepping inside. "Hi, Champs," she said, zooming in

on the can of beer in Hannah's hand. "Nice of you to get your fourth-grader granddaughter drunk on this hot afternoon." She took the can away from Hannah and held it against her cheek to cool down.

"Mooomm," Hannah said, "don't get mad at Champs. I wasn't gonna drink it. Duh." She made a face at her mother.

"I wasn't aware that you acquired a dog," Laura said.

"Her name's Millie," said Champs.

His stomach roared like the Metro-Goldwyn-Mayer lion at the start of a movie.

"Did you have any lunch, Champs? You look a little pale," Laura said. "I have an extra sandwich in the *Flying Cloud*. I'll go get it if you want."

"*Flying Cloud*, eh? Sounds more like a fart than a trailer to me. Okay, I'll take the sandwich." He wanted to ask what kind of sandwich it was before committing—she might serve him up a shit sandwich for all he knew. But he wasn't one to look a gift horse in the mouth.

"Oh, by the way," Laura remarked as she stepped out of the tent, "there's a crack in the camper's door window. You wouldn't happen to know anything about that, would you? I didn't notice it the last time I was here."

"Maybe Larry knows what happened," Champs replied. Technically, that wasn't a lie.

"I'll ask him then," said Laura, and walked off with Hannah's beer still in hand.

Champs cracked jokes with Hannah and Zoe about the *Flying Cloud* while Laura got him a sandwich. She returned with a kaiser roll, stacked high with turkey, lettuce, tomatoes, and dill pickle chips. It was damn good. He washed it down with his cold beer while Laura sent the girls off to Josanne's for a tea party so she and Champs could talk in private, he supposed.

She perched on a folding chair after scrubbing it with an antibacterial wipe. "So. I didn't leave here last time on the best of terms."

Champs shrugged, hoping to move on from that painful moment. He considered the sandwich enough of an olive branch. Yawning, he hoped Laura would get the hint that all was well and he needed his nap. It didn't work.

"I'm sorry about what I said, Champs. I was just in shock." She took a deep breath. "I understand now you don't want to live at Egret's Pond and I want you to know I took care of all the remaining paperwork and outstanding bills."

Laura leaned forward and put her sticky antiseptic-gel hands on his knees. "I accept that you want to live down here by yourself and you don't want to rent out the cottage as a vacation home."

Champs nodded. So far, so reasonable. He wondered what had changed her mind.

Laura removed her hands. She sat upright and crossed her arms on her chest.

Here we go, thought Champs. He braced himself for her next move.

"But, the fact is," Laura went on, "that you're getting older and Mom is not here anymore to take care of you and manage things. I realize you don't need round-the-clock care yet, but I've set up interviews with home health aides who would come daily and help you to—"

"Don't need that," interrupted Champs.

"Yes, I'm afraid you do," said Laura, as if addressing a client who claimed he didn't need to make provisions for alimony in his will. "And even if you don't, *I* need it, Champs. Please. Be sensible. I have enough to worry about with the kids and the . . . well, a million other things. Don't you see I'm trying as hard as I can to make sure you are well cared for and you have a regular source of support in case—"

"Told you. Don't need it," Champs interrupted again. "I've got Jeffrey, so my care and safety are in good hands. Quit worrying about me."

"Jeffrey? *Jeffrey?* Champs, he lives in the Poconos. Where he has a job. And a girlfriend. And a life. I know he comes down here once a week, but he's not a reliable source of support. Now, if you'd just hear—"

"Nope," Champs cut in. "He lives here now. Got fired and moved into the lower cabin today. I don't know about any girlfriend—unless you're talking about Millie?" He leaned over and scratched Millie's ear, finding another tick. She hadn't been invited to Josanne's tea party and sat next to him, panting and ready to bare her teeth.

Laura wrinkled her nose. "Well, I guess I need to catch up with Jeffrey. Anyway, there's something else we need to talk about. Mom's ashes. I know you have the urn somewhere since I couldn't find it at Egret's Pond." She paused to wipe away the sweat pouring down her face. "Jesus Christ, it's boiling in here. How can you stand it? I need more water before we get through all this. Do you want anything?"

"Beer," Champs replied as Laura zipped herself out of the screen tent. He sighed.

There was nothing in Pat's goldfinch notebook about how to deal with their children's "issues." Why hadn't Pat briefed him on what Laura, David, and Jeffrey would need from him in her absence? A few hints or background details so he could've prepared himself to step center stage. She'd known he wasn't good at "talks." He was good at fixing things, solving logistical problems, and helping with math homework. Champs was the chief provider and had no aptitude for the chief carer role. Why couldn't people be more like equations? Or fish?

He decided a silent defense was the best offense. Champs helped Millie onto his lap, where she rolled into a ball with a paw over her muzzle. He let his chin slump forward and pretended he was fast asleep.

"Shit," said Laura as she approached the screen tent.

Champs snored for added authenticity.

He heard her water bottle land with blunt force somewhere on the lawn. He listened to the refreshing crack-hiss of his beer and Laura's desperate gulping. There was a pause that seemed to stretch for hours. Champs resisted scratching his head or adjusting Millie on his lap. He had the distinct feeling that Laura was staring right at him. About to give in, he heard her flip-flop toward his main tent. She unzipped the tent flap, and he listened to her rifling through his things. After a few minutes, Laura gasped and broke out in sobs.

Champs's heart dropped to the pit of his stomach. He knew she'd found the urn. Found her dead mother. In a hiding spot at the corner of his tent. Beneath a pile of dirty clothes. Covered by sweat-soaked shirts, Sassafras-stained shorts, and skid-marked skivvies. Shame prickled his skin.

As Laura cried, Champs panicked. His mind raced between the desire to comfort her and the fear she might dump Pat's ashes over his head or stab his eyes out with a tent pole. He risked a peek at Millie, who jumped off his lap and nudged his legs with a low growl. Champs scrunched as low as possible in his chair.

"How will she ever forgive me?" he asked Millie, who whimpered at the door. He leaned over to unzip the tent, thinking she needed a potty break.

Millie barked and charged at Laura, who had lurched out of the main tent, holding the urn and running toward the cabin. They collided in the old vegetable patch.

"Get away from me, you filthy mutt!" Laura shouted, holding tight to the urn.

Millie yipped and retreated to the screen tent, ears down.

Champs watched Laura stumble to the real porch and into the cabin, cursing him or Millie, he couldn't tell. No doubt she would turn on the air-conditioning full blast to cool down before getting the girls back from Josanne. Champs hated air-conditioning. Laura and David had installed it in the cabin several years ago as a surprise birthday gift for Pat. Champs had declared recirculated air a suspicious ploy by the energy fat cats to run up gas and electric bills. He'd refused to use it and switched it off if someone else had the nerve to turn it on.

Hearing the condenser kick into high gear, Champs wondered how many ways Laura would make him pay for burying her mother in his dirty laundry.

14

Third-Degree Burns

Champs rose early the next morning with a dry mouth and a throbbing headache. He brewed a pot of coffee in his grandmother's enamelware percolator and slurped a can of mandarin oranges. As he drove down to the dock, Millie riding shotgun, the radio informed him it was the first day of summer break, and therefore time to get out the Coppertone and lemonade, 'cause it would be a scorcher. Champs turned off the radio. He knew damn well what kind of day it would be just by stepping outside his tent. Why did people need a cocaine-fueled disc jockey sitting in some air-conditioned studio up in Dover to tell them what the weather was like in their own backyards? Idiots.

He had a hazy memory of waking last night to the smell of meatball sandwiches he'd been too drunk to eat. Jeffrey must have helped him into the tent and tucked him into his cot. Champs felt ashamed and wondered if Laura had taken the girls home after finding the urn. He hoped not, though he deserved nothing less.

"We better keep a low profile today, Millie. And no beer drinking until dinner, at least."

Jeffrey was pulling his hand-built wooden canoe on shore when Champs and Millie caught up to him on their way to *Tetanus*. He lifted up a five-gallon bucket containing two beautiful striped bass still flipping their tails.

"Why'd you keep 'em?" Champs asked.

These were the first decent fish he'd seen all season, but keeping any fish caught in the Sassafras was a thing of the past. There'd been a ban on striper fishing at one point because they were a threatened species. Then the largemouth bass had developed parasitic worms in their flesh. All the other fish, including the catfish, had diminished over the years in number, size, and suitability for eating unless you were fond of stomach cramps and diarrhea. They fished for sport, not for food.

"Figured I'd impress the girls, then teach them how to clean a fish. Just for fun," Jeffrey replied.

"And Laura's okay with that?" Champs ventured.

Jeffrey said nothing.

"Guess you already heard," Champs continued. "I upset her. Surprised she's still here."

Millie left the dock, wandered down to the river's edge, and crunched on a dead blue crab abandoned on the sand by the receding tide. Jeffrey grabbed his tackle and made for his truck. He got partway there and turned around.

"I don't know what it is with you two and I don't wanna know either," he said. "But you better make it right, or you'll never see Laura and the girls again. You think you've earned the right to live out your life however the hell you choose without regard to anyone else. I get that. But ask yourself this: Do you really want to die a lonely old drunk? Shouting obscenities at the nurses paid to clean you up when you shit your pants? Just like your father?"

Champs sputtered.

Millie yacked up a crab claw.

Shoulders slumped, Jeffrey walked on to his truck. He drove away, glaring at Champs in his rearview mirror.

Out on the water, Champs motored downriver. For the first time, he didn't want to fish. He wanted to be mad at Jeffrey. What right did his son have to speak to him like that? How dare Jeffrey suggest that he was anything like his father? But it wasn't anger that arose. Instead, Champs had a sinking feeling that Jeffrey had only pointed out the hard, cold truth.

Champs was thirteen when he went to visit his mom in the hospital, where she was suffering from a severe case of bronchitis. This wasn't unusual. June had been a chain-smoker since she was seventeen and was always coughing and sick. Teenage Champs kept his mother company all afternoon as she reminisced about the past.

According to June, Champs Senior and his younger brother, Stuart, had grown up in a brick row house with a skinny backyard that opened onto a dirt alley and railroad tracks in Downingtown, Pennsylvania. Champs Senior had finished high school as a football hero with poor grades and a reputation for playing the field. After high school, he'd gone to work at the refinery and joined the Alert Fire Company as a volunteer fireman.

"Big and strong, he was then. Boastful, too," Champs's mother recalled. She'd known Champs Senior in high school, but it wasn't until one summer at the fire company carnival, not long after his first promotion, that they'd gone up the hill together.

"Do you know what that means?" June asked her teenage son. Champs blushed and looked at the floor.

"Three months later, I found out I was pregnant," she continued. "We eloped to Elkton, Maryland. Your father made it clear he was only marrying me because he had to. I thanked him. Being an unwed mother was scandalous back then. Guess it still is."

At the next fire company carnival, Champs's mother and father had both been wheeled into emergency screaming and yelling. June's waters had burst at home, and her mother had driven her straight to the hospital. Champs Senior had been drunk and goofing around at the hot dog stand when his antics knocked over the hot dog pot. Thirty gallons of boiling water later, he'd sustained third-degree burns and was rushed to the hospital in an ambulance. He never ate a hot dog again.

After a long and painful labor, a midwife wheeled June and infant Champs to the burn unit, where Champs Senior sat propped up on a gurney. He'd been drugged with morphine, wrapped in gauze like a mummy, and attached to a drip bag. June had attempted to put baby Champs in his arms, but Champs Senior had turned away, already disappointed in his son for being underweight at birth.

"He called you a runt," Champs's mother said. "He said, 'None of us Nolands are runts. You're sure that boy is mine, now, aren't you, June?' I stayed by his side for a few minutes, hoping he'd warm up to you, but he stared at the wall and said nothing."

Champs learned that his father had returned to work after discharging himself from the hospital, demoted to the mailroom because of his injuries. He'd also had to resign as a firefighter. The scarring had disfigured parts of the right side of his body, including his face, neck, arm, and hand.

It was the first time his father's ugly scars had been explained to Champs.

"He wasn't the same man after that," his mother said. "When the pain pills ran out, he turned to the bottle."

"But why does he hate *me* so much?" Champs asked.

"Guess he's always blamed you for the accident."

"But it wasn't my fault!"

"It was his own damn fault, Champs. A clown at a carnival. Downright foolish. But you were born right there in the middle of it." She paused. "I reckon he blames you for his problems 'cause it's easier than owning up to them himself. That way he never has to change."

She finished the story by recounting Peety's birth, two years later. "Your brother. Now, he weighed in at nine pounds, seven ounces—a big boy by any standard. Your daddy held him high in the air like a trophy for all the family to see. 'A prime number one Jimmy,' he said. I never seen him more proud."

Champs remembered June had coughed up blood and he'd run to

get the nurse. He also recalled the hurt in his chest, as if his mother had planted a seed of shame that rubbed up against his heart.

From that day on, Champs had known he was the throw-back and Peety the prized crab. He had vivid memories of the pride his father had expressed for Peety, who was strong and competitive in all the ways Champs would never be. Peety had been the star quarterback of the varsity high school football team. Champs had only played one season of JV baseball as a benchwarmer.

Champs Senior had rubbed Peety's accomplishments in Champs's face whenever he got the chance. When Champs turned eighteen, he stopped competing with Peety for his father's attention. He reckoned he could cope with the scorn his father heaped on him, but he wouldn't lose a brother because of it.

"Yeah, it's like you're a scab he can't stop picking," Peety said when Champs broached the topic of their father. They made a truce, agreeing that they'd never let Champs Senior's cruelty come between them. It got to where they could almost laugh about it. Almost. Then, the storm. Peety came crashing down from the pedestal Champs Senior had put him on, and Champs did nothing to break his brother's fall. Nothing at all.

After Peety walked out the door that night, never to return, Champs Senior grew more bitter and angry. The family did what they could to avoid him during the winter months and placate him during summer to avoid his ire or ridicule. He continued to drink. By the time Jeffrey was a senior in high school, the Sassafras Natural Resources Police had issued Champs Senior three warnings for driving his boat while intoxicated.

"Goddamn communists!" Champs Senior complained. "They don't know shit."

The laws toughened on drunk drivers, so to keep Champs Senior out of jail, Champs hid the boat key and relegated his father to dock fishing only. Champs Senior declared it was fine by him since there was no law against a drunk man fishing on land.

But there was a law against drunk and disorderly conduct on land. After a woman complained to Larry about an old geezer on the dock waving his privates at her, the Deadrise Cove Association held an emergency meeting. Larry informed Champs that his father was no longer welcome in the public areas around Deadrise Cove. He could stay within the confines of the cabin and backyard, but if he ventured anywhere else, drunk or sober, they'd call the real police and have him thrown in jail.

Later that summer, David arrived at the cabin with his wife and baby daughter, Samantha. He was walking up from Hill Beach to make lunch for the family when he witnessed Champs Senior slap June so hard she fell over on the porch. David yelled back to the beach, bringing Champs and Larry sprinting up the hill.

By then, Champs Senior was in the backyard, yanking hillbilly tomatoes off the vine and hurling them against the boat shed, where they exploded in a spray of seeds, pulp, and blood-red juice. Champs ran past him onto the porch to make sure his mom was okay. He and David lifted her like a child and carried her into the cabin so she could rest while they went outside to deal with Champs Senior. They found him on his back in the vegetable garden, pinned down by Larry's foot and his Winchester Super X2.

"It's time for you to leave," Larry said. "Do we understand each other?"

Champs Senior nodded. David half-supported, half-dragged his grandfather to the car as if strong-arming a stun-gunned protestor to a police van. Champs packed a duffel bag full of his father's clothes and toiletries, then grabbed the keys and drove him back to Pennsylvania. Champs's uncle Stuart took over from there. He rented a cheap, month-to-month apartment for Champs Senior in Downingtown. Laura arranged a restraining order.

June went to live with Pat and Champs after that. She passed away six months later from pneumonia, which she'd contracted during a hospital stay for emphysema. Champs sold his childhood home and used the money to supply round-the-clock nursing care for Champs Senior as he continued to drink and deteriorate. He died two years later. The daily caregiver found him stone cold and naked on the floor in a pile of his own excrement. The coroner declared "wet brain" as the cause of death. Champs buried his father alone and then stayed out all night obliterating himself with a bottle of bourbon until he threw up, utterly aware of the irony of the situation.

"I'd like to forget all of it, Millie," Champs said now, steering the Sea Nymph into Deadrise Cove. "But there's not enough beer in the world to get the job done."

The dog whined in sympathy.

Champs looked at the gas gauge hovering on empty. He calculated he must have motored on autopilot to Betterton and back, a twelve-mile round-trip. The Sea Nymph rocked him like a cradle while he sat idle in his boat for a few minutes. As predicted, the day was a scorcher. The sun throbbed down on his forearms and knees. A slick of Sassafras sheen covered his skin. Despite the discomfort, relief flooded his body as if he'd made it through the fires of hell and purged something poisonous.

"My father was an asshole, Millie," Champs said. "That's on him."

15

Red Kayaks

N o one was around when Champs and Millie got back to the cabin.

"Must've all gone down to Hill Beach," Champs muttered.

He longed for a beer or two and a nap in his rocking chair in his screen-tent porch. Champs thought he was a six-pack behind his regular consumption, maybe more. He stood on the lawn for five minutes, not trusting himself to go near his makeshift kitchen, where the beer cooler was, but not sure about another confrontation with Laura down on the beach.

"What d'ya think, Millie?" he asked.

Millie had an orange plastic shovel in her mouth. She looked at Champs, then at the beer cooler, then turned and headed toward Hill Beach, her tail wagging.

Champs sighed. If he'd had a tail, it wouldn't have been wagging.

The trail down to the beach wound through a mixed forest of cedar, oak, hickory, mulberry, and sassafras trees. Brambly thickets of winter-berry and blackberry shrubs prevented any shortcuts through the trees. The ground under the trees was a tangled, damp place, full of ivy, felled branches, rotting leaves, and the occasional northern water snake. In the spring and summer months, blue flag irises and cardinal flowers bloomed. Though the watershed forest thrived, the path to the beach was in disrepair. Champs twisted his ankle on the uneven gravel trying to steer clear of a poison ivy vine that stretched across the trail like a tripwire.

The Deadrise Cove Association had been chartered to collect annual dues from residents to fund regular maintenance of the community path. But Larry had mentioned to Champs he'd found it difficult to demand that people pay up, so funding was scarce. The association focused its limited resources on asphalt and rocks to fill the crater-sized potholes that pockmarked the roads after winter.

Champs had zero interest in being the community tax collector. But something needed doing about the state of neglect in the neighborhood. Otherwise, they'd have a lawsuit on their hands if some idiot got hurt. He arrived on the beach still muttering about it, rehearsing the lecture he would give to Larry.

"Miiilleee!" squealed Zo-Zo. She galloped out of the river, pigtails streaming behind her and bright orange water wings pumping the air.

Millie bolted toward her, shovel in her mouth, and the two collided like sumo wrestlers. The corner of the shovel popped one of Zo-Zo's inflatable water wings. She screamed and fell back as if she'd been shot. Laura gasped. Jeffrey and Hannah dropped the minnow net they were dragging and ran to Zoe's side. Millie grabbed the shovel like a bone and bolted to the far side of the beach.

All but Champs burst out laughing.

"Look, Champs!" cried Hannah. "Millie is hiding the murder weapon!"

Champs walked further down the beach and leaned around a patch of reeds to see Millie drop the shovel into a hole she'd dug. She turned around and buried it by kicking up sand with her hind legs. Then she curled in her trademark ball on top of the concealed evidence, paw over muzzle as if this rendered her invisible. Champs chuckled, for the first time in many moons.

As the laughter subsided, Laura called out to Champs. "I know you came down here for a sandwich. Here it is."

She waved a Ziploc bag in the air, and Champs wondered if she'd make him beg like a dog, but she didn't, so he assumed Laura had forgiven him. They sat down together on the threadbare brown bedspread. Champs opened his mouth to apologize. The words wouldn't come, so he bit into the ham-and-cheese sandwich instead. It had farm-fresh tomato slices, red onions, and sweet pickles. He was in heaven. Mustard, mayonnaise, and vinegar dripped down his wrists. He licked it up between bites.

Laura ignored him, crossed her arms, and stared across the glinting river, the hot sun reflecting off the light chop like diamonds. He saw veins bulging at her temples. Her jaw clenched as she ground her teeth. She looked just like Pat had whenever she'd held her ground on some decision they'd had to make. It wasn't often, but when Pat got like that, Champs had known she wouldn't budge. He'd caved every time. Goddamn it, Pat, where are you now?

"Larry ever say anything to you about the association?" Champs asked with his mouth full.

"Not that I remember," Laura replied without looking at him. "Why do you care?"

"Path down here's a mess. Dock's not too good either."

"So it's Larry's fault, is it? God, Champs, you're unbelievable!" She pushed herself up from the blanket and stomped away.

Stomping wasn't so effective in the soft sand, Champs noted, but he got the point. He stopped himself from following her to clarify the situation. It wasn't worth it: no matter what he said or didn't say to Laura, he was always in the wrong. He finished the sandwich and wiped his hands on the picnic quilt.

Jeffrey jogged up toward the red plastic kayaks lying upside down on a bank of grass above the beach.

"Give me a hand with these, will ya?" he said to Champs.

They each dragged one down to the river.

"Yay! Boats!" said Zo-Zo.

"They're called kayaks, Zo-Zo the Bozo," taunted Hannah. "I'm riding with Champs."

"Oh no, not until I race you and your mother," Jeffrey called out. "C'mon, Zo-Zo the Bozo! You're on my team. Did I mention? The winning team." He lifted his niece under the arms and plonked her down in the front seat of his kayak, posing behind it, raring to go.

"Champs, throw me my water shoes," said Laura.

Champs went back to the beach blanket and tossed the smooth black slip-ons in her direction. He wondered if they were made from killer-whale skins.

Hannah stepped into the water like a fawn. She tested the sturdiness of the kayak, then turned her back to the boat, squatted into the seat, and swiveled her legs over the side in one graceful motion.

"Uh-oh," said Jeffrey. "I think we gotta pro here. Champs, give us a push! We're gonna need all the help we can get."

"No fair!" cried Laura.

Champs lumbered forward and shoved Zo-Zo and Jeffrey's kayak into the river. Zo-Zo was more interested in splashing Champs with her paddle than racing, so it ended up an even start by the time Laura got her water shoes on and pushed off the sand. She and Hannah paddled in sync, a powerful and precise rhythm. Millie walked into the river as far as possible, then doggie-paddled in circles, whining. She gave up, waded back to the beach, and barked at the receding kayaks.

Gazing at the back of Laura's blond head, Champs tried to hold on to her as long as he could before she became a dot in the middle of the river. He wished he could talk to Pat about Laura. Perhaps Laura thought about him the way he'd thought about Champs Senior. He remembered one particular time he'd been the champion of assholes to her. Maybe that had set the tone for their whole relationship. The thought filled him with shame.

16

Role Casting

On David's tenth birthday, Champs gave him a fishing rod and tackle box. From that day on, when the men went out on the river, so did David. He woke at six a.m., packed the boat snacks, and filled the cooler with beer and one can of 7Up for himself. Pat joked that it was the powdered mini-donuts and soda that David loved far more than fishing. She was right about that.

According to Pat, there were many mornings when Laura snuck out of bed and followed the fishermen to the dock on her bike. She watched with envy as the orange and white Regal tri-hull sped off downriver. But it never occurred to Champs that his daughter would want to join them. Only the men went out fishing in the early morning hours. That was how it had always been, and no female in history had ever questioned it as far as Champs was aware.

So, when it was Laura's tenth birthday, he was baffled when she ripped the paper off a brand-new Schwinn ten-speed and kicked the tire before running to her room in tears. Pat and Champs looked to David for an explanation.

"I think she wanted a fishing rod," he said.

"What for?" Champs asked. He cringed at the thought of it now.

Pat did what she could to comfort Laura, but she refused to come out of her room even as her friends arrived for her birthday party. David saved the day. He'd graduated to an adult-sized pole and used Champs's old fishing vest with lots of pockets to carry his lures and neon-colored spongy worms. David dug out his battered plastic tackle box and warped rod and reel from the garage and brought them to Laura. She beamed. After dinner, to his credit, Champs spent two hours in the backyard teaching her the basics of bait, lures, and casting for different fish.

Laura practiced every moment she could, much like Champs had done as a boy. She made collages with pictures cut from *Field and Stream* magazine and nailed them to her bedroom walls. Tape never works, she told her mother.

Laura asked Champs to draw the Sassafras River on a piece of paper so she could memorize its every nook and cranny. He found it all very amusing until she asked him to mark the hottest fishing spots with a red pen. There was no way Champs would reveal those secrets to anyone, kin or no kin. He'd have rather had his hand chopped off than give up hard-earned Sassafras intelligence. Who did she think she was? Laura didn't press the issue.

Summer came. They packed the van, hitched up the Regal, and drove to the cabin one weekend as usual. Champs Senior and Uncle Stuart had arrived a few days earlier. The next morning, Laura rose before anyone. She gathered the rods and tackle boxes and packed the snack bag and cooler, remembering to add an extra 7Up for herself. She put everything in the van and sat on the porch waiting for the others to rise, groan, and make their coffee.

Champs was proud of Laura for getting everything ready for them. But also suspicious. He wondered if she was buttering him up for the swing set she'd been pestering him about. Champs didn't believe in swing sets or monkey bars. That was what trees were for. He made a mental note to fix a rope swing at Hill Beach so they could enjoy flying into the river at high tide.

As the others whipped through the porch and clambered into the van, Laura pulled on Champs's sleeve. "I'm ready to go, too," she announced.

"Go where?" he replied.

"Fishing. I get to go now, don't I?"

Champs had thought she was joking and laughed.

Now he wished he could reach back through time and stop his younger self from saying what he'd said next.

"Laura, I don't know what you were thinking, but you can't come out on the boat with us. You're a girl, right?"

"But I can cast better than David now. You said so yourself."

"Tell you what," Champs suggested. "Grab yourself a life jacket and jump in the van. We'll give you a ride down to the dock, and you can fish from there until you get tired. Then you can walk back to the cabin all by yourself. How's that sound?"

"That sounds like shit!" Laura stormed back into the house yelling for her mother.

Champs remembered he'd stood frozen in disbelief while his uncle, father, and David chortled away at Laura's retort. In retrospect, it was kinda funny, he had to admit.

"Guess she told you what's what!" Champs Senior said. "Now get in the car, we're done fartin' around here. Let's go catch us some fish!"

Champs learned later that Laura had barged into her mother's bedroom and insisted she get the kayak out right that minute, at 6:21 in the morning. Pat had dragged it down the path to Hill Beach, where Laura got in and practiced paddling all day long.

The next morning, when the fishermen set off in the van, Laura was waiting at Hill Beach in the red kayak with her rod duct-taped to the plastic hull. As soon as she heard the car engine, she paddled as fast as she could into the middle of the river, then followed the Regal when it left the dock.

Champs and his crew were chucking lures to shore at the mouth of Mill Creek when a rogue cast glided across their lines—a big no-no on the river. The men turned in unison, ready to give the perpetrator a good dressing-down. Staring back at them, in her unicorn pajamas and pink life vest was Laura.

They carried on fishing, ignoring her as she followed the boat around and did the same. She accepted a tow-ride home, sunburned and dehydrated, hands so blistered it took two weeks before she could use them again.

When Laura recovered, she got right back into the kayak to follow the fishing boat. Champs was ready to break the unspoken rules and let her join them. But he didn't have the guts to stand up to his father, who'd already made his thoughts clear. Females on the fishing boat? "Over your dead body," were Champs Senior's exact words. So Champs did nothing. And knew he was a coward for it.

One morning, Champs Senior gunned the boat all the way to Turner's Creek before stopping. Laura was a determined little girl, but she couldn't make it that far in her kayak. She gave up pursuing the man boat and explored the creeks of the Upper Sassafras instead, fishing wherever she wanted. Much to Champs Senior's embarrassment, Laura often brought home more keepers than him. Much to Champs's chagrin, she refused to share her map of the best fishing spots marked in red pen.

Laura's love of paddling the dawn river and the strength she built in her arms, back, and legs had served her well when she took up rowing. Her freshman year at the University of Delaware, she'd walked straight onto the varsity-eight crew team with a partial scholarship.

"See, Millie, something good came of it all," said Champs, hoping for redemption, if only from the dog.

Millie squatted in the sand to pee. She wasn't buying it.

The kayakers had reached the other side of the river and were on their way back to the finish line. Laura and Hannah had a clear lead. Champs turned away and humphed himself back up the hill, where he went straight into his stifling tent house and collapsed on his cot.

17

Dirty Girls

Three hours later, he woke up to Laura squirting him in the face with a small water pistol. He smelled barbecue, and his stomach flailed around like a fish in a livewell. Laura handed him a bottle of mineral water.

"If you don't get up and interact with your grandchildren, you won't get any dinner," she threatened.

"What?" said Champs, blocking the spray gun with his hands.

"Now!" she commanded.

He left the tent and made a beeline to the beer cooler under the Coleman stove. Jeffrey intercepted him, extending a croquet mallet in his direction. Champs spied the slick brown beer bottle in Jeffrey's other hand and considered snatching it and running down to the lower cabin. One look at Hannah put him off the idea. Her powers of observation were off the charts. He could tell from her expression he'd be letting her down if he ran off with a beer to get buzzed.

Champs took the mallet and studied the course layout, a higgledy-piggledy maze of silver wickets winding through the lawn and his encampment. It was his turn. With a series of precision hits and strategic continuations, he caught up with the others. When his break ended, Hannah and Zoe exchanged glances, winks, and giggles.

"Oh boy," said Jeffrey. "You're in for it now, Champs."

The girls teamed up with one purpose: to croquet Champs's ball as far away as possible and laugh while he tried to maneuver it back into play. Champs went along with it for a while—it wasn't a real match. But it annoyed him. Croquet was the one ball game he could play well. He'd won all the time against his father, grandfather, uncle, and brother when he was younger. Until his father had put an end to it by cheating. Whenever it was Champs Senior's turn, he'd carry his ball and place it next to Champs's, then whack it into the bushes or under the shed. Champs had complained it was cheating, but his father only laughed. When Champs had stopped playing, Champs Senior called him a quitter.

Forgetting he was with his granddaughters, Champs went in hard for a win. He'd show them all the right way to play this game. Fair and square. First, he scored a wicket, and his ball knocked Hannah's. He croqueted her ball deep under the hedge. Hannah frowned. Champs made another successful run, earning himself a continuation shot. His ball rolled up against Zoe's with a soft click. He positioned himself for his best stop shot, a move guaranteed to knock her ball so far out of bounds, she'd never get back in the game. It was one of his favorite plays. Champs was so absorbed in its execution, he didn't bother to check his surroundings before clobbering the ball with his mallet. He looked up after the satisfying crack to see Zoe's ball speeding through the air like a cruise missile. The hairs raised on the back of his neck right before the ball plowed straight into the *Flying Cloud*, making a massive dent in its aluminum siding.

"Shit," he muttered.

Jeffrey and the girls tried not to laugh.

Laura barged off the porch, a raging bull.

"What in the hell do you think you're doing?" she yelled.

"I didn't mean to hit the thing. I just—" Champs tried to explain.

"Shut up, Champs!" Laura interrupted. "Goddamn you!"

She picked up an errant croquet ball and threw it at his head. He ducked, then dodged the next one right behind it. It hit the ground and rolled into Millie, who was running to defend Champs. She yelped.

"Stupid dog!" shouted Laura, and picked up a mallet, as if she needed sturdier weaponry to mount a successful offense.

"Whoa!" Champs yelled, his arm outstretched in the "stop" position.

"Mom, stop it!" shouted Hannah. "It was an accident!"

"Laura! Drop it. Now!" said Jeffrey.

Laura lowered the mallet and locked eyes with Champs. He didn't know what to do next. He felt like he was in a movie, in the middle of an action scene, and had forgotten his line. Was he the hero or the villain? The cop or the robber? Fight or flight? He stood there and did nothing.

Zo-Zo sprinted to Millie and gave her a fierce embrace. "You okay, Millsy? It's all right, Millsy," she said soothingly.

"Can I help at all?" It was Larry, carrying a Benelli shotgun. "I heard the commotion. Everything okay over here?"

"Everything's fine, Larry," said Laura, recovering herself. "It's nothing. Really. Get rid of that gun for God's sake, and then join us on the porch for a beer."

Champs watched Larry jog to his house to lock up his gun and lope back, joining Jeffrey on the porch to accept a bottle of Victory Golden Monkey, a 9.5 percent Belgian-style tripel. Brewed in Champs's hometown of Downingtown, Pennsylvania, the Golden Monkey was a beer you didn't drink: it drank you. God help the man who had more than two. Champs tried not to drool. It was the one bottled beer he allowed at the cabin.

Turning away, Champs watched Hannah and Laura join the heap that was Millie and Zo-Zo.

Laura bent down to stroke the dog. "I'm sorry, Millie. I'm sorry, girls. That was not okay. I messed up. That won't happen again. I'm sorry." She pulled her daughters in tight. "I love you both so much.

And you, Millie . . . well, I guess I have a lot of making up to do. Would a hamburger make things better?"

Millie perked up, and the girls wore giant smiles as they followed Laura back inside the screened porch.

Champs stood forgotten in the yard. "I'm sorry, too," he mumbled.

He set to work collecting wickets, balls, and mallets. Sweating beyond Sassafras-sheen level, he noticed a slight tremor in his hands. Champs bent over, heart racing, hands on knees, to catch his breath. He lifted his head to gaze at his family on the porch and felt pulled back into another dimension. His family appeared like tiny matchstick figures on a minuscule stage at the end of a tunnel.

Hannah approached, placing a frozen can of Sprite in his hand. "Mom says it's time to eat."

"Okay." Champs removed his sweat-stained cap and rolled the chilly can across his forehead, a brief respite from the sweltering day. He took Hannah's hand, happy to have someone by his side.

At the picnic table, Champs dug in like a starving soldier. The sweet-savory flavor of sun and vine exploded on his tongue with every bite of sliced tomato. He hadn't tasted anything like it in years. He remembered his mother's tomatoes, her specialty. Picking them right off their sturdy, fuzzy stems, young Champs had eaten them like apples, red juice and seeds trickling down his forearm and dripping off his elbow in the sticky heat of August. He glanced at the empty rectangles where the garden used to be. They looked like giant grave sites.

"Where'd you get these?" Champs asked, helping himself to a fifth slice of tomato.

"At that new place in Galena," Laura said.

"What new place?" Champs slathered an ear of corn with butter.

"The Donovan and Marcosi girls—remember them? The farm stand girls?" Laura said. "They turned the stand into a market, open year-round. It's more of an organic grocery slash nursery. They upgraded the greenhouses, fields, and gardens behind it. There's no name for it yet, but they've got a contest going to pick one. Hey, girls —what d'ya think we should name the store?"

"Dirty Girls," blurted Champs.

Jeffrey sprayed a mouthful of beer across the table. Laura and Larry snickered.

"Good heavens!" said Josanne, who just that moment joined them on the porch.

"Uh, Champs? Something you'd like to share with us about farmers' daughters?" Larry joked.

"Watch it, Larry," Jeffrey warned. "You're talking about my mother there." He snorted, and giggles erupted around the table. But not from Champs.

"I didn't mean 'dirty' like that," he snapped.

Champs knew the farmers from way back—both were on the river whenever they could snatch a couple of hours away from their farms. Chuck Donovan was a first-rate bass fisherman, and Marcosi had a knack for knowing where the crabs were hot. Champs couldn't remember when he'd last seen either one.

"What *did* you mean, darlin'?" asked Josanne as she passed him a glass of her famous sweet tea.

"It's dirty work, farming," explained Champs. "Get dirty doing a day's work on a farm. Doesn't matter what you're growing—corn, tomatoes, soybeans, chickens. Those gals, they run the market *and* dig in the dirt, so . . . it popped into my mind, that's all."

"I like it," said Jeffrey. He pounded his fists on the table and chanted, "Dir-tee Girls! Dir-tee Girls! Dir-tee Girls!"

Hannah, Zo-Zo, and Larry joined in the chant.

"Okay. Okay. All right," said Laura, rolling her eyes. "Dirty Girls it is. I'll stop in on our way home tomorrow and enter the contest." She high-fived her girls and raised her chardonnay glass to Jeffrey and Larry.

Champs didn't notice. He stared at the sweet corn and tomatoes on his plate, thinking about his dead dirty girl, Pat.

Pat was born and raised on a family farm in Southeastern Pennsylvania. Her father's name was Nicholas, but everyone called him Nickleby, based on the Charles Dickens character of the same name. Nickleby's Farm was a right-sized mixture of dairy cows, layers, and canning crops including peas, tomatoes, and sweet corn.

As an only child, Pat worked side by side with her mother and father in all aspects of the farming business from the moment she was born. She grew up thinking of herself as just another farm animal that required regular feeding and occasional grooming to check for unwanted parasites. It was no surprise to anyone when she excelled at animal husbandry in the 4-H club. One entire wall of her bedroom had been papered with blue ribbons. She'd been a dirty girl, indeed—at least by Champs's definition.

As an adult, Pat became a 4-H volunteer teacher and the Pennsylvania state coordinator until a sudden tragedy put an end to it. In the late seventies, she read an article about the Vietnam veterans who lingered in the system unable to get the mental health care they needed to make a full recovery. Their suffering moved her to write to the 4-H national council suggesting they form a program for veterans. She never heard back from them.

Undeterred, Pat pinned up a flyer at the local veterans' center requesting any volunteers interested in farmwork to meet her in the general-purpose room at four p.m. that Friday. A man called Bobby turned up. Every Tuesday, Wednesday, and Thursday while the kids were in school, she picked Bobby up at the center and drove him to Nickleby's Farm to teach him to care for the animals and gardens. She structured her intervention as a twelve-week program.

At the end of Bobby's term, he thanked her and told her he was a new man. Then he introduced her to Keith, with similar results. Sometimes there was a break in her schedule, but she continued her work until her last client, JP, shot himself in the head during the seventh week of her program.

Champs was ill prepared to deal with the distress and upset that followed. He didn't understand the depth of Pat's devastation. The language of mental illness and suicide was beyond his experience. It was a terrible tragedy, he knew that. But why did Pat take it so personally? It baffled him, how she blamed herself for JP's death. From Champs's perspective, she barely even knew the man. Every time Champs tried to make her feel better or suggest she move on, Pat cried even more and isolated herself in their bedroom. She didn't want the kids to know about it, so she tried to act like everything was normal when they were around. But it took a toll on all of them.

Several weeks went by before Pat's doctor told Champs she was headed for a breakdown. Pat was the expert on healing through animals, but Champs believed the Sassafras was the best cure for all ailments. He packed up Pat's things, took David and Laura out of school a month early, and drove them down to the cabin for the whole summer. Champs made visits on the weekends and took a one-week vacation but otherwise lived as a single man back home in Downingtown.

It turned out that Champs's intuition was right, at least in part. Pat recovered that summer. But she claimed it was due to taking a dose of her own medicine—that was the summer she helped Chicken Ray get his poultry business in working order.

"It was the chickens that did the trick," she said.

Champs didn't care what had prompted Pat's turnaround. He was happy to have his wife back to normal and discouraged her from continuing her work with veterans.

That September, Pat told Champs she was pregnant. Her pregnancy with Jeffrey was one of the happiest times of their marriage.

"Penny for your thoughts," Josanne said to Champs.

"Huh? Oh," he replied, doing his best to refocus on the present.

"Well, we best be going now," said Larry. "Thank you, Laura, for this delicious dinner. It's been a real pleasure."

Before leaving the porch, Josanne turned to Champs.

"Toodle-oo, Champs. See you on Wednesday?"

Champs nodded, trying to remember what the hell was on Wednesday.

Humble Pie

"She's looking tired," Laura said when Larry and Josanne were out of hearing range.

"It's arthritis," said Jeffrey. "Larry says it's getting hard for her to keep up with the sampler work she loves. Her hands are just too painful. But you know Josanne—she's not one to complain."

"Or slow down," added Laura. She looked at Champs. "Well, Champs, if you have any room left, Dirty Girls was also selling home-baked pies. I bought a strawberry-rhubarb one. I know it's your favorite."

Champs couldn't believe his luck. He salivated at the thought. His mother may have had her shortcomings, but she'd known her way around a pie crust and used to bake the best strawberry-rhubarb pie in Pennsylvania. She'd have won blue ribbons with it if she'd been the kind of woman to take part in county fairs. Champs knew the Dirty Girls pie wouldn't come close, but Laura had remembered his favorite flavor, and that was a good sign in his book.

Laura left to get the pie.

Hannah returned to the Agatha Christie book that had been on her lap throughout dinner.

Zoe gave Millie her medicine: lemonade administered through a straw, drop by drop, on the dog's tongue. Champs gave the dog a stern look, but she ignored him. He turned to Jeffrey.

"Larry mention anything to you about the association?"

"He said it's not been easy. Told me he went to collect from Carl's boys last year. They haven't paid dues since Carl passed away four years ago. Anyway, the big one, what's his name?"

"Dex?"

"Yeah, him. Larry says Dex answered the door in nothing but his boxer shorts and a Wilson Combat 1911. A Classic Supergrade, no less."

"A what?" asked Champs.

"It's a pistol, Champs, a powerful one. One of those would set you back about six grand. I'm not even sure if they're legal here. Larry practically shit his pants. Anyway, the whole place smelled like weed."

Jeffrey was at the refrigerator getting himself another Golden Monkey. He offered one to Champs, who accepted on instinct.

"Did Larry get the money?" Champs asked.

"No, he made some excuse about seeing a used Pontiac Fiero that Dex might wanna look at sometime. Dex just glared at him with 'zombie eyes,' and that's when Larry turned around and left."

"Humph," Champs muttered. He took a satisfying gulp of beer.

Laura returned to the porch. "Here you go," she said, and slammed Pat's urn down on the picnic table just in front of Champs. "Oh, I forgot. I didn't get strawberry-rhubarb after all. I got humble. Humble pie. And now you're gonna eat it, Champs."

The cicadas, racketing all evening, came to an abrupt halt. Silence was the loudest sound on the porch. The girls, wide-eyed, stared back and forth between the urn and their mother. Jeffrey was slack-jawed.

Champs lifted his eyes from the urn and looked straight at Laura. "There's no pie?"

"Is that all you can say?" Laura exploded, her eyes aflame.

"There's no pie? Your dead wife is sitting on the table in front of you, and all you can think about is your goddamn pie?"

Jeffrey attempted to stand.

"Sit down," Laura commanded. "This concerns you, too."

Champs crossed his arms in front of his chest and thrust the deep frown on his face forward.

"Mom died two months ago, and you all seem fine to carry on as if nothing happened. She died, for chrissake!" Laura looked at the urn and stabbed her finger at Champs, who tried hard not to flinch. "And you! You refused, flat-out refused to have a funeral, a ceremony . . . anything! Fine, that's you. You do you, Champs. Come down here against her wishes and drink your life away. Treat this place like a goddamn swamp, bury our mom—your wife—under a stinking pile of dirty underwear!"

Laura swiped Jeffrey's beer from the table, glugged it like water, and threw the empty bottle across the porch, where it hit the indoor fountain and smashed to pieces.

Hannah startled.

Zoe covered her ears and shut her eyes.

Jeffrey winced.

Champs didn't bat an eyelid. Been there, done that, he thought, recalling his own adventures in bottle smashing.

Laura continued her rant. "But what about the rest of us, huh? Your children? Your grandchildren? We're all supposed to do what? Just walk on eggshells around you and pretend like everything is normal? Do you seriously think we're okay? Do you even think about us at all?"

"It wasn't in the plan," Champs offered.

"We're not in the fucking plan?" Laura screeched. "You have no idea wh—"

"He means the funeral, Laura, not us," Jeffrey interrupted. "Calm down. Remember? It was Mom who said she didn't want us making a fuss with any services or funeral. It was in the plan."

"Well, I'll tell you what wasn't in the plan!" Laura redirected. "Him running out of Egret's Pond in the middle of the night to live down here like a . . . like a . . . like a goddamn bum! That was not in the plan, was it? But you didn't seem to note that detail, did you, Champs?"

Champs studied the floor as if it had only just appeared under his feet.

"What's in the jar?" Zoe asked.

"Grandma," said Hannah.

"How did Grandma get in that jar, Mommy?" asked Zoe. "I thought you said she was in heaven with the angels and unicorns."

No one spoke. No one moved, except for Millie, who scratched at a flea. A motorcycle roared to life somewhere across the street while the cicadas picked up their screeching fiddles.

"She is, Zo-Zo. Grandma is in heaven," said Laura, defeated.

She sat down between her girls, pulled Zoe onto her lap, and gathered Hannah up close. Hannah's book, *Peril at End House*, slid to the floor.

"I can't go on like this anymore," Laura said in a strained voice, verging on tears. "I'm so tired, and I miss Mom so much. Sometimes, I can't even breathe. I can't eat. I have so much to talk to her about. Sometimes, I call her, and when she doesn't pick up, the fact she died hits me all over again."

Jeffrey's eyes moistened.

Champs pressed his fingertips into his forehead. It pounded as if being hit repeatedly by an anvil. Unable to meet Laura's eyes, he tracked a single firefly as it flashed on and off across the backyard.

"Look at me. I'm a mess," she said.

She blew her nose in a napkin and patted away her tears, then squirted her hands with antibacterial gel. After turning on the fountain and bringing the overhead fans to life, she settled down between the girls and spoke in a soft voice.

"I know Mom didn't want a fuss, but I need to say goodbye. I need closure. I think she would feel good knowing we came together to support each other. She needs to know how much we love her and miss her. I can't do this on my own anymore."

Zoe's lids drooped with sleep.

Hannah leaned her head on her mother's shoulder.

Champs stared at Pat's urn. He wanted to greet her but thought it might get him in more trouble with Laura.

"What can I do?" said Jeffrey.

"I've talked to David, and he said he has vacation time after the Fourth. Samantha and Ryan can't come because they have summer things going on. I don't know what the situation is with Kimmie. But we're coming down for a week. I'm assuming you and Champs don't have plans to be away then. I want us all to be together like we used to be every summer . . . when Mom was here. And I want us to celebrate her life. I want to let go of her ashes in the river. Have a short ceremony or something. Is that okay with you, Champs?"

Champs nodded and pushed himself up from the table. "I'm tired. Going to bed."

He picked up Pat-in-the-urn and carried her back to his main tent. Champs had no intention of fouling up the river with a sunken urn that would leak out Pat's ashes. How the hell could they expect him to fish in there after that? He would be terrified of reeling in his line, never knowing if Pat's head would be at the end. Was Laura out of her goddamn mind?

That

When Champs woke the next morning, Laura and the girls were gone. The air was still and cloaked as the sky darkened to a slate blue. The calm before the storm. Champs made his coffee and breakfasted on Stagg chili straight from the can, sharing some with Millie. He watched a pick-up truck pull into the driveway of the lower cabin to collect Jeffrey. Champs recognized the driver—it was Chicken Ray. He wondered what Chicken Ray and Jeffrey were up to. They must have hit it off on the *Duchess* the other day.

Millie nudged Champs's leg, looked at the Windstar, and barked once.

"Maybe later, Millie. Maybe later," said Champs, who was still not in the mood to fish.

He rooted around in a tackle box, retrieving a pencil stub and a yellowed index card. After pouring another coffee, Champs sat down in his screened tent to make a to-do list. It usually set his mind at ease once he'd written things down, even if he never looked at the list again and forgot to do everything on it. In fact, sometimes that was the best part.

Ten minutes later, there was nothing on the list. There had to be something he could do, something that required his attention and skill set, he thought. Champs leaned back in the rocker, shoved the pencil and index card into his pocket, and finished his coffee. Images from the past popped into his head like an erratic slide show.

He flashed on a woman with a hard hat whom he'd known in his early days as a lab assistant at Air Products. He flashed on old Ken Vernon, the Riverkeeper, pulling invasive water chestnut out of the Sassafras. He flashed on a classmate with pronounced buckteeth who'd sat next to him in advanced chemistry at college. He flashed on Pat, wearing a broad sunhat, dumping a half-bushel basket of crabs into the steamy cook pot.

A mosquito hovered at his ear with its high-pitched buzzing. It reminded Champs of the static-like ringing sound before a blackout. He reached for his flyswatter and smacked himself across the side of the head. Dead mosquito.

The slide show continued, one flash after another, accelerating right up to present events. Champs felt like he was in a boxing ring as the last set of images hit. The urn—a right uppercut. Jeffrey's moving in—a left hook. Laura's plan for a family reunion—a right cross. David's coming—jab. Ashes in the Sassafras—jab. Soon—jab.

His head spun. His hands trembled. Confused, he called out for Pat, thinking she'd be able to take care of all this. It calmed him down for a minute, and he took a deep breath and closed his eyes while he waited for her. Time passed. His mind went blank, leaving him wide open for the knockout punch, a powerful hit to his solar plexus—a kill shot.

Pat is not coming. She's dead!

Champs crumpled over. He tried to catch his breath, but it felt as if his whole torso were being squeezed by a constrictor knot. His heart slowed, longer and longer intervals between each muffled beat. A sharp pain raced down one side of his body. Was this it? The end of the line? He wasn't ready!

He gasped for air until a wheezy inhale somehow filled his lungs. The air rushed out of him again. He felt like a pair of bellows operated by an unknown hand. As his breathing stabilized, giant waves of grief hit. They crested then bottomed out in a trough, rose again, and dropped out from under him. Again and again, he rode the swells, sweating and convulsing in dry-heaves between sets.

Slowly, the pain settled and the craving for alcohol took over the anguish of loss. Champs tried to ride that out, too. But he was alone. He thought of heading over to Larry's, but the sky chose that moment to release sheets of rain. Thunder rumbled. Somewhere in the far back of his brain, a bugler played *taps*.

God help me, Champs thought as he ran to his real porch and threw open the SMEG refrigerator. The cold beer soothed his raw throat and stricken nerves. He savored it. And the next one. He took the third beer and sat down at the picnic table, his back supported by the cabin. If he was good at anything, it was numbing his emotions. From his pocket, he pulled out the pencil and dampened index card and wrote: *hide urn, cancel reunion, buy beer*.

A lightning bolt crashed to the ground in the woods behind Larry's house. Two seconds later, a deafening boom of thunder shook the cabin. Champs jumped up from the picnic bench and scanned the back-yard. Adrenaline coursed through his body as the memory of a different storm flashed in his mind.

Champs's brother, Peety, had been a popular guy in high school; he had a date for every occasion. A cheerleader with glossy black ringlets and rosy cheeks at his junior prom. A beautiful and impossibly thin French exchange student at the homecoming dance his senior year. At the senior prom, a curvy blonde with drool-worthy cleavage who, it was said, never wore panties. Ever. Peety refused to confirm or deny the rumor, no matter how much Champs Senior teased and prodded. Champs thought his father's interest was creepy.

At the end of high school, Peety showed no appetite for college, though he had his choice of Division 1 football scholarships. Peety wanted to earn a living and get out of the family house; he wanted independence. Through one of Champs Senior's old contacts at the fire department, Peety secured an apprenticeship at a small construction firm. A quick learner, he was strong and able to manipulate machinery and tools as if they were extensions of his own body. He had an eye for proportion and a knack for putting uptight contractors and homeowners at ease.

Peety developed a close circle of friends, whom Champs Senior encouraged him to bring to the cabin, sometimes for a day or two of fishing, sometimes for crabbing, and always for rowdy beer drinking, men and women alike. On those occasions, the lawn was full of tents to accommodate the overflow from the cabin.

Eventually, Champs Senior gave Peety the green light and a small budget to build a second cabin on the double lot, partway down the hill to the beach, shaded by sizable oaks and cedars. Champs found out later that his father had been hoping to arouse Peety's nesting instinct. Champs Senior had thought the project would nudge Peety into proposing to Susan, the knockout real estate agent he'd introduced as his girlfriend.

Peety worked on the cabin every weekend he could. With the help of his coworkers and a handful of other friends in construction, it was finished in three months: a two-bedroom bungalow with a full-sized bathroom and open-plan kitchen, dining, and living room. Sliding glass doors led to a covered wooden deck at the back, screened on three sides. There was a partial river view through the trees. Champs Senior had griped that he wouldn't pay for the porch, so Peety paid for it himself.

Champs and Pat used the cabin on weekends if Peety wasn't there. When David and then Laura came along, it had been a relief to spread out and escape the commands and mean-spirited comments that Champs Senior made when he'd had too much to drink. Ol' Champs, who was still alive at that point, did his best to keep his son in check, but he grew too old and sick to come down to the Sassafras much.

In the spring of 1974, Peety announced that he'd accepted an offer to work for a developer in Middletown, Delaware who had contracts to build several subdivisions in the area. It was better pay and meant that Peety could live full-time in the lower cabin. A handful of Peety's construction buddies and real estate friends made the same decision—it was boom time on the Eastern Shore. Peety rented out the second bedroom to another builder, a man named Rick. Champs Senior disapproved.

"How the hell's that boy ever gonna find a wife when he's got that goddamn Rick hanging around him all the time?" he complained, over and over, to Champs.

Then came the storm—a freak storm, a mix of hurricane and tornado. It hit Deadrise Cove in the middle of the night with lashing rain, powerful gusts of wind, and Ping Pong–ball-sized hailstones. Champs, Pat, Champs Senior, and June were startled awake in the early hours by what sounded like a freight train careening off a railroad bridge into a granite-strewn forest below. It was terrifying. Thunder and lightning crashed around the cabin.

Pat woke the children and gathered them under the kitchen table.

Champs's mother paced the cabin smoking a cigarette.

Champs Senior and Champs went out on the screened back porch to watch the storm, undeterred by its violence. They saw a flashlight beam charge toward them from the lower cabin. Behind it, Peety screamed for help.

Champs Senior and Champs sprinted off the porch toward Peety.

Larry barreled across the lawn from his cottage with an industrial-sized flashlight and an ax.

The men followed Peety as he barged through the front door of the lower cabin. Flashlights scanned a massive oak tree that had crashed through the master bedroom, ending its fall in the main living area. Wet tree trunk, splintered roof beams, insulation, dense branches, shattered ceiling panels, and drywall filled the back half of the cabin. Rain poured through the collapsed roof.

"In here!" Peety indicated the crushed door frame of the master bedroom. "Help me! Rick's pinned under the tree, and I can't get him out!"

"I can't see anything!" shouted Champs Senior, who entered the room first.

Larry and Peety lifted their flashlights.

The mighty oak had collapsed the exterior master bedroom wall and flattened the roof and ceiling on its way down to the living room. On the double bed, under the rubble and tree trunk, Rick wasn't moving.

"Get out of the way!" shouted Larry, and shoved Champs Senior to the side. He knelt on the sodden bed and hacked at the oak tree.

"What the fuck are you doing? You're gonna kill him!" shouted Peety.

Another section of the roof buckled.

"We have to get out of here, now!" screamed Champs Senior. "C'mon, Peety, let's go!"

"No! I'm not leaving Rick!" Peety said.

"Wait!" Champs yelled from the back of the room. He lifted a thick branch out of the wreckage and wedged it between the floor and the tree trunk. "This won't hold for long, but if you chop the legs of the bed, we'll have a split second to pull him out when the bed tilts. Hurry!"

Champs Senior took the flashlights and aimed them at Larry, who cleared through the debris as if he were parting the Red Sea and chopped at the legs of the bed.

Champs and Peety positioned themselves to pull Rick out as soon as the mattress dropped.

Rick moaned in pain.

"It's okay, Ricky. I'm right here. You're gonna make it, I promise. We'll get through this," Peety said in a tone of voice that Champs didn't recognize.

Champs Senior flashed his torch on Peety as the bed gave way.

Peety and Champs pulled Rick free. He was naked, marked by bleeding gashes, scratches, and a rib poking out of his chest. He appeared unconscious.

Sirens approached the cabin. Pat had called the fire department, who'd dispatched an ambulance and fire engine. Two paramedics carried Rick out on a stretcher. There wasn't a fire but the firefighters worked to stabilize the cabin.

Peety climbed into the ambulance with Rick. It sped off to the hospital, sirens wailing.

Champs and Larry stood in the rain, not sure what to do next. They trudged back into the lower cabin to see if they could be of any use.

Champs Senior stood rigid in the doorway of the second bedroom, which was undamaged by the fallen tree. He trained both flashlights on the untouched, perfectly made bed. Larry and Champs exchanged a grim-faced look.

At daybreak, Champs sent Pat and the kids home. Peety arrived back from the hospital reporting that Rick was in serious but stable condition. Over the next few days, Champs and Peety met a steady stream of insurance men, reporters, contractors, inspectors, electric and gas company reps, builders, and scores of neighbors who wandered in and out of the lower cabin. They signed all the paperwork and wrote checks for the necessary cleanup to secure what was left of the cabin. Casseroles and cakes from Josanne and her church community filled the refrigerator and countertops. Larry and Chicken Ray were around, lending what support they could.

At every opportunity, Peety stood outside his father's door imploring him to come out and talk. Champs listened as Peety tried to explain himself and begged Champs Senior to understand. It was futile. The door remained locked, the man on the other side of it silent and smoldering.

"Please, Mom, talk to him. Help him understand. I'm the same person I was before. Nothing has to change," Peety begged his mother, over and over.

"I can't," she repeated each time. She sat wedged in the corner of the sofa, a frozen rabbit, chain-smoking Marlboro Lights with trembling hands. The air in the cabin turned hazy and sour.

"Champs? Can you talk to him?" Peety asked.

Champs dropped his head and said nothing. What could he say? They both knew Champs Senior would no sooner listen to him than he would a raisin.

When Champs Senior did speak, after three days of drinking and seething in his room, his words hit Peety like buckshot, releasing a spray of disgust and self-righteous anger on a son who had shamed him and made a mockery of everything he valued.

"I didn't raise you to be *that*!" he shouted, gesturing at Peety with a half-empty bottle of Jim Beam. "It's an abomination. It's against nature. You make me sick!" He drew out the last word in a twisted snarl.

He took a long pull from the bottle, then lobbed it at Peety's head. Champs ducked, and his mother cowered, but Peety caught it and tucked it under his arm as if he might run it in for a touchdown. Whiskey dribbled onto the carpet. Champs's mother wept.

"Now get the hell outta here!" Champs Senior yelled. "I never want to see you again!"

Peety set the empty whiskey bottle down on the cinder-block side table. He held Champs's gaze for what seemed an eternity. Champs turned away. Peety left the cabin, got in his truck, and disappeared.

A week later, back in Downingtown, Champs received a postcard with a Florida PO box address. It said, *Please tell Mom I'm fine, and it's not her fault.*

"I should have written to him, Millie," Champs said now, shaking his head. "That's all there is to it."

Chock Full o'Nuts

C hamps was on the back porch about to get up and fix his lunch at his encampment when Jeffrey arrived.

"Hey, Champs," Jeffrey said. "Got your mail for you."

He flopped an electric bill, an envelope addressed in a child's hand, a flyer for the Galena Fire Department's pancake breakfast, and the latest issue of *National Geographic* onto the table.

"My mail?" Champs eyed the stack.

"Yep, your mail," Jeffrey said. "Laura told me she got the cabin set up with the post office, so now all your mail will come straight to this address. You'll need some new numbers on the mailbox down the end of the road, but otherwise, you're all set."

Champs poked at the pile of mail, lifted the bright orange pancake-breakfast flyer, and stared at it.

"You want me to add that to your list?" Jeffrey asked. He scribbled something on the card before Champs could stop him. "I crossed out 'cancel reunion' 'cause that's not gonna happen. And I added 'plant the garden,' 'buy crab pots,' and 'poker night slash pancake breakfast,' your choice."

"Let me see that," said Champs, and snatched the index card out of Jeffrey's hand. He was about to protest the edits when Jeffrey spoke up.

"I think it's about time for some lunch. You want tuna salad?"

"Are you gay?" Champs blurted.

Jeffrey snorted. "You mean because I like tuna salad?"

"No. Just generally speaking. 'Cause if you are—"

"Hold it right there, Champs. I'm not gay. I just haven't found the right woman. Like Chicken Ray. He never found the right woman either, but that doesn't make him gay."

"Humph," Champs muttered. He wasn't sure he wanted Chicken Ray to be the role model for his son.

The storm cleared, and Millie wagged her tail and pawed at the screen door. Champs let her out and watched her sprint down to the lower cabin.

"You know, it's never too late to contact him," said Jeffrey.

"Contact who?"

"Uncle Peety."

"You know about him?"

"Mom told us the whole story a long time ago. She also told us it didn't matter whether we loved men, women, or goats—it was all the same to her."

"Goats?"

"Whatever. Maybe she said chickens. We all got the point. She said you felt the same."

Champs bobbed his head up and down. He picked up the *National Geographic* and flipped it open to the cover article, "Destination Pluto." He looked out at the forlorn vegetable beds. Since Pat had died, life felt more like outer space every day. His stomach groaned.

"You say you're making sandwiches?" Champs prompted.

After the tuna, Champs took his to-do list back to his main tent. He didn't want Jeffrey coming up with any more bad ideas. The yellow urn leaned into the corner of his open suitcase where he'd left it last night. Jeffrey had clarified during lunch that the reunion was going ahead whether or not Champs wanted it to. That meant Laura would be back for her mother. She had been clear enough about her plans for the ceremony. Champs picked up the urn and sat down on his cot to contemplate his options.

He'd have to hide it where Laura would never go. The Sea Nymph was a possibility, but if the urn got knocked over, there would be the problem of cleaning Pat out of his boat. Perhaps he could hide it somewhere inside the cabin? He decided that wouldn't work since Laura knew every nook and cranny of the place and could search the whole thing in a matter of minutes. It was damn hard to hide a dead wife.

He had an idea. So far he'd been thinking about where to hide the urn, but what mattered most to him were the contents. What if . . .

"What if I leave the urn in plain view and just hide Pat?" he said to Millie, who had followed him into the tent, panting.

Lunging out of the tent, Champs scanned the yard to make sure no one was watching. He took a gallon-sized Ziploc bag from his kitchen-supplies bin and peeled away the masking tape on the urn. Removing the lid, he poured Pat's ashes into the baggie. It was dustier than he'd expected. Then Champs emptied the ground coffee from a new Chock Full o'Nuts canister into the urn. Laura would be onto him if it felt empty. He replaced the urn's lid and put the masking tape back in place. The Ziploc bag of Pat went into the empty Chock Full o'Nuts canister. He pushed his thumb around the yellow plastic lid and stowed it behind a can of baked beans on his camp shelf. Champs walked the coffee-filled urn over to the cabin and left it on the picnic table, where Jeffrey would find it and put it somewhere safe for Laura.

Feeling pleased, Champs crossed off the first item on his to-do list. Then he added *talk to Larry* and marched over to his neighbor's house. He pounded on the door. After several minutes, he banged again. The house had a doorbell, but Champs hated doorbells after his time in Regret's Pond. They reminded him of death and unwelcome surprises.

"Well, hello, Champs. What a nice surprise. C'mon in here," said Josanne when she answered the door. A blast of frigid air nearly knocked him over. He took in her slurred words and disheveled appearance.

"Oh, um, sorry to disturb you. I came to see Larry," he said, peering over Josanne's shoulder. "He here?"

"Yes, darlin'. He's out in his man cave, I think. I'll go get him." Josanne stood there as if she'd forgotten where she was. Or had finally frozen on the spot in the polar vortex effect of her air-conditioning. Champs thought he might be on the verge of frostbite if he stayed there any longer.

"I got this. I'll find him, Josanne. You get back inside," he said.

Champs made a hasty retreat to Larry's man cave, a.k.a. the garage, where he kept his vintage Jaguar XJ12. He had never seen Larry drive the car. What was the appeal of tinkering with a vehicle you'd never drive? At least Larry used the guns he polished all the time. Even if only to accessorize his outfits on some days. Champs thought the Jag would be put to better use as scrap metal in a welding yard. He didn't share his opinion with Larry, though; he wasn't an idiot.

Inside the garage, an overhead fan made a small dent in the otherwise stifling air that reeked of lube oil and old tires. Larry was bent under the hood. "Hey there, Champs. Can you hand me those boot clamp pliers over there?" he asked.

Champs passed the pliers to Larry. "Just knocked on your door. Is Josanne okay?"

"Think so. Why d'ya ask?"

"She didn't look so good."

Larry stood up and wiped his hands with a filthy rag. He looked hard at Champs. "That's the pain pills. For arthritis. Some days her hands hurt so much, she has to take an extra dose to get any relief. Must be one of those days."

"I didn't know it was that bad," said Champs.

"Comes and goes. Like the tide, I guess. Only at least with the tide you've got a rough idea of when and why. Not so with arthritis. I'll check on her in a minute." Larry sighed. "What brings you over here, Champs? Ready to trade in that Windstar?"

"Wondering about the association," said Champs.

"What about it?" Larry went back to work under the hood.

"You still running it?"

"What's left of it, yeah."

"Path down to Hill Beach needs work," Champs said. "And there's that pile of rubble over by the boat launch, too."

"Yep. There's plenty needs doin' around here. And plenty of nothing to get it done." Larry stood back from the Jag engine and nodded, apparently satisfied. After putting his tools away and slamming the hood down, he walked over to his minifridge and pulled out a beer. "Want one?"

Champs sure as hell did, but he tried to hold back, remembering he'd moved "buy beer" from his to-do list over to his to-don't list earlier, hoping to clean up his act. Technically, he'd promised himself not to *buy* any beer, so this didn't count. Plus, it was just plain weird to refuse another man's offer of a beer from his man cave. Champs had his reputation to think about.

"Sure. Thanks," he said, accepting the cold brew.

They left the garage and headed to the veranda.

"Ya know, Champs, things have changed around here," Larry began, settling into a cushy floral chair and putting his feet up on an ottoman. "Folks have changed. I'm used to all the bitchers, and I got no problem with assholes—seen plenty in the dealership, sold 'em all cars and trucks just the same. Bitchers and assholes? I can handle them fine. Used to enjoy winding them up and watching the show." Larry chuckled.

Champs leaned forward. "Jeffrey told me about Dex."

"Dex? Yeah, he's all right. I mean he's scary as hell and God knows what's going on over there. He won't be winning any awards for community service, sure enough, but he paid his dues. And then some. After I went over there that time, a fat envelope of cash showed up in my mailbox. Five hundred dollars, it was. And a doobie as thick as my thumb. I didn't know what to do with it."

"The doobie?"

"No, the money. It's still sitting in the association safe. Couldn't bring myself to walk up to the teller at the bank with a wad of green-backs smelling to high heaven of illegal substances."

"What'd you do with the doobie?"

"Smoked it. With Chicken Ray in one of his bird sheds—more like a shit shed if you ask me. We figured it would cover up the skunky smell of the weed. Didn't figure on the effect it had on all them birds though. Funniest damn day of my life, that was."

"Humph," Champs muttered. "From what you're saying, the association's got five hundred dollars at least. Why aren't the repairs being made?"

"Like I said, Champs. Folks have changed around here. We kept the dues so low because there were men around who would show up and pitch in—do the work, donate time and materials—you remember. That's all gone now. No one wants to lift a finger. No one knows how to get the job done. No one has time."

Champs remembered the main community event each year at Deadrise Cove. The third Saturday in April marked the official start of the summer season, when folks gathered to put the floating docks and dock fingers back in the river next to the launch ramp. It used to be a festive event. The men showed up at eleven a.m., each with a case of Yuengling or Natty Boh, the regional favorites, and plenty of grit to drag the docks from the shed into the Sassafras, making repairs as they went. Champs pictured his mother and the other women—rain or shine —setting out card tables crowded with Jell-O salads, cold cuts, white bread, potato chips, and plenty of gossip.

As a child, he'd run around with the other boys. They sized each other up, rode bikes, threw rocks, and dared each other to sneak sips of beer. Games of kick-the-can involved hours of arguing over the rules rather than much kicking of any can. In high school, they'd sneak off to smoke cigarettes, swig from a pilfered Four Roses whiskey bottle, and engage in the occasional fisticuffs. There was a lot of making out, too, he remembered now with a smirk. The docks were returned to the shed to overwinter on the third Saturday of October. That was a men-only event with no fanfare.

The community tradition had stood firm when he and Pat had kids.

Champs knew David had had his first real kiss at the dock-launch picnic when he was fifteen years old. The girl he'd kissed had turned out to be the crush of a local ruffian. David had staggered home that evening with a shiner and a split lip, nonetheless beaming and singing *Foreigner's* "Feels Like the First Time" using an empty bottle of Rolling Rock as a mic. Those days were long gone now. Champs, Jeffrey, Larry, and one other man had put the docks in this year on a drizzly morning at the end of April. There was no beer.

"There's hardly any point in keeping the monthly association meetings going," Larry continued. "Only three of us show up: me, Josanne, and that geezer always complaining about his neighbor's trespassing."

"That still going on, huh?"

"Every month. We don't have the heart to tell him his sworn enemy passed away nine years ago. He makes his motion to have 'that son of a bitch' arrested for trespassing. I second it. The three of us vote in favor of the matter. Then Josanne pretends to write it down in the book, has him sign our electric bill, and gives him a glass of sherry and a chunky square of pineapple upside-down cake. After that, he excuses himself and walks home." Larry shrugged.

"Why don't you hire some contractors to get the work done?"

"I did that once or twice, even pitched in my own money to get things done right. No one said a damn word of thanks. Fact is, things are falling apart all the time around here. It's near impossible to get any help, paid or otherwise. I tried to find a fella to come out and repair the docks? He wouldn't do it unless I got the hornet hive removed first. Tried to find a fella to come out and remove the hive and he wouldn't come unless I fixed the dock first. Price of things gone up so much. That wad of bills sitting in the safe? Wouldn't even pay for the nails to make a new dock, let alone the labor to get it done. The association is dead, Champs. And I'm sick of being the asshole who knocks on doors begging for more money and help."

Champs wasn't sure how to respond, and since he didn't want to get involved, he got up to leave. "Thanks for the beer, Larry. You're probably wanting to get on inside and check on Josanne," he said.

"Hold up a minute, Champs. There's something I've been meaning to tell you. Me and Josanne? We're thinking about selling up. It's just not the same anymore, and we're not on the river so much like we used to be. With her arthritis and all, well . . ."

"Where you headed?" asked Champs.

"Florida, most likely."

"Good luck with that." Champs hated Florida. It reminded him of a long-lost brother and those idiotic pink herons that only knew how to stand on one leg.

21

Sowing Seeds

The next morning, Champs got up early to resume his regular fishing routine. He'd intended to go trolling downriver Shell-cross-way, but he puttered upriver instead. Anchoring just off Wilson Point, he waded into the narrow strip of beach. Millie disappeared into a stand of cattails. Champs clambered into an old duck blind and watched the herons fly in and out of their rookery in the trees on Hen Island. Goddamn pterodactyls.

Maybe he would take Larry up on his offer to learn how to shoot. How hard could it be to hit one of them? He imagined himself dressed head to toe in camouflage, machine-gunning them down like Rambo. There was probably some idiotic Department of Natural Resources law about not killing herons. He doubted Millie would make a good retriever, anyway.

She came out of the reeds and rubbed her back in the sand, legs in the air, tongue lolling. Champs had half a mind to try it himself. Pat used to scratch his back all the time. With her gone, he imagined himself sitting on the fake porch, a flyswatter in one hand and one of those wooden back scratchers in the other. It had come to this.

Leaving the blind, Champs stood on the shoreline cracking the peanuts he'd shoved into his pocket earlier. Larry's intentions to sell and move to Florida had caught him off guard. He tried to imagine what it would be like without them next door. It didn't feel right, but why should he care? It wasn't like they were close friends. No, the real problem was that he didn't want to get used to anyone new at this stage.

"What if they're golfers, Millie?" he said. It was the worst thing he could imagine. Other than more herons. Or hippies. Champs hated hippies.

"Guess we better head back," he said, although he wasn't sure why. He waded out to *Tetanus* and pulled up anchor, having not so much as dipped a lure in the river. His hands shook as he got behind the wheel.

Jeffrey's truck, filled with fresh lumber and bags of potting soil, greeted Champs when he returned to his campsite. The door of the lower cabin slammed shut, and Jeffrey bounded up the rotting stairs toward Champs and Millie. He passed Champs an icy can of O'Doul's.

"What the hell's this?" said Champs. He knew a nonalcoholic brew when he saw one.

Jeffrey rolled his eyes. "Just drink it, Champs. I'm not serving anything else, and you're gonna need it to stay hydrated—we've got a lot of work to do. Chicken Ray'll be here any minute to help, so let's get started."

"This was your idea. I'm not getting involved in this."

"Shut up and go get the tools or I'll dig a hole right here and bury you in it," Jeffrey said.

Champs raised his eyebrows. "Fine. But call off the chicken man. We don't need any help from him."

Jeffrey smirked. "Too late."

Chicken Ray pulled in behind the Windstar.

Three hours later, red-faced, soaked in sweat, and smeared with dirt, they'd completed the job. The raised beds were restored to their former glory, brimming with fresh black soil and leaf mulch. Champs had enjoyed the physical labor, the earthy smells, and the camaraderie of his son and Chicken Ray. He felt purposeful, and his mind didn't wander over the past or worry about the future.

Josanne called the men onto the porch. She'd set up a buffet of sandwiches, cookies, and sweet tea.

"Thanks, Josanne. How are you feeling today?" asked Champs, surprised by the note of actual concern in his voice.

"Why, I'm feeling just wonderful, honey. Been working all morning on Mrs. Anderson's memorial sampler for her dog, Bessie. Poor thing up and died a few weeks ago. The dog, I mean. She was devastated, of course. Mrs. Anderson, I mean. Lives down Betterton way. Bessie was a golden retriever—a big one, too. Nearly cleaned me clear out of DMC Old Gold floss. What do y'all think of this for the epitaph: 'Bessie was Better in Betterton.'"

Jeffrey choked on a piece of rye bread.

"Better than what?" asked Chicken Ray as he stuffed a peanut butter cookie in his mouth to stop himself from cracking up.

"Well, better than dead, of course," said Josanne, indignant.

Jeffrey and Chicken Ray couldn't contain their laughter.

"Sounds real nice, Josanne," said Champs, ignoring the two idiots on the porch.

"Oh, Raymond darlin', before I forget, I heard folks talking the other day said you had that chicken farm of yours up for sale. Is that true?" asked Josanne. She was the only one allowed to call him Raymond.

Chicken Ray cleared his throat. "Yes, ma'am. But they don't call it a chicken farm anymore—it's a poultry production facility, according to industry folks nowadays. I've got two of 'em. Capacity to manufacture over forty thousand broilers three times a year."

"Like a chicken factory?" prompted Jeffrey.

"That's right. I'm not considered a farmer anymore. In fact, the only thing I take care of now is the computers and machines that run the whole operation."

"You don't handle the chickens?" asked Champs.

"Oh, I get to handle them all right. Every day, I get to walk the flock and wring the necks of any units—that's what the birds are called —that don't look right. Seems that's the only thing their robots can't figure out how to do," said Chicken Ray.

"How so?" asked Jeffrey.

"It takes experience to know just what and when to cull. Used to be a matter of keeping all the birds as healthy as possible. Now it's all about efficiency—how fast can a unit turn feed into meat. The robots they tested couldn't tell the difference between a chicken stressed by disease and all the rest of them stressed by their living conditions. Killed one out of every three birds. I hear they're getting better, though," Chicken Ray explained.

"Sounds awful, Raymond. Those poor chickens. I had no idea," said Josanne.

"Been like that for a while now. The kind of chicken farm Pat helped me set up is no more. At least not around here. Don't get me wrong, I made a good living at it. Just don't have the stomach for it anymore. Two sheds isn't enough either. Whoever buys my place will prolly build two or three more right off the bat. Realtor says I'll get a good price—there's a ton of Asians wanting in on this now, apparently. A lot of cash to spend. That's what they say, anyway."

"Then what're you gonna do?" asked Champs. He bit into a cookie and chased it with a gulp of sweet tea.

"Actually, Champs," Jeffrey interjected, "Chicken Ray and I have been weighing up the costs involved in getting Uncle Hessie's old boat repair business going again," said Jeffrey.

"What for?" said Champs.

"Things are different now," Chicken Ray replied. "Used to be things took ten years to develop around here. Now everything changes fast as a woman changes her mind. Two years from now, there's gonna be a line of pricey condos and a sparkling new marina tucked in there in front of the Kitty Knight House. They have to wait for the new sewer system and up it goes. What's the word for it, when the rich folks move in, and the locals move out?"

"Gentrification," said Jeffrey.

Just then Larry entered the porch with a six-pack of real beer in hand. "Speaking of gentrification, I was just at a jam-packed town council meeting—apparently Starbucks is interested in coming to Galena," he said, passing out the beer.

"Well, I'll be damned," said Chicken Ray.

"What's this got to do with wooden boats?" asked Champs, who sure as hell wouldn't be forking out four dollars for a recycled-cardboard cup of joe any time soon. He reached for one of Larry's beers and opened it under the table, as if no one would notice.

"There's a market for them again. This time it's a premium market, not a working waterman's market. Classic wooden boats. Repair and new build," answered Jeffrey. "Quite a few contracts out there. I've got a meeting next week with those condo developers. They're interested in amenities. Reckon I can sell them a fleet of handcrafted wooden canoes."

Champs chuckled. "You're pulling my leg."

"No," said Jeffrey. "I was hoping you'd invest."

Champs missed his mouth and beer trickled down his chin. Josanne passed him a napkin. "Invest with what?" he asked. "I think you forget I live in a tent, piss in the bushes, and eat from a can!"

"Honey, please tell me you don't really relieve yourself in the shrubbery," said Josanne.

"And, um, just outta curiosity, Champs. Where you layin' down those number twos?" asked Larry, snorting.

"Well, from now on," said Champs, "I'll be laying 'em down in your goddamn begonias!"

Knee-slapping laughter filled the porch. Champs managed a satisfied grin, then grabbed another beer. Larry picked up the last one and the two men, neighbors for over forty years, raised their cans.

"A toast," said Larry. "To my good friend Champs and his future success as the world's first homeless venture capitalist!"

"To Champs!"

"Cheers!"

"Cheers!"

Champs had no intention of investing in anything, ever, but at that moment he didn't care. He felt warmed by the toast and the real beer.

"Lord have mercy," said Josanne, "I don't know about all this wheeling and dealing, but I must get back to my sampler, and y'all got to figure out what's going in that new garden of yours and get it in there before it's too late."

On her way out, Josanne gathered up the empty paper plates and swept the crumbs onto the floor, where Millie scarfed them up, tail wagging.

"I best get back to my birds," said Chicken Ray. "Larry, Jeffrey, I'll see you tonight. You coming, Champs?"

"Coming to what?"

"Poker night. We meet at the Catholic church now. Reverend lets us use the conference room there as long as we attend a Sunday service now and then," said Chicken Ray.

"That and leave him a fifth of Fireball every month," said Larry.

"He'll be there," Jeffrey said as Chicken Ray and Larry walked out. He turned to Champs and smiled. "It's on your list."

Champs grunted.

"Speaking of your list," Jeffrey continued, "I picked up the new numbers for the mailbox. Why don't you walk down there with Millie, stick them on, and get your mail?"

"You do it," said Champs. "I'm terribly busy. Why don't you drive over to the nursery and buy the plants while you're at it? No point raising from seed at this stage. Tomatoes, bell peppers, zucchinis—the usual."

He dug in his cargo shorts for cash, handed it to Jeffrey, and shooed him off the porch. After updating his to-do list, Champs attacked the remaining beer in the SMEGerator, as he now referred to it.

22

Exposed

At dusk, Jeffrey arrived with two cans of Kutztown Birch Beer, a bag of meatball sandwiches, and a large cushioned mailer. Champs had just showered and was sitting on his screen-tent porch wrapped in a beach towel. He oozed a new Sassafras sheen in the oppressive heat that lingered even at sunset. The cicadas chirred in full chorus. Champs dabbed calamine lotion on the swollen mosquito bites that dotted his legs and arms.

"You got a package in the mail," Jeffrey said as he unzipped the screen door.

"Quick! Zip that damn door shut! Can't have more of these blood-suckers getting through the screen!" said Champs.

Jeffrey unwrapped the sandwiches and opened the sodas.

"Did you get the plants?" asked Champs, his mouth full of meatballs.

Jeffrey nodded and washed down a bite of sandwich with a swallow of birch beer. "Bought them from Dirty Girls. They're doing great. Not just with the produce and nursery, but with a whole range of premium organic products. Jill Marcosi said to say hi. She sends her condolences."

Champs clapped his hands on a mosquito, leaving them smeared with blood. "Goddamn skeeters," he said, and picked up the other half of his sandwich.

"I'm serious about that business with Chicken Ray. We don't have to fix up the entire wharf area and warehouse all at once. I was telling Jill about it, and she offered to help me with all the paperwork—business plan, legal stuff, back-office systems for a small business," Jeffrey said.

He switched on a camping lantern on the floor of the porch tent.

Champs smacked another mosquito on his arm and scratched at a bite on his ankle until it bled. Pouring calamine lotion into his cupped palm, he slathered it like sunscreen on his skin until his chest, arms, and beer belly were painted in it. Lit from below, he resembled a giant pink glowworm.

"A pyrosome," Champs said, recalling the bioluminescent sea pickles he'd seen in a *National Geographic* article. He thought he would make a great new character on *SpongeBob SquarePants*. Champs loved watching that show with his grandkids. He had a real affinity for Squidward.

"Are you even listening, Champs?" asked Jeffrey.

"What do you think that package is all about?" Champs replied.

He'd learned that the best answer to a pointless yes-or-no question was an open-ended question that changed the subject. Worked every time.

"Looks like it came from Egret's Pond," said Jeffrey. "Aren't you gonna open it?"

"Maybe tomorrow," Champs said.

"Your choice," said Jeffrey. "It's time we got over to the poker game, anyway."

Champs shook his head. "Not me."

Before Jeffrey could protest, Champs leaned forward to unzip the tent flap. He grabbed the lantern and his package and lumbered across the grass to his main tent. Partway there, his towel fell away, mooning Jeffrey, who yelled, "Nice one, Champs!"

Champs sat naked and aglow on his cot and tore open the thick mailer. Inside, there was another package addressed to Pat at their former Egret's Pond address. He squinted to read the return address. Nickleby's Farm. How could that be? Pat had sold her father's farm after her parents had died. They'd put the proceeds into a retirement account, which had dwindled somewhat given the high cost of Egret's Pond and Pat's cancer treatments.

The envelope was bulky. Champs thought he could feel the outline of small books inside. He brought it up to his nose for a good sniff.

"Should I open it, Millie?"

She wagged her tail and licked the back of his hand.

Champs opened the inner package to discover a letter and a stack of notebooks, each one with a different bird sticker on the cover. He recognized them as a match to Pat's death-plan notebook, the one with the goldfinch on it. Setting the journals aside, he tore open the letter.

Dear Mrs. Noland,

We hope you are well and that these notebooks reach you in good condition. We found them tucked into a niche in the main barn when we tore it down. We only read enough to understand what they were and who they belonged to. Your compassion for our veterans moved us to tears. Thank you for your service. God bless you, and God bless America. Sincerely, Mr. and Mrs. Jonathan Curtis.

"Well, I'll be damned," said Champs.

He ate his way through a package of marshmallows while skimming through the notebooks, each one dedicated to a veteran Pat had worked with at the farm. The first page of the notebook detailed the vet's biographical details, including a description of what they looked like. After that, she had recorded dates and farm activities along with brief feedback from the veteran, like a science report.

When he opened a notebook about a vet called Hal, Champs noticed an alarming change in Pat's tone. She'd moved from record keeping to detailed reflections on conversations and shared moments with her clients. It was like reading her private diary. She'd written about feelings and used too many intimate words for Champs's liking. In one passage, Pat expressed the love she felt as Hal brushed a cow for the first time, his trembling hand guided by hers.

"What is this bullshit?" Champs exclaimed.

Millie put a paw over her muzzle and farted.

Champs shoved her out of the tent and returned to his reading with a sense of dread.

He reached Pat's final client notebook, JP's. The man who'd shot himself in the head and brought Pat's program to an end. It had a dove on its front cover. Champs opened it to the first page and felt his heart rate rise along with a good deal of bile. "JP" was a nickname for Jeffrey Powell. Pat had described him as tall and handsome with dark wavy hair and hazel eyes that changed color depending on how the light hit them. It sounded like a goddamn romance book.

Several images fused together in Champs's brain, overloading his mental circuitry. In the electrical pop that followed, something blew wide open. Some part of him had known it all along. He'd pushed it away over and over, deciding he was crazy to even imagine such a thing. He'd never mentioned it to anyone. But here it was, staring him in the face.

He counted the months out on his fingers between JP's death and Jeffrey's birth. It was possible. Yes, it was entirely possible that Champs was not Jeffrey's father.

"Son of a bitch!" he yelled, and threw the notebook across the tent, where it landed on top of his dirty clothes pile.

Zappers

Over the next four weeks, Champs drove himself to the edge of madness. He felt like a two-headed snake: one head full of his life as he'd known it and the other full of a different life—the one where he wasn't Jeffrey's father. The schism left him in a constant state of peril, an existential unknowing. Was it true? Or was he imagining things? How could Pat keep a secret like this all these years?

He drank throughout the day and couldn't sleep through the night. Furtive and exhausted, he paced in front of the Chock Full o'Nuts coffee can, mumbling and gesturing. Some nights, he sat from midnight until two or three in the morning in his screen tent listening to the mosquitoes electrocute themselves on the high-voltage metal grids inside the fluorescent zapping device he'd installed. Champs sometimes lulled himself to sleep by counting the sizzle of fried insects. It was comforting.

With no one he could trust to ask, Champs lost the ability to think rationally about the issue. Instead, he looked for signs that would answer his question, as if he could divine the truth in a formation of stars or the hooting of an owl. One afternoon, he walked to the end of the street and brought back a fistful of black-eyed Susans. He sat on the grass with them like Ferdinand the Bull and picked off each golden petal, alternating "he is," "he isn't," until he got to the last one: "he is." Champs convinced himself his sample size was too small to confirm the validity of his analysis.

He decided that if he finally caught a fish, it would mean that Jeffrey was his. But what if he caught an eel? Or a tiny sunfish that hardly counted as a real catch? Or what if he caught the fish and it escaped before he landed it in the boat? What would that mean? He continued to motor around the river for a couple of hours most mornings but refused himself the pleasure of fishing because there was just too much riding on the outcome.

Larry, Josanne, Jeffrey, and Chicken Ray attempted to pull him out of what they called his "funk." Champs joined in just enough so it would seem like he was trying. He didn't need to do much since Larry and Josanne were preoccupied with the sale of their house and move to Florida. Jeffrey, Jill, and Chicken Ray were caught up in creating a business and cleaning up Hessie's old place.

Champs tended the garden and drove himself to Save-Cave now and then to stock up on food and drink. He did his own laundry with a bar of soap in a galvanized metal pot they'd once used for steaming crabs. He left it pegged on the clothesline, his permanent closet. The weather made its way across June in a muggy rhythm of sun, shower, thunder, repeat.

Nobody mentioned anything about the reunion or the ceremony over those weeks, so it was a surprise when Laura and Brian arrived on a Friday afternoon with the girls in tow. At the request of Larry and Josanne, they moved the *Flying Cloud* to a flat part of the grass between the upper and lower cabins where it wasn't visible to potential buyers. Unfortunately, this move opened up the view of Champs's homeless encampment, which was the topic of conversation when they all sat down for dinner together that night.

Champs knew something was up when Josanne and Larry carried platter after platter of buttermilk fried chicken, bourbon baked beans, honey corn bread, and sliced yellow tomatoes over to the cabin. Brian poured him a Guinness in a real glass. Laura sat her girls on either side of him. Jeffrey was out with Chicken Ray going over the developer's contract details—if everything went well, he was on to build a fleet of canoes painted in retro colors.

The conversation started neutrally enough when Champs asked Hannah about the book on her lap.

"It's a stupid Nancy Drew book," she replied.

"What happened to Hercule Poirot?" Champs asked. He wondered how Hercule Poirot would go about investigating "Jeffreygate."

"I love Hercule Poirot, but Nana doesn't think it's appropriate for my age. She talked to my teachers about it, and they told me for the summer I had to do a book report on this," Hannah said, holding up the book as if it were a dead rat.

"Brian's mother has a big influence at the school," Laura explained.

"Well, I don't know why a young woman such as yourself is interested in all that murder and detective nonsense," Josanne said. "What you need is some good ol'-fashioned romance. I have a whole box full of Harlequins. You come on over after dinner, darlin', and we'll get you all sorted out. Put some fun back into your summer."

Laura and Brian shot disapproving looks in Josanne's direction.

"Okay," said Hannah, sounding skeptical.

"What about me?" asked Zoe. "I hate reading, but I want something special, too."

"Zoe!" Laura scolded. "You're being greedy. Just because Hannah gets some—"

"You leave that to me," Larry interrupted. "I have something special just for Zo-Zo."

"What about me?" Champs asked. Everyone laughed.

"Champs, darlin', you've already got so much special baked into you, there's no need to go begging for any more," Josanne said, loading his plate with another piece of corn bread.

"Speaking of which," Larry added, "we have a special favor to ask you, Champs."

"Told you before, Larry. I'm not interested in getting involved in association matters. Maybe Brian here can help out. We could rough him up a little, make him look like an Irish mobster, and send him around with one of your duck guns to collect dues," said Champs.

He wasn't kidding, but everyone laughed again. He wondered if he should consider stand-up as an encore career.

"No, no. This isn't about the Deadrise Cove Association. It's about your tent situation over there," Larry said.

"What about it?"

"Wondering if you could temporarily move it?"

"Move it?"

"Just for a little while, Champs," Josanne said. "While we get the house sold, is all. Folks might not want to buy next to a homeless shelter. You know how prejudiced people can be."

"I can help you get it cleared out tomorrow," offered Brian.

"It's better if you use the real kitchen and bathroom anyway," said Laura. "When it gets colder, you will need to move inside, no matter how much you hate the thought."

"What d'ya say, Champs?" prompted Larry.

Champs had a flash of déjà vu. Hadn't he been here before when they were trying to talk him into staying at Regret's Pond? Now they were trying to talk him out of staying in his own tent on his private property? He felt like a piece in a game of checkers. Pushed and prodded here and there across the board, given false hope he'd one day be king, only to find himself jumped over and removed from the game board.

"What the hell, I don't give a shit," he said. "I'll sleep on my goddamn boat."

Champs would have left, but he spotted a peach cobbler on the wooden games table and wasn't about to miss out on that.

"Thank you, Champs. We are ever so grateful that you can accommodate us while we're in need. You're our hero. Now, let me get that peach cobbler, and we can all have dessert," said Josanne.

Champs expected someone to protest his threat to bivouac on *Tetanus* amid a hornet-filled dock, but no one did. The next day he and Brian cleared the backyard. Champs packed a cooler full of beer and a suitcase full of canned food, clothes, and his coffee-scented dead wife. He put his valuables in the Windstar and drove to the Sea Nymph. At twilight, he erected a one-pole, one-man tent that resembled a body bag on the aft deck of his boat. Rocked by the lapping tide and a lullaby of crickets and croaking frogs, he slept like a baby.

24

Venus de Lilo

At 6:13 on Sunday evening, four pounds of marinated skirt steak sputtered on the grill, and a mix of new potatoes, green beans, and chives swam in a buttery sauce on the set picnic table. David's rental car pulled into the driveway.

"He's here!" shouted Hannah, who ran toward the car still gripping her badminton racket.

Zoe followed, her sundress pockets full of shuttlecocks that she'd refused to hit back to her big sister because she felt sorry for the little "birdies."

Laura and Brian went to the side yard to welcome David. Jeffrey and Champs joined them. Laura had informed Champs that David would come on his own this time because of unforeseen complications. When Champs had asked for more details, Laura told him he'd have to ask David about that.

"Uncle David!" squealed Zoe, running into his arms as he got out of the car.

He lifted her in a bear hug and made a show of poking, tickling, and kissing her.

Just then, the passenger-side door opened and a woman with frizzy brown hair half-controlled by an elastic, red-rimmed sunglasses, and an army-green tank top appeared. She waved at the dumbstruck Nolands on the other side of the car.

"Who is that?" asked Zoe, pointing an incriminating finger at the unexpected guest.

"That must be his secret lover," announced Hannah, who'd spent the previous forty-eight hours reading Josanne's romance novels.

That must be the unforeseen complication, thought Champs.

The woman laughed and walked around the front of the car to introduce herself.

"Holy shit," said Jeffrey.

Laura gasped.

Brian dropped his can of Guinness.

Champs shook his head and looked at David.

"Surprise!" said David.

"You didn't tell them I was coming, did you?" asked the heavily pregnant woman who lifted her sunglasses to glare at David. She had round blue eyes like Pat's and a smattering of freckles.

"No, he didn't," said Laura. She stepped forward and extended her hand. "I'm Laura, David's sister. I'm guessing you're Mel?"

"Yes, plus one," said Mel, pointing to her protruding belly, then shaking Laura's hand. "Nice to meet you, Laura. I've heard a lot about you."

"Well, let's hope some of it was good," said Laura with a sideways glance at David. "This is my daughter Hannah and my other daughter, Zoe . . ."

Champs eyed Mel with suspicion. She was taller than Laura, with tanned, muscular limbs that reminded him of a mountain lion. He noticed the bell-bottom hem on her purple stretchy pants, her beat-up leather sandals, and a gold ring on the second toe of her right foot. When she turned to shake hands with Jeffrey, Champs saw a small yellow butterfly tattooed on the back of her shoulder.

". . . And this is my father, Champs," said Laura, who had continued with the introductions.

"You a hippie?" he blurted.

"Champs!" three people shouted at once.

Mel looked amused. "I hate hippies," she said. "Nice to meet you, Champs."

She didn't try to shake hands with him or touch him or apologize for his loss. He liked her already.

"Okay," said David, clapping his hands together. "Thanks for the introductions, Laura. I'm ready for a beer. I forgot how stinking hot it is here this time of year."

He set Zoe down and plowed through to the porch.

Zoe took Mel's hand and led her to the porch sofa. The girls sat down either side of her. Champs sat at the picnic table and resumed reading *The Salty Dog*, a newsprint magazine of advertisements and boats for sale. Jeffrey refilled Laura's wineglass, gave Hannah and Zoe cans of Sprite, and passed fresh beers to the men. He held one out to Mel.

"Oh my God, Jeffrey. She's pregnant. She can't drink beer!" said Laura. "Would you like a bottle of sparkling water, Mel?"

"No, thanks. Beer is great," Mel replied. She cracked open the sweaty, cold can and downed half of it with obvious pleasure before propping it on top of her swollen stomach.

"Don't you think that's a bad idea given your condition?" Laura asked.

"Don't you think you should mind your own business?" David cut in.

Laura shot him a withering glance.

"But, hey," David continued. "Look what you've done to the place, Laura—it's amazing. Is that a waterfall feature over there?"

Laura nodded and turned it on. Champs grimaced behind his magazine. He hated the fake sound of the fountain because it gave him the urge to urinate at all times. Getting old was hell.

"David, can you take a look at these steaks?" said Brian. "I remember you're the Weber expert around here."

The two men headed for the barbecue on the lawn.

Jeffrey's phone buzzed, and he excused himself to take the call in the cabin.

Zoe placed her hand on Mel's stomach. "Is that a baby in there?" she asked.

Champs peered over the top of *The Salty Dog*.

"Yes, it is," said Mel.

She lifted her tight tank top, pulled the fabric of her stretchy pants down, and pressed Zoe's hand into her blue-veined bump. To Champs, it appeared as if the full moon had landed on Mel's lap, right there on his porch in Galena, Maryland.

"Oh! I felt it kick my hand!" Zoe said with a mixture of awe, surprise, and delight.

"Zoe, go get another place setting for Mel," Laura said like a drill sergeant.

Zoe frowned but did as she was told.

"Can I feel it, too?" asked Hannah.

"No! Hannah, leave Mel alone and go help your sister," ordered Laura.

Hannah rolled her eyes and went into the cabin.

Champs continued to ogle the planetary orb that was Mel's exposed belly.

"Do you want to feel it?" she asked him.

He disappeared behind his magazine as if to pretend he wasn't there and the question did not pertain to him.

"How far along are you?" asked Laura, refilling her wineglass.

"I'm not really sure. Maybe seven, eight months."

"And you got on an airplane?" Laura sounded furious.

Champs peered over the top of *The Salty Dog* again and watched Mel finish her beer. Laura's behavior confused him. He understood her anger at David for having an affair and breaking up his family—that's what he assumed had happened. Champs could admit to similar feelings. But Laura had never liked David's wife, Kimmie, so it didn't make sense that she would be mean to Mel right off the bat. And what was all this fuss about the pregnancy? The baby was innocent in this. What the hell was going on with Laura?

The girls came through with an extra place setting, arguing about how babies got made.

"You're so stupid, Zoe. The man has to put his sperm in the woman's vagina," Hannah said.

"How does he put it there?" asked Zoe.

"He flickers his tongue on the woman's nipples, and she gets really wet, and there's a lot of moaning, and then he penetrates her with his stiff—"

"Hannah! Stop! What the hell are you talking about?" Laura exclaimed.

Mel giggled.

"That's what it says in those books Josanne gave me. It's the same every time," said Hannah.

Before Laura could respond, Jeffrey pushed through the main door and interrupted.

"Hey, Laura. That was Chicken Ray on the phone. I invited him and Jill for dinner. They're on their way."

"Great," said Laura in a deadpan voice.

Champs watched Jeffrey stare at Mel's naked belly. His son seemed mesmerized by it, as if in the presence of the eighth wonder of the world. Mel grinned and waved Jeffrey over. She put his hands on the bare bump. Smitten, Jeffrey knelt before her and pressed his ear on her stretched skin, his face an expression of pure worship.

"Oh, for God's sake," said Laura. "She's just a pregnant woman, not the fucking Venus de Milo."

"Who's fucking Venus de Lilo?" asked Zoe.

"Nobody," said Mel.

"Yeah, she's a stone-cold lover," said Jeffrey.

He and Mel cracked up and high-fived like they'd known each other for years.

Champs ducked behind his classified ads to hide his smirk from Laura's seething eyes.

"I think I'm going to be sick," she announced, and stomped into the cabin.

25

Pinkie

When Jill and Chicken Ray arrived, Jeffrey introduced them to David and Mel as his business partners, and they all sat down to eat. Laura rubbed her hands and the girls' hands with antibacterial wipes. She offered one to Mel, who turned it down.

As polite chatter rippled across the table, Champs noticed Mel decline the skirt steak. He wondered if she was one of those vegemetarian types. He'd heard there were a lot of them out in California. Champs thought it would be better to find out now, rather than waste his energy liking Mel if it turned out she was a meat hater. Not that she'd be there that long, but still.

He waggled a piece of steak in the air and called out for Millie, knowing full well this would attract Laura's ire.

"What the hell are you doing with that steak, Champs?" she asked.

Her voice brought all other conversation to a standstill.

"I'm feeding it to Millie," he replied.

He let the dog jump onto his lap, where she pulled another piece of steak from his plate.

Laura glared at him.

"What?" Champs said. "I'm a vegemetarian."

"Bullshit!" said Laura. "Put the dog down. Now!"

Millie jumped down and ran behind Zoe's legs, sensing an immediate threat to her safety.

"Well, Mel is a vegemetarian, so I thought I'd make her feel comfortable," said Champs.

"Me? I'm not vege . . . vegetarian. Where'd you get that idea?" asked Mel.

"You don't have any meat," said Champs, pointing to her plate.

"Oh, right. No offense to the chef, it's just that I prefer my beef on the rare side," Mel said, and bit into her corn. "This is amazing corn. Is it locally grown?"

Champs admired her redirection technique and her palate. Mel was right about the steak. It was so well done it qualified as jerky. He noticed Mel and Jeffrey exchange a glance. Jeffrey blushed. Was she flirting with him? This would be one hell of a week, Champs thought.

"Sure is," said Jill, talking about the corn. "Grown right down the road on Dad's farm. We sell it at our new market over in—"

"How did you two meet?" Laura interrupted, pointing to Mel and David with her wineglass.

"Jesus Christ, Laura!" David said. "Is this really necessary?"

"It's fine," said Mel. "I met him in the office when I came to service his pinkie," she said.

Jeffrey spewed a mouthful of beer.

Brian coughed into his fist.

Chicken Ray and Jill snorted.

Champs and the girls shrugged at each other.

"Service his pinkie, huh?" Laura said. "Is that what they call it these days?"

She threw back the rest of her chardonnay. Brian tried to remove her glass, but Laura clung to it. They played tug-of-war until Brian let go. Laura fell back against Champs, who farted. It was another fun fact about the aging process, he'd observed: difficulty controlling certain bodily emanations.

"Ew. You farted! You farted!" Zoe held her nose with one hand and pointed at Champs with another.

"That was Millie," he said.

The dog barked in protest.

Another round of laughter.

Except for Laura. She shot daggers at Mel over her fresh glass of wine. She wasn't about to lose an evil-eye contest, Champs thought. This was predator against predator as far as he could tell. Things could get bloody.

"Go on," Laura said. "You were saying? About David's pinkie?"

"Yes. I'm an art teacher part-time, so I have to supplement my income. I have a good green thumb and used to work at a gardening center. Raj—he's the owner—also rented indoor plants to the managers of office buildings and retirement homes. Part of the contract included taking care of the plants. 'Pinkie' is just shorthand for pink rubber trees —a variety of *ficus*. They like a lot of natural light, so David's office, since it's a corner one, was an ideal location for pinkie number nine— she's one of my favorites. I met David when I came in to service his plant." Mel popped a new potato into her mouth and locked eyes with David.

"And it was what—love at first sight?" Laura's combination of sneer and slurred words made her seem like an evil witch. "Didn't you notice his wedding ring before you wrapped your—"

"That's enough, Laura!" said Champs.

Laura giggled, but the giggles turned to sobs.

"What the hell's wrong with you?" asked David.

Laura reached for her wineglass, only to knock it over. Mel was quick to mop up the spill with her napkin. Jeffrey was quick to help Mel with his napkin, Champs noticed. Brian lifted Laura by the elbow and guided her away from the table.

"I'm sorry for my wife's behavior," he said to Mel. "She's obviously upset and has had too much to drink. Please excuse us. Girls, come along now, it's time for bed."

Brian maneuvered Laura through the screen door, then lifted her in his arms and strode through the evening twilight toward the Airstream. Hannah lifted a bewildered Zoe in the same way. They made an odd procession, like soldiers carrying the wounded off a battlefield.

"You've just given me a great idea, Mel," said Jill, breaking the tension. "Been thinking about how to expand Dirty Girls—shame we couldn't use that name for real—to keep the cash flow coming in the winter. The possibility of renting out and servicing indoor plants might be a good fit for us. Mind if I pick your brain about that later?"

"Sure, no problem," said Mel.

"Well, we better be getting back," Chicken Ray said. He and Jill said their goodbyes.

David and Mel excused themselves to get settled in the main cabin.

Jeffrey jumped up to clear the table.

Champs helped himself to another beer and tried to process the evening's events. His thoughts returned to JP. It crossed his mind that he might never know if Jeffrey was his or JP's. He felt dizzy and disoriented, lost in outer space, destination Pluto. He wanted it all to stop.

He left the table, stretched out on the sofa, and closed his eyes. He imagined sitting with Pat on a wooden terrace high in the branches of a loblolly pine. He held her yellow-mittened hand, and they looked out over a vast, empty silver lake. He felt calm such as he'd never known in his life. Take me now, he thought, and passed out.

pH Balance

C hamps woke an hour before daybreak. Someone had thrown a blanket over him. After letting Millie out, he took a bottled water out of the SMEGerator.

David stepped out of the house wearing sweatpants and a T-shirt, his running shoes in hand. He acknowledged Champs with a nod and Champs grunted back. David sat down to lace up his sneakers, but five minutes later he still hadn't accomplished the task.

"Fuck it," he said, and disappeared into the cabin.

Champs relieved himself through the screen, thinking his spray would shower the pachysandra on the other side. Instead, most of it dribbled down onto the porch. He washed it away with sparkling mineral water. Large shapes moved in the dawn light across the dewy lawn. Doe and buck.

David returned with two chipped shot glasses and an unopened bottle of Woodford Reserve—a Christmas gift he'd bought for Champs five years ago. He filled both glasses to the rim and handed one to his father before knocking back half his pour. Champs did the same, grimacing as the acrid liquid snaked its way down to his empty stomach.

"I guess I'll start," David said. He gulped his bourbon and refilled the shot glass. "I wanted to tell you about the problems Kimmie and I were having. But then we came out here to see Mom for the last time and then the whole Mel thing happened, and Mom died, and you moved here, and . . . it's just been difficult. It's a fucking mess. I tried to call you, but you didn't answer. I left messages, but you didn't call back."

Champs said nothing. He stared at his son and felt like he was sitting with a complete stranger. Was David even his? What the hell, maybe Pat had tricked him all three times. David could be the son of the garbageman for all he knew. Would Pat betray him like that? Not the Pat he thought he'd married. It must have been the whiskey clouding his logic, playing on his doubts.

"Aren't you going to say something?" David prompted.

"Did Laura know?" Champs wondered how much his daughter had hidden from him.

"She knew some. Kimmie called her after she found out about Mel and kicked me out of the house. You know Laura—she was hardly on my side of this. Anyway, she didn't know about the pregnancy, if that's what you mean."

"Did Pat know?"

"No, thank God. Here's the thing. I want to make it right with Kim. I want to get back together with her. She's changed since this happened. She went off on some empowerment hiking thing in the Canadian wilderness. Can you imagine that? Kimmie? She went back to work, too. Full-time. CMO for a well-funded startup."

"What about the kids?" Champs asked.

"They're fine, Champs. Samantha just finished her freshman year at San Diego State. She stayed down there for the summer. She has a great internship. Ryan has one more year of high school. He's traveling around France with his girlfriend right now. This has nothing to do with them."

Champs finished his bourbon, and David refilled his glass.

"Look, Champs. I made a huge mistake. I know that. My therapist says affairs are a common reaction when a parent dies. I'm not blaming Mom, of course."

"Do you remember anything unusual about your mom the summer after JP died?" Champs thought he would try a direct approach. David might remember something—after all, he was almost twelve that summer.

"What? Who's JP? I don't know what you're talking about, Champs. Look, I need your advice. Mel is a nice person, but the fact is I don't even love her. I doubt she has significant feelings for me, either. It all got complicated with the pregnancy. I'm trying to be responsible, here."

"Responsible, eh? I'll tell you something about responsible, David. I've been responsible all my goddamn life. You know what responsible is? Responsible is a license for folks to walk all over you."

The bitterness of his outburst shocked Champs. It was as if he'd been possessed by his father. Hands shaking, he hit the bourbon again. Might as well go all in, he thought.

"I'm sorry. I know I let you down," said David, and put the cork back into the bottle.

"You let yourself down, son."

Champs wasn't sure if he meant the words for David or himself. He wished he hadn't started the day with whiskey. Or with David. He got up to leave, felt the floor roll beneath him, and heaved to the side like the long boom of a skipjack.

David broke his fall.

They stood in a clumsy embrace, clinging to each other as if neither of them knew who was supporting whom. Champs hadn't held his son in decades and felt a profound urge to pull him in close and protect him from all the storms to come. He regained his balance and crushed David to his chest. David put his arms around Champs.

Just then, Mel came through the door in a yellow nightie with a steaming-hot mug of Constant Comment tea. "Oh, I'm sorry. I didn't realize you were . . ."

Champs pushed David away, bolted off the porch, and vomited into the vegetable garden. He'd never been able to keep down hard liquor.

Mel ran out to him as David uncorked the Woodford Reserve and collapsed into a club chair nursing the bottle.

"Okay, Champs," Mel said. "It's okay. I noticed the garden's pH was off anyway, so you picked a good place to hurl. I'll help you get back into the cottage before anyone wakes up and makes a fuss."

She put her arm around his waist and draped his arm across the back of her neck. They hobbled together toward the porch: a pregnant jungle cat and an old-man rag doll.

"Get the damn door," Mel shouted to David.

A few hours later, Champs woke up for the second time that day. He was in the bed he used to share with Pat, a wet cloth draped across his forehead, wearing only his underwear. The blinds were closed, so it was dim. He fumbled for his glasses, scratched the sides of his head, and drank the mug of water left on the night table. Someone knocked on the door.

It was Jeffrey and Mel with a tray of hot chicken broth, saltine crackers, and a glass of sweet tea.

"This is from Josanne," Mel said. "How are you feeling?"

"Old," said Champs. He took the tray onto his lap and stared at the food. "What are you two doing here? Where's Laura? Where's David?"

"They're all out on the river for the day—on the Yammy. Don't worry about them," said Jeffrey.

"Guess Laura didn't get around to redecorating this room," Champs said after scanning his environment for any signs of blue paint, wicker, or whitewashed woodwork.

He sipped at the broth, nibbled on a cracker, then put the tray aside.

"Now, if you'll excuse me, I need to get dressed and get back to my boat."

Jeffrey and Mel tried to protest, but he shooed them away so he could get his pants on in privacy. He noticed a foam pad and sleeping bag stretched out against the far side of the room. How would Mel and David parent together when they couldn't even share the same bed? David's words came back to him: *I don't even love her.*

Champs gulped down the sweet tea and crammed the saltines into a pocket of his cargo shorts before leaving the room. He switched off the air-conditioning, found his keys on the kitchen counter, and walked out to the porch. Jeffrey and Mel were at the picnic table staring at something on the computer. Was it his imagination or were they sitting a little too close together?

"Why don't you take Mel out on one of your canoes, Jeffrey? Show her your new buildings," Champs said before whistling for Millie and climbing into the Windstar.

He didn't know what Pat would have done about David's "unforeseen circumstances." There was no way he could bring it up with Laura. So it was up to him to put a plan into action. He'd need advice from Hannah about romantic matchmaking—she'd be an expert after reading all those Harlequins. But judging by the pheromones in the air, Champs didn't think it would take much effort on his part.

Rippling

On Wednesday, Champs sat on Josanne's veranda and bit into a heavenly square of chocolate-mayonnaise sheet cake. He watched her struggle to make stitches on the sampler she was preparing for a mother whose infant had died. Josanne seemed exhausted by the effort. She set the embroidery down and flopped back into her cushioned chair, reminding Champs of a collapsed spinnaker.

"Not much wind in my sails for sewing today, Champs," she said, and sighed. "How are you doing after your spell yesterday, darlin'?"

"Fine," said Champs. "Is there any more cake?"

Josanne ignored the request. "Say, Champs, I've been pondering something. You've been over here enjoying my baking now for several weeks, isn't that right?"

Champs nodded and shifted uncomfortably in his seat.

"The truth is, I need your help. Honey, I can't keep up both the baking and the sewing anymore. My hands just aren't what they used to be. I sure am committed to my beloveds though. I simply can't imagine letting them down in their time of grief. You wouldn't want me to do that, would you now, Champs?"

Champs shook his head. What else could he do? He knew he was being reeled in. But how was a man supposed to resist a Southern woman's charms? Josanne bent over to pour him more sweet tea. She smelled spicy. He stared at the tender, pale strip of skin between the lacy edge of her bra and the rosy, sun-kissed part of her chest. His mouth watered. Jesus Christ, he thought, this woman is a pro. Champs knew he was gut-hooked and would soon be landed in the boat. He surrendered. Whatever Josanne wanted, she'd get, as far as he was concerned.

"Well, how about I teach you to do a simple cross-stitch, and you can help me get through this last batch of work? That way I can keep baking these fine cakes just for you." Josanne slid another square of chocolate goodness onto Champs's plate.

He nodded as if it were the best idea he'd ever heard.

"Oh, darlin', bless your sweet heart. Aren't you so kind to offer?" she said. "Now, you finish up your treat, and I'll get you started in no time. We'll have so much fun together!"

She passed him the sampler she was working on, and with her instruction, Champs made his first cross-stitch. It wasn't bad, he thought.

Later that afternoon, as the sky clouded over, Champs asked Hannah to take a walk with him to get the mail. He hadn't checked it since Jeffrey had brought him the package. He told Hannah he needed her help to carry back the pile.

Laura, deep in conversation with David, nodded her permission. It was perfect timing as Zoe was in the middle of a shooting lesson with Larry and his ancient Red Rider BB gun. Jeffrey and Mel had gone to Dirty Girls to get corn and tomatoes and talk to Jill about renting plants.

"How are those romance books coming along?" Champs asked once they were clear of the yard.

"Mom made me give them all back to Josanne," said Hannah. "It's okay because I was getting bored with them, anyway."

"Doesn't hurt to take a break from reading now and then," said Champs.

"Yeah, Mom says I have no more excuses for not getting exercise. She wants me to be on the track team at school."

"Do you like running?"

"Not really, but it won't be for long since we're moving and all," Hannah said.

"Oh, that's right, the move," Champs said, somehow keeping his voice neutral while his pulse ran like a Thoroughbred racehorse in the Kentucky Derby.

He had no idea about any move. Another thing he'd been kept in the dark about. There were too many secrets in this family. They obviously thought he was a goddamn idiot.

"Yeah, Mom says Daddy has a new job saving the environment, and it will be good because we won't have to wear uniforms to school anymore. She told Zoe we could get a dog, too. I hope my new school allows Agatha Christie books," Hannah remarked with a sigh.

"You'll still be able to see all your friends, though, on the weekends?" Champs felt guilty for manipulating his granddaughter, but he was desperate to get his hands on some facts.

"Champs! Don't be silly. You know I can't see my friends on the weekends if I live all the way across—" Hannah came to a halt and pushed her glasses back into position on her nose.

Champs prompted her. "All the way across . . ."

"Wait a minute." Hannah folded her arms against her chest. "You didn't know about this, did you? Mom's gonna be mad at me for telling."

"I won't tell her you told me. There's something else I need your help on," Champs said. "In those books you read, the ones from Josanne, what did the men do to get the women to fall in love with them? I mean at the beginning, not the parts where they were, um, well, you know what I mean."

He turned tomato red. What kind of weirdo asks his granddaughter about romance? They'd have him locked up in no time. He really needed a filter.

"Hmmm," said Hannah, who didn't seem worried by Champs's question. "Flowers and jewelry really impressed the ladies in the books, and when the men opened doors for them. Um, they seemed to like seeing the men's muscles all the time, especially if they were sweaty. Like this one time, the lady fell in love when she watched the man chopping wood for her. It didn't make sense because it was summer and she didn't have a fireplace or anything. Oh, I know—another time this lady thought she was in love with this rich man but when this poor man with holes in his shirt rowed her out to the middle of the lake to see the moon, she got all lovey-dovey over the rippling in the water and the rippling on his arm muscles, and, well, there was a lot of rippling. Stuff like that."

"Okay, thanks. I can work with that."

He opened his mailbox and loaded Hannah's arms with leaflets, bills, and magazines.

"Reckon it will rain any second now. Why don't you and Millie run on ahead, so the mail doesn't get wet."

"Okay, and don't worry, Champs. I'm good at keeping secrets," Hannah said.

"Secrets? What secrets?"

"I won't tell anyone about you and Josanne." She winked at Champs, then ran down the road like a natural born sprinter, Millie bounding at her side.

"Wait a minute! It's not about me and . . ." Champs realized it was too late; she was out of hearing range. He would correct the misunderstanding later. In the meantime, he had a lot of new information to consider.

Freddy the Frog

T he drizzle turned to thrashing rain as he made his way back to the cabin. A gust of wind pushed him through the porch door, where Mel, wearing not much more than a moth-eaten wool cardigan of Pat's, looked up from the *National Geographic* she was reading. Thunder tumbled across the darkened sky. The smell of skunk filled the air. He hoped Millie hadn't been sprayed.

"There's been a fight," she said. "Everyone scattered."

"Oh," Champs said. "Any dinner?"

"Dinner didn't happen. I can make you some scrambled eggs and sliced tomato if you want."

"What happened?"

Champs regretted the question. He didn't want to know what had happened. He wanted to get in his Windstar and drive out to Middletown for a truck-stop burger and a beer. Pretend he didn't have a family. Pretend his dead wife wasn't in a coffee canister. Pretend he wasn't just now standing on his fisherman cabin's porch with his cheating son's pregnant lover. Pretend he wasn't trying to figure out how to set up his cheating son's pregnant lover with his illegitimate, homeless, jobless other son. Pretend he hadn't had a verging-on-pornographic conversation about bulging muscles with his nine-year-old granddaughter, who'd assumed he was lusting after his rifle-toting neighbor's wife. When did it all get so goddamn complicated?

"David and Laura," Mel said. "They went at each other's throats. Brian took the girls back to the trailer. Jeffrey took off in his truck. The neighbor guy—Larry, is it? He came over with a shotgun asking what all the ruckus was about. Anyway, I went inside to take a shower and when I came back out David waved me out of the bedroom because he was talking to Kim. Laura was gone. Sorry about the sweater, but it was all I could find in the other bedroom."

It made little sense to Champs that a pregnant woman would fly across the country with a man who didn't love her. But what did he know? He thought he'd take advantage of the opportunity to talk to Mel alone. "Why did you come out here with David?"

"Good question. I don't know. The school district ran out of money for art next year, and Raj's place got shut down. The circumstances weren't ideal, and Raj advised me to make myself scarce. I guess David didn't tell you this, but my mom died not too long ago—I used to live with her. I know that's weird for someone my age—I'm thirty-four, in case you were wondering. Anyway, coming here just seemed the best option. I needed the break, I guess."

Champs sat down on the sofa and massaged his temples. The pain was diamond-like in its precision. He felt Pat's absence like a clean cut. There was so much he wanted to talk to her about. More than anything, he longed to be with her, hold her hand, listen to the storm pass across the sky together.

"It's a little chilly out here," Mel said. "I've brewed up some herbal tea. Let me get you some and a plate of eggs. I'll try to dig up aspirin, too, for that headache of yours. It will give me something useful to do."

Champs didn't protest. He hated herbal tea, but the eggs sounded good. Maybe he could ask her to make a pot of coffee. There were a lot of things he wanted to ask her. Mel would soon be the mother of his fifth grandchild. David had made his position clear, but Champs wondered what Mel was thinking. He also wanted to make sure Mel wasn't a serial killer or a gold-digger before she got any closer to Jeffrey. Now would be a good time to investigate.

Mel returned with a mug of tea and a plate of eggs. The tea smelled like berry pie, fresh out of the oven with a buttery crust. He took a sip and let the warm liquid smooth his nerves.

"Did you find any aspirin?" he asked.

"Sorry, no. But see if that tea helps."

"Have you met Kim or the kids—Samantha and Ryan?" Champs asked.

He liked to ask yes-or-no questions. Most folks felt obligated to answer with more than one word.

"No," Mel replied.

Champs took a gulp of hot tea, thinking Mel would explain more, but she didn't.

"Are you and David planning to shack up together after that baby's born?" Had he just said "shack up"?

Mel tilted her head and raised an eyebrow. Champs waited, inhaling the blueberry steam from his mug. Five minutes passed, marked only by the sound of rain and Champs's sipping tea.

"I know what this must look like," Mel said. "But it's not what you think. Or whatever Laura thinks. David will go back to Kim, probably when we get back from this trip. Hopefully, they will move on and forget all about me. I never intended for him to even know about the pregnancy, let alone get involved with it. I plan on raising this child all on my own, just like my mom did with me. It's what I've always wanted to do. I'm just sorry my mom won't be around to be part of it —she would have been so thrilled to have a grandchild."

Champs finished his tea. His lips were greasy, as if he'd eaten a plate of buttered biscuits. He felt warm and relaxed. "Is there butter in this tea?"

"Yes, that's how I've always had it. Do you like it?"

"It's terrific. My headache is gone," Champs replied as a happy clown smile spread across his face.

He couldn't think of any more questions to ask Mel. His urgency to figure her out had melted away.

Mel giggled.

"What?"

"You've been staring into space with that goofy smile of yours for about ten minutes. It's cute."

"It's cute," Champs repeated, and kept on smiling.

"I don't have siblings, so maybe that's just how it is—but is it always so tense when your three kids get together?"

As long as he could remember, David and Laura had been at each other's throats. Pat used to beg, plead, and bribe to get them to stop arguing. Sometimes they'd come to a truce. Laura to make Pat happy, and David because he loved ice cream. Champs never had much say in the matter. Jeffrey had arrived so much later it was as if they'd raised him as an only child.

"Pat used to keep them all together," he said. "I guess I'm a poor substitute. Funny how it's true. That old saying—you don't know what you got until it's gone. Our family was always like a good wholesome slice of American cheese. Now Pat's gone, it feels more like Swiss."

Champs wasn't sure where his cheesy clichés and metaphors were coming from. Or why he couldn't stop smiling. He felt like he was in front of a campfire, roasting marshmallows and laughing at jokes his brother made.

"I remember Laura was always inventing games to prove she was better than David. But he was older and stronger, so she'd always lose and complain it wasn't fair. She was obsessed with fairness and winning. Still is." Champs chuckled.

"What's so funny?"

"Well, Laura figured out she'd have a better chance of winning if she switched to less physical games. She came up with this court-house game where she'd lock up one of her stuffed animals in a steel dog cage and declare it guilty of a crime. I remember when she accused Mr. Rabbit of stealing the neighbor's carrots. She was the prosecutor. David was the defense attorney. She made me be the judge."

"Sounds a lot more creative than the online shooting games kids play these days," said Mel.

"Oh, sure. Pat and I used to laugh about the different cases. The kids came up with hilarious witnesses and evidence. I've never looked at a stuffed animal the same since," Champs laughed. It felt good to share a joke with someone rather than be the butt of one in front of everyone.

Mel adjusted the porch lights, so they weren't so glaring, and lit a citronella candle she'd picked up at Dirty Girls. She didn't turn on the fountain, and Champs was grateful for that.

"Go on," she said.

"One time David put his pet rock on the stand as a last-minute witness to clear his client, Freddy the Frog, of lily-pad trespassing. On cross-examination by Laura, David claimed that Rock took the fifth and thereby maintained his right to a stony silence."

Mel laughed. "That's too funny. How did you keep a straight face?"

"It was hard, especially when Laura didn't get the joke and jumped up yelling, 'Objection!'" Champs warmed to his story. "I overruled. Laura got so mad. She picked up Rock and threw him at David. She almost hit his head. I had no choice but to hold her in contempt. I sentenced her to three hours of community service."

"Oh, poor Laura."

"She spent the entire afternoon weeding the vegetable garden under the watchful eye of Freddy the Frog. David tied him in one of the nearby tomato plants to supervise her. She was so damn mad. I could see the steam shooting out of her ears!"

Champs and Mel shared another laugh.

"What's going on in here?" asked Jeffrey as he entered the porch. "Let me in on the joke."

"Get me some water, Jeffrey," Champs said, pointing to the SMEGerator.

"Okay, but tell me what's going on," Jeffrey said.

"Your dad was just telling me some crazy stories about this *Law &*

Order game that David and Laura played when they were younger. So funny," said Mel.

"Did he tell you about the Case of the Vandalized Couch?" asked Jeffrey, passing a bottle of water to Champs.

Mel shook her head.

"Well, I was still a baby, so I only know the story from Laura repeating it thousands of times. It was the only case she ever won, right, Champs?"

"That's right."

Champs's headache had vanished, and he couldn't remember why he'd been in such a bad mood earlier. His eyelids were a little heavy for this time of night. Briefly, he wondered how his tent bag was holding up in the storm, but even that seemed like a worry for another day. He could always sleep in the Windstar with Pat and his emergency blanket again.

"So, apparently Laura put me in the dog cage once," Jeffrey said. "She accused me of projectile-vomiting on the couch. It was true. The whole family saw it happen. David agreed to be the defense attorney. He thought he would win again because there was no way Champs would find me guilty and keep me locked up in the dog cage for twenty-four hours. That was the mandatory sentence."

"Oh my God, this is almost like the argument they had this afternoon," said Mel. "How did you rule, Champs?"

"I could tell that David thought he had it in the bag, but so did Laura. I had to go with the facts. Laura got the win she thought she deserved, and David just shrugged and went back to his *Space Invaders* game."

"But what happened to Jeffrey?" asked Mel.

"He was guilty! He had to pay his debt to society. Otherwise, Laura would've bitched all night that it wasn't fair," said Champs.

"You mean you left your baby locked up outside in a dog cage for twenty-four hours?"

"No," Jeffrey answered. "But he did leave me most of the afternoon. Mom found me when she came out to get Champs for dinner.

Apparently, I had a dirty diaper, sunburn, and a huge appetite that night. Otherwise, I survived."

"See that, Mel? He's a strong one, that Jeffrey," Champs said. "Good with an ax, too, I've heard. You should see his muscles when he chops wood. They ripple, I'm telling you."

Champs beamed at his son, who flexed his muscles for Mel in the dancing light of the candle. They all laughed. He felt rosy all over and pleasantly drowsy. His cheeks ached from all the smiling but his body was free of pain. He yawned.

"C'mon, Champs, let's get you into a bed tonight. There's no way we're leaving you to sleep on your boat in the middle of a rainstorm," said Jeffrey.

He helped him into the second bedroom and pulled back the blue covers. Champs felt as if he were being poured into the bed, like syrup on fluffy pancakes.

"Fluffy pancakes," he muttered.

"Yes, that's right. Fluffy pancakes. Good night, Champs," Jeffrey said, but Champs was already sound asleep.

Coming Clean

The next day broke sunny and mild with no threat of stagnant humidity. Champs was late to rise and found Laura nursing a hangover on the porch.

"Where is everyone?" he asked, stretching his arms above his head. His joints cracked like popcorn kernels over a hot fire.

"Jeffrey and Brian went off to buy new traps so we can crab later. The girls went with them. I don't know where David and Mel are. Are you making coffee?"

"I'll make some," Champs replied. "I see you've made peace with Millie."

The dog was curled up next to Laura on the porch sofa, and she stroked its back from time to time.

"It's temporary," said Laura. "I'm lulling her into a false sense of security so I can give her a proper bath before the girls get back."

"Good luck with that," Champs said, and went inside to put the coffee on.

When he came out again, Laura was in the yard wearing rubber gloves, soaping down a miserable-looking Millie. Champs wandered out to help.

Partway through, Millie gave a vigorous shake and bolted off unrinsed toward Hill Beach. Soaked and covered in suds, Champs and Laura shared a much-needed laugh. It seemed to break the tension that had stretched between them for the last three years.

"C'mon," said Champs. "I bet the coffee's ready now." He stood and offered his hand to Laura, who took it.

Minutes later, he felt like Millie must have done. That is to say, tricked. As they sat down with their coffee, Laura blasted him with a request to help plan the ceremony to release Pat's ashes in the Sassafras. It was a nasty shock. He'd forgotten the real intent behind this family reunion but he remembered something else.

"Not so fast," he said. "Let's talk about your plans to move first."

Laura flinched. "Hannah told you, didn't she?"

"She did not," lied Champs.

"Well, how did you find out?"

"Well, when were you going to tell me?"

"After the ceremony," Laura said, and steadied herself with an elongated inhale and exhale. "I wanted to put one major life transition behind us before launching into the next one."

"It might surprise you to learn one day that life does not conform to an orderly manner of one thing before another like the proceedings in a courtroom." Champs finished his coffee and stood up to leave.

Laura glared at him. "That's the most condescending thing you've ever said to me, Champs. I am well aware of the chaos inherent in living and dying. More so than you'll ever know. But rather than drown in the futility and overwhelm of it all, I prefer to set out the stepping stones to recovery. We all have to move on somehow."

"And you're moving on to where?" Champs crossed his arms in front of his chest.

"You say that like I'm running away." Laura sighed. "But it's not like that. This has been in the works for a long time. Brian's sick of living in his father's shadow, and he's sick of working against his values. We live like puppets on his parents' social stage, paraded around at the right clubs, in the right clothes, with the right cars and right vacations. They pay for all of it, did you know that? They insist. My daughter can't even read a book without interference from my vampire of a mother-in-law, trying to prove her moral superiority. She's got her nose stuck so far in the air she can't smell the shit that's piled up to her knees."

This was all new to Champs, and it confused him. He sat back down. "So this is not about your mother and me at all?"

"Oh, God, Champs!" Laura slammed her hands on the table.

Champs startled.

"This is about me! Don't you get that? It's about me and my husband and my kids for once, not about what everyone else wants. This is normal, Champs. It's healthy." She stood up to get a sparkling water from the fridge. "We need to move on. *I* need to move on. I was hoping to do it with your blessing. I was hoping to do it without feeling guilty about leaving you."

"How far are you going?" Champs asked.

He preferred to discuss the facts—the ones relevant to him.

"Seattle," said Laura.

"Seattle, Washington?"

"That's the only one I'm aware of."

"When?"

"October first."

Laura turned on the ceiling fans and water fountain. It was getting hotter outside but Champs suspected she'd done it to annoy him.

He couldn't quiz her any further as David and Mel entered the porch with tense expressions and Brian pulled up with the girls to unload the truck.

"I'm going to go make the sandwiches," Laura said and went inside.

Champs took off his cap, wiped his forehead free of sweat, and repositioned it. He supposed he had really screwed up Laura's plans this time. She'd wanted a guiltless escape where everything was in its place as she saw fit. Him in a Regret's Pond prison cell. His boat in the boneyard. His cabin rented to strangers. His wife dumped in the river. Laura wanted to cut her losses and wash her hands of the filthy mess that was her family. Champs saw now that she'd been trying to clean them up, sanitize them, purify them, since that summer when she'd arrived in a snit and left in rubber gloves and a cloud of Lysol. What kind of monster had he raised?

American Lotus

"Not a chance in hell we'll catch any crabs today. It's too early in the season," said Champs. He'd just returned from the community dock with *Tetanus*, ready to load her up for the day.

"It's just for fun, okay? Doesn't matter about the crabs," said Jeffrey. "Besides, it's a beautiful day to be out on the water."

Mel sat on the grass next to Jeffrey wearing one of Pat's bathing suits. She helped him tie empty laundry detergent bottles onto the twine attached to each collapsible, circular crab trap. Champs stared at the faded gold one-piece stretching over Mel's stomach. She reminded him of the urn.

"Laura found it for me," Mel said. "The bathing suit? I hope it's okay. I didn't bring one."

Champs nodded and turned away. He didn't see what was fun about crabbing when there was nothing to catch. Sounded to him like a lot of work for nothing. When he was a kid, they'd bring home two dozen number ones after a few hours of crabbing. Nothing beat leaning over the gunnel and yanking up a crab trap of glistening blue claws on a hot afternoon. Except cracking them open all evening long, using your fingers to dip the sweet meat in melted butter, and washing it all down with a cold beer. It was a visceral experience in eating. Crack, bang, scratch, pick, slosh, scrape, pinch, suck, swallow, cut, burn, bleed. Not for the faint of heart. By the time Jeffrey could pull a trap, they could still count on a baker's dozen of Jimmies after an afternoon downriver in August and September. But nowadays? In July? He would be gobsmacked if there was a single keeper in the entire Upper Chesapeake watershed.

"You don't have to come if you've got something better to do, Champs," said Laura.

Champs ignored her and lifted the grocery bag of raw chicken necks into his boat, followed by Millie. She'd rinsed herself in the algae-covered low tide at Hill Beach, acquiring a pungent stench and bright green highlights. He added a cooler of beer and a stack of life vests. The adults didn't wear them, but he had to have one per passenger on the boat by law.

Laura and David packed the food, sodas, water, and beach towels into the new boat. Brian inflated the donut-shaped rings the girls wore around their waists like Michelin-tire-sized hula hoops. When everyone had slathered themselves in sun cream, per Laura's orders, they drove down to the landing ramp, launched the boats, and set off for Pond Bar.

"Okay, who's crabbing and who's swimming?" David called out from the Yammy as they approached the sandbar opposite Ordinary Point. It formed a partial barrier between the Sassafras and a tidal pond.

"Everyone's swimming while you and I bait and sink the traps," said Champs.

Once David was aboard the Sea Nymph, Champs motored three hundred feet offshore, where the river was twelve feet deep. He and David established a natural rhythm of securing a raw chicken neck to the bottom of a trap and tossing it overboard at twenty-foot intervals.

Millie treated herself to any necks that slimed their way out of David's fingers and onto the boat deck. When they finished, a line of three dozen floating Tide bottles ran horizontal to the riverbank.

Back on the beach, Millie ran off to join Jeffrey, Brian, and the girls, who were digging a large hole at one end of the sandbar. David and Champs joined Mel and Laura, who sat side by side on the brown bedspread, midconversation.

"I think it will be fine. You worry too much," said Mel.

"It's just not safe for you, Mel. There's a reason we call it *Tetanus*, okay? Not to mention all the bacteria from the raw chicken," Laura said.

"What's this? You going all wacko about germs again, Laura?" asked David.

"I'm not 'wacko about germs,' David. I know a thing or two about pregnancies, and I don't want Mel to expose her baby—your baby—to any risks."

"Just leave her alone, Laura. She's an adult and capable of weighing up the risks herself," David said.

"She might not be aware of the risks is what I'm saying. So how the hell is she supposed to weigh up what she doesn't even know about?"

"Hey, Mel. I wanna show you something," said Champs, *sotto voce*.

Mel followed him over the sandbar to the pond, where hundreds of pale yellow flowers, some of them ten inches wide, were in full blossom three feet above the water. Their saucer-shaped leaves, like lily pads, filled the pond almost to its edge.

"Oh my God! What are these?" said Mel. "Lily pads?"

Champs stared across the pond and remembered the first time he'd brought Pat here.

They were on their honeymoon, an extended weekend stay at the Kitty Knight House, the infamous inn and restaurant in Georgetown. Infamous because it was haunted by the late Catherine "Kitty" Knight. She had saved her brick colonial home from being burned down by the British when they'd rampaged through towns along the Sassafras during the War of 1812. When Champs was growing up, it was a salacious tale of Kitty's defending her community by offering sexual favors to the aptly named Admiral Cockburn. In exchange, he sent his troops back to their barges and left what became Kitty's house, and two other buildings behind it, unharmed.

At some point, the narrative had changed to a G-rated version. In the kid-friendly story, Kitty had begged the admiral to stop on account of an old lady trapped inside one of the houses who would burn to death if he proceeded. If Champs were in charge, he'd have stuck to the original version. Inns haunted by a begging, Goody Two-shoes woman were one thing, and inns haunted by a hot-to-trot, corseted damsel in distress were a whole other kettle of fish.

During their honeymoon, on a bright, hot day in mid-July, Champs had taken Pat out in one of the hotel's canoes. Love-struck, he'd marveled at her beauty as he rowed all the way to Pond Bar. He'd covered Pat's eyes with his hands and walked her over the sand until her toes were in the pond. "Tada!" he'd said, removing his hands. Pure joy had spread across his beloved's face as she took in the hundreds of bursting lotus flowers gathered in the pond like a crowd of yellow-haired maidens in bright green skirts.

"Oh, Champs. These are beautiful," he thought he heard Pat say once again.

He turned to embrace her and tell her how much he loved her as he'd done on that same spot fifty years ago. But it was Mel who stood beside him now, frizzy haired, sunburned, and pregnant with his next grandchild. The romantic memory faded.

"These are American lotus blossoms," he explained. "The native tribes around here ate the roots like sweet potatoes and ground the pod seeds into flour. Or they roasted them like nuts. Alligator corn, they call it down south."

"Alligator corn? I like that," Mel said, placing a hand on her belly.

"These flowers came from ancient seeds—several hundred years old, some of them. The dried pods drop their seeds into the water, where they hibernate in the mud until one day, when they're good and ready, they bloom."

Champs wondered if any of today's flowers were offspring of the yellow blossoms he and Pat had admired on their honeymoon. That day had been so filled with promise. What other seeds had been planted then? What other flowers were yet to bloom before his time was up? He watched Mel stroke her bulging bump.

Jeffrey ran up beside them with a bottle of water for her.

Champs left them alone. With each stride away from the pond, he felt himself slipping out of the scene. Was this what death would feel like? A sensation of fading out of the many canvases on which his life had been painted, receding moment by moment from his memories? He shook his head to clear the thought, alarmed at how much reflecting he'd been doing lately. Maybe he was closer to death than he realized. Closer to Pat.

Man Overboard

"Where is Mel?" asked David as Champs neared the beach blanket.

"She's checking out the pond."

Champs heard Zo-Zo's squeals as she floated in her tube through the narrow channel of swift current that emptied the pond as the tide went out. They called it the lazy river.

"As I was saying, David, I'm only trying to protect Mel, but she won't listen and neither will you. At this rate, you won't have to worry about having another child to raise," Laura said, biting into a turkey-and-Swiss-cheese sandwich.

"That's ugly, Laura. Even for you," David said.

"Why did you even bring her here to begin with?" asked Laura.

She handed the sandwich, one bite down, to Champs and necked her can of sparkling wine.

"Why not?" said David. "I think she's enjoying it and she needed a change in scenery. Her mother died recently, you know. You two have more in common than you think."

"I have nothing in common with Mel, and I'm surprised you want to defend her. She broke up your marriage and trapped you by getting pregnant. Don't you care about Kim, Samantha, and Ryan at all?"

"Shut up, Laura!" said David. "Mel didn't break up our marriage. Kim and I managed that all on our own. Mel didn't trap me by getting pregnant—if anything I trapped her. Not that it's any of your business, but when Kim kicked me out, I tracked Mel down. Showed up at her house with my suitcase, unannounced. She's never asked me for so much as a dime, let alone a commitment to raise a baby with her. Jesus Christ, Laura, when did you become such a judgmental bitch?"

"I don't know, David. When did you become such a cheating bastard?"

"Stop it!" Champs thundered. "You're acting like children, both of you. This time, you've got Mel in the damned dog cage, and you've put her on trial. For what? I will not play judge, so just give up the act. As far as I'm concerned, you're both losers right now. Your mother would be ashamed of you!"

"She'd be ashamed of all of us," said Jeffrey. He and Mel had returned from the pond, unnoticed. "We're supposed to be here to remember her and support each other while we say our goodbyes and instead we're tearing each other apart."

"I think it's best if I go back to California," said Mel. "You need the time together as a family without me complicating everything."

"If you're going back, I'm going with you," said David.

"Nobody's going anywhere," Laura said. "Please. Look, I'm sorry, Mel, for what I said earlier. For everything I've said since you arrived. It's a very difficult time and I . . . I don't know . . . I guess I'm not coping very well. Please don't go. You're part of our family now."

Mel nodded.

Laura turned to David. "I apologize for being such a jerk, David."

"It's a little late for that," he replied. "But we'll stay. For Mom's sake, not for yours."

"Who's for crabbing?" said Champs, clapping his hands together. He relished a great diversion.

Laura and Brian stayed behind on the beach with Millie and the girls, while Champs pulled anchor and zoomed *Tetanus* in a giant loop to the start of the crab pot line with Jeffrey, David, and Mel on board. He handed everyone a beer, and they toasted to a good catch.

"Jeffrey and Mel—take the port side. David, you're on starboard," said Champs.

He idled the boat forward so the first floating Tide bottle was within Jeffrey's reach. Jeffrey bent a knee on the gunwale and reached over to grab the twine underneath the float. With a firm yank, he pulled the trap to the surface in a rapid hand-under-hand motion.

"Nothing," he said, and let it drop into the river, tossing the float away from the boat.

David pulled the next trap, leaning over the starboard side of the boat.

"Nobody's home," he said, and let it go.

After a few more empty traps, Mel announced that she wanted to try.

The wake of a passing boat rocked the Sea Nymph.

"Hold on," said Jeffrey. "Just let this pass before you pull one, Mel."

"Okay, Mel. Bring in a good one!" Champs called out over his shoulder.

He watched as Mel tried to find a comfortable position given her baby bulge. She wasn't balanced when the Tide bottle drifted past her but lurched toward it anyway like a wide receiver diving for the football. Her weight over the gunwale as another wake wave passed under the hull caused the Sea Nymph to tip precariously.

"Grab her!" shouted Jeffrey.

It was too late. Mel flailed out of the boat and splashed into the river like a lucky tuna.

"Man overboard! She can't swim!" David yelled. "Call nine-one-one!"

Champs cut the engine, grabbed a life jacket from under the cockpit, and hurled himself into the water in one instinctive move. Jeffrey did the same. In a frenzy, David threw the remaining life vests into the water, then screamed toward the shore.

"Laura! Help! Help! Brian!" He waved his arms to attract their attention.

"We've got her, David. Calm down!" yelled Jeffrey.

Treading water, Champs struggled into a life jacket while Jeffrey secured one around a spluttering Mel. Getting a life vest on in the river was no easy task.

"Are you okay, Mel? Is the baby okay?" David asked.

"Yes, I think so," said Mel, and turned to Champs. "I'm sorry, Champs. I ruined the crabbing."

The Yammy came up beside them.

"What the hell, David?" shouted Jeffrey. "She can't swim? And you let her get on the boat without a life vest on? Pregnant? Are you a fucking moron?"

"This isn't my fault, Jeffrey. Don't you try to pin this on me. Besides, she's fine. We're all fine."

"It's no one's fault, it's just an accident. I should've asked for a life vest. It just didn't occur to me because no one else was wearing one," Mel said as Jeffrey guided her toward the boat ladder.

Champs didn't feel fine. He'd lost his glasses in the rescue attempt and couldn't see beyond his elbow. He felt like he was slipping out of the scene again, borne away by some stygian current to places unknown. A great pain radiated outward from the center of his chest. Water moccasin, he thought. I've been bitten. His head filled with a shrill ringing sound, and then everything went black.

Jeffrey's voice called out to him. Champs tried to propel himself forward to meet the voice. He tried to yell back but no sound came from his mouth. He felt someone jerk his life vest forward.

"Champs! Champs? Okay, good. There you are. C'mon, I've got you," said Jeffrey.

"What happened?" Champs wondered how long he'd been out.

"You blacked out, just for a split second. Shit, you look pale."

"My glasses. I can't see."

"Just reach your arms out and I'll push you into the swim ladder on the Yammy. It's coming up now. Got it?"

"I'm not blind! I can't drive the boat back, though," Champs said.

"Reach up. I'll help you get in," said Brian somewhere above him.

Champs stuck his arm out. With Brian pulling and Jeffrey pushing, he rolled onto the swim deck of the Yammy like a beached whale.

"Is Mel okay?" he said. "She fell out of the boat."

"She's fine," Laura said. "Get this towel around you and come sit next to me. We need to get you home now."

"Home? What home?" Champs said. "Where's Millie?"

"She's leaving now with David, Mel, and the girls on *Tetanus*."

Jeffrey climbed aboard and stowed the swim ladder. Brian roared the motor to life and sped away from the shore, following in the wake of *Tetanus*.

"What about the crab traps? We can't leave them out there," said Champs.

"I called Chicken Ray. He's coming to get them. We might pass him on the way back," Jeffrey said.

Champs felt cold. He pulled the beach towel tighter around him and hunkered down into his seat. The great Chicken Ray to the rescue, he thought. He'd probably haul in a bushel's worth of crabs in those pots and be in the goddamn newspaper again. Champs was imagining the headline when it occurred to him that Pat had spent a lot of time with Chicken Ray that summer after JP died. Maybe Chicken Ray knew something. It was a long shot; Pat wasn't a woman who went around airing her dirty laundry, especially to another man. In fact, if she'd confided in anyone at all, it was most likely Josanne. Come to think of it, he'd seen Pat on Josanne's veranda a lot that summer. Josanne was probably making a JP memorial sampler. He couldn't recall the finished product. Pat must have kept it hidden.

By the time they returned to the dock, Champs was shaking and burning up with fever. Brian and Jeffrey helped him into the Lexus. He listened to Laura and Jeffrey argue over whether they should take him home or straight to the ER.

"You tell me now he's been having blackouts since he got down here?" Laura spoke as if accusing Jeffrey of negligence. "I told you he needed to stay at Egret's Pond. He needs to go to the hospital and get checked out. What if these blackouts are mini heart attacks or strokes?"

"You're blowing it out of proportion, Laura. I agree he should be checked out by a doctor, but this isn't an emergency. He's just run-down from sleeping outdoors and dealing with all of us. Let's get him home and in bed and see how he is in the morning," Jeffrey said.

"Okay, fine. We'll do it your way. But if he strokes out in the middle of the night, it's on you!"

"Just get in the car, Laura," said Jeffrey.

Champs felt weak and confused. Why couldn't they take him to his real bed in Downingtown, where Pat was alive and everything was warm and safe? He would wake up to her confident smile and every-thing in the past two and a half years would be explained by a fever-induced delirium. Please, he pleaded in his head. Just one more day with her.

Jeffrey's strong arms enveloped him to ward off the chill. Champs felt the whole car spin. He looked down to see ruby slippers on his feet, but they weren't his feet, they were Pat's feet attached to his legs. Champs watched the heels click together and heard himself say, "There's no place like home. There's no place like home. There's no . . ."

Conowingo Dam

N ineteen hours later, Champs woke in the spare bedroom, tucked into blue sheets and covered in moth-eaten blankets. Without glasses, he could just about make out the shape of Josanne cross-stitching in a chair in the corner of the room.

"Josanne?" he croaked.

"Oh, my! Yes, darlin'. I'm right here." She stood and put her stitching down. "Let me help you with some water."

Champs turned onto his side and propped himself up with an elbow as Josanne held up a glass of water and helped him get hold of the straw. He emptied it, feeling like a kid home sick from school.

"More?" she asked.

"Not unless you can make it a root beer float," Champs said, easing himself back into the bed.

"Very funny, darlin'. Let's take this one step at a time. How are you feeling?"

"What time is it?"

"It's almost lunchtime. You've been asleep since late yesterday afternoon. Brian and Jeffrey carried you in here, got you changed and into bed. You were delirious from the fever, kept going on about red slippers and tornados and goodness knows what else. Jeffrey stayed at your side until five this morning, when Laura came in to relieve him. I took over from her about an hour ago. I should let them know you're awake now."

"Not yet. Please, Josanne. Just sit with me a few minutes."

"Of course, hon. Are you okay, considering?"

"Tired, old, and foolish is what I am."

"C'mon now, this is no time to beat yourself up. You saved a pregnant lady from drowning in the Sassafras. You're a hero, Champs."

"If I'm a hero, then we're all screwed."

Josanne fussed around him, feeling his forehead, removing a blanket, opening the curtains to let a slant of sunshine into the dim room.

"Laura wants to release Pat in the Sassafras. She thinks a little ceremony will help us all feel better and move on," Champs said.

"Mmm-hmm." Josanne picked up her cross-stitch and moved her chair closer to Champs.

"I tried to move on. All I saw in front of me at Egret's Pond was dying into a smaller and smaller box. So I came here, thought I'd be free from all that. Expected this place to be just like it always was and me to be just like I always was in it. Think I half-convinced myself that Pat would be here, too. Like she always was."

Josanne placed her hand on top of Champs's for a moment before resuming a steady rhythm of cross-stitching—puncturing the fabric with the needle, pulling the thread through, and plunging the needle and thread back underneath the surface. It reminded Champs of the to-and-fro of small waves lapping on the shore of Hill Beach.

"I don't recognize myself here, Josanne. I don't recognize my wife, and I don't recognize my children. Seems I must have sleepwalked through my life. Everything's moved on without me, especially Pat. I'm all out of answers, but the questions keep coming."

"I know, dear. I know. Thoughts like these come to all of us, sometimes more than once. We want so bad to figure out death, to get away from the hurt, to make it something else. I think death is a great fissure thrown in our path, like a crack in the earth. Now, some of us are gonna spend the rest of our time looking into that crack paralyzed and full of fear. Others are gonna be drawn into it and disappear in the blackness. There's some fools gonna try to jump over it to the other side, where the grass is always greener, but they never really make it. Only way to move on, Champs, the only way I've seen it work, is to build a bridge. And to build a bridge takes time, it takes materials, and most of all it takes other people. You can't do it alone."

There was a knock on the door.

"Come on in," said Josanne.

Jeffrey poked his head through.

"Oh, you're awake. How you feeling?" he asked.

"Hungry," said Champs. "And I need the facilities."

"Well, let me get on out of the way now. I've got chicken noodle soup for y'all. I'll bring that right over. You take it easy there, Champs." Josanne gathered her cross-stitch and bustled out of the room.

"Thank you, Josanne!" Champs called out.

"Here, let me help you get up," Jeffrey said.

"Thanks, son," said Champs, accepting Jeffrey's support. "Can you find my spare glasses?"

"They're right here on the dresser. Laura found them in the Windstar earlier and brought them in. Here you go."

Champs put his eyeglasses on and the small room rematerialized. He saw his suitcase open on the floor against the wall. Laura must have brought it in from the Windstar. His scruffy clothes were thrown to either side. Pat's bird notebooks, the food supplies, and the Chock Full o'Nuts urn were gone. There was no sense worrying about it, Champs reasoned. He'd find out who had them soon enough.

He showered and dressed, then joined the rest of his family partway through their lunch on the porch. The heat and humidity hit him like a city bus after the subzero atmosphere of his air-conditioned cabin. Millie barked and wagged her tail from the other side of the porch screen.

"Champs! Champs!" Zoe yelled. She wriggled out of her seat on the picnic bench and ran to give him a big hug. "Mommy made us draw pictures for you. So you'll get better faster." Zoe skipped to the game table and back again with a piece of paper. "Here's mine. It's better than Hannah's. She can't draw good."

"She can't draw *well*, Zoe. We don't say 'draw good.' It's 'draw well,'" Laura said, correcting her.

"Really, Mom?" said Hannah.

"This is very nice, Zoe. Is this me here, under the water?" asked Champs.

"Yeah, that's you. You're sinking to the bottom, and this is Uncle Jeffrey jumping in to save you. And that's a big shark that's coming. That's blood coming out of its mouth. Do you like it?"

"Yes, it's fantastic. Especially the shark. Thank you," said Champs.

"All right, Zoe. Sit back down and let Champs get his food," Brian said.

"There's a space for you right here," said David, indicating a seat on the bench next to him.

Champs sat down. Laura passed him a Gatorade.

"Josanne's coming out in a minute with some soup for you," she said, and offered a brief smile. "I'm glad you're okay. You scared the heck out of us."

"Thank you for diving in after me, Champs. I'm sorry I fell. It was stupid of me to be on the boat in the first place without a life vest. I'm really sorry," said Mel.

"Good to see you up and about, though," said David, putting his arm around Champs's shoulders. Champs let it stay there. Josanne's advice came back to him: *You can't do it alone.*

Larry held the porch door open for Josanne, who placed a hot bowl of chicken noodle soup in front of Champs. He let the steam fog up his glasses while sipping it.

"Hey, girls," said Mel. "I checked with your mom, and she says it's okay for me to take you over to that bead shop by the library. Wanna go make bracelets?"

"Yay! I'll make one for you, Mommy," said Zoe. "C'mon, Hannah, let's go, let's go, let's go!"

Mel left in the rental car with the girls while Josanne and Larry found seats around the table.

Champs knew he had some reconciling to do with his family—it was time for him to start building bridges. It lifted his spirits to see that Laura had softened toward Mel. He'd try to follow her example.

"Did Chicken Ray find any crabs in the pots?" he asked.

Good-humored laughter followed like the relief of a cool breeze.

"Well, did he?"

"Nope. Not a single one," said Jeffrey.

"I reckon if we're gonna catch crabs this time of year, we'd have to go on out to the bay. Not sure the Sea Nymph is up to that journey," Champs said.

"I think we're done with crabbing this trip," said David.

"Yeah. Sounds about right," Champs replied. "If it's all the same to you, I think I'm done with sleeping outside, too. Figure I'll move into the second bedroom until you and Mel go home."

"Good idea. Fine with us," said David.

"And you can make me that doctor's appointment, Laura. I better get myself checked out before you all disappear and the weather turns. Jeffrey, I'll need your help to get this place winterized."

"Sure. I can do that," said Jeffrey.

Champs finished his soup, patted his mouth with a napkin, then mopped his brow and neck. He cleared his throat.

"Brian, I understand you're planning to take my daughter and granddaughters to Seattle, Washington. That right?"

"Yes. I'm sorry we didn't tell you about it from the beginning, Champs. There never seemed to be the right time. I'd like—well, we'd like, Laura and I, to explain our decision to you. I value your opinion and wish I would have sought it out long before it came to this," Brian explained.

Champs nodded. He didn't need an explanation. He knew he and Pat were lucky their children had stayed this close to them for so long. It had upset them when David and Kimmie moved to California with

Samantha and Ryan. Champs realized now they'd taken Jeffrey's and Laura's proximity for granted. As if he and Pat had paid their dues by letting go of one child and therefore the other two were guaranteed to stay near.

"I've got brownies at the house," said Josanne. "Champs, darlin', Larry and I have news to share. I know you're tired, but it won't take more than a minute, then y'all can get on with your afternoon together," Josanne said.

Laura and Brian whisked around clearing up lunch.

David and Jeffrey cracked open fresh cans of beer and settled onto the sofa talking about Jeffrey's business plan.

Champs tried to picture Peety. What he might look like now. What he might be doing. His mind kept bringing him back to the Peety who stood in the cabin, cradling a dripping bottle of whiskey like a football, gazing straight into Champs's eyes, waiting. Waiting. Was he still out there waiting?

And what about Laura? Wasn't Laura waiting, too? Waiting for him to let go of her mother's ashes so she could move on? Waiting for him to acknowledge her grief, and what else? There was something else, too. He couldn't put his finger on it. He felt like the Conowingo Dam, holding back 464 miles of Susquehanna River water. Maybe it was time to open a floodgate or two.

"Have you thought about the ceremony for your mother yet, Laura?" he said.

"Oh, um, yes, a little. But we don't have to talk about that now, Champs. It's been a long day already. I don't want to tire you out and here comes Josanne with the brownies, anyway. You need any help, Josanne?" Laura called out.

Champs realized Laura had probably opened the coffee can and knew about Pat's ashes. He wasn't sure how to handle that, but there wasn't much he could do about it now. It surprised him to realize what a relief it was to surrender the fight. A small thought cloud hovered in his field of awareness. What else could he stop fighting?

"We've had an early offer on our house," announced Larry once Josanne had passed around the brownies.

"What?"

"Wow!"

"Congratulations!"

"But you haven't even got it up for sale," Champs pointed out.

"Well, that's true. But our agent's been approached by a buyer who'd heard we were putting it on the market," Larry said.

"Who is it?" Laura asked. "Someone we know?"

"Is it a good offer?" asked David.

"What are these stringy things in the brownies?" Champs asked. He hadn't noticed them at first, but now he was concerned something unsavory had fallen into Josanne's cake batter.

"Oh, that's shredded carrot," said Josanne. "One of my dear friends at church told me all about the wonders of beta-carotene for arthritis. I'm not one for vegetables, so I'm trying it out in my baking. These went down real well at yesterday's annual fund meeting. I think they taste marvelous, don't you?"

"Oh, sure," said Champs.

About as marvelous as strawberry lentil shortcake, in his opinion, but he wasn't going to spoil the afternoon by making a fuss. He crumpled his napkin around the last morsel of brownie. He then spent a few minutes sucking at his teeth and rolling bits of carrot to the tip of his tongue, where he picked them off with his fingers and flicked them onto the coir mat. They blended in just fine. He'd begun to appreciate this rug for all the unpleasant things it could absorb.

"So, it's an unusual offer, and we were going to reject it outright. But then we thought we'd better run it past you folks first. The offer is from a prominent Maryland General Assembly member who also sits on the Chesapeake Watershed Conservancy board of directors," Larry explained.

Champs's eyebrows pinched together, scrunching his face into a sour frown. He was suspicious of all politicians. "Go on, Larry."

"The offer is substantial, but he's got a bigger project in mind," Larry said. "He only wants our property if you're willing to sell up, too. He already has tentative agreements with both properties on the other side of me."

"Sell up, huh? I think you mean sell out, Larry." Champs felt his temper rise and the floodgates shut down. "I see what's going on here. Fancy-pants Annapolis politician thinks he can barge in here and take advantage of old folks, steal the land right out from under us, and turn Deadrise Cove into a development so those bureau fat cats can make millions. They'll force us all out, rename the place after the developer who ruined everything, paint a goddamn blue heron on the sign, and—"

"Just hold on, Champs," interrupted David. "Let's get the facts straight before we disappear in a cloud of conspiracy theory. Now, just how much are we talking, Larry?"

"Doesn't matter how much we're talking," Champs fumed. "My family's owned this property for more than half a century! I live here. This is my home, for chrissake. It's all I got left. Where am I supposed to go if I sell this place?"

"Florida?" offered Larry.

"Florida?" said Champs, disgusted.

"Now, what you got against Florida, Champs?" asked Josanne.

"Florida is full of old people and pink herons that haven't got the sense to keep two feet firmly planted on the ground when they take a shit."

Larry choked on his beer.

Laura rolled her eyes and shook her head.

David, Brian, and Jeffrey chuckled.

Champs placed his bifocals on the coffee table, rubbed his eyes, and positioned the glasses back on his face. He felt surrounded by strangers.

"Well, bless your heart, Champs. No one here's gonna force you to sell your property, and we're not gonna drag you kicking and screaming to the Sunshine State," said Josanne.

"By the way," said Larry. "Flamingos aren't related at all to herons. They're not even considered waterfowl. They don't even eat fish. They eat algae and mollusks."

"Well, I'll keep that in mind," said Champs.

"I think it's worth hearing them out, Champs. This could be a good way to help us all move on from the past," said Laura.

Champs stood up, powered by adrenaline or sugar or beta-carotene, he didn't know what and didn't care.

"I have moved on, Laura. I've moved on to here. To this. To being an independent old man who drinks too much beer, likes *National Geographic*, and loves to fish. Most people would consider that a well-earned retirement. If that's not good enough for you, well too bad. It's your turn to move on, so go! What's stopping you? You've got the coffee can, her notebooks, and my blessing. But you're not getting my freedom. That's not for sale at any price!"

Champs looked at the stunned and stricken faces on his porch. His intentions to build bridges and give up the fight had backfired. Self-awareness was for idiots, he thought. Grabbing another beer and his keys, he left them all behind.

Millie settled in the passenger seat of the Windstar as Champs reached for his "Who Gives a Carp?" baseball cap. He put it on and headed to the dock for some much-needed time alone on the fishing boat that fit him like a glove.

33

First Mate

Chicken Ray, shirtless and wearing tropical-patterned swim trunks, approached Champs as he stepped down from the Windstar.

"Hey there, Champs. I was just about to stop by your place. I'm afraid there's bad news."

Ray removed his Miami Dolphins cap and placed it over his heart as if he were a police officer about to inform a mother that her child had been mortally injured. Champs's heart sank like an anchor.

"It's your boat. The Sea Nymph? She's swamped."

"Swamped?" Champs repeated, and peered across the floating docks to his boat slip.

He saw the front third of *Tetanus* poking its bow up like a dolphin awaiting a fish from its trainer. The rest of the boat was underwater.

"Shit!"

Champs jogged to his drowned beloved for a closer look.

"You must've had a leak or something," said Chicken Ray, who'd caught up to Champs on the dock, and placed a hand on his shoulder.

Champs shrugged him off. He stared at the sunken mess that was his pride and joy. Anger at his own stupidity overshadowed the loss he might have felt.

"Damn it! I should've replaced those cracked lines to the water pump after I dragged her out of Swansong Marina last spring." He scrunched up his face and massaged a crick in his neck. "I'm guessing the deadwell flooded, and the battery gave out on the bilge pump after all that rain."

"Well, it's better she sank here than rusting to hell in that damn boatyard," said Chicken Ray.

"Now I'm a fisherman without a boat."

Chicken Ray placed his hand on Champs's shoulder again. One look from Champs and he removed it and backed away.

"I'll have to get a wreckage crew to haul her back to Swansong Marina for good. I bet the Nurps are already on their way to paste my ass with fines and citations. What a goddamn mess."

"Nurps?"

"Natural Resources Police." Champs took off his cap, wiped the beads of sweat off his forehead with an equally sweaty forearm, put the cap back on, and adjusted it.

"Hey, I know a guy who can get her out, and it won't cost you much. Just better if we're not here when he does it. Want me to make a call?"

Champs was reluctant to accept help from one of Chicken Ray's "guys." He didn't want to owe anybody anything. But it had to be better than an afternoon wasted with smirking county officials. He nodded at Ray, who walked back to his truck to make the call.

Millie splashed through the low tide, barking at a pair of mallards. She startled the resident blue heron from its perch. With a throaty squawk, it soared across the dazzled surface of the Sassafras. Champs mumbled a goodbye to the Sea Nymph and trudged back to shore as Chicken Ray ended his call.

"It's done. How 'bout we transfer your crab pots to the back of the Windstar before getting the hell out of here?"

"Any crabs in them when you hauled them out of the river?"

"Nah, not a one."

Champs wanted to believe Chicken Ray, but he found it hard to trust a man wearing reflective sports sunglasses. It was suspicious. Why cover your eyes unless you had something to hide?

He caught a sickening whiff of offal emanating from the storage buckets containing his collapsed crab rings in the back of Chicken Ray's pickup.

"Jesus Christ, you didn't get the necks out of these?" he asked.

"Hell no! I didn't want you laying into me for stealing your bait."

"Well, I'm sure as hell not putting these into the back of my van."

Champs staggered away from the truck with his nose tucked under his T-shirt. He thought he might vomit.

Chicken Ray dug out two nearly frozen cans of beer from a cooler in his truck. He handed one to Champs. "Here. Looks like you could use one of these. It's hotter than hell today."

They stood in the beating sun, slick with Sassafras sheen, slurping beer slushies. Champs watched Millie wiggle on her back in the sand while the heron returned to its post. Out on the river, a speedboat smoked past, and a Bayliner pulled a water-skier over its wake. Kids were diving off a private dock that jutted out from a riverside cottage a few hundred feet to the right. Their bright voices and excited squeals filled the air with the sounds of summer vacation.

"Remember when that was us?" Champs asked. It seemed like such a long time ago, like the Byzantine Empire or the Ice Age.

"Just about," said Chicken Ray. "You got any plans for today?"

Champs shook his head. He wondered if there was such a thing as a cremation service for boats. It might be nice to have the Sea Nymph's ashes nearby, like Pat's. He made a mental note to look into it.

"Tell you what I'm thinking," said Chicken Ray. "Let's put these traps on the *Duchess* and give them a final soak out in the bay. We prolly won't catch a damn thing given the rot on these necks and the time of day, but I'm all provisioned up"—he gestured to the cooler and several Save-Cave bags of peanuts and Doritos—"so what d'ya say?"

"Yeah, all right." It surprised Champs to hear himself agree. "But those are my traps and my bait, so anything we catch belongs to me. I don't give a damn if we're on your boat. I want to make that clear."

"Ha! If I'm hauling your ass—not to mention that filthy dog of yours—all the way out to the bay, then half those crabs are mine."

Champs mumbled but then agreed to the arrangement. He knew there wouldn't be any crabs worth having a prolonged negotiation about. It was too hot and too late in the afternoon, and crabs preferred fresh bait, as Chicken Ray had already mentioned.

They loaded the traps, dog, cooler, and snacks onto the *Duchess*. She purred to life, and Ray carved a turn out of Deadrise Cove heading to the wide open mouth of the Sassafras.

There wasn't any shade on the fishing boat unless Champs sat right next to Chicken Ray on the center console's command bench under the bimini. He perched on the end of it, angled away from Chicken Ray. It was the second time in twenty-four hours he'd been a passenger on another man's boat—the second time in twenty-four years, actually. Champs found he didn't care about his downgrade in status to first mate. In fact, it was a relief to sit back and surrender to the leisurely ride.

He helped himself to another beer and studied the yachts, sports cruisers, sailboats, and catamarans as they slowly motored by Sassafras Harbor Marina and Georgetown Yacht Basin. When they were through the no-wake zone, Champs observed the forested shoreline and occasional strips of sandy beach framed by cattail and native grasses. Lifting his head, he watched an osprey chase a bald eagle against the cloudless blue sky. Champs noticed the exact moment when the air whooshing past him changed from the musky smell of river headwaters to the brackish scent downriver to the salty tang of open bay. This is freedom, he thought. This is my home.

Chicken Ray slowed the *Duchess* near Meeks Point on the eastern shore of the bay. "Let's put 'em in here. There won't be time to get to the Chester River and back today."

He and Champs worked seamlessly to get all thirty-six traps spaced apart in a smooth curve roughly one hundred feet offshore around the entrance to Still Pond. With no need to chop necks and tie them to the bottom of the traps, they finished the job in less than ten minutes. They left the line and joined several other boats and raft-ups anchored in the sheltered cove between two necks of land.

Champs and Chicken Ray submerged themselves in the water to cool down. With only their eyes, ears, and nostrils exposed, they resembled subaquatic hippos with ball caps. It was the best relief you could get from the ninety-eight-degree-heat haze.

Millie took to the shore, dog-paddling and loping through the water toward a golden retriever. Rap music blared from a flotilla of three small houseboats nearby.

"Got any bites on that chicken factory of yours?" asked Champs.

"Pretty damn near to closing on it. A matter of weeks, now."

"You think this boatbuilding scheme of Jeffrey's is gonna work out?"

"The warehouse and docks need a lot more work than he thought. Codes have changed since that place went up. I got him fixed up with a couple of my guys to keep the costs low. Jeffrey's focused on building the retro canoes for the marina and condo developers."

"What's your interest in all this?"

Chicken Ray cocked his head. "My interest?"

"Cut the bullshit, Ray. What are you getting out of it?"

"I'm doing it for Pat."

"Pat?" Champs had been prepared for a variety of scenarios, but not this one.

"Yeah, Pat. She helped me with the chicken farm all those years ago. I never thanked her for that while she was alive. Now I found a way. Helping her son get his business off the ground. Simple as that."

"Yeah, but Pat didn't spend any money or offer you low rent on valuable riverfront property."

"Nah, she gave me her time. Way I see it, that's the most valuable thing of all. You got any other questions for me or can we get on with the crabbing now?"

Champs stared hard into the mirrored surface of Chicken Ray's sunnies, then whistled for Millie and helped her into the boat.

Chicken Ray pulled anchor, and they got under way.

"Haul 'em in the boat, Champs, whether or not they got any keepers. It's a one-run-and-done job today."

Not only had it been a long time since Champs was a passenger on a boat, but it had also been at least as long since he'd pulled the traps on a crabbing trip. He leaned over and gave the rope under the first float a sharp tug, surprised by the anticipation he felt bringing the pot to the surface. It was empty but the chicken neck was gone. He turned and let the crab ring collapse in its plastic storage bin.

The rhythm of reaching over the gunwale, grabbing a float, hauling in the trap, releasing any nubs of neck meat, pivoting into the boat, dropping the empty cage on top of the last one, and taking a swig of suds before repeating the sequence was like a drug. Champs felt useful and engaged, at work instead of idle, at ease for the first time in years. He relished the Sassafras sheen, his ability to balance in the rocking boat, the spray in his face as the waves slapped against the hull, the burn on the back of his neck, the smell of motor exhaust.

At the seventeenth pot, Champs hauled in two crabs. They both escaped the trap and skittled along the fiberglass bottom of the boat. Millie backed away and barked.

"They're keepers," Chicken Ray said, handing the heavy-duty crab tongs to Champs.

Champs estimated their size: just under the five-inch legal minimum when measured point to point across their hard shell. There wasn't a crab ruler on the *Duchess*, but, like his father before him and his grandfather before him, Champs believed anything a recreational fisherman landed by any means was de facto a keeper, the Nurps be damned.

He shook the crab off the tongs into a bushel basket. He did the same with the second crab, then dunked a faded beach towel into the bay and draped it across the basket to keep the crabs alive.

Chicken Ray cracked open another round of beer, and they toasted to their good luck. Two was better than none.

"Let's keep it going," said Ray.

Champs kept it going on and off until the end of the line. They'd caught nine crabs in total, which posed an interesting problem. Who would get four crabs and who would get five? Both men knew this was the kind of argument that made foes out of friends. There would be blood. They stood in silence staring into the bushel basket as the blue-tipped crabs fought to climb on top of each other to escape.

"Count 'em again," said Chicken Ray.

"Won't make a damn bit of difference. Sure we didn't miss a pot?" Champs swiveled his head and scrutinized the surface of the bay. Nothing.

Chicken Ray opened a bag of Doritos and another can of beer. Champs opened the peanuts. For several minutes there was only the sound of cracking, crunching, guzzling, and the click-clacking of crustaceans, claws raised in battle.

Since it was sacrilegious for a fisherman to throw anything edible back in the water, that wasn't an option. Neither man could afford to be generous in this situation either, since that would upset the balance of the relationship and cause simmering resentment for the next three generations. They'd both seen that happen too many times. Never mind that Chicken Ray had no generations.

It was unclear what the trigger was that broke the tension of two buzzed old salts locked in a dangerous stalemate over nine not entirely legal blue crabs on a sizzling-hot July afternoon. But within milliseconds of each other, Champs and Chicken Ray started snorting, chuckling, and guffawing, then made their way through another two beers and three bags of salty snacks.

On their way back, the sun let go of its grip on the river and slipped beneath the horizon, leaving behind an inky blue sky streaked with vibrant purple, pink, and orange hues. There was nothing like a Sassafras sunset.

Back at Deadrise Cove, the Sea Nymph was gone from her slip, hauled back to Swansong Marina, where all good intentions went to die. A lone boy was line-fishing for crabs at the end of the dock. With a nod of approval from Ray, Champs handed over their catch.

He loaded Millie and the empty crab rings into the Windstar, exchanged satisfied nods with Chicken Ray, and drove back to the cabin, tired in every good way a fisherman should be.

34

Who Knows About Birds?

"Where the hell have you been?" demanded Laura when Champs and Millie returned to the cabin. It was eight thirty p.m., and she was alone at the cluttered picnic table with a scratched plastic tumbler full of white wine.

Champs took the role reversal in stride: Laura the angry parent and him the recalcitrant teenager who'd slept half the day, then left in a huff, returning several hours later with alcohol on his breath, having told no one where he was or who he was with.

"Out," he said, and headed inside to scrounge up dinner. He was starving after a full day on nothing but a bowl of soup, a shit brownie, and a sack of peanuts.

"Not so fast, Champs. We need to talk."

Ah, the worst four words to come from a woman's mouth. Champs winced. Most men would rather hear "I want a divorce," or "The toilet needs plunging," or just about anything else besides the dreaded "We need to talk." What that really meant was: "I need to yell at you about some terrible thing I'm feeling that is all your fault and can't be fixed and if you so much as hint I'm exaggerating or tell me to calm down, I will scream and jab my finger at you for an additional forty minutes, then slam things and refuse to feed you." Champs had experienced no other outcome to the "We need to talk" talk. He doubted this evening would break the trend.

"Where's everyone else?" He knew Laura was too sophisticated to fall for a redirect, but it gave him a few seconds to snatch a beer and a fistful of string cheeses and Peperami sticks from the SMEGerator.

"Brian's putting the girls to bed and the rest of them went out to meet up with the dirty girls at some Irish pub in Middletown. You've been gone so long, I was about to call search and rescue. Where the hell did you go?"

Champs bit the top off his meat-flavored snack and chased it with a bite of string cheese. He chewed them together as he would a sandwich —without the bread and other accompaniments. If there'd been a jar of pickle slices handy, he'd have popped in one or two of those.

While his mouth was full, he decided not to answer her questions. His delay tactic lasted for all of five seconds. When he was midswallow, she continued.

"What did you mean about the coffee can and the notebooks? You know, before you told me to get the hell out of town?"

Confused, Champs popped open his beer, took a slurp, then filled his mouth again with Peperami and cheese. If Laura didn't have his dead-wife-in-a-can and her scandalous bird notebooks, then who did?

"Fine, don't answer me. Why respect me now? After all, I'm only trying to help you grieve the loss of your beloved wife. I'm only trying to bring us together as a family since without Mom we are all falling apart."

Champs cleared his throat. "You're trying to take the place of your mother? My Pat?"

"She wasn't just your Pat. She was all of ours. And yes, I'm trying to replace her, because if I didn't step up to the plate, who would? I deserve credit for this, a pat on the back, a 'good girl, Laura,' some appreciation for what I'm putting myself through for the sake of all of you. Goddamn it! I deserve your respect, and all you can offer is stubborn silence or random outbursts or bad manners. There are things we need to settle, Champs. It's for your own good."

"You mean it's for *your* own good. Nobody asked you to take over where your mother left off, so stop pointing out how grateful I should be. I told you earlier, you have my full approval to do what you need to do as part of your grieving process or whatever it is you call it and move on to Seattle. Just leave me out of it."

"Leave you *out* of it? That's the opposite of what I need. I already lost one parent and I don't want to lose another. I want you to be entirely *in* it. Right here with me, by me, for me. You're my dad for fuck's sake, and I need you." Laura began to cry.

"Please don't cry, Laura."

"Are you out of your mind? Crying is exactly what I should do. For your information, when people are sad and mourning, they cry! It's a normal response to the death of a loved one. You should be crying. You should have been crying for months. How else are you going to release the pain? How else are you going to grieve?"

Champs had had enough of this. He wasn't a touchy-feely man, true, and perhaps his emotional intelligence needed an upgrade, but he knew one thing for sure: there was no normal response to the death of a loved one. Josanne and her damn dead-people samplers had taught him that. Not to mention over seven decades of life experience, including the loss of his grandfather, both his parents, his childhood dog, a smattering of tadpoles, his only brother, and now Pat.

He stood up and jabbed his finger at Laura, aware that he'd turned the tables on her "We need to talk" talk. He looked around for something to slam, just in case. "Stop telling me how I should grieve! I don't need your help. I don't want your help. I don't want anyone's help. What do you know about loss, anyway?"

It had slipped out in anger, and instantly he regretted it, knew it was a terrible, terrible thing to have asked his daughter, who, he should have realized all along, was in crisis and pain. She'd just lost her mother, the most essential and irreplaceable person in her life. But it was too late to take it back.

"What did you say?" Laura seethed. "What do *I* know about loss?" She flung her cup of white wine at Champs. It bounced off his chest and onto the woven carpet. He'd forgotten that Laura was a thrower like his father, not a slammer like Pat and most women he knew.

"You son of a bitch!" she shouted, and hurled *The Tycoon's Pregnant Mistress*, one of Josanne's Harlequin paperbacks. It struck him hard on the right shoulder.

"What do *I* know about loss? I'll tell you what *I* know about loss, you, you . . ." Laura was spitting her words now, punctuating each insult by throwing anything she could reach at Champs.

"You nasty . . ."—a *National Geographic* headlined "Who Knows About Birds?" hit Champs in the groin—"selfish . . ."—Champs withstood a deep cut to his palm as he deflected the metal pliers that sliced like an errant baseball pitch straight toward his forehead—"bitter . . ."—Laura struggled with the wooden end seat of the picnic table; she got it overhead just in time for ". . . old man!"

Champs lurched to the side, cradling his bleeding hand. The bench shot across the porch, busting through the screening and landing deep in the hedge. Having run out of objects, Laura threw herself at Champs, hammering her fists on his chest as he fell backward from the strength of her blows into the club chair.

"I lost my baby, goddamn it! Okay? Is that enough loss for you? Losing a child? What can you say about that, Champs? Huh? Ever lost a child? I lost my son. Mom was there for all of it. But where were you? My son, my beautiful Thomas . . ."

Laura collapsed into sobs.

Champs sat stunned and stiff. Son? What son? What was she talking about?

Laura pushed herself away from him. "Oh, and then then there's Mom. You weren't the only one to lose her, okay? She was my mom! My mother! Does that even count for anything in your little fucking scrooge world?" Laura could barely get the words out as rage twisted her throat.

"I'll never see her again. She's dead. Just like Thomas. Dead. I can't do anything about it. A million times a day I go to call her, get her advice, tell her something funny about the girls, just hear her voice, and every time it feels like she dies again. I tried to tell you this before. And *you*, you say nothing, never ask, never think for a second about what I might be feeling. No, you sit here in this germ-infested dump, get drunk, fish, and put me down. You keep her ashes under your goddamn dirty underwear!"

Spent, Laura slumped down on the concrete in a puddle of wine and wept.

Champs's heart swelled and burst. His body flash-flooded with emotions: shame, sorrow, dread, regret, loss, fear, and something else. He couldn't put his finger on it, but that something else moved him to action.

He bent over, maneuvered his arms around his daughter's shoulders and under her kneecaps, and lifted her onto his lap. He held her close to his chest and rocked her. She felt as fragile as a tiny bird pummeled in a hailstorm. Champs smoothed her hair with his bloody palm, kissed her forehead. Ray's words rushed back to him: *She gave me her time. Way I see it, that's the most valuable thing of all.*

"I'm here now, Laura," he said softly. "I'm right here."

"Daddy?" Her voice was the cracked whisper of a distraught child.

"Yes, honey. I'm right here. I've got you now."

She flung her arms around his neck.

Birthday Surprise

On Saturday morning, Champs rose early to make blueberry pancakes and bacon for his whole brood. He hadn't cooked a family breakfast since Samantha and Ryan, David's children, were little. He remembered when his grandchildren had wanted pancakes shaped like animals. Pat had happily taken on feeding her family, but she had no patience for special requests. You ate what she cooked, and if you didn't like it, you were welcome to make yourself something else. She was a pragmatic nurturer.

So it was Champs who'd made the special pancakes for the kids. He'd discovered he could modify the basic Mickey Mouse shape to make most mammals with ears: bears, cats, rabbits, dogs. He'd used blueberries, chocolate chips, whipped cream, and licorice whips to animate his creations. Bored with his usual repertoire, he'd expanded his portfolio to include fish, crabs, and once, a seahorse. When he'd attempted a shrimp, Ryan had complained that it looked like his penis. Eventually, Champs had moved on to more abstract objects, and breakfast became a guessing game like charades. When he'd stumped them all with a toilet-plunger pancake, Pat put her foot down and told the kids they were having cereal from then on.

It occurred to Champs, as he turned the sizzling bacon over on the electric griddle, that apart from summer visits, it was Pat's relationships with family members that had kept him feeling connected and involved—albeit at a distance. She'd stayed in regular touch with not only David but also his wife, Kimmie, and the grandkids. Pat had remembered their birthdays and graduations, their teachers' and friends' names, their hobbies, sports, and anniversaries. Same for Laura, Brian, the girls, and Jeffrey, too. Pat could tell Champs what Jeffrey was for Halloween when he was four. She could tell him who Laura's first roommate was in college. Right now, Pat would probably have been handing him a pen to sign his name on Brian's birthday card. Champs wished he had paid more attention. He also wished Pat had written it all down in an addendum to the goldfinch notebook— maybe a blue-footed booby notebook.

David and Mel, closest to the delicious aromas filling the cabin, were the first to join Champs in the kitchen. He hadn't heard them come in last night but gathered it had a been a late one given the mumbled greetings, red eyes, and rush to the coffeepot. Mel wandered out to the porch with her steaming cup and a piece of bacon. David sat down at the dining table facing Champs.

"This is impressive," he said. "What's the occasion?"

"Uh, Brian's birthday."

"Oh. Does he know it's his birthday?"

Champs shrugged. "It's a surprise." He emptied the coffeepot, giving his mug an extra dollop of whipped cream. "You mind making another pot while I finish up breakfast?"

"Sure." David squeezed himself into the small kitchen area. "Mel and I are flying back to SFO tomorrow night. She's got to see the OB on Monday, and I've got a new client. A company called CGX. They're in the IoT space, which is a great opportu . . . what the fuck?"

Champs looked over his shoulder to see David peering into a Chock Full o'Nuts coffee can.

"What the hell do you call this?" David said, pulling the Ziploc bag free of the canister. "Are these . . . no, it can't be . . . oh my God . . . are these Mom's ashes?" he shouted in alarm.

Before Champs could reply, Zoe and Hannah barged through the door, followed by a bewildered Brian and Laura, eyes drawn to the dangling bag that David held like a rabbit he'd just pulled out of a magic black hat.

"Surprise!" said Champs. He flipped the pancakes on the griddle.

"What's in the bag?" asked Zoe. "Let me see! Let me see!"

"That's just coffee, Zo-Zo, not a surprise," said Hannah.

"Aww. What's the surprise then?" Zoe asked Champs.

"It's your dad's birthday, and I'm making breakfast. Happy birthday, Brian!" Champs raised his coffee mug, hoping he was somewhere in the right ballpark date-wise.

"Daddy's birthday? Yay! A birthday party! I already made a present. C'mon, Hannah, let's go get Daddy's presents." Zoe yanked her sister's arm and whispered in her ear, while Hannah locked eyes with Champs.

He sent her a look he hoped would communicate his urgent need for her complicity. She nodded once, then hustled her sister out of the cabin in a mock display of excitement. Thank God for Hannah.

"Brian's birthday is in February," said Laura when the door slammed behind the girls.

"It's okay, Champs. I don't mind celebrating a little early while we're all together," said Brian. "Uh, how about I get the table ready?" He didn't wait for a reply and left the cabin as if escaping a fire.

"I did it a while ago," Champs confessed, and poured the remaining batter onto the spitting grease in the pan. The last pancake was always a giant one. "Panzilla," the kids used to call it. They'd always made Champs eat every bite.

"What the hell for?" David asked.

"To stop Laura from dumping Pat into the Sassafras. Figured I'd hide the urn so you couldn't do it. It was too big to hide, so I just hid Pat. Her ashes, I mean." He gestured to the Chock Full o'Nuts can with his spatula.

"So, the actual urn is filled with ground coffee?" David asked, incredulous.

Champs nodded.

"Did you think I wouldn't notice?" Laura asked.

"I didn't expect the damn thing to end up here where someone would open it to make a pot of coffee!"

"I think Laura means did you not think she'd notice when she released ground coffee into the river instead of Mom's ashes?" said David, gathering handfuls of knives and forks.

"Why would anyone notice what was in the urn?" Champs was confused.

When Laura had mentioned releasing Pat's ashes, he'd assumed that meant dropping the urn, lid secured, into the river, where it would land in the muck on the bottom like pirate booty. He'd been worried that the idiot treasure hunters would dig it up one day with their oyster rakes.

"Champs, you don't drop the whole urn," Laura said. "You release the ashes. Only the ashes. You like, well, sprinkle them on the surface. Not 'sprinkle,' that's the wrong word. They sort of fall through your fingers, like—"

"Well, how the hell was I supposed to know that? Only dead people I've ever seen were buried in a coffin at the cemetery or put to rest in a morgue, frozen on a silver platter."

David let the cutlery drop with a clatter onto the counter. He and Laura tried to hold back their snickering.

"No one gets put to rest on a silver platter in the morgue," Laura said, trying to straighten her face. "The morgue is a temporary place before burial or cremation. People go there to identify their loved ones. Sometimes the deceased are there awaiting autopsy. Either way, the bodies are on stainless steel trays. No silver platters are involved."

"I'll keep that in mind," said Champs.

He'd had enough of the processing-dead-people conversation and focused his attention on Panzilla, flipping the pancake high in the air. He liked to add some drama on the last one. Panzilla missed the skillet and landed with a splat on the floor. Millie, waiting at Champs's feet for just this opportunity, ate it with a happy dog grin and a wagging tail. Champs saw Laura and David exchange an eye-roll.

Jeffrey pushed through the door wearing a faded Philadelphia Eagles cap and an "Only Dead Fish Go with the Flow" T-shirt, which had belonged to Peety. It was remarkable how well he fit in Peety's clothes, Champs thought. And he smelled like Champs Senior, he thought, picking up a whiff of what must have been a heavy night. Champs had the nose of a hound dog.

"I hear we're celebrating a birthday today!" Jeffrey said cheerily. "Is there any coffee in here?"

Champs ducked behind the counter.

"Um," Laura said.

David stifled a laugh.

"What? What's going on?" Jeffrey asked.

"Nothing, nothing. You had to be there," David said. "Here, go set the table. We're out of coffee unless you want instant."

"How are we out of coffee already? I put a new can in the cupboard yesterday. It was in your suitcase, Champs." Jeffrey took the silverware from his brother. "It's right there, you idiots." He pointed to the Chock Full o'Nuts canister.

"Nope, that's the empty one," David said, placing his hand on top of the can. "You want instant or not?"

"Sure. Instant is better than nothing." Jeffrey headed outside with the knives and forks.

David gathered butter, syrup, napkins, and paper plates and followed his brother, winking at Laura on the way out.

"Champs, can I put these back in the urn now?" Laura asked, reaching for her mother. "I'll trade you for some real coffee."

Champs's eyes opened wide.

"No, no, no! Not from the urn. Jesus Christ, that wouldn't be sanitary! I mean, I have another bag of coffee, in the *Flying Cloud*. A new one. I'll run and get it while you bring out the breakfast."

Relieved, Champs watched his daughter leave the cabin with his dead wife. It seemed right that Laura would have time alone with her mother. Pat would enjoy that. He hoped it would be a comfort to Laura, too. A rush of love for the two most important women in his life colored his neck and face. He maneuvered his way through the porch door with two loaded platters of food.

Brian was admiring the new bracelet that Zoe had made for him at the bead shop. Mel was showing Jeffrey the logo designs she'd sketched for his new business. David and Hannah were playing hangman. Laura came running across the lawn with a bag of gourmet ground coffee.

Champs paused to take a mental picture and send it to Pat. He smiled, imagining her receiving it and clutching it to her heart. Then he scrunched his eyebrows together, worried that Pat wouldn't recognize Mel. It was damn difficult navigating the uncharted waters of his new relationship with Pat. He wondered if it was difficult for her, too.

36

Fowl Play

Partway through the cheerful fat-and-sugar feast, Chicken Ray
arrived carrying a dog kennel with four chickens inside.

"Where's Millie?" he said, looking around for the dog.

Champs shook his head and indicated with a forkful of pancake
that Millie was in the cabin.

Chicken Ray set the kennel down on the concrete porch.

"Daddy, look! Chicken Ray brought you chickens for your birthday
present!" Zoe jumped down from the table and ran toward the cage.
"Let them out, let them out, Chicken Ray! I want to hold one. Look,
Daddy! Oh, please let me name them, please, please, please, please,
please."

"There's no point in naming them, Zo-Zo. Duh," said Hannah.
"Chicken Ray's birds are for eating. They'll be killed soon, and you'll
starve because every time you bite into your chicken nuggets, you'll be
like, 'Oh no! This is Eloise! I can't eat poor Eloise! Why did she have
to die?'" Hannah drew the last word out into a moan and sniffly cry.

She was a good actress, Champs thought, although he noticed a strain in her voice.

"Hannah! That's a terrible thing to say. What's wrong with you?" Laura said.

"Well, it's true. Right, Chicken Ray?" Hannah turned to Chicken Ray for confirmation.

"It used to be true," said Chicken Ray. "These chickens aren't for eating."

He warned Zoe not to stick her finger in the cage in case the birds mistook it for a worm and gave her a nasty peck.

Champs poured him a mug of coffee and motioned for him to have a seat. He glanced at Hannah, who was glaring at her mother.

"Happy birthday, Brian," said Chicken Ray. "Didn't mean to crash your party here." He shook Brian's hand before sitting on the sofa and sipping his coffee.

"Are the rest of the birds safely at Jill's?" Mel asked.

"Yep. It will take them a while to settle into their new digs, but I think they'll be happy there. Happier than dead, anyway."

"What's all this about?" asked Laura.

"Seems like 'fowl' play," Champs said with a smirk.

There was a collective groan around the table.

"That's 'eggsactly' what I was thinking," said Brian, and smiled, pleased with himself, as more groans and a giggle from Hannah filled the porch.

"All right, all right, you two. Quit your 'yoking,'" said Laura.

This earned her a round of applause.

"'Shell-y' get back to eating these pancakes?" asked Mel, winking at Hannah.

"Okay," said Hannah, "but they're not as good as they're 'cracked' up to be."

Everyone laughed, and Brian gave his daughter a high five.

"Good one, Hannah," said Champs.

She smiled briefly, then resumed her moody posture. Champs detected that something was bothering her, but he couldn't put his finger on it.

"Oh, no! Stop that, Zoe. No! You can't feed that to the chickens!" Laura exclaimed.

"Why not? They like it," Zoe said. She ripped off another strip of bacon and dangled it through the bars of the kennel, where a bright orange beak snapped it up.

"It's fine," said Chicken Ray. "Backyard chickens will eat anything —even chicken!"

"Ew, gross," said Zoe. "Daddy, can I keep one in my room when we get home? I promise I'll feed it and take care of it."

"Sorry, Zo-Zo, those chickens are staying right here at the cabin with Champs and me," said Jeffrey.

"Says who?" Champs wasn't sure he liked the idea of turning his yard over to orphaned farm animals. Millie was one thing, but a flock of chickens? Who knew where that would lead? Pigs? Donkeys? Cattle? He hoped there were zoning laws in effect to prevent things from going too far.

"C'mon, Champs. Don't be a party pooper," said Jeffrey. "Having chickens will be fun. They're healing birds. I got the idea from those notebooks of Mom's I found in the Windstar," said Jeffrey.

Champs froze.

"What notebooks?" asked David and Laura.

"They were Mom's notebooks from when she used to work with the Vietnam vets before I was born. She kept records—kind of like diaries, I guess. The chickens, according to Mom, were great for healing PTSD—course, they didn't call it that back then." Jeffrey took a bite of bacon and handed the rest to Mel, who beamed at him, took a bite, and joined Zoe in feeding the birds.

"And you read them all?" asked Champs. His stomach did a cartwheel, and he waited for the sky to fall.

"Yeah, it was fascinating. Hey, I was wondering. Was I named after JP? The journal says the 'J' stood for 'Jeffrey.'" Jeffrey folded a pancake around a slice of bacon and bit into it like a taco.

"Who's JP?" asked David and Laura.

Champs had a mouth full of food, so he didn't answer. Not that he knew much about JP anyway, except that he was probably Jeffrey's real father and he'd shot himself in the head after Pat had started helping him. He glanced at Chicken Ray, wondering if he could put any meat on the bones of this story.

"I can answer this one," said Chicken Ray. "JP was the last man your mother tried to help. I don't know what she wrote in her notebook about him, but he was different from the others."

"Different how?" asked Laura.

"He wasn't a Vietnam veteran."

"Well, what was he?" asked David, an edge to his voice.

"He was the younger brother of a soldier who was tortured and killed at the Hanoi Hilton," Chicken Ray explained. "JP blamed himself for his brother's death and so did his parents. According to Pat, JP thought he should have been the one to die, although he never said why. She said his guilt left him more traumatized than those who'd been to war. Way I see it, some wounds are too deep to heal."

"How do you know about this?" said David.

"She talked some the summer after JP died. When we worked on the chicken farm. Like you said, Jeffrey, chickens can be healers. My little brothers died in Vietnam. I guess she thought I would have some answers. Course I didn't." Chicken Ray shrugged and finished his coffee.

Laura refilled his mug.

Champs noticed that Hannah and Zoe had pricked up their ears. Hannah's face was bright red, her jaw locked and grinding. Zoe stabbed her finger in and out of the chicken cage, attempting to poke the birds.

"Well, none of that was in the notebook," Jeffrey said. "Mom described a few sessions with him on the farm, but her notes were vague—except that he seemed uninterested in the animals."

Champs was alarmed at the track this story was taking. Bile rose in his throat. Could it be that Chicken Ray had known all along that JP was Jeffrey's father? Who else knew? Why was he the last to know about anything? He shot an evil eye at Chicken Ray.

"All I know about JP," Champs blurted, "is that he let your mother down and caused her a lot of pain. The man was a screwup if you ask me. He shot himself in the head, and we all moved on. End of story. C'mon, we're having a birthday party here. Pat would roll over in her grave if she knew we were dredging all this up. Do we have any candles, Laura?"

"She doesn't have a grave," said Hannah.

"Hannah!" Laura scolded.

"Well it's true, you said so yourself. You keep talking like Zoe and me aren't here. We're kids, you know. You're not supposed to tell us about people shooting their heads off and graves and war and torture and ground-up Grandma." Hannah's eyes filled with tears behind her glasses. She sniffled, crossed her arms in a defiant manner, then added, "And it's not really Daddy's birthday, either."

"Yes it is!" said Zoe, on the edge of a tantrum.

Champs felt an urge to wrap her up in his arms, bring her down to the beach, and build sand castles with her all day long. Zoe was a bright, happy child who needed grown-ups to be reliable, kind, and fun. He remembered that feeling all too well.

Zoe broke into sobs and ran for cover in the cabin.

Millie spotted her chance and ran onto the porch, snarling like an attack dog at the four caged chickens. They panicked in a flurry of wings, feathers, and alarming shrieks as if they were in the throes of dying.

Mel jumped back in alarm with a sharp shriek of her own.

Champs leaped forward to grab Millie, shouting, "No, Millie! No! Stop that!" His head smacked against Chicken Ray's as Ray lunged for the birdcage. They both fell back uttering obscenities.

Laura hustled to Champs's side and Brian to Chicken Ray's side.

David lifted the cage of hysterical birds and maneuvered them into the yard away from Millie's squirming in Champs's arms.

Mel yelled again. She fell into a squatting position, grabbing the side of a club chair for support.

"What is it? Are you bitten?" cried Jeffrey, dashing to her side, like a knight in shining armor.

"No, my waters broke!" She attempted a grin. "Surprise!"

"I guess we're going to have a birthday after all," Laura said.

Gunshot

Champs's eyes bulged like a cartoon character's.

David dropped the kennel on the lawn. The crash landing jiggled the cage door open, and chickens burst forth squawking in four directions.

Millie leaped out of Champs's grasp and bolted through the torn screening in hot pursuit.

"Call nine-one-one!" yelled David, rushing back onto the porch.

"No! No ambulance! I've got this," cried Mel, wincing with the next contraction.

"Don't push, Mel! Don't push!" Laura shouted.

Zo-Zo poked her head out of the cabin door and screamed.

"Stop screaming, Zoe! She's just having a baby," said Hannah, rolling her eyes.

"No! The chickens!" Zoe said. "The chickens are loose, and Millie's chasing them! We have to save them!" She bolted into the yard.

Hannah ran after her sister, who ran after Millie, who ran after her dinner.

Larry's garage door opened. He stumbled toward the porch dressed in full camouflage, including a camo "Duck Hunting . . . It's a Calling" hat and a Browning A5 camo shotgun. He stopped short of entering when Mel moaned in the throes of another contraction.

"It's okay, Mel. You're doing just fine. Keep breathing. That's it. Good girl," coached Laura.

Jeffrey rubbed Mel's back and shoulders between contractions.

"We've got to do something!" David said. He sounded like a panicked Chicken Little. "She can't have this baby now! She can't. It's way too early! Something's wrong. The baby will die. I'm calling nine-one-one! Where's my goddamn phone?"

"Do something, Ray!" Champs hissed. He and Chicken Ray hadn't moved from their spots on the concrete porch.

"Me? What am I supposed to do?"

"You're a farmer! You know about these things! Do something! Help get it out!"

"I'm a chicken farmer, you moron! Chickens lay eggs, not babies! I don't know jack shit about getting anything out of a vagina—human or animal. You do something!"

"Mel, I think it's best if we drive you to the ER," Brian said, taking control. "We can get a nine-one-one operator on the cell phone to help us on the way to the hospital. No ambulance. It's the safest option right now. Okay?"

Mel nodded and groaned at the onset of more labor pains.

Crack! The sound of gunshot splintered the air.

Mel and Laura screamed.

Jeffrey, David, Champs, and Chicken Ray ducked for cover.

Millie bolted around the side of the cabin. Zoe and Hannah were right behind her.

"Millie! Fetch!" Larry commanded, pointing to the dead bird at the back of the yard. The girls stopped in their tracks while Millie retrieved the chicken, dropping it at Larry's feet.

"Good girl," Larry said, giving Millie a pat on the head. He lifted his rifle and took aim at another chicken.

"Nooooo!" cried Zoe, darting to the middle of the yard as if to form a human shield between Larry's gun and the three remaining chickens.

"Stooooop!" cried Laura.

"Larry! Put your gun down!"

"Don't shoot!"

"Oh my God!"

David lunged through the screening to tackle Larry.

Hannah bolted across the yard to save her sister.

Crack! The shotgun went off again as David knocked Larry to the ground and Hannah delivered Zoe to safety behind the boathouse.

"What the fuck do you think you're doing?" David yelled. He had Larry pinned on his back to the ground and shook him hard by the shoulders. "Are you fucking insane? You almost killed Zoe!"

"I didn't almost kill anyone, you son of a bitch!" Larry flipped David off of him and both men jumped to their feet prepared to fight. "You're the one who almost killed her! You set the gun off when you jumped me, asshole."

"Stop it!" Champs barged outside. "Stop it! Both of you. Get control of yourselves." He grabbed the shirts of both men and forced them away from each other.

Brian emerged from behind the boathouse carrying his two stricken, sobbing daughters, one in each arm.

Mel screamed and twisted her body as if Jeffrey and Laura, who held her in a supported squat position, were roasting her over an open flame.

"Shit," said Laura. "She's closer than I thought. We need to get her to a hospital, now!"

"Don't you dare move me! I'm staying like this. I have to stay like this," Mel insisted.

Champs gave David and Larry a final shove. "Laura and Jeffrey, get Mel in the Windstar. Now! Walk her over there, and she can stay squatting like that in the back of the van. Ray, get the door for them, then get in the passenger seat and call nine-one-one! Quick! Let's go."

Chicken Ray threw his keys at David. "Move my truck. It's blocking the van."

David caught the keys and ran to the Dodge pickup.

Larry picked up his gun and staggered behind David.

Laura and Jeffrey helped a panting, sweat-drenched Mel into the back of the Windstar.

"Get in! Quick!" Laura motioned for Brian and the girls to get into the van while the V-6 engine choked to life.

Zoe scrambled on hands and knees to her mother's leg and clung to it, whimpering. Hannah tried to spread a *Kent County Crier* newspaper on the filthy bottom of the van between Mel's legs. As soon as Brian shut the doors, Champs shifted the Windstar into reverse and shot out of the driveway.

"Brace yourselves!" he warned, ramming the gearshift into drive.

Nosy neighbors, three distraught chickens, and rampaging Millie— gawking, squawking, and barking—made an obstacle course of the gravel road ahead. Champs leaned hard and long on the horn, then slammed his foot down on the accelerator as Mel screamed through another contraction. David blared his horn and screeched the pickup's tires as he and Larry barreled out of Deadrise Cove on the heels of the Windstar ambulance.

Forty minutes later, Champs skidded to a stop at the hospital's emergency entrance in Middletown. He raced with the alacrity of a much younger man to open the back of the van.

Laura and Jeffrey waddled Mel through the automatic glass doors of the hospital. Her shouts had subsided to whimpers but Champs didn't know if that was a good thing or a bad thing.

"Do we wait here?" asked Hannah.

"Can I get out?" asked Zoe. "I want to see the baby."

"First we need to park," said Champs as a hospital guard blew his whistle and gestured to a *Visitors Parking* sign.

By the time they reached the maternity ward, David and Larry were already there. Laura explained that Jeffrey, mistaken for the father, had been whisked into a delivery room with Mel.

"What happens now, Mommy?" said Zoe, kicking the metal leg on a row of welded-together hospital chairs.

"Now we're in the waiting room, so we wait," Laura answered. "Stop kicking the furniture."

"How much longer? I'm hungry," said Hannah.

"Brian, can you take the girls to get something to eat? It could be a while, depending on what's going on in there."

Champs watched Brian and the girls leave the waiting room on the way to food. He wished he could go with them.

"I'm surprised that Mel's contractions intensified so fast like that," Laura said. "Normally, it takes a lot longer the first time."

"I think we can abandon 'normally' at this stage. There's nothing normal about any of this," David observed.

"True." Laura nodded. "I guess you missed your chance at a shotgun wedding."

David gave his sister the middle finger.

"Is this her first birth?" asked Larry.

"She never let on about any other kids," David replied. "And speaking of shotguns, what in the hell were you thinking when you decided to make a shooting range out of our backyard?"

"Everything was under control until you lunged at me. I'm an excellent marksman and bringing down those crazy-ass chickens was instinctual. No one was in any danger."

"The girls were in danger!" said David. "And don't you talk to me about being in control. You look stoned as hell."

"You're stoned?" asked Laura, incredulous. "And you came to the hospital?"

"Oh for God's sake, Laura," said David. "It doesn't matter about the hospital. It matters about shooting chickens!"

"Instinct," said Larry. "A hunter sees a bird on the loose, he's gonna shoot it down. It's what we do. Pure instinct." He extended his arm like a rifle and tracked an imaginary bird across the waiting room.

"Pure bullshit," Champs said. "You ever shoot that thing near my house again, I'll—"

"What? Shoot me?" Larry laughed so hard he doubled over.

"It's not funny," said Laura.

"Yeah, it is," said Chicken Ray, snorting and chuckling.

"No, it's not!" Laura tried again.

All four men cracked up, made their arms into rifles, and shot at each other. Gallows humor. Several minutes passed as the laughter subsided and the anxiety of not knowing what was happening coupled with the restlessness of not having anything to do took over. The room was silent until Champs broke through the nervous tension.

"What are your plans, son?"

"Plans?"

"You're about to be a father again. What are your plans for the baby and Mel?"

"I don't know. This all happened so fast. I thought we'd have time to work something out."

"What's there to work out?" asked Chicken Ray. "Way I see it, shit happens. You deal with it where you are."

"My life sure as hell isn't here if that's what you're implying. I've got a flight to catch tomorrow, an important new client to meet on Monday, and it looks like Kim's ready to give me a second chance."

"Jesus Christ, David. You can't just pretend that your girlfriend isn't giving birth in there to a child you fathered, then abandon them while you fly home to pick up where you left off as if nothing ever happened!" Laura was livid.

"He could," said Larry.

"It's your child, David!" Laura implored. "For God's sake, can you hear yourself? Your newborn son or daughter. Your flesh and blood. How can you even imagine not wanting to hold him and know him and cherish him every single moment?" Laura's eyes flooded with tears.

David looked baffled at Laura's outburst.

Champs put his arm around her shoulders. He understood that he couldn't do anything to change the reality of a dead son and a dead mother. Those weren't things that could be fixed. Not by him, not by anyone. His job, as a man and a father, was to be there next to her and provide a calm harbor for her pain, a safety net when things went wrong.

"It's okay, Laura," Champs said, his voice just above a whisper. "Thomas is held and loved. He's up there right now in Pat's arms. And that baby being born in there—we're gonna hold it and love it no matter what David does."

Champs looked to his son, his neighbor, and his friend. Was there a wise man among them? David walked away toward the water cooler. Larry stared at the floor, stifling a yawn. But Chicken Ray, eyes welling, met his gaze with an intensity Champs had experienced only once before in his life. He glanced away, uneasy without knowing why.

"Champs Noland?" called a nurse-midwife in scrubs who emerged from the door leading to the delivery rooms. "Champs Noland?"

Champs raised his arm as if responding to roll call in fourth grade. "Yes. Here."

He stood, removed his cap, and straightened his shirt like a young man about to meet his future father-in-law.

"Oh, good," said the nurse, walking toward Champs with a smile and an outstretched hand. "Let me be the first to congratulate you on the birth of your grandson. It was a tough labor, but in the end, he shot out like a bullet from a gun. Mom, Dad, and baby are doing fine."

"Jeffrey's not the dad," blurted David.

"Well, obviously, he's not the bio dad," she said. "But Jeffrey's definitely got the look of a wonderful father. Come, see for yourself."

Bio Dad

Champs had less than two minutes to consider what the midwife meant by "obviously, he's not the bio dad" as he, David, Laura, Larry, and Chicken Ray followed her through the doors of the labor ward and entered the second room on the right.

Mel was propped up in a hospital bed, hair unkempt, cheeks rosy red, beaming at Jeffrey, who stroked the cheek of a dark brown infant cradled in his arms.

Laura drew a sharp breath and brought her hand to her mouth.

David shook his head in an explicit negation of everything he saw before him.

Chicken Ray grinned like a benefic angel.

And Larry whistled a bird call that sounded like "uh-oh."

"Is he black?" Champs asked, approaching the bed.

"No, silly," Mel replied, waving him forward. "He's half Indian."

"You mean Native American?"

"No, Champs," Jeffrey laughed as he deftly handed the baby back to Mel. "Benji Raj here is part Indian, as in the country of India. In South Asia? Maybe you've heard of it?"

"You mean this isn't David's baby?" asked Laura.

"Wait a minute," said David. "Did you just say Benji Raj? As in Raj? Your recent boss Raj? From the garden center? Why the hell didn't you tell me it wasn't my kid?"

"You never asked," said Mel, undisturbed by David's tone. "And besides, I didn't know until today. Champs?"

Mel offered Benji Raj up like a present. Without hesitation, Champs took the infant in his arms, careful to support his head. Benji Raj opened his new blue eyes for the second time in his life. Champs saw Pat staring back at him, full of wonder, peace, and joy. His heart stretched as wide as the smile that spread across his face. He couldn't help it.

Laura leaned over Mel to give her a hug.

Chicken Ray moved to peer over Champs's shoulder and admire Benji Raj.

Larry congratulated Mel and shook hands with Jeffrey. There was nothing like the atmosphere of a brand-new baby—innocent and miraculous—in the room. It was a unique bubble where goodwill did not feel faked or forced. At least for some.

"This is crazy," David barked from the other side of the room. "This is outrageous! That baby has nothing to do with us. It's not even a Noland. I don't know what you're thinking, but you can't expect me to raise a child that isn't even mine."

"Why not?" Champs heard himself say. "I did."

Everyone stared at Champs. The moment seemed endless to him, but less than a heartbeat passed before Larry spoke.

"Champs," he whispered. "Now's not the time."

"The time for what?" Laura asked. "What are you saying, Champs?"

Lifting his gaze from Benji Raj to Jeffrey, Champs said, "It's you, Jeffrey. I love you as a son. But I'm not your real father."

"What?" said Jeffrey, bewildered.

"Hang on a minute," said David. "If you're not Jeffrey's dad, then who is?"

"JP," replied Champs. He handed the newborn to Mel, who lifted one end of her sweat-stained tank top and brought Benji Raj to her breast.

Laura, Jeffrey, and David sat heavily on the edges of Mel's hospital bed with arms crossed and worried expressions.

Champs felt relieved he could finally speak the truth out loud, even if this wasn't the appropriate time or place. Another floodgate opened wide. "I never knew for sure, but I always had a feeling, ever since you were born, Jeffrey. I only discovered it was JP—"

"It's not him," interrupted Chicken Ray.

"What?" It was Champs's turn to look bewildered.

He watched Chicken Ray and Larry exchange a knowing glance. Champs felt like the accused in a courtroom on the verge of receiving the verdict.

"It's not JP," said Chicken Ray. "It's me. I'm Jeffrey's biological father. But he's your son, Champs. You're his real dad. That's how Pat wanted it, and I agreed. It was a one-night stand, both of us three sheets to the wind. That's all. Pat loved you, Champs. She never wanted to be with anyone else. She chose life, and she chose you. Simple as that."

Champs gasped for air and staggered backward, clutching his chest. Something wrapped around his heart, something intent on squeezing the life out of him. He stumbled backward and landed hard, unable to break his fall. He clawed at his throat as if he could loosen the binds that threatened to strangle him.

"Champs!" Laura screamed, flinging herself to his side.

"Nooooo!" cried Jeffrey, leaping impossibly over the bed toward Champs.

"Call nine-one-one!" shouted David. "He's having a heart attack!"

"We're at the hospital already, you goddamn moron," said Larry. "Ray, run out there and call for—"

"Fire! Fire!" Chicken Ray yelled down the hallway. He activated a nearby fire alarm. "In here! Help!"

The sudden blare of the alarm was nothing compared to the sound of the blood that rushed to Champs's head like he was an erupting volcano. He thought his brain would explode. Whoever held the cruel belt around his heart tightened it another notch. Images of encroaching flames filled his line of vision. He shook them away and locked eyes with Jeffrey, desperate to find the best parts of himself reflected there despite the lack of a genetic connection.

He was dimly aware of the chaos of nurses and doctors, Laura, Chicken Ray, and Larry trying to save him. Someone covered his mouth and nose with an oxygen mask. The alarm continued to shriek in urgency as he was lifted onto a gurney. It was so hot and unbearably stifling in his body. Jeffrey stared helplessly back at him.

"I'm sorry," Champs tried to say. "I love you. I love all of you."

But he knew it was too late. These were his last seconds on Earth. He couldn't take it, couldn't bear any of it, but he couldn't stop it; there was so much left to say, he didn't want to go; his heart shredded; he was terrified, and the darkness kept coming, closer and closer still. He closed his eyes. In the minuscule beat between life and death, he felt rainfall on his skin—sweet and cooling spring rain—the blessed beginnings of everything made new. He stopped fighting and let go.

Octopus Trap

"**A**m I dead?" Champs croaked.

He was in a white room on a white bed with white sheets. An angel dressed in white hovered over him. The angel was overweight, and this surprised Champs; he had imagined that angels would be slim. And blond. This mousy-haired, chunk-o angel didn't have a halo or wings either. It was extremely suspicious.

It also concerned Champs that his vision was blurry. He'd expected that in death he would be free from all bodily malfunctions. Restored to health if not youth. But he felt as if he'd had too long of a journey to the pearly gates: delays, missed connections, harrowing flights clutching the sick bag with no entertainment screen, forced to sit folded in on himself like bad origami in the back of economy next to a screaming baby. There was only one logical conclusion: he hadn't qualified for heaven, so this was purgatory.

"Just rest," said the disappointing angel. She had crooked teeth and bad breath.

Or maybe hell.

The next time Champs awoke, a warm, slim hand held his. This angel was no disappointment. She had a beautiful head of blond hair and bent over his white bed as if in prayer. He wondered what this angel was praying for. It couldn't be for him since he was already dead. Wings? A time-share in Fort Lauderdale? Angels seemed far too human to him so far. At least this one was better than the last.

Perhaps if he closed his eyes and drifted back to sleep, he'd wake again to further improvements in his life-after-death environment. Maybe he'd wake on a brand-new *Tetanus*, with tanned, rippling muscles, reeling in a thirty-pound striped bass, buxom models on deck making sandwiches and refilling his beer mug from the onboard keg of Dogfish Head 60 Minute IPA.

"Champs? Can you hear me?" The blond angel lifted her head, revealing her halo. It was Laura.

"Laura? Are you dead?"

"Oh, Champs. Oh, thank God. No, I'm not dead." Laura threw herself on Champs's chest. He winced at the pressure and squinted as bright sunlight streamed through the window into his face.

"How do you feel? Can I get you anything? Water? The nurse?"

"A sandwich?" replied Champs. He ached in every nerve, tendon, bone, and blood vessel. A weary ache that didn't feel like pain so much as exhaustion. He was wiped out. His stomach growled. At least there was nothing wrong with his appetite.

"That's a good sign, Mr. Noland. Welcome back," said the disappointing angel, who'd slipped into the room unnoticed.

Champs groaned and shut his eyes. Why was the disappointing angel here, mixed in with the real Laura? It was too confusing, this mix of life and death. He should be alive or dead, simple as that. He had expected clarity in the afterlife, even if it was the clarity of hell. At least you would know for sure where you were and what to expect.

Instead, the same moronic real-life trends of "all-in-one" this and "multiuse" that were in effect on the other side. He blamed the Swiss. They'd paved the way with a pocketknife that could also be a screwdriver or scissors or tweezers or a corkscrew or a saw! Next there were the computer guys who'd created a telephone that was also a flashlight, multiplex (itself an abomination of a movie theater), radio, camera, postal service, and spying device, if you only knew the correct combination of dance moves—one touch, tap, double-click, swipe—and avoided the unavoidable side button, which turned the whole damn thing off. Now here he was in some complex version of heaven, hell, purgatory, and life before.

"Where am I?" Champs expected a complicated acronym. He wondered if perpetual weariness was the sentence for someone between alive and dead.

Laura looked worried. "You're in the hospital, Champs. We thought you had a heart attack after Mel's baby was born. Benji Raj? Do you remember?"

It all came flooding back to him. The brown baby with Pat's eyes, the chicken farmer with Jeffrey's eyes, the pain in his chest, something about a fire, and then rain.

"A fire?"

"Yes, but there wasn't an actual fire," Laura responded. "Chicken Ray yelled 'fire' because yelling 'help' in a hospital doesn't raise any eyebrows. We thought you were dying. You terrified us."

"I wouldn't recommend trying that kind of stunt again," scolded the disappointing nurse. Champs was delighted she wasn't an angel after all. "Water birth is a thing, I grant you that, but laboring under ceiling sprinklers to the sound of an air-raid siren is not ideal. I expect there will be lawsuits. My health insurance premium will go up. Yours, too."

So the sweet rain was not heaven-sent, thought Champs. He hadn't been blessed after all. Or had he? He was alive. That was better than dead. Perhaps the ceiling-sprinkler blessing was not an initiation into death. Maybe it was a baptism to new life? A wake-up call? But what had he awakened to?

"Not a heart attack? Then what?" Champs worried about his diminished physical state, recovery time, and unpleasant lifestyle changes.

"Takotsubo cardiomyopathy," said the disappointing nurse. "I'll let your daughter explain. You missed breakfast. The next meal is lunch, unless one of your family members smuggles something in from Denny's. I'll be back later to check on you." She scribbled on her clipboard and left the room.

"'Takotsubo' is a Japanese—"

"Can you use normal words? I'm tired."

"Yes, sorry. It's called broken-heart syndrome. It mostly happens to women, but some men, too, usually after an emotional shock. The symptoms mimic a heart attack, but there is no heart disease present so no long-term implications. The doctors want to monitor you for a few days. They want you to rest. Then you can come home and return to your normal life. Although they recommend stress counseling."

This all sounded like bullshit to Champs. Either you had a heart attack, or you didn't. He felt ill enough to call it a heart attack. The expression "hitting rock bottom" seemed apropos. He felt weak, and good God, tears streamed down his cheeks. Maybe doctors didn't consider uncontrollable tear production a serious long-term implication, but Champs did. He grasped at something to engage his mind.

"Taco scuba. Is that what you said?"

Laura chuckled before explaining. "No, takotsubo. It's a Japanese word for 'octopus trap.' Your heart looks like an octopus trap—kinda squeezed in the middle like you tightened a belt—when you have an attack. The blood can't pump through, and it feels like a heart attack, but it isn't. They really don't know a lot about it."

This new information struck Champs as karmic retribution for all the seafood he'd trapped and eaten throughout his life. He imagined the ghosts of long-digested Maryland crabs and Maine lobsters approaching a Wizard of Oz–like octopus to request revenge on a particularly ruthless fisherman. He thought it would work well as a mobster-style film starring Al Pacino. Champs loved Al Pacino.

Laura's cell phone chirped. "Ready for some visitors?"

Champs couldn't think of anything worse. His eyes watered and threatened to spill again. For some inexplicable reason, he thought of his mother and longed for her presence. The need was visceral and heartbreaking. Laura had said this octopus thing usually happened to women. Was that because they were naturally overemotional? Was this what women felt like? He forced himself to stop sniveling.

"Oh, Champs, I'm sorry. Everyone can wait while you get some rest. Here, let's tuck you in, and I'll stay until you fall asleep. It's okay. I'll be right here."

Laura patted his tears away, wrapped a hospital blanket around his shoulders, and held his hand in hers. He was too exhausted to feel embarrassed or push her away. He let Laura comfort him like he was a child, closed his eyes, and surrendered to sleep.

Faith

Champs opened his eyes and tried to locate the source of the smell pervading the room. He saw a Josanne shape sitting near him, working on one of her samplers. A blurry, but recognizable, red and white Chick-fil-A bag was at the bottom of his bed. Now, this was a heaven he could appreciate.

"Josanne? That you?" he mumbled, unable to generate any volume. He felt old and weakened by a broken heart, a dragon slain not by St. George, but by a trap-wielding Octopus of Oz. He wasn't overall dead, but he knew something in him had died, or died down, anyway. It was time to not expect much.

"Yes, darlin'. How are you feeling?" Josanne replied.

Champs coughed. "Blind. My glasses anywhere around here?"

Josanne located his glasses in the top drawer of the hospital night-stand. She placed them on his face, and his fuzzy surroundings came into sharp focus. Hospital room: machines, tubes, puke colors. A prisonlike cell on a ward. Some places were best seen without clarity. He took his glasses off, propped himself up, and reached for the food bag.

"They wanted to wake you up to feed you their hospital food, but I insisted they leave you alone. You need your rest, and I know when a man wakes up proper in a hospital bed, he needs good ol' fried food to stir the appetite. So you enjoy it. That's root beer in the cup there."

Champs sucked on the straw and let the fizzy, cold, sweet liquid tingle down his throat. He chomped into the fried chicken sandwich and stuffed in two waffle fries for good measure. It took so long to chew it all that by the time he swallowed, he'd lost interest in eating any more. He sighed.

"Don't worry, sweetheart. It's the nature of being in a hospital. Everything feels tiresome for a while, but you'll get your mojo back. You're gonna need it to see you through those sleepless nights with a new baby. He is such an angel, that Benji Raj. I told Larry it was a shame we'll be going just when that sweet babe arrived. Jeffrey and Mel are besotted with each other and with that dumplin' Benji Raj. That's the Lord's work, there. Who woulda thought a young gal would come out here with one brother's baby in her belly and fall in love with the other brother just in time for the birth of an Arabian angel to bless their new romance? It's just like one of my Harlequins. Shame on me, babbling like this. I can't believe I missed the whole thing. I know if Pat were still alive, she'd be pleased as punch. Aren't you, darlin'?"

"I don't know what to be anymore, Josanne." Champs took a deep breath. "Turns out I'm not Jeffrey's father, and David's not Benji Raj's father, but I am the grandfather of a little boy named Thomas who died before I met him. And Pat is dead." He put a waffle fry on his tongue and let it dissolve like a fast-food communion. It helped hold back his tears.

"That sure is a lot to come to terms with. But you will. Trust me, I've seen it happen again and again. But you have to learn some new skills, Champs. You've got to get yourself some faith."

Champs shook his head. "You know I don't believe in all that God stuff. No offense."

"None taken. Darlin', faith isn't a matter of belief. It's a matter of practice. Like a muscle that needs strengthening in order to carry you through the hard times. I told you before, death is like an earthquake. It shifts the plates underneath us for good. There's no reverse button, no predictable sequence of steps that repairs or restores things. And meanwhile with your foundation in pieces, there's nothing left to prop up all the other crapola you've been storing away in the attic for years. The whole house, and everything in it, crumbles to dust. You can't stop it."

Champs placed another waffle fry on his tongue. If this was a pep talk, he wasn't feeling it. Tears rolled down his cheeks, and he made a slurping sound with his straw, hoping that would cheer him up. It didn't.

Josanne continued. "The fact is, Champs, you aren't the person you were before. Maybe you never were the person you thought you were before. You've got to accept it and stop looking over your shoulder. Tend to who you are now. Tend to what's in front of you. Remember, you're not alone. I'm gonna help you and Larry's gonna help you. And Laura's gonna help you and Zoe and Hannah and Brian will help you. And Jeffrey and Mel and Benji Raj will help you. And Raymond's gonna help you, too—if you'll let him. So right now you're crying. Go on and tend to your crying. Tend to each new thing as it arises with all the faith you can muster. Practice. It gets easier, I promise."

Champs let a high tide of tears overflow and run down his cheeks. He sobbed as Josanne picked up a sampler and stitched. She stayed near him but did not try to calm him. His body heaved; his nose and eyes became the heads of rivers that snaked down his T-shirt, turning it to marshland. It was a relief to tend to his crying instead of holding it back. He let his body do what it needed to do. He rode his grief like a current to the wide open mouth of the river. And he didn't drown.

When he finished, he wiped his face and put his glasses on, ready for whatever aftershock came next. Josanne was prepared with a glass of water. He drank as if from the fountain of youth. She sat down to put the finishing stitches on the sampler. He watched her tie off the yellow thread. For a moment it appeared to him like a strand of spun gold. He imagined a long-haired woman with full cherry lips playing the harp in the corner of the room.

Josanne removed the embroidery frame and fit the finished canvas into its final frame behind glass. "This is for you, Champs. I hope I captured the everlasting bond between you and Pat."

He took the sampler and held it as tenderly as he'd held Benji Raj the day before. In golden thread, it said, "In Loving Memory of Pat, the River That Runs Through Me." Josanne had cross-stitched the Sassafras River across the middle of the sampler, end to end. She'd captured its forested red banks, sandy shoals, and rippling, brown-green surface.

There was a density to the sampler. It was full of love. The river was framed by a border motif of goldfinches alternating with leaves from the sassafras tree, recognizable by their distinct yellow mitten shape. Champs felt his heart grow big, like a blimp inside his chest.

"Oh, Josanne," he said, "This is . . . This is . . ."

They held each other's gaze with teary eyes, overcome with bitter-sweet emotions.

Later, when it was time, Champs would reflect on his afternoon in the hospital with Josanne. All along he'd been suspicious of the fight-or-flight instinct. Now he knew why. There was a third option: faith. And he didn't need to join a church to find it. Thank God for that.

Visiting Hours

Laura came back in the evening as Champs woke from another nap. She brought clean clothes, toiletries, and a new pair of pajamas and slippers. They were old man's pajamas, standard-issue for Egret's Pond geezers in Ruston Hall. And slippers? Jesus Christ! Only Ol' Champs wore slippers. But Champs didn't feel like arguing. In fact, he felt very mellow.

As Laura stepped out, the disappointing nurse took over. She removed his catheter, heart monitor, and IV. Then she helped him use the facilities and change into the new pajamas. Surprising himself, Champs delighted in the soft comfort and dignity provided by his new nightclothes, slippers and all. Freshly shaven, smelling like Irish Spring soap, Champs left his made-up hospital bed intact and sat in a chair by the window, ready to receive his visitors. He felt like a king.

David came first. Champs stood up to greet his son with as manly a hug as he could manage; he was new to this kind of thing, after all. David leaned on the edge of the hospital bed facing Champs, who settled back into his chair. He asked the usual questions. Champs answered in brief. There wasn't much to report, and David wasn't a student of irony, so Champs skipped the part about the octopus trap.

"I'm going back to Kimmie," David announced. "Mel is fine with it. Kim wants me to keep seeing the therapist. She thinks we both need outside support to work through everything, especially Mom passing away. It hit her hard, too, and the kids. I fly back tonight."

"Good. When you and Kim are ready, I want to visit. Maybe we could go back to that lodge again. The one on the big blue lake?"

"You'd do that? You'd fly out on your own to see us? I thought you hated California."

Champs answered with a chuckle. "Oh sure, that hasn't changed. Goddamn hippies and communists."

"I can't wait to tell Kimmie. She'll be so happy. And me. And the kids. We've missed you. Thank you, Champs. Thank you for everything." David leaned over to give his father one more hug before leaving.

Champs felt like he was glowing from the inside. Anything seemed possible. He wanted to give thanks to the Octopus of Oz. He was a different man, a hopeful man. And a different man deserved a different name. What the hell, he'd give it a try.

"David? There's one thing I'd like to ask you before you go."

"Sure, anything."

"Can you call me Dad from now on?"

David grinned. "Of course. What do you want the kids to call you?"

"How about Gramps?"

"Done. Goodbye, Dad. I'll see you soon."

Champs gave him an approving nod.

The disappointing nurse came in to take his vitals, give him a dose of codeine, and hand him a tray of hospital food. She stood over him with her hands on her hips, glaring, until he ate a few bites of the tasteless shepherd's pie and soggy green beans. The nurse seemed satisfied with that and took the tray away, leaving him with the Jell-O cup, a plastic spoon, and a fresh glass of water.

"We want you in bed and ready to sleep by eight p.m.," she said. "I'll be back one last time tonight with a sleeping tablet. If you don't have a BM in the morning, let me know, and I'll get you some Metamucil for that. Push that button over there if you need me to clear out any visitors. You need your rest."

Champs nodded. Despite her gruff tone, he appreciated the matter-of-fact way she dealt with his body. It gave him confidence that the physical part of his recovery was in good hands. This nurse knew how to take care of things.

Laura, Brian, Zoe, and Hannah came next. Zoe galloped her imaginary horse across the floor, dismounted, and flung herself into Champs. Hannah approached him skeptically with a stack of boat classified ads and fishing magazines.

"You look bad," she said.

"Hannah!" Laura scolded. "That's not nice."

Champs winked at Hannah to let her know he was just fine with her assessment. He would always value her pragmatic perspective. It reminded him of Pat.

"Can I have this Jell-O, Champs?" asked Zoe. She didn't wait for an answer and tucked herself into the hospital bed as if she were the patient. "Mommy, call the nurse. I need her to check my heart and temperature and bring me more Jell-O. Where's the TV? Want me to ask the nurse for a TV, too? I can do that. Is she mean to you, Champs? I'll kick her butt."

Champs smiled. "No, she's just efficient."

Hannah sat cross-legged at the bottom of the bed. Laura took the remaining chair, and Brian rocked back and forth on his heels with his hands clasped behind his back.

"Not a big fan of hospitals, huh, Brian?" Champs asked.

"No, I'm not. Do you mind if I use your bathroom?"

"Go for it."

Champs raised an eyebrow at Laura.

"I think he's having issues with the cafeteria food he ate last night," she said.

"Yeah, Daddy has the squirts," said Zoe, making a wet farting sound to emphasize her point.

"Ah," said Champs, smothering a giggle. He would never be too old for toilet humor.

"That's enough, Zoe," Laura said.

Zoe ended her noisemaking, exchanging frowns with Champs.

Laura picked up the framed memorial sampler from the nightstand and studied it. Tears gathered in her eyes. "This sampler is beautiful. Josanne really captured you and Mom. I can feel it."

"Josanne and I had a long chat this afternoon. Never thought I'd hear myself say this, but I'll miss her when they leave." Champs smiled and changed the subject. "So, what are your plans?"

"Brian will drive home tomorrow with the girls. His mother will stay with them for a few days to help out while I'm looking after you and helping Mel and Jeffrey with Benji Raj. They'll come to visit you before they leave the hospital. I don't know if they discussed it with you, but the plan is for them to move into the master bedroom in the main cabin, at least until they can find a place of their own. Are you okay with the second bedroom when you're cleared to leave here?"

"I have a different plan in mind." Champs didn't have a plan so much as an impulse. He decided to tend to it.

Brian emerged from the bathroom and Laura invited him to take her seat. She joined her daughters on the bed, handing over her cell phone to Zoe, who wanted access to her Pokémon account. Hannah poured her dad a glass of water.

"A different plan?" Laura prompted, her jaw clenched.

Champs shifted in his chair and cleared his throat. "I don't know if it's too late, but I've had a change of heart, you might say. I'm thinking about moving back to Egret's Pond. Taking up that apartment in Ruston Hall."

"Really? Are you serious?" Laura sounded both hopeful and dubious.

"Oh, sure. I'm serious. It's not working out for me at the cabin. It's not like it used to be. It feels like I'm trying too hard to swim upstream, to re-create the past. Soon it will be cold, too. And with Larry and

Josanne moving on and you moving away, I think I'll be more comfortable where I have more time to tend to myself. I've got this nifty new outfit, too. I'll fit right in at Ruston!"

Laura ignored the joke. "Wow, Champs. This is a big decision. I mean, I agree with you. But you hated it at Egret's Pond. Are you sure about this?"

"Laura, the only thing I'm sure about is that I'm tired of fighting. I need a simple base to make a fresh start. Figure things out. Can you get me that apartment?"

"Yes, but not immediately. I kept your name and deposit on the waiting list just in case. I'll call tomorrow and find out how long it will be. You may have to spend a few more weeks in your cabin, but hopefully not too long."

"Good. I'm glad that's settled. Thank you, Laura. I know I've been a real pain in the ass about this. I'm sorry. You didn't deserve all that hassle. And you did a nice job with all that redecorating."

"Are you gonna get a girlfriend at the bird puddle place?" asked Zoe.

"Zoe, that's none of your business," said Laura.

"Only if you and Hannah pick out a good one for me!" Champs said with a wink to Hannah.

Brian and Laura laughed.

Champs stifled a yawn. Cheerfulness was tiring.

"Well, we better get going. Leave you to your rest," said Brian.

"You better get some rest yourself, Brian," Champs chided. "You look worse than I feel and that can't be good. Let me know if you need any help with your move. I think you're making a good decision, there, son. I'm proud of you and Laura. Real proud."

"Thanks, Champs. That means a lot. I hope you'll visit us often. I think you'll like salmon fishing in the Columbia River in Washington. C'mon, girls, let's rally!"

Champs pushed himself off the chair to shake Brian's hand and give Zoe and Hannah a hug goodbye. He embraced Laura and told her he loved her.

"I love you, too, Champs."

"Oh, that's another thing."

Laura looked at him sideways.

"If it's okay with you, I don't want you to call me Champs anymore. I never liked it. Call me Dad, instead."

Laura stifled a sob. Champs drew her in for another hug.

"Can we call you something else, too? I know, I know, how about Gramps?" offered Zoe.

"Gramps sounds perfect," said Gramps. He looked at Hannah, who gave him a winning smile and two thumbs up.

They whooshed out the door, and Champs eased himself back into the chair. He sipped from his water glass and let his eyes rest on the new sampler. He imagined the river running through him as he allowed himself to sink under the surface. In the current, in the flow, he found Pat. Not the Pat he'd married or the one he'd always counted on to take care of things. Not imaginary Pat or a memory of Pat. Not the urn Pat, either. Just Her. And he knew Her for the first time. And he did not have to grasp at the knowing nor let go of the knowing nor alter the knowing nor question it. He could visit again whenever he wanted and stay as long as he needed. The same was true of the Sassafras. In fact, Pat and the river were inseparable.

The disappointing nurse returned. "Visiting hours are over," she said.

Champs emerged from the river feeling a little raunchy. He decided to tend to it.

"Have you come to tuck me in?" He winked twice.

"Don't you get all snarky with me, Mr. Noland. Remember I'm the one with the needles and the restraints and I'm not afraid to use them."

Champs replied with a cheesy smile. "Is that a threat or a promise?"

"God help us. We've got another pervert on the ward."

Bird Dog

"Dad? Of course, I'll call you Dad," Jeffrey said at the end of his visit the next morning. Champs hadn't ventured into a more extended conversation about Chicken Ray's revelation because of the peachy glow that had surrounded Mel, Jeffrey, and Benji Raj when they'd arrived in his room. He hadn't wanted to pop the bubble. Not yet. Maybe never.

He spent another four days in the hospital in his own bubble. Everything appeared in soft focus and suspended. He thought he was falling in love with the disappointing nurse. After confessing his feelings, she immediately reduced his pain relief in half. Then half again the next day. The day before the doctor released him, she gave him nothing. His lovey-dovey feelings vanished. The bubble burst.

Champs decided to pull out some of his "act like an old man to annoy people" moves. He may have been a new man in some ways, but he wasn't completely reformed. Kicks were kicks. He pretended he was deaf and blind.

"I think I liked the pervert better," the disappointing nurse said.

"What?" Champs cupped his ear and squinted at the chair as if he'd mistaken it for the nurse.

She raised her voice. "I said, I think I liked the pervert better."

"You like pervert butter?" Champs pushed the call button.

The nurse slapped his hand away from the buzzer. "What do you think you're doing, Mr. Noland? I'm right here. I know you can see me. Stop calling another nurse. We're short-staffed as it is."

A second nurse rushed in. "What is it, Mr. Noland? Are you okay?"

"I want to talk to the shift supervisor. This nurse here just told me she likes to butter perverts and then hit me. I'm afraid of what she's gonna do next. Also, I'm blind."

"Mr. Noland. If you're blind and Nurse Caroline likes to butter perverts, I don't give a good goddamn." The second nurse glared at him and left the room.

"That didn't work out well for you, did it, Mr. Noland?" said pervert Nurse Caroline.

"What?" Champs feigned hearing loss again and lifted his right buttock to toot. Well, she did keep giving him that wretched Metamucil.

On the day of his release, Laura packed up his belongings, stowed the Pat sampler in a cardboard box for safe transit, and wheeled him out of the hospital into a used, pea-soup-colored Subaru with beige cloth seats. It smelled like Old Spice aftershave.

"Whose car is this?" he asked.

"It's yours," Laura replied, starting the car with a push of a button. "The registration on the Windstar lapsed fourteen months ago. I had to get it inspected, and it didn't pass. The repairs were too costly. They don't even make half the parts it would need. Anyway, Larry helped me trade it in for this. It's fun to drive and economical, too. You'll see."

"Huh," Champs said. It was a foreign-make car but it wasn't too bad and came with a well-worn feeling he appreciated. A little on the small side though. "How am I gonna fit my golf clubs in the back of here?"

"Golf clubs? What golf clubs? You don't even play golf, Cham—I mean, Dad." Laura blushed.

"Well, I'm moving to a retirement community, I drink eight ounces of Metamucil every day, I wear pajamas and slippers, and my goddamn boat is in the boneyard. It's a perfect time to take up golf."

Laura laughed. "I'll get you one of those matching plaid golfer outfits for Christmas."

"Oh sure. Maybe they'll put me on the front cover of the Egret's Pond brochure under the headline 'Old dogs can learn new tricks.'" He snorted. "So, thank you for staying back this week and helping out. I'm sorry we didn't get to do that service for your mom."

"It's okay. I don't know why I was in such a hurry. As Josanne says, 'there's time for everything if you take it stitch by stitch.' She's doing a lot better with her arthritis. Mel's been making her a special tea that works wonders for her pain."

"I'm gonna guess that Larry's been dipping his cup in that teapot."

Laura nodded. "I don't know what worries me more: a stoned, gun-toting neighbor or a nursing, drug-dealing sister-in-law."

"Purely medicinal drug-dealing. Did you say sister-in-law?"

"Well, it's a little early to call it, but I have a feeling it might turn out that way."

Champs smiled. "How's Benji Raj?"

"Oh, Benji Raj is doing great. The parents? They haven't got a clue! Jeffrey can build boats and houses from scratch, but putting an IKEA crib together just about undid him. I think 'fuck' will be Benji Raj's first word." They both laughed. "Anyway, he put the whole contraption into the back of his pickup, along with all the cloth diapers, wrappers, and paraphernalia which Mel had insisted they use, and drove it all to the dump. He came back with a truckload of Huggies and beer!"

"That's my son, all right. Good for him. So where does the baby sleep?"

"Jeffrey built him a small canoe, and he sleeps in that. It's clever. You can rock it and everything."

"Chicken Ray around much?" Champs was afraid to ask, but he

wanted to know the lay of the land before arriving to crash the party. He wondered if the ache of knowing he wasn't Jeffrey's biological father would ever go away. Maybe he'd carry it with him for the rest of his life.

"Here and there, yeah. He works with Jeffrey a lot at the warehouse. If you want to talk about any of that with me, you know, the Chicken Ray thing, I'm happy to listen. Anytime."

"Never mind that. It's my turn to listen. Tell me more about Thomas."

It took the whole ride back to the cabin for Laura to finish. Champs hadn't interrupted once.

"I wish I'd met him," he said as they pulled into the overgrown driveway tracks.

"Me too, Dad. Thanks for listening." Laura wiped the tears and mascara stains from her cheeks.

Larry and Millie greeted Champs as he got out of the car. At least, he thought it was Millie. She stood at attention at Larry's side, shorn like a sheep and wearing a thick camouflage-patterned collar with two metal studs on the inside.

"What the hell did you do to my dog?" Champs barked.

"Laura asked me to take care of her. Millie's a good bird dog, you know. I've been training her. All she needed was a little grooming and some discipline to get in shape."

"Doesn't she look great, Champs?" said Laura. "She smells good, too. She's been dewormed, neutered, and treated for ticks and fleas. And Chicken Ray knows a guy who installed an invisible fence so she can't get out anymore." She pointed to the flags that dotted the yard, defining Millie's boundaries.

Champs noticed Millie's lip curl up in disgust, but she refrained from baring her teeth.

"C'mon," said Larry. "Let's get you a beer." He opened the porch door, and Champs waited for Millie to enter first. She put her tail between her legs and walked away.

"Oh, she's got her own door now," Larry explained. "Chicken Ray knows a guy who fixed the screening on your porch and installed a durable doggie flap. You can lock it at night, so she doesn't wander out, and unwanted visitors don't wander in."

"It's worked out well," said Laura. "I'll see if Benji Raj and his parents are awake." She hurried into the cabin.

Millie pushed through the dog door and curled up in her odor-controlled dog bed. Champs looked around his porch while Larry got the beers. Did something always have to change every time he left the cabin? He noticed three ten-pound bags of dry dog food for overweight dogs, a large box of mint dental chews, two metal dog bowls, and a brown leash attached to a harness hanging from a duck-shaped hook near the SMEGerator. Champs thought if he ever got dementia, they could fit him with an electric collar and throw him out here with Millie; she seemed to have all the essentials. He'd been through hell in the hospital, but it didn't compare to the hell his dog had been through in the last week.

"I'm sorry about this, Millie," he whispered, bending down to scratch her belly. She gave him the silent treatment.

Champs stood up and accepted a beer from Larry. He cracked it open, enjoying the hiss and the feel of the cold can. After seven days in a controlled climate, the heat and humidity enveloped him like rising bread dough. "What happened to the other chickens?" he asked.

Larry confessed that he'd shot the remaining three and turned them into broilers after watching a how-to video on YouTube. They were in his freezer, ready to roast when the weather cooled. Champs wondered why someone would delay a good chicken dinner because of the weather. He was about to suggest they try smoking one on the barbecue when Mel, Jeffrey, and Laura—proudly holding her new nephew, Benji Raj—came out of the cabin. It was his best homecoming ever.

Heartleaf Philodendron

Over the next several weeks, Champs did his best to fit into the whirlwind of activity at the cabin. But the chaos of an infant was jarring. Champs had gone straight back to work when his children were born, so he'd been spared the minute-by-minute drama, exhaustion, and mess that taking care of a baby all day entailed. Just watching it wore him out. He marveled at Mel's stamina and did his best to keep things clean and put away. Including himself.

A new routine helped. Champs tucked himself into his room at eight p.m. and stayed there until six a.m. The first few nights, he'd disturbed the baby with his frequent trips to the bathroom. So Champs had found an old bucket in the boat shed, which he'd moved to his bedroom for nighttime use. Sometimes he heard Benji Raj crying in the night or Mel or Jeffrey pacing around the cabin at odd hours. It was comforting to Champs. The sounds of other people nearby, their shushing and shuffling, gave him a sense of companionship during his bouts of insomnia.

Jeffrey and Mel's romance blossomed despite the lack of sleep. Jeffrey told Champs they were taking it slow and seeing where things led. But Champs knew that was an understatement; they fawned over each other like love-struck teens, just as he and Pat had done. Love at first sight. The rest of the time, Jeffrey worked long hours at the warehouse repairing and building boats, hiring and training staff.

Champs took it slow. He watched a lot of TV with Benji Raj in his lap while Mel took a shower, had a nap, or made a short trip to Dirty Girls. Mostly, though, Benji Raj was on the breast, in his canoe bed, or tied to the front of Mel in a strappy fabric contraption called a Wilkinet. She didn't look much like a drug dealer, medicinal or otherwise. Champs wondered where she got her supply and who else was on her client list. He didn't want to get arrested. Although it occurred to him that there wasn't much difference between life in prison and life in Egret's Pond.

One day, when it was too hot and sticky outside even for Champs, he turned off the TV and asked Mel for details about the special tea.

Mel laughed. "I was wondering when you'd ask about that. You know I have a green thumb, right?"

Champs nodded.

"Well, back in California, I kept an herb garden at Raj's nursery. When a friend asked me to grow marijuana to help with her migraines, I agreed. It's just another herb, as far as I'm concerned. It didn't take long for Raj to get wind of it, so to speak. I thought he'd fire me, but he didn't. He came up with a business plan to sell to uptight professionals with chronic stress and depressed old folks with chronic pain. No offense."

"None taken." Champs was fascinated. "Go on."

"Raj set up a grow house at the nursery, bought the seeds and supplies, and paid the bills. I grew, processed, and packaged the product, and buried it in the soil while servicing the plants. Only people with heartleaf philodendrons were clients. I was prepared to claim it was biodegradable, biodynamic fertilizer if anyone got suspicious."

"I take it someone got suspicious and pointed in Raj's direction?" Champs saw that coming a mile away. He felt like Hercule Poirot.

"Yep. Raj's dick of a brother-in-law figured it out and tipped off the police. That's when Raj closed the nursery and told me to make myself scarce. I stuffed the last harvest of buds into Ziploc baggies and hid them in Band-Aid tins in my suitcase."

"But what about the sniffer dogs?"

"They're trained to sniff for explosives and heroin now. Nobody cares about weed anymore." Mel patted Champs on the knee. "And don't worry, you can tell Laura I'm not growing here, and my California supply is nearly gone. Only you and your neighbors have been the beneficiaries."

"Oh, that's too bad. I was hoping to get a heartleaf philodendron in here."

Their laughter woke Benji Raj. While Mel tended to her baby, Champs headed over to Josanne's for cross-stitching and what he presumed would be the last of the special tea. He enjoyed his visits and went two or three times a week for an hour or two of needlework. They didn't always have special tea. But when they did, there was plenty of chuckling and not much stitching.

Champs had continued his work on the sampler for the mother who'd lost her child. The third time he picked it up, he realized he was working on Thomas's memorial sampler. He tried to give it back to Josanne, telling her he couldn't do it justice. She handed him a needle threaded with blue floss and told him he was the *only* one who could do it justice. Stitch by stitch, he felt closer and closer to Thomas and Laura.

One evening, while he was pondering what image to feature on the sampler, a great blue heron appeared in his mind. It flew out of a sassafras tree into an apricot-colored sunset. Champs knew that the heron was Thomas. Inspired, he took the idea to Josanne, who created a blue heron pattern for him to follow. Since then, the pterodactyls on the river had no longer bothered him. They were talented fishermen, after all. They deserved his respect.

Chicken Ray made himself scarce at first. Champs assumed that Mel or Jeffrey took Benji Raj to the warehouse for visits. Then one morning, Champs emerged from the bedroom with his makeshift latrine to find Chicken Ray in the kitchen with a pink box of donuts and two jumbo Styrofoam cups of coffee. It was awkward. Champs wasn't ready for a truce.

Chicken Ray offered a coffee to Champs. He responded by offering his pee-bucket to Ray as if signaling a duel. Chicken Ray accepted the challenge. He poured Champs's urine down the sink, rinsed the bucket, and dried it with a paper towel. Then he looked at Champs as if to say, "Now what?" Champs wasn't sure what the code of dueling required him to do next. Parry a blow with a wooden spoon? Blind his opponent with a hot cup of coffee? What would the swashbuckling Errol Flynn do?

"Donut?" Chicken Ray gestured to the pink box. Champs had never refused a donut and wasn't about to start then. He put down his proverbial sword, nodded, and bit into a cruller. Honor restored, they resumed their friendship as if nothing had ever happened.

4 4

Molting

At the crack of dawn near the end of August, Champs was in bed clamping a pillow over his head to muffle the sounds of Benji Raj's screaming. In the last few days, six-week-old Benji Raj had found his lungs and decided it was his job to scream nonstop. Mel had rushed him to the hospital one morning, to be sent back with a diagnosis of "babies cry a lot" and a prognosis of "it will get better." It didn't seem to be getting better.

The more Mel worried, the more Benji Raj fussed. She tried to soothe him with her breast, but he refused to take it. She changed his diaper every four minutes, and that only advanced his diaper rash. She jiggled keys in front of him, put him in the sink for a warm baking soda bath, rocked him, swaddled him, but nothing seemed to work. Champs wondered whether there was any special tea left. Maybe a teaspoon or two would soothe the kid so they could all get some rest.

His door swung open, and Mel yanked the pillow from his head.

She stood over him, a red-eyed monster, his wailing grandson in one arm and the Wilkinet contraption in the other.

"You have to help me," she pleaded. "I can't stand it another second. Take him away from me. Please."

"Let me get dressed first, woman!" Champs yelled over the squalling baby.

He had been planning on taking the Yammy out today. He was feeling a lot better and thought a short boat ride and some sunshine would do him good. Champs sighed, disappointed. What the hell was he supposed to do with a crying Benji Raj at the crack of dawn? He found his glasses and threw on some shorts, a grubby T-shirt, and a "Don't Be a Dumb Bass" fishing cap before stumbling out of the bedroom.

Mel pressed the squirming baby face-first into his chest, then pushed the Wilkinet against Benji Raj's back and commanded Champs to hold it in place. He did his best as she wound the straps over his shoulders, through some loops, and around his waist before tightening them like a corset in a complicated combination of crisscrossing fabric and a double knot. Champs could hardly breathe, and Benji Raj kept right on wailing.

"There," she said. "Take him out of here. Go!"

"What if he needs feeding?"

"There's some formula in the kitchen and a bottle. We've never used it before, so you'll have to figure that out. You're a chemist, right? Pretend you're in the lab. I don't care what you do with him, just bring him back alive." Mel ran into the bathroom. He heard her sobbing over the sound of the shower. Steam escaped from under the door.

Champs figured as long as the baby was hollering, it was still alive, so he chose to ignore the fuss and pursue his earlier plan. It was difficult moving around with an active howler monkey bandaged to his torso, but he got the hang of it soon enough. His years of maneuvering with a solid beer belly came in handy. He prepared a bottle of formula and a liverwurst sandwich on pumpernickel. Tossing both in the cooler, he added two light beers and a tray of ice. As he left the porch, he grabbed a sun hat for Benji Raj and a bottle of baby sunscreen. Champs gave himself a mental high five for remembering protection for his grandson.

Millie followed him across the dewy lawn. As they approached the car, she dropped her ears and tucked her tail between her legs.

"Is it your haircut or this screaming kid you don't like?" asked Champs. "I'm gonna assume it's both. C'mon then, girl, jump in."

Champs set the cooler in the backseat and waited patiently for Millie to board. She whimpered her refusal.

"I know it's not the Windstar, but *Swee'Pea* here is a real hummer. And you can jump in all by yourself." Champs had named his new car *Swee'Pea* after Popeye's mischievous adopted "boy-kid." To his constant annoyance, everyone assumed he'd meant Sweet Pea, as in the garden vegetable.

The dog wouldn't budge.

"Fine, then. Suit yourself. If you want a boat ride, you can walk down to the dock."

Champs looked at the car and frowned. "Okay, Benji Raj. You and I have to figure out how we're gonna get in this thing."

So far, he noted, taking care of a baby was only a matter of logistics, as long as you didn't mind the noise. He was good at logistics. "Easy peasy," he said, full of confidence. Champs moved the driver's seat as far back as it would go and ducked into the seat. With his arms and legs stretched straight out, he could still reach the steering wheel and the pedals. It was awkward, but it worked. Fortunately, the seat belt was long enough to accommodate his baby-bulked torso. He clicked it in place and eased *Swee'Pea* onto the gravel road. "And we're off!"

Within seconds, Benji Raj was asleep.

They reached the turn for the dock in three minutes, but Champs didn't want to risk waking up the baby, so he did another lap around Deadrise Cove. As they passed the cabin, Millie ran barking toward the car, slamming on her dog brakes right before reaching the edge of the lawn. It dawned on Champs why she hadn't joined them in the first place.

He stopped and got out of the car, careful not to bump Benji Raj's head on the car frame.

"To hell with this thing," he said as he threw Millie's shock collar into the thick ivy hedge. It disappeared things as well as the coir rug on his porch.

The dog rode shotgun to the dock, sticking her head out of the open window, tongue lolling to enjoy the breeze.

Benji Raj continued to sleep while Champs balanced his extra weight along the unstable and splintering dock. Millie took advantage of the time to splash in the river, roll in the sand, and crunch a fish head on shore. She was like a soldier on furlough, Champs thought. So was he. He prepared the Yammy to leave and whistled for Millie. On their way out of the cove, Champs saluted the blue heron in its usual perch on the bank of the river.

"Great morning for fishing," he called out.

The new boat glided across the smooth, silky river. Champs was eager to hammer the throttle and see how fast the highfalutin speedboat could go. But he didn't risk it—there was a baby on board, after all. Cruising downriver, he opened a beer. It was on the early side for beer drinking, but it was summer, and he was on an excursion. What difference did it make when he drank a beer? There were no rules to follow here and nobody watching. It was the "freestyle lifestyle" he'd dreamed about with the bonus of a grandson to share it with.

Champs admired how responsive the Yammy was to his handling. He remembered when he'd first driven an automatic car with power steering after years of busting his ass on a manual everything. This felt the same: effortless compared to *Tetanus*. Surprisingly, he liked the polished and conditioned materials, the understated design, and the sportiness of the Yamaha. It was a relief to be rid of the cranky old hulls of the Windstar and the Sea Nymph, he realized.

A relief, too, to be rid of his own crusty shell. Champs had long admired the cussedness of the blue crab. Its ornery personality and refusal to submit to rhyme or reason. The hard shell it wielded to ward off an attack and prevent injury. Like the crab, he'd built a solid outer shield for protection and had nurtured an attitude of scorn toward change. That was the way to stay safe, he'd thought: Resist! Resist! He'd forgotten along the way that crabs must molt to survive. When their carapace threatens their survival by restricting growth, they molt. The crabs risk being naked and soft while a new shell takes shape.

"I should've molted a long time ago," he said to the river, the sleeping infant, and the shaved dog.

Champs thought about how much enjoyment he'd denied himself by holding on to his aging cabin, van, and fishing boat—not to mention his crusty old self. It occurred to him it was Laura who'd initiated these changes. She'd been trying to help him, not hurt him. In his cussedness, he'd decided she was selfish and greedy—that nothing was ever good enough for her. In fact, what was not good enough for her was his steady slide into laziness, loss of self-respect, and loneliness. Pat had taught their daughter well. So what if Laura was obsessed with antibacterials? She had her reasons for that. Her doctor had told her a bacterial infection could have been the cause of Thomas's stillbirth. When your dad ran a boat called *Tetanus*, it was a natural step to assume his whole lifestyle was at fault.

It was high tide, so Champs flipped open his clamshell to call the drawbridge operator. While he waited, he tooled around in circles near Jeffrey's boatbuilding warehouse. The rotten pilings and collapsed wharf were gone, replaced by a sizable dock and a pier with numbered boat slips. A tall, covered working bay with a boat lift that could accommodate everything from a canoe to a Chesapeake Bay skipjack flanked one side of the dockyard like a sturdy sentinel. On shore, the rusted, corrugated-metal-roofed warehouse and peeling, warped outbuildings had been bulldozed and trucked away. A repurposed, arching airplane hangar painted sky blue with enormous front-and-back aluminum sliding doors was open to the river. Inside, Jeffrey and two other boatbuilders were already at work. The smell of sawdust and the sound of sanding machines drifted toward Champs, who smiled with pride for his son. He wondered what Chicken Ray's old uncle Hessie would've made of the place.

The drawbridge keeper sounded one long and one short blaring horn noise. Champs steered the boat under the bridge and through the marina's no-wake zone. Once through, he opened up the engines and smoked down an empty river to buoy ten, which wasn't a buoy at all but a pile day marker. Champs had long ago given up trying to explain that to folks.

When the motor stopped, Benji Raj stirred like a lizard wiggling free of a young boy's fist. Champs anchored and got himself, the baby, and the cooler onto the beach. Millie belly-flopped into the river and ran off to inspect the shoreline. Judging by Benji Raj's all-out wail, it was time for a feed.

Champs had no idea how to get out of the complicated wrapped-and-double-knotted cage tied to his chest. He twisted and yanked it and pulled straps through other straps for five minutes in the warming sun, but it wouldn't budge. Damn women and their stupid weaving! A man would use bungee cords, simple as that. Sweaty and exhausted from the effort, he waded to the boat and retrieved a fishing knife from the glove compartment. Back on shore, Champs sawed himself and Benji Raj out of the Wilkinet corset.

"I'll tell you what, son. Bungee cords and a fishing knife. All the tools a man really needs. You remember that."

He sat on top of the cooler under the dappled shade of a sassafras tree and fed his grandson. Benji Raj took well to the bottle and was soon slurping and suckling at one end and burbling and squirting at the other.

"Good man," said Champs, and then remembered he'd have to change the diaper. "Shit."

45

Dawn Fishin'

Thirty minutes and two trips back to the boat later, Benji Raj cooed and hiccuped on a towel in his personal sand pit, dug expertly by Millie. He was slathered in sun cream and diapered in a chamois cloth and bungee cords, but otherwise naked. Champs sat next to him enjoying his suds-and-sandwich picnic. It was the best picnic he'd had in a long time.

No one had to know that minutes before he'd cleaned his grandson's yellow-spackled bottom in the river. Champs had remembered a *National Geographic* photo of Indian people bathing in the Ganges River. If it was okay for the Ganges, it was okay for the Sassafras. Benji Raj seemed to love being dangled by his armpits and swooshed around in the bath-temperature water. Champs had felt Pat all around them.

He stretched out on his back next to Benji Raj, mimicking his babbling noises and waving, occasionally jerking, arms and legs. Together, their eyes tracked a spicebush swallowtail butterfly as it flitted above them. Champs turned onto his side, propped his head up with his weathered hand, and talked to his grandson about his upcoming move back to Egret's Pond.

"I know it makes sense. It's the right thing to do. But I'm not looking forward to it, Benji Raj. It could be another twenty years before I bite the bullet. If it's twenty, it might as well be twenty-one so I can buy you a beer in a bar, assuming they still have beer, bars, and beer in bars. I'll be riding one of those motorcycle wheelchairs by then. Christ, I'll probably be wearing Huggies, too. If that's the case, you remember this day and bring me out here, dig me a sand pit, and let me lay in it to stare through the tree branches at the sky."

After a smile, the frown lines deepened on Champs's face. Twenty-one years in a one-bedroom unit in Ruston Hall. What a shitload of days immersed in lousy food and smells. He wanted to make Laura happy. He wanted a simple base so he could focus on doing the things he wanted to do. But what were those things? He hadn't even had his last hurrah, whatever that was.

From the standpoint of a hospital bed, feeling weak and hobbled by the Octopus of Oz, Egret's Pond was a sensible choice. A responsible choice. A good decision. A way to tend to the challenges in front of him. What if this was his last hurrah? Why did it have to end? His legs still worked, his ticker was fine, he knew what a sock was for, and he'd just gotten a new car. Hell, he was out here in the wild entrusted with the care of an infant. Maybe he could talk to Mel and Jeffrey, see if they'd be happy for him to stay with them. He could babysit Benji Raj while Mel polished pinkies for Dirty Girls and Jeffrey built his boats.

"What d'ya say, Benji Raj? You and me? Shooting the breeze together?" The baby grinned and grasped Champs's outstretched finger. They shook on it.

Feeling sleepy, Champs considered trusting Millie to watch over Benji Raj while he closed his eyes and dozed off. Just for a few minutes. Fortunately, his grandson had a solid preservation instinct and fussed as soon as the thought had crossed Champs's mind. It was time to get back.

He left the baby kicking and screaming while he splashed through the water to grab a life vest and more bungee cords from the boat. Back on the beach, he swaddled Benji Raj in the towel, loaded him into the life vest, pulled the straps tight, and pressed him face-first against his chest, using the bungee cords to fasten the makeshift Wilkinet to his torso. So simple! Champs kept one arm underneath the life vest to make sure Benji Raj wouldn't slip through the bottom. It reminded him of when he'd carried Pat's urn under his winter coat to Blue Claw. That seemed like lifetimes ago.

Once the boat was under way, Benji Raj fell sound asleep. The sun had finished preheating the air; it was baking time on the river. Champs worried he'd been gone too long. If it were Laura's baby, he would have already been hunted down by a hostage rescue team in military helicopters. What if they were met at the dock by a harrowed Mel surrounded by ambulances, fire engines, and police cars? She'd rip Benji Raj away from him and run up the hill while an officer cuffed him and took him to the county jail to await charges. What charges, he wasn't sure. Probably contamination because of the baby poo he'd deposited in the watershed. Champs thought the environmental movement had gotten so out of hand that he'd be locked up for littering long before they came after him for child endangerment.

But the dock was empty when they arrived.

Benji Raj woke up and seemed alive enough to meet Mel's only requirement. When they got back to the cabin, she was hunched over the picnic table with a sweating can of beer, a length of rope, a wooden dowel, and his ancient copy of *The Ashley Book of Knots*. It looked like she was making a mess of the clove hitch. Champs wasn't surprised. In his experience, women sucked at knots, except for the dreaded double knot he'd had to cut himself out of earlier. They were great at folding, though, so that was something.

He cleared his throat to get her attention. Mel took one look at Champs carrying her son in a jerry-rigged life-vest baby carrier and howled with laughter.

The next morning, she emerged smiling and rested—Benji Raj had slept through the night for the first time.

After that, she fastened the life-jacketed Benji Raj to Champs every morning and sent them out on the river for a boat ride and brunch. It was only a few days before Champs bought some bloodworms and began teaching his grandson how to catfish. And so it was that Benji Raj had the distinction of being the youngest Noland ever to earn his spot as a fisherman on the early morning boat.

46

Humping Rabbits

Champs rarely thought about "Jeffreygate" during the day, but at night he was tortured by lurid dreams featuring an evil Chicken Ray. Their friendship had moved on, but some dark part of Champs had yet to let go of the betrayal. He dreamed of Chicken Ray's snatching baby Jeffrey, who morphed into a fluffy chick that went to market while Chicken Ray counted his money at a poker table with an evil laugh.

Another recurring nightmare featured Pat and Ray as vampires making out at the morgue, which morphed into Champs *in flagrante* with the disappointing nurse. When he woke with a racing heartbeat and a woodie one morning, Champs decided he needed to talk to someone. Not about the woodie, of course, but about the unanswered questions that lurked under his dreams.

There were plenty of opportunities to talk to Mel, so Champs started with her when they were weeding the garden one afternoon. He figured if things got awkward he could feign an insect bite or heatstroke.

"Think you can answer some questions I have about Jeffrey?" he asked.

Mel peered out from under her sun hat. "I'll try."

"What's he think about Chicken Ray being his dad?"

"Oh, that's easy. I'd sum it up as 'So what?'" Mel returned to her weeding.

"Humph." Champs picked ripe cherry tomatoes off the vine, trying to think of another way to approach the topic.

"You're still his real dad, if that's what you're worried about," Mel continued. "He thinks it's great that Benji Raj gets to grow up with two grandpas. Cool, isn't it?"

"Cool. Yeah, it's cool," Champs said, trying to act cool. He felt like an idiot.

"It's hard for me to tell if Jeffrey's changed or not since I didn't know him before. He told me it's the first time in his life he's felt settled and happy. 'At home,' he said. Can you hand me that spade over there?"

Champs retrieved it for her. "At home, huh? Makes sense. He's a Sassafras true-blood after all. That's a certain kind of breed, Mel. I can see why he's shooting down roots like eelgrass in the riverbed. Hope you love it here, too, 'cause a waterman like Jeffrey? He's never gonna leave."

"Just like you," Mel said, and smiled.

He couldn't have been happier for Jeffrey, but there was still an affair and a secret love child to reckon with. Champs couldn't bring himself to ask Chicken Ray. That would be humiliating. It would be the same with Larry, although he seemed to have known all along. No, this was a perfect job for Josanne.

He brought it up at their usual Wednesday afternoon teatime. He could always blame the special tea if he later regretted the conversation. Josanne laid it out for him in the same way she'd taught him how to sew and how to grieve and how to live again after an unbearable loss.

"Did she love him?" he asked.

"No, not in the way I think you're worried about, anyway."

"Did he love her?"

"Yes, I think he did. But he let go of that long ago, first out of respect for you and Pat, and then out of respect for himself."

"I can't get the image of them humping like rabbits all summer long out of my mind," he blurted, and flushed with embarrassment. Still, it was a relief to say it to someone out loud. Someone he trusted.

Josanne burst out laughing. "Well, butter my butt and call me a biscuit, Champs! You sure have one heck of an active imagination. Get it through your head, darlin', it was only one hump, okay?"

Champs wasn't sure how one hump was better than many when it came right down to it. Was he supposed to feel relieved by that? This wasn't the quality of advice he'd come to expect from Josanne. Perhaps she'd had too much special tea to be of any use. He got up to leave.

"No, don't go. Please, sit back down, Champs. Go on, sit," said Josanne.

He sat.

"That's better. Good. I'm sorry. I didn't mean to laugh at you. This is a hard thing to get your head around, I know. Let me tell you what I know for certain. It was one drunken night when things got very dark. They used to talk about that awful war all the time. You know his brothers were killed in Vietnam, right? It was only when Pat found out she had a bun in the oven that they talked about that night and decided to part ways. When y'all went back to Pennsylvania that summer, Raymond came over here one day after lunch. Sat right where you're sittin' now and cried like a baby in front of Larry and me. When he finished, I gave him a piece of coconut cream cake, Larry took him to the shooting range, and we haven't talked of it since."

Champs exhaled and took a long drink of sweet relief tea. It all made sense to him now. All except two things.

"How'd she know it was Ray's baby? I mean, I could've been—"

"She knew, Champs. And all you gotta do is look at Jeffrey. He's the spittin' image of a young Raymond."

"I never noticed." That wasn't entirely true, but Champs was ready to move on to his last question. "But why'd Ray get so involved with us now, after all this time?" he asked.

"I don't know. Maybe Pat wrote to him when she was sick. Maybe it's a coincidence. Maybe it's the Lord's work."

"Or maybe it was you." Champs could see right through her.

"Well, the Lord does work in mysterious ways. Now, help me get these dishes inside, I'm ready for a nap."

Champs smiled and cleared the dishes, happy to have something practical to tend to. As he walked back to the cabin, his cell phone buzzed. It was Laura, excited to share the good news: Champs could move into his new apartment in Ruston Hall on October 1.

"That soon?" he asked.

"C'mon, Dad. It's perfect timing. I can help you pack up before we leave for Seattle. Oh, on that note, we'll be down for Labor Day weekend. We'll take the *Flying Cloud* back with us when we leave. One less thing you have to worry about."

Champs ended the call as soon as he could. He was a man condemned. It felt like he'd just been given five weeks to live. After his handshake agreement with Benji Raj, Champs had never gotten up the nerve to ask Jeffrey and Mel about the possibility of living with them. He'd known it wasn't a realistic option. They'd made it work so far, but sometimes he felt in the way. Not a burden to them, but more like a wet sock left in the corner of the room. Harmless enough, until it began to stink.

He'd be packed away in Regret's Pond before winter rolled around, but he couldn't imagine Mel, Jeffrey, and Benji Raj in the cabin long-term. It was too small, too drafty, and too remote for a family. What they really needed was a proper house in a nice community with other young families.

Champs heard Chicken Ray's truck pull up in the driveway. He waved him onto the porch with a cold can of beer. They stood drinking together in the muggy heat, watching the sky turn gray.

"I think we're in for a belter by dinnertime," Champs remarked. "Mel and Benji Raj are out if you were hoping to see them."

"No, I came to see you," Ray said, taking a seat on a club chair and propping up his work boots on the glass coffee table. He removed his "Rise and Shine Mother Cluckers" ball cap and scratched behind his ear. "What do you think of that name? Benji Raj?"

"I think he'll get his head flushed down the toilet when he's in middle school." Champs finished his beer and took a seat across from Chicken Ray.

"Yeah, you're right. Kids are cruel. They'll probably shorten Benji to BJ."

"BJ Raj."

"The King of Blow Jobs."

"That's bad."

"How 'bout you and me call him Ben, see if it sticks?" Ray suggested. "Way I see it, grandpas should have a say in the matter."

"Agreed. Ben it is."

Ten minutes passed as the two men steamed on the porch and drank another beer in companionable silence. Millie amused herself dismembering a teddy bear left unattended on the porch.

"Laura called. I've got five weeks to live," Champs said.

"Is that right? Well, you better get your shit in order then. Speaking of which, I got something I wanna show you. Are you busy right now?"

They both burst out laughing.

Champs fidgeted in the passenger seat as Ray barreled down the road toward Galena. He still didn't like surprises.

"Where'd you say we're going?" he asked.

"I didn't," replied Ray. "But here's the thing. I've been doing a little thinking, about Ben and Jeffrey and Mel. Seems to me they need a proper house. No offense to your cabin but it's not the right place to raise a kid around here, least not when winter comes around."

"Well, I'll be damned, Ray. I was just thinking the same thing." Champs thought it was interesting how much they agreed on what was best for their grandson. He also realized that he didn't miss Pat as much when he was with Ray. It was almost like a part of her lived on in him.

"Yep, so I was thinking about my house," Ray said.

"What about your house? Don't you live in it?"

"It's a nice house. Two stories, three good-sized bedrooms, two bathrooms, a large kitchen and family room, huge flat lawn, and that separate garage where Uncle Hessie and me used to sell bait— remember that?"

"Oh sure, I remember. But doesn't matter how nice and big it is if you're still living in it. Those two young folks need privacy to have a little fun as a couple, if you know what I'm saying. Geezers like us? We put a damper on that kind of thing. Believe me, I've noticed."

They crossed the drawbridge into Fredericktown. Champs figured Ray was taking him to see his house and relaxed. Instead, Chicken Ray pulled off to the right into the gravel lot behind Jeffrey's warehouse.

"And what if I'm not?" Ray asked.

A few drops of rain plopped on the windshield.

"Not what? I don't follow." Champs was confused.

"What if I'm not gonna be living in it?"

"Oh, your house. Well, then I think it's a great idea. Why the hell not?"

"Exactly what I thought," said Ray. "Let's go give them the good news together."

"Wait a minute, if you're not living in your house, then where are you gonna be living?"

"Oh, right next door to you."

"In Ruston Hall?"

Ray chuckled. "Not on your life."

"Damn it, Ray. What the hell's going on?"

"You'll see," said Ray, and before Champs could press him any further, he scrambled out of the car and ran across the parking lot.

Himalayan Salt

L abor Day weekend was always packed on the Sassafras. It marked the end of the summer even though the floating docks at Deadrise Cove didn't come out until mid-October. For the lucky retired and year-round resident fishermen, the six weeks between back-to-school and Halloween marked the prime striper season. During that time, fall unfolded with warm weather and mellow light filtering through red, gold, and orange leaves. Nights cooled and brought a tinge of crispness to the dawn air. There were plenty of fat fish and crabs for the taking. Or, there used to be. The absence of party boats, water-skiers, tubers, and children or grandchildren to entertain was idyllic. Often, the surface of the river was so still you could mistake it for glass. It was the season Champs—and every Sassafras fisherman— looked forward to the most. But first, there was one more loud, crowded, scorching weekend to get through.

Champs had stocked the SMEGerator with all the food and alcohol they could possibly need. He'd asked Mel to help him with a meal plan and begged Josanne to fill Pat's old cookie jar with white chocolate chip sugar cookies just for the girls. He had everyone's favorite on hand, including white wine and watermelon-flavored Perrier for Laura.

She arrived at noon on Saturday with Brian riding shotgun and the girls sporting back-to-school haircuts. They'd cut Zoe's curly red locks so short she looked like Orphan Annie, Champs observed. Just a trim for scholarly Hannah, in keeping with her sensible personality. As if on cue, Hannah repositioned her glasses and scanned her surroundings; forewarned is forearmed. Champs's stomach twisted like a Palomar knot thinking about how little he would see her in the coming months and years. Not only Hannah, but all four of them. He resolved to make every minute of this weekend count.

"You made it!" he said, and welcomed everyone with a hug, including Brian, who looked a little surprised at first, then smiled with twinkling eyes. "Ready for a Guinness?" Champs asked him, clapping him on the shoulder.

"Always ready for a Guinness," Brian replied.

The girls ran in to attack the cookie jar while Champs handed out cold drinks and made sure everyone was comfortable on the porch. He even turned on the fans and the fountain.

"You look good, Dad," Laura commented.

"Oh, sure. After those new pajamas and slippers you bought me, I thought I'd better spiff up the rest of my act. Went shopping with Josanne and got all new shorts, sweaters, jeans, T-shirts, underwear, and socks. Josanne's real handy with the coupons and sales."

Laura laughed. "Oh, I bet. But I was talking about you, your health. You look great. Younger."

"Must be Ben rubbing off on me," Champs said, demurring, although he knew there was more to it.

Since the heart attack that wasn't a heart attack, some of Champs's worst habits had changed for the better. For every beer he drank, he drank a bottle of water. This had cut his alcohol consumption in half. Thanks to Mel, there was a hot bowl of steel-cut oatmeal and a toppings bar waiting for him every morning. On weekends, he cooked eggs and bacon for everyone.

By far the most significant and most delicious change was the bounty of fresh vegetables and herbs that Mel nurtured with her green thumb in the raised beds. Under her tutelage, Champs now cooked with extra-virgin olive oil instead of butter. He thought the term "extra virgin" was suspicious but delighted in his new vocabulary of spices—turmeric, za'atar, cumin, and garam masala. He ate less meat and didn't miss it one bit. Mel had even convinced him to buy Himalayan salt—imported, pink salt! Jesus Christ, he'd be wearing a nose ring, wooden beads, and huarache sandals next.

Champs still had his suspicions that Mel was more of a hippie than she'd let on. But one thing was for sure: Mel was no lazy-pants drifter. She worked hard and got her hands dirty. Champs respected that. She still sucked at knots though.

"Where are Jeffrey, Mel, and Benji . . . Did you just call him Ben?" Laura asked.

"Where's Millie?" asked Zoe, stepping back onto the porch, hands full of cookies.

"Yeah, Ray and I call him Ben now. It was an executive grandpas' decision. We don't want him getting bullied at school. Anyway, they'll be back any minute. They drove over to the new house to take measurements for furniture. Millie rode along to mark her territory."

"A new house?" said Brian, while Laura spewed her Perrier.

"Oh sure. They're moving into Ray's old place in Fredericktown this weekend."

"With Chicken Ray?"

"Nah, he's moving out. Another executive grandpas' decision. They can't stay here year-round and raise a kid. Ray's house has three bedrooms, reliable plumbing, it's on a paved street with neighbors who have young families and a school bus that stops a few blocks from the house. Jeffrey can walk to work from there. It's perfect for them."

"Oh, well I'll look forward to seeing it then, I guess," Laura said. "Where's Chicken Ray going to live?"

"Here," said Champs.

Brian choked on his Guinness. "Chicken Ray's going to live here?"

Champs laughed. "Why not?"

"But you're moving to Egret's Pond, right?" Laura sounded panicked. "Or has that changed? Oh my God, it's like musical houses around here. I can't keep it all straight!"

"Can we stay here, too, Mommy? I don't want to live in Seattle," said Zoe.

"Great idea, Zoe," Hannah said in her deadpan voice. "Mom and Dad can just buy Uncle Larry and Aunt Josanne's place."

"Yay! For real?"

"No, not for real, Zoe. Hannah, stop teasing her like that. We are moving to Seattle in three weeks. You're gonna love it there, Zo-Zo," said Laura. She turned to Champs. "Please tell me you are still moving to Egret's Pond on October first like we planned."

"Yes, I still am. I called them yesterday and signed myself up for Recycling Club. Their Halloween meeting is on October fifteenth. We're supposed to reuse garbage to make a unique costume. There'll be prizes and everything. I can't wait."

Champs winked at Hannah, who tried to hide her giggles.

"Seriously, Dad?" Laura looked doubtful.

"Yes, yes. Seriously. I'm moving to Rust in Hell just like we planned. Relax, Laura."

"And Chicken Ray? Is he really going to live here?"

"Temporarily. Then he's off on a grand adventure to find Uncle Hessie."

"Isn't Hessie dead?" asked Laura.

"Who's to say?" Champs replied, affecting a mysterious tone.

"Who's Uncle Hessie?" asked Hannah.

"He was a friend of the family and he's Chicken Ray's uncle," Laura replied.

Champs watched Hannah think for a minute. She was the smartest girl he knew—just like her mother.

"So, let's see. If Hessie is Chicken Ray's uncle, that makes Hessie . . . baby Ben's great-great-uncle, right?" Hannah asked.

Brian nodded.

"So if Hessie is Ben's great-great-uncle and Ben is my baby cousin . . . that makes Hessie my—"

"Hold it right there, Hannah. Let's find out if Hessie's alive first before we draw up a new family tree, okay? It's confusing enough already," said Laura.

"Can we go to the beach now?" Zoe whined. "I'm bored."

Blazed

Champs packed a picnic in his new yellow Coleman cooler. He'd had to replace the ten-year-old red one he'd used on his first boat ride with Ben because he'd stuffed the river-rinsed dirty diaper in the cooler and left it in *Swee'Pea* for three days. Mel had found him trying to rescue the cooler with bleach and the garden hose. She'd sent him straight to Save-Cave to buy a new one.

He chuckled, remembering the fun he'd had with the unlucky teenage sales associate in the seasonal aisle that day.

"Hello, thank you for shopping at Save-Cave. Can I interest you in a Playmate?" the slouched young man with his hands shoved in his pockets had said.

Champs had known the clerk meant a Playmate-brand cooler. He hated them. They all had a pitched-roof lid design, a significant engineering flaw in Champs's opinion. What kind of moron would buy a picnic cooler you couldn't even sit on? But Champs hadn't been in an educating frame of mind.

Instead, he'd decided to give the boy a hard time by pretending to interpret Playmate in a very different way. He'd squinted at the name tag on the sales clerk's shirt.

"You some kind of a pervert, Jason? You trying to sell me an inflatable 'bunny' sex toy I can ride down the river on?" Champs had said.

Jason had turned red as a fire engine and attempted a stuttered response.

Champs had interrupted him. "You asked me if I was interested in a Playmate, didn't you? Well, didn't you?"

"No, sir. Uh, yes, sir. But, I didn't mean—"

"Well, what the hell did you mean, Jason? Either you have Playboy centerfolds for sale in this aisle or you don't. Which is it, Jason? 'Cause between you and me, I just might be interested. It's been a while, you know what I'm saying?" He'd winked and taken a jab at Jason's shoulder.

Shrinking away, Jason had shoved his hands deeper into his pockets and stared at the floor, mortified.

Champs had snorted before letting him off the hook. "Ah, it's okay, Jason. Don't you worry. I'm just pulling your leg. I don't have much use for a Playmate-brand cooler, but I'll take that yellow Coleman one over there."

It had been his best day at Save-Cave, ever.

When he finished packing the cooler, Zoe, Hannah and David walked with him to Hill Beach carrying bright-colored beach towels and sand toys. Josanne and Larry were near the river in matching webbed lawn chairs drinking from a king-sized insulated Thermos. A family-sized bag of Cheetos Puffs sat on the damp sand between them. Cheese dust stained their fingers and orange crumbs littered Larry's thin chest hair and Josanne's deep-canyon cleavage. It wasn't a good look.

"Oh, Champs, darlin'. We were just talking about you, weren't we, Larry?" Josanne said, and hiccup-burped.

Larry chuckled, giving Josanne's shoulder a little push. She hiccuped again and launched into a fit of giggles. Larry reached down for another Cheetos Puff and tried to stick it into Josanne's nostril, claiming it was a hiccup cure. When he landed it, she sneezed and sent the orange snack flying out like a Nerf gun bullet. It hit Larry in the forehead, which they both found hysterical. Champs watched in horror as Larry and Josanne continued to load their nostrils with Cheetos bullets and sneeze them out at each other. They laughed so hard their laughs became silent convulsions and tears ran down their cheeks.

"What's wrong with them?" Hannah asked Champs.

"Maybe they've had too much to drink," he said.

The *Duchess*, carrying Chicken Ray, Mel, Jeffrey, Benji Raj, and Millie, approached the beach.

Laura and Brian emerged from the hill path carrying what looked to Champs like two huge surfboards and a couple of kayak paddles.

"Well, the gang's all here," Champs said.

Hannah crossed her arms, pushed her glasses up, and stared at Champs. "You're not really going in the old people's home, are you?" she asked.

He bent down and whispered in her ear. "I may have another option."

"What is it?"

"Later," he replied, putting his pointer finger to his mouth in a "hush" position.

"What are you two conspiring about?" Laura asked as she dropped her surfboard.

"Not another surprise birthday party, I hope," Brian added, laying out a new beach blanket on the sand and arranging the boards and beach bags around its perimeter.

"Conspiring?" Champs asked. He redirected. "Why the surfboards? Last I checked, there wasn't much of a swell predicted on the Sassafras."

"They aren't surfboards, they're SUPs," Laura informed him. "They're kinda like flat, stand-up kayaks with a different paddle."

Champs thought a stand-up boat with one oar was the stupidest idea he'd ever come across. "Is 'SUP' short for 'stupid'?" he asked.

Laura gave him an exasperated look.

He watched Mel wade through the river to the beach with Benji Raj and Millie. Millie made a beeline for the Cheetos party and crunched on the spent missiles. Laura took the baby in her arms and joined Zoe, who was building an elaborate sand fortress. Brian grabbed a beer from the cooler and waded out to David, Chicken Ray, and Jeffrey, who were doing the hippo to keep cool. Hannah threw herself on the beach blanket and rummaged in her backpack for a book.

"Did you make the tea extra strong today?" Champs asked Mel, gesturing to the cheese-dust-covered stoners in matching lawn chairs.

"Oh, them. Hmm. I gave Josanne the last fat bud and taught her how to make the special tea to ease her arthritis pain. Looks like she got the measurements wrong."

Josanne and Larry crawled on all fours into the river. They sat in the lapping waves and squealed like children. "I peed!" said Josanne, chortling and splashing water on Larry.

"Looks like she got the measurements very wrong," said Champs, grinning. "How's that new house of yours?"

"It's wonderful. Chicken Ray knows a guy who put a fresh coat of paint on the walls and trim. The furniture is in good shape. A friend of mine is helping me with the sale of my mom's house back in Oakland. We're happy, Champs. Thank you." Mel leaned in and gave Champs a kiss on the cheek.

He blushed. "That Raj fella—is he okay with, well, you know, the baby and all?"

Mel nodded. "We have a unique friendship, I guess you could call it. Let's just say he was a satisfied donor. He's got three kids and raising another isn't in his game plan. I'm so glad that Jeffrey and I found each other. Life's funny, isn't it? The way things happen when you least expect them to?"

Champs agreed. He'd been so focused on his own misery, he'd forgotten to take in some of the good happening all around him.

A deafening blast shook the sand beneath them.

Swansong Marina went up in raging flames and thick smoke.

"Fire! Fire!" Zoe shouted.

"*Ray!*" Champs boomed, swiveling his head to stare down the town's most notorious arsonist.

"I had nothing to do with it!" Chicken Ray yelled. "I swear!"

"Call nine-one-one!" shouted David.

"Get on the goddamn boat and make yourself useful," Chicken Ray said, shoving David into action.

Brian and Jeffrey flew out of the water toward their children. Laura raced to Mel, handing over Benji Raj, then ran back for Zoe. Brian held Hannah's hand, and they hurried across the sand behind the others toward the boat.

Seconds later, Jeffrey gunned the motor, and the *Duchess* sped away from the beach.

Champs yelled at the nine-one-one operator over the roar of the fire.

"You two. Out of the river!" Chicken Ray shouted. "C'mon! We gotta go. *Now!*"

Josanne and Larry sat couch-locked in the sand staring at the raging marina with saucer-shaped eyes. Champs grabbed Josanne under the arms and half-dragged, half-lifted her to standing. Chicken Ray did the same for Larry.

Sirens blared while they staggered up the hill path to safety. Champs wondered what the hell had happened and whether his home was in danger of burning to the ground. He turned around once to look for Millie, but there was no sign of her. Where was his goddamn dog?

The firefighters came in engines by land and Coast Guard boats upriver. By the time they'd put the fire out, Swansong Marina was destroyed. Its entire inventory of rotting pleasure yachts, rusted fishing vessels, and abandoned sailing craft had burned to blackened stubs or fire-damaged aluminum and fiberglass hulls. The gas fires created by the fifty or so motorboat engines in the marina wreaked enough havoc and environmental degradation to keep the Deadrise Cove shoreline closed for two years.

Project Bald Eagle

There were two days of Labor Day weekend left, but the heat on Saturday gave way to a torrential downpour on Sunday morning that helped put out the remnants of the Swansong fire. Champs got up early and brewed his coffee. He chatted softly to Millie who'd returned in the evening, covered in soot, with a patch of singed fur, but otherwise unharmed.

Laura walked in dripping wet, rubbing her bloodshot eyes. "We're going to Twinny's Place for breakfast. Do you want to come?"

"No, thanks. You go ahead." He followed her out of the cabin and sat down on the porch to watch the rain.

Larry jogged over, holding a *Kent County Crier* above his head. "Josanne wants me to go to some damn emergency community meeting. She says the mayor, the sheriff, and a Department of Natural Resources rep will be there to answer questions about the explosion. You coming?"

"I don't have any questions," Champs said, draining his coffee mug.

"I don't have any questions, either. But it should be a good shit show. You don't wanna miss that."

Champs put on his "Fish Forever, Work Whenever" cap and followed Larry out to his truck.

The church hall was booming when they arrived. Champs reckoned everyone with a Galena zip code who wasn't at Twinny's eating pancakes was there. After a two-hour shouting match, a fistfight broke out between the DNR rep and Dex, the neighborhood pothead. The meeting was adjourned. By the time Champs returned to the cabin, Mel, Jeffrey, and Benji Raj had gone out, taking Millie with them. Laura and Brian were packed and ready to leave. They said their good-byes—no point in staying when the weather and the explosion had shut down the river.

Champs looked around the empty cabin. The silence was painful, and since he'd missed breakfast, he decided to treat himself with a trip to the donut shop.

Although he'd assured Laura that he would return to Egret's Pond, the truth was he'd had another offer. It was time to make a decision. And serious decisions like this one required a glazed cruller or two, he reasoned. Champs retrieved a thick manila envelope from under his mattress and fired up *Swee'Pea*.

His favorite donut shop was in Middletown. When he arrived, he almost didn't recognize the place. The shop had a brand-new, gleaming white façade with banners announcing organic smoothies and gluten-free croissants. Inside, the sticky, low orange and brown booths had been replaced with long, modern tables in retro colors with uncomfort-able-looking stools. Champs was most perturbed by the giant self-service ceramic cow with several nozzles attached like teats, each labeled with a different kind of milk. He scanned the options: whole milk, 2 percent milk, nonfat milk, coconut milk, almond milk, soybean milk, hemp milk, rice milk, and pea milk.

"Pea milk, my ass," he muttered.

Champs thought it was ludicrous to call the watery substance somehow squeezed from coconuts, almonds, and soybeans milk. Milk came from the mammary glands of ungulate animals, particularly those of the bovine persuasion who were "milked" for that purpose. The liquids squeezed out of nuts, vegetables, and grains should be called juice. Or maybe not. He didn't relish drinking "nut juice" as a substitute creamer.

Deciding to enjoy his coffee black, Champs balanced himself on a stool at the far end of a back table. He stared at the manila envelope. After Ray and Champs had announced the new housing arrangements to Jeffrey and Mel, Ray had taken Champs for a beer at the Sassafras Grill. Two pints each of IPA later, Ray had come out with an extraordinary proposition. Stunned, Champs had asked for time to think about it. Now was the time. But Champs couldn't bring himself to open the envelope. He absentmindedly ripped his fat man's donut in tiny pieces like some people twist their napkins or pick the labels on their beer bottles.

The last envelope he'd opened had contained Pat's bird notebooks. He couldn't imagine the Pat of all those years ago who'd risked her own well-being to improve the lives of veterans and others traumatized by Vietnam. What would have happened if JP hadn't died? Champs knew animal therapy—including with chickens—was now an approved, sought-after treatment for mental illness, especially PTSD. If JP had lived, Pat might have been an expert in animal therapy, a leader in the movement. But that would have taken her far from home and far from him. He frowned. He didn't like himself for resenting his dead wife's never-realized potential.

Sweeping the donut crumbs aside, Champs opened the envelope and pulled out the two items inside. A glossy sales brochure for the Beneteau Swift Trawler 34, a luxury two-cabin, one-head powerboat cruiser, flybridge optional. And a spiral-bound Waterway Guide on the Intracoastal Waterway, a three-thousand-mile boating highway of inlets, bays, canals, and rivers along the Atlantic coast and the Gulf of Mexico. Nicknamed *the Ditch*, it was easily accessible from the

Sassafras since the Chesapeake Bay was part of the waterway. A sticky note on the brochure in Ray's chicken-scratch handwriting read, "Departs Sassafras for FL on October 15." This was Champs's ultimate ticket to an epic "freestyle lifestyle." A new beginning for a new man unconstrained by the past.

He didn't know if he buzzed with excitement or too much caffeine, but either way Champs's heart pounded. He knew he would go. He couldn't wait to go. All he had to do was convince Laura to let go of Egret's Pond. And figure out what to do with the cabin now that the dock and beach were a safety hazard. Champs decided to tackle the Laura problem first. He hatched a plan—*Project Bald Eagle*—and hurried out of the donut shop to buy a notebook and a sticker of the national bird at Save-Cave.

Every so often, Champs's strategy of ignoring a problem in the hopes that it would go away paid off. So it was with the cabin. Several days after he'd finished Project Bald Eagle, Champs was at Otwell's when he glanced at the *Kent County Crier*. A large photo of Swansong Marina in flames graced the front page. Next to it was a smaller photo of a much younger Chicken Ray. The headline read, "Celebrity Arsonist Has Alibi." Champs laughed and bought a copy.

The cops had deemed the explosion an accident—spontaneous combustion of two propane tanks in ninety-plus-degree heat. "Spontaneous combustion, my ass," Champs muttered as he read the full article on his porch, slurping an icy-cold Diet Coke. What kind of idiot investigators had declared this an accident? The kind that were paid off, he concluded. Champs wondered who stood to gain by this whole fiasco.

At sunset, Larry arrived with a bag of meatball sandwiches and a sixty-four-ounce growler of Dogfish Head 60 Minute IPA straight from the brewery in Delaware. Champs waved him in, delighted at the opportunity to drink and eat for free with a man his age. They talked about the weather for five minutes before Champs told Larry about Project Bald Eagle.

"Oh, so you're joining the search for Uncle Hessie?" asked Larry.

"What do you know about it?"

"Chicken Ray finally came clean. He told me Hessie escaped that hotel fire unharmed. He's got an address for him somewhere down in the Florida Keys. Marathon, I want to say? Have I got that right?"

"Yeah. I didn't know it was common knowledge, but that's the main purpose of the trip. Me? I'm going along for the ride. Exercising my faith muscles. It's not about the destination, it's about the journey. That's what I always say," said Champs, who'd just then remembered the quote from the Regret's Pond wall calendar.

Larry smiled. "Sure. Uh-huh. And what about Peety?"

Champs eyed him suspiciously. "What about Peety?"

"You ever think of looking him up?"

Champs poured himself another beer before answering. "Florida's a big state, Larry, and that was a long time ago."

"You didn't answer my question."

"Don't suppose I did."

Larry changed the subject and asked Champs what he planned to do with the cabin now that no one would rent it for a vacation home given the Hill Beach closure. Champs shrugged.

"You got any ideas?"

"There is one thing," Larry said, refilling his beer glass.

"Oh yeah?" Champs shoved the remaining meatball sandwich into his mouth.

"Turns out that politician, Jack, who gave us the earlier offer? He's got investors and preapproved plans to remake the marina, Hill Beach, and Deadrise Cove into a sustainable, eco-friendly-living community, complete with a river ecology research center. Jack's got the conservationists on his side, developers and builders lined up, and a bill in the legislature that changes the zoning laws. I've seen the plans. They're calling it a green tech investment. Phase one will open in two years if it all goes through."

"What's that gotta do with me?"

"Depends on what you think half a million dollars in your pocket has to do with you," Larry replied. "Almost everyone is ready to ink the deal. Except you."

"When did all this come about?"

"It's been brewing since you turned down the first offer, but Jack couldn't make the numbers work without the Swansong Marina property and at least ten Deadrise Cove lot owners closest to the water selling up. He'd given up and was on the lookout for another property when the marina exploded. Now here we are."

When Laura arrived on October 1, hoping to move him into Egret's Pond, Champs explained the offer to her. She got Jeffrey and David on speakerphone, and together they agreed to take it.

"There's something else," Champs said when Laura ended the call.

She turned pale and asked him hesitantly if he was dying. He reassured her that wasn't the case and gave her the Thomas memorial sampler, framed and wrapped in blue tissue paper. Afterward, he felt a little slimy for buttering her up that way, but not enough to ruin his memory of the look in her eyes when she gazed at the cross-stitched version of a great blue heron and the words, "Beautiful Thomas. Born to Fly Free."

Her eyes filled with a mixture of love, loss, and hope all at once. "Radiant crossover" came to his mind.

Laura hugged the sampler close to her heart. "Thank you, Dad. This is just what I needed. I love you."

Champs wiped his wet eyes and blew his nose.

"I have something else for you," he said, and handed her the notebook with the bald eagle sticker on it.

"What's this?" Laura asked. "Another one of Mom's notebooks?"

"Go ahead, open it," he urged.

She turned to the first page, where Champs had written his name, his age, and a brief description like a personal ad: "An extremely handsome retired man with not very much hair. Beer drinker. Strong of heart and limb. Blessed with three wonderful children, their incredible partners, and five wonderful grandchildren. Desires freedom from early incarceration to fish with ex–chicken farmer and possible arsonist on luxury trawler bound for Florida."

"But you hate Florida," Laura said, puzzled.

"Oh, sure. But like I always say, it's not about the destination, it's about the journey."

Laura smirked and shook her head in apparent surrender. "Okay, then. But you're a pain in the ass, you know that, right?"

"So are you," Champs responded.

They both laughed.

Bon Voyage

On the morning of October 15, Champs parted the curtains in the guest bedroom of Jeffrey and Mel's house in Fredericktown. It was a sunny and blustery fall day, judging from the bright maple leaves stirred into action by the wind. His eyes fell on a group of three giant, lopsided pumpkins awaiting carving on the flagstone back porch.

Mel had already assembled Ben's Halloween costume. He would make his first trick-or-treat appearance as a hot dog—swaddled in a reddish-brown, hooded towel with two pieces of Styrofoam, shaved to resemble a bun, on either side of him. Champs and Chicken Ray had pleaded with Mel to change her mind about the costume. They'd told her Ben looked more like an enlarged and garish close-up of lady parts. "Something you'd find in a lesbian art exhibit," Ray had said. That comment had earned him a kick in the shins from Mel and an alarmed look from Champs, who'd wondered what the hell Ray was doing hanging out in lesbian art museums.

After a quick shower and shave, Champs dressed in a long-sleeved, burgundy T-shirt tucked and belted into clean jeans, a storm-colored down vest, and his new bungee boat shoes, a present from Laura to keep him safe on deck. He put on a cap with a picture of a tarpon and the words "Size Matters," a gift from Chicken Ray. Champs made the bed and headed downstairs, where Mel greeted him with a travel mug of hot coffee.

"Are you ready?" she asked, hefting Benji Raj higher on her hip.

"I wish I could take you and Ben with us," he replied. He felt tears prickle in the back of his eyes.

"We'll be here when you get back. Right, Benji Raj?" The baby smiled and leaned toward Champs, who scooped him up for one last cuddle and a few words of wisdom.

After a hug from Mel, he walked out of the house and down the paved road to Jeffrey's wooden-boat warehouse. There he would say goodbye to Jeffrey and join Captain Ray on board *Sassy Pat*, their preowned 2011 Beneteau Swift Trawler 34 bound for the Florida Keys. Larry had worked his connections to find a seller in Annapolis willing to provide a substantial discount on the Beneteau in exchange for a cash deal and the *Duchess*. Champs and Ray had split the cost of the boat and its necessary repairs on a one-third, two-thirds basis. The two-thirds ownership entitled Ray to the bigger stateroom and the right to call himself "Captain." Champs was relegated to first mate and head chef. He couldn't have been happier and had already stocked the boat with exotic seasonings and pancake mix.

Sassy Pat was ready for her maiden voyage following a two-week berth at Jeffrey's, where she'd been polished and loaded for the journey. Besides stowing his clothes and personal items, Champs had hung two framed pieces in his new home: Pat's memorial sampler, in his tiny stateroom, and the crappie print on the door of the head.

With his family cabins sold and scheduled for bulldozing, a generous retirement fund in the bank, partial ownership of a luxury yacht, and a new adventure ahead of him, Champs allowed himself a big smile of satisfaction. He was getting good at tending to the things in front of him.

Millie met him at the edge of the back parking lot, barking and wagging her tail.

"Good dog, Millie." Champs squatted to scratch her behind the ears. "I'm gonna miss you, but Ben needs you now. I know you'll do a great job looking after him."

She gave his face a few slobbery licks.

"All right then, Millie," he said, standing and wiping his face with his sleeve. "Time to get me the hell outta Dodge." They walked across the empty parking lot. Champs opened the side door leading to the central warehouse space.

"Surprise!" shouted a throng of people who emerged from under worktables, inside canoes, and behind stacks of lumber.

Champs nearly wet his pants. He still hated surprises. Besides, it wasn't even his birthday. As the crowd broke out laughing, clapping, and cheering, he saw the bright banner duct-taped to the far side of the hangar: *Bon Voyage!*

"Well, I'll be damned!" he said, and tipped his hat to the crowd.

Laura approached him with a bright orange life vest she secured around his torso.

"You're supposed to be in Seattle," he said.

"What? We couldn't miss your bon voyage party! Now come on over to the stage." She led him to a raised platform where Captain Ray stood wearing an identical life vest and bewildered expression. They shrugged and shook hands. Jeffrey and Laura joined them on the makeshift stage as the audience, such as it was, grew silent.

"David, come on down!" Laura shouted.

Champs was stunned when David appeared and jogged toward the platform. He gave his son a bear hug and saw over his shoulder that Kimmie, and his grandchildren Samantha and Ryan, were there, too. This was the kind of surprise he could get used to.

The atmosphere felt like a wedding, but Champs hoped no one thought he and Ray were a couple leaving on their honeymoon. On the other hand, what the hell? There was nothing wrong with *that*, after all. He scanned the faces with a rising heartbeat, hoping to meet Peety's eyes. But Peety wasn't there, and Champs felt silly for his childish hopes.

Jeffrey gave a short speech followed by some words from Laura and David acknowledging Champs and Captain Ray with the same pride and excitement. Fortunately, Champs didn't have to speak beyond a red-faced "Thank you" and "This means a lot." They all stepped down to clapping and cheers.

Laura told Champs that Larry and Josanne had organized the whole thing. It was their last week in Deadrise Cove before moving into their new bungalow in St. Augustine, Florida. Champs and Ray would visit on their way to the Keys. Laura excused herself to help Brian open the warehouse's sliding doors facing the river.

Champs rushed to David and his family first. Ryan and Samantha gave Champs an iPad for a going-away present. Samantha gave him a quick tour of Facebook, where he was already "friends" with all his family members, plus Larry, Josanne, Ray, and pervert Nurse Caroline. Champs burst out laughing. He chatted to Kimmie about her new job and when he could visit them in California.

When he looked up, Laura, Brian, and the girls were in a huddle with Jeffrey on the boat dock near the Yammy. Larry stood at the helm of his boat with Josanne and Captain Ray aboard.

"C'mon, Dad," said David. "There's a little something we have to do before you leave."

Champs was reluctant to leave the party, but David insisted.

Twenty minutes later, the boats anchored just offshore from the sandbar that separated the Sassafras from the tidal American lotus pond. There weren't any blooms this time of year, just large, dried pods bent over their stems, ready to release their seeds. Laura led them to the edge of the pond, carrying the golden urn. She'd explained on the way over how she'd combined Thomas's and her mother's ashes, so that they'd be together. Champs let a breeze sweep away the tears that rolled down his cheeks.

Laura opened the urn. They took it in turns to release the ashes into the still, shallow pond: Laura, Champs, Jeffrey, David, Kimmie, Brian,

Samantha, Hannah, Ryan, Zo-Zo, Captain Ray, Larry, and Josanne. They all held hands and watched as the ashes settled on the silty bottom of the pond, where they'd one day bloom with the American lotus seeds into sunny yellow maidens. It was the perfect memorial for his golden-haired farmer's daughter, Champs thought.

"I love you, Pat," he choked out through tears. "Bon voyage!"

They returned to the warehouse docks with bright eyes and light hearts, renewed and ready to celebrate life in Pat's honor.

Josanne and Larry had gathered an eclectic group of locals, including Jill Marcosi and her dad. There were other folks from Dirty Girls and several men whom Champs didn't know but understood to be Captain Ray's "guys." He shook hands with all of them, grateful for their help over the years.

Chuck Donovan, the retired farmer Champs knew from his fishing days long ago, stopped by with his third wife. She had breast implants the size of cantaloupes and dyed hair that resembled the floss poking out of fresh-picked corn. Champs didn't realize he was eyeing up her ripe melons until Chuck cleared his throat and gave him a stern look of warning.

An older man in a wheelchair turned out to be Frank Pruitt, the former owner-operator of the crab hauler *Emi-Lee*. He was mostly deaf, wore a "Got Crabs?" cap, and introduced his overweight female caregiver as Jumbo Jimmy. Champs shook his head and exchanged an eye-roll with Kristen; her name was embroidered on her yellow polo shirt. She winked back. Champs blushed and later asked Samantha to get Kristen on his iFad thingamajig.

Ken Vernon, the retired Riverkeeper from back in the day, was there with his daughter, Cheryl, the current Riverkeeper. Champs was delighted to see Ken, who had been one of Pat's favorite people on the Sassafras. He shook hands with Cheryl and got a brief update on the river before a nearby commotion interrupted their conversation.

They turned to see a reporter and film crew interviewing Jeffrey about the grand opening of Tockwogh Wooden Boats next week. Jeffrey explained how he'd chosen the name of his business in honor of the Native tribe who'd first made their homes and livelihoods on the Sassafras.

What a goddamn good day to be alive, Champs thought.

I'll Be Back

I t was time to go.

Champs found it hardest to say goodbye to Zoe and Hannah.

"You're on Faceplace, right?" he asked Hannah.

She giggled. "It's Facebook, Gramps, and Mom said I could create an account just to keep in touch with you. Here, I have a present for you."

Champs unwrapped the small box and found what looked to him like a credit card inside.

"It's a gift card for your iPad. You can get *National Geographic* on it. And Harlequin romances, too. You know—if you need any more advice on catching a girlfriend." Hannah winked. "It worked for Jeffrey and Mel, right?"

Champs chuckled and gave her a huge squeeze.

"Open mine! Open mine! Open mine!" squealed Zoe. She pushed her sister aside and handed Champs a large, flat box.

"What's this?" he said, removing the lid and pulling out a folded, bright pink piece of heavy-duty plastic.

"You blow it up! It's a decoration for your new boat. It's a pink flamingo! Do you like it?"

Champs threw his arms around Zoe. "I love it!" he said.

As Captain Ray and First Mate Champs boarded *Sassy Pat*, Josanne waved Champs up to the flybridge. "There's one more thing I've been fixin' to give you."

"Oh, Josanne," he said. "You've already given me so much, and this party . . . I loved it. Thank you."

She motioned for him to sit down and handed him a yellowed envelope. "I have no illusions about how you will receive this or what you will do with it. That's gonna be up to you, darlin'. I do pray you make peace with this part of your life, whatever you choose. God bless you, Champs."

Her expression was hard to read. Worry? Hope? She'd been his anchor and his guiding light through everything. She was, he realized, his best friend.

Swallowing hard, he opened the envelope and took out the small, folded piece of paper inside.

He hesitated. "What's this about, Josanne?"

"Honey, you're gonna have to read it, and then you'll know," she said with soft eyes and the kindest smile he'd ever seen.

He took a deep breath and unfolded the paper.

It was a street address and phone number in Miami Beach, Florida.

Peety's address and phone number.

Champs felt his heart explode like a firecracker, showering every cell in his body with warm light. He broke into what he would later understand to be tears of joy, taking Josanne's hands in his.

"Thank you, Josanne," he said. "This is just what I needed. What am I gonna do without you?"

"You're gonna do just fine, Champs. Now, help me off this boat so y'all can get going on your adventure."

Minutes later, Champs and Ray waved goodbye to their family and friends on the dock. Captain Ray engaged the motor and steered *Sassy*

Pat downriver on course for their "freestyle lifestyle." Once they'd cleared the no-wake zone, the luxury cruiser picked up speed. Champs climbed to the flybridge again for a 360-degree view of the Sassafras and the landscape that had shaped his life.

"Isn't it beautiful, Pat?" The wind carried his words away.

He imagined the warmth of her smile and sparkling blue eyes. Wherever Pat was now, Champs knew she was delighted with how everything had turned out. He breathed in deep and felt her love swell inside him, and after a moment, he gently exhaled and let her image fade. He let her go.

At Lloyd Creek, a bald eagle soared high in front of the boat, guiding them downriver. As *Sassy Pat* reached the mouth of the Sassafras, the magnificent bird swooped into a stand of loblolly pines on shore. Champs recalled a *National Geographic* article that described bald eagles, particularly older eagles, as birds with high "site fidelity." No matter where they roamed, their instinct always brought them back to where they'd fledged.

Captain Ray pointed the boat toward the lower Chesapeake and the Atlantic Ocean beyond.

Champs waved goodbye to his beloved Sassafras. For now.

In his best Arnold Schwarzenegger impersonation, he shouted, "I'll be back!"

A NOTE TO READERS

Thank you for spending time with Champs on the Sassafras River. A book is nothing without its readers. If you enjoyed *Sassafras*, will you please consider writing a review on Amazon and Goodreads? Reviews help independent authors make their books more visible to new readers.

ACKNOWLEDGMENTS

Like Champs, several generations of my family have spent all or part of their summers in a (newly refurbished!) cabin on the Sassafras River. Thank you to my grandparents for paving the way and my uncles and aunts for keeping the traditions alive.

My heartfelt thanks to Keith. Without his love, support, stories, and generosity, *Sassafras* would not have been written. His passionate knowledge of the Sassafras River is unsurpassed. Our hilarious text exchanges were the highlight of this project. (All mistakes are, of course, mine.)

Moon-sized thank yous to content editors Andi Cumbo-Floyd and Wendy Craig, copy editor Aja Pollock, proofreaders Lindsey Wood and Courtney Wood, and cover illustrator Andy Bridge. I can't imagine *Sassafras* without your expertise, excellence, and enthusiasm.

A thousand thank yous to my writing teacher Pamela Eakins and her Sisters of the Holy Pen writing circle (especially Wendy, Maya, raVen, and Amanda). All writers need encouragement and feedback, and these women are my lifeline.

Thank you to Shayla Raquel, a consummate marketing and book launch genius who also designed and produced an excellent author website for me.

My husband, Paul, never lost faith in me or the book. He encouraged me when I lost confidence, contributed to plot and character development when I got tangled, and loved me unconditionally through the whole messy process. He's waited a long time for this. To him, my forever love and gratitude.

Big love and embarrassing hugs to my kids—Ella, Theo, and Luke. They cheer me on, accept my weirdness (most of the time), and keep me laughing (book or no book) no matter what life brings. You three are at the heart of everything.

ABOUT THE AUTHOR

Trish Heald is a former strategic business advisor, writer, and editor who turned her hand to fiction after an MA in Psychology revealed a passion for helping flawed characters through crises and renewal. Trish lives in the San Francisco Bay area with her husband, three screen-addicted teenagers, and a narcoleptic beagle. *Sassafras* is her debut novel.

CONNECT WITH THE AUTHOR:

trishhealdauthor.com

🅕 facebook.com/fictionbytrishheald

🅞 instagram.com/trishhealdauthor

🅖 goodreads.com/trishheald

CPSIA information can be obtained
at www.ICGtesting.com
Printed in the USA
FSHW011255201219
65318FS